TATTOOS AND TIES

ORDER

KINDLE ALEXANDER

Edited by Jae Ashley
www.jaeashley.com
Cover art by Reese Dante
http://www.reesedante.com
Cover content is for illustrative purposes only. Any person depicted in
the content is a model.

ISBN Print: 978-1-941450-19-2
ISBN ebook: 978-1-941450-20-8

This is a work of fiction. Names, characters, places and incidents are
either the product of the author's imagination or are used fictitiously,
and any resemblance to any actual persons, living or dead, events, or
locales is entirely coincidental.

TRADEMARK ACKNOWLEDGEMENTS

The author acknowledges the trademarked status and trademark owners of the following trademarks mentioned in this work of fiction:

Alexa, Echo: Amazon Technologies, Inc.
Batman and Robin: DC Comics Partnership
Bluetooth: Bluetooth Sig, Inc.
Bud Light: Anheuser-Busch, Incorporated
Captain America: Marvel Characters, Inc.
Carhartt: Carhartt, Inc.
Clive Christian: Clive Christian Limited Public Company
Crown: Diageo North America, Inc.
Disney: Disney Enterprises, Inc.
Ferrari: Ferrari S.p.A. Corporation
Ford F-250: Ford Motor Company
Google, Google Maps: Google, Inc.
Harley: H-D USA, LLC
Hilton: HLT Domestic IP LLC
Hulk: Marvel Characters, Inc.
Keurig: Keurig, Inc.
La-Z-Boy: La-Z-Boy, Inc.
Marvel: Marvel Characters, Inc.
Mercedes Benz: Daimler AG Corporation
NASCAR: National Association for Stock Car Auto Racing, Inc.
Red Bull: Red Bull GMBH LLC
Samurai Jack: Cartoon Network, Inc.
Shelby Cobra: Carroll Hall Shelby Trust
Spider-Man: Marvel Characters, Inc.
Viceland: Vice Media Canada, Inc.
Whole Foods: Whole Foods Market IP, L.P.
Wonder Woman: DC Comics, Inc.
Word: Microsoft Corporation

A SPECIAL THANKS

Steve Wiscaver, Jae Ashley and Olivia Lindsey, thank you for your help with our legal research. This book wouldn't be here today without your support.

DEDICATION

Kindle, you're forever in our hearts.

Perry, you're missed every day.

NOTE FROM
THE AUTHOR

This is not a motorcycle club or legal bible – please don't use as such. Creative license was taken with this story. It's a work of fiction.

CHAPTER 1

The idea of losing sleep while holding a man in his arms all night long was about as foreign an idea as falling hopelessly in love, but Alec Pierce had managed to do both in a relatively short time. The love part had happened months ago, but last night had been the first time he'd said the words aloud.

As for losing sleep and holding his biker through the long hours of the night, well honestly, he'd done quite a bit of that over the last several months too. Tonight, though, was different. His cup runneth over so to speak, and as Keyes Dixon slept like a baby in his arms, Alec lay awake, lost in the warmth of their great love story.

Alec smiled and angled his head, kissing the top of Key's soft hair, certain if Shakespeare were alive today, he would want to write his next great masterpiece based on the Pierce and Dixon coupling. His grin turned a bit wicked at the mental image of Key wearing the tight-fitting men's leggings so popular in the Elizabethan era. No matter how

Alec loved their story, he did recognize the ridiculousness of his overactive imagination and rolled his eyes as a soft chuckle welled up from his chest while imagining the possibility of their bedroom sword play.

Key stirred. With Key stretched across his body, his face buried in the crook of Alec's neck, both the rumble of Alec's chest as well as the quiet noise of the soft chuckle would have woken his always-light-sleeping boyfriend.

"You good?" Key lifted his head, cracking open sleepy eyes as he scanned Alec's face to find the answer to his question.

"I'm good. Go back to sleep. You still have a few hours before you have to leave."

Key's brows dropped into a solid V as he assessed Alec's answer. He must have decided Alec was on the up-and-up when his eyes slid closed and he tilted his chin up. Alec obliged and granted him the kiss. Key turned, tucking an arm under Alec's shoulder, bringing him to where they were face to face, intimately sharing a single pillow. Key fell back asleep almost instantly.

Funny, Alec had never slept in a bed with another person. Even during grade school sleepovers, Blaine would take the floor of Alec's bedroom—or vice versa when he stayed at Blaine's—but not now, hopefully never again. His oversized California king could have been a twin bed for all the space he and Key used when sleeping together.

Alec ran his fingertips over Key's scraggly beard, marveling at the multitude of colors reflected there. Key's hair had been darker when they'd first met, but with all the time they had spent in Alec's secluded backyard, swimming, grilling, and just being together outside like Key enjoyed doing, his hair had turned different shades from honey to blond. Alec lifted a piece of Key's long hair, letting it filter through his fingers. He loved the wild, silky strands. From the first minute he laid eyes on his biker man to right this second, Key just did it for Alec.

"You aren't sleepin'," Key mumbled, his eyes remaining closed.

"I'm admiring," Alec answered, cupping Key's cheek with his hand.

"Why're you awake? You're gonna be tired tomorrow," Key grumbled, this time cracking his eyes open again. Alec noted even Key's eyelashes had changed colors. It was an extraordinary thing for a man who had spent most of his life outdoors.

"I'm committing our love story to memory," Alec teased. He leaned in to kiss Key's soft lips. Key's eyes opened wider, and he cocked a single brow as he scanned Alec's face again.

Maybe as long as a minute passed before Key rolled his eyes and jostled Alec as he turned a hundred eighty degrees, giving him his back. "When you're rememberin' shit, remember it wasn't my fault that those damn two by fours were in the road no matter what the fuck Blaine says."

Alec laughed and kissed Key's shoulder, coming in behind his biker who pressed lovingly against his chest. "I'm quite thankful for those two by fours." Alec moved Key's hair to lay his whiskered cheek along Key's neck and upper back and tightened his hold.

"Go to sleep, Alec. You'll be too tired tomorrow for your important case or whatever you said you had to do."

Seconds later, Key's soft snores returned in a comforting cadence. Key was right, he should sleep. He just didn't want to miss any time he had with Key.

As much as Alec had decided to read Key's loving actions, not go by his lack of words committing them together, they still had so many obstacles that could rip their relationship apart before they ever got fully started. From this point forward, there would be no more sticking his head in the sand, avoiding the destructive elements within his or Key's lives.

If Key had five years before he could retire from the motorcycle club, then Alec had to prepare his own life. He had to get his affairs in order to distance himself from his employment at the Dallas County District Attorney's office, and end his beyond stupid bid for a federal judge nomination. That last one had Alec's gut twisting, and he settled back on his pillow, staring at Key's strong muscular back.

Yeah, that was the wet blanket suffocating his fantasy. The constant worry swirling around their relationship remained no matter how many times he pretended their differences didn't matter. He pushed the heel of his palm against the aching pressure growing in his head. What would Key's motorcycle club—Alec rolled his eyes knowing most of the civilized world would definitely call that rough and rowdy bunch of men a biker gang no matter how many times Key denounced the idea—do to Key if they found out about Alec?

And if that time came, how could he protect Key?

He'd had this internal conversation with himself dozens of times. He'd even considered hiring protection, but Key's so-called brothers would spot a security detail in a minute, creating more questions than either of them wanted to answer. Plus, Alec had seen the DA's surveillance photos of the biker club members. At six-four, Key towered over the next tallest member of the club by several inches. His sheer size dwarfed all his brothers. To say Key was a big guy with brute strength on his side put it mildly. Key would believe he could take care of himself. In most cases, there was little doubt he could, but not against the ten or twelve members of that club intent on causing him harm.

Stop, Alec. Have faith. It's been your motto since you two met.

That was damn hard to do. The magic of the night faded under the heavy weight of uncertainty. Alec closed his eyes and tucked in around Key. Fate wouldn't have given him this perfect man to just take him away. Alec had to believe that. There was no other choice.

The cell phone rattling on the nightstand caused Keyes Dixon to open his eyes and begrudgingly watch the device rumble against the polished wood. It stopped moving only to immediately begin again. Dammit, whoever was on the other end seemed determined to get his attention, but he was just that committed to ignoring them. The phone stopped buzzing, and he waited a second or two. Nothing more came through, and Keyes closed his eyes, mentally settling back against Alec's comforting warmth. It wouldn't take much to fall back asleep.

Keyes sighed as the fucking phone started again.

Goddammit, Keyes mentally yelled. He stretched an arm across the mattress only because the phone might wake Alec who had been up late, doing that weird middle of the night waking thing again. Not the first time Keyes had caught Alec awake at all hours of the night, but last night, Alec was right in his face, staring at him with all that doe-eyed, newly stated devotion in his eyes. Keyes's heart twisted at the sweet sentiment on Alec's handsome face, and maybe for the first time in his life, the ache in his chest was a good thing. At least it seemed good right now.

As Keyes moved, Alec followed. He grabbed the phone. Alec instinctively rolled with him until Keyes settled with Alec's body curling back around his. They slept about the same way they were when awake, staying close to one another. It seemed an unconscious thing. Keyes hadn't let himself question it before. Now, it seemed like a big warning sign, something he should have paid closer attention too if he had truly meant to keep himself at a distance.

He'd been such a dumbass not to protect his heart better than he had. Keyes knew the deal when he'd started showing up regularly at the attorney's house. This was only supposed to be sex, nothing more, but the sexy, smart, up for anything Alec Pierce became sexier and smarter with each passing day. How had he managed that? Alec drew him in like a fly to some of the sweetest honey he'd ever known.

He guessed all that fell solidly into the *best laid plans* category.

What a joke.

The reality had Keyes serving up his fragile heart on one of Alec's fancy silver platters, readily handing it over without a backward glance.

Keyes scrubbed a hand over his face, fighting a yawn, trying to adjust his eyes to the sudden bright light of the phone screen in his hand. The damn thing started vibrating again. With a press of the button, Keyes silenced the phone and stared at the screen. Six o'clock in the morning.

"Don't leave yet. Another thirty minutes," Alec murmured, moving them both to where he entangled himself around Keyes's body, keeping him right there. It didn't take long for Alec's deep even breaths to again coat and caress Keyes's skin, letting him know how tired his mister must be from staying awake so late last night.

Keyes slid his thumb over his screensaver. Seventeen missed text messages, but no missed calls. He pushed the messages icon, opening the text messages to see his father's cell phone number. Anxiety double timed it throughout his body, waking his ass right up. Nothing good could come from looking at anything his shitty old man had sent. His father was a fuck-with-his-head kind of guy, and Keyes was already dealing with a growing mountain of emotional bullshit with Alec's I-love-you confession last night.

Don't do it. Do not open the messages.

Keyes pulled his finger away from the screen and lifted his gaze to the bedroom ceiling. His life was already so fucked with trying to balance the secrecy of Alec along with his responsibilities to the bike club and the day-to-day operations of the tire shop. He was seriously living on the edge all the damn time. He didn't need any more baggage weighing his stressed-out ass down. And since his brothers would never understand his relationship with an assistant district attorney, one of Keyes's biggest worries involved Alec's safety.

But the texts could be a warning. No, his old man would never warn him of a pending strike, but that bad temper would get the best of him and he wouldn't be able to hold back. He'd most definitely ridicule Keyes, and that would give him all the heads up he needed to keep Alec safe.

Keyes nodded to himself, lifted a finger, and swiped to open the message.

"god 4 nothing cocksuker cant keep me from a buiznes I fuckin started."

Keyes let out a breath. Same old shit. He refused to read any more, not sure why it had taken his father this long to complain about being kept away from the tire shop. Instead, he went through the steps of blocking his old man from further text messages and deleting all the messages he'd ever sent. He should have done that a long time ago.

Honestly, he'd been surprised Fox, his motorcycle club's president, had kept such a tight hold on his father, also a patched-in member of the club. It had been six months since Keyes had kicked his abusive father to the curb. Of course, he saw his old man at the clubhouse, in all their meetings, and sometimes when they rode out together, but his father had remarkably kept his distance. Keyes just had to put up with his offensive mouth. It was honestly a miracle the man had voted for Keyes to become a full patch member. He always wondered what kind of deal Fox had made with his father to get his acceptance vote.

This morning's timing though...yeah, that seemed cosmic. The fact that his old man picked today to start shit again—there was no coincidence there. Keyes dropped the phone on the mattress and lifted his head to look down at Alec. Even sleeping, Alec was the most beautiful man in the world—his sunny blond looks just did it for him. Keyes's arm tightened around Alec in protection. Alec was so damn special to the world—his life mattered. He had meaning and purpose. He made a difference to mankind. If good versus evil existed, Alec landed in the top side of good. Keyes went the exact opposite direction. Even on his best day, he lived his life firmly on the side of evil.

Why Alec had confessed his love last night, Keyes wasn't sure, but he believed Alec or at least he wanted to. He couldn't remember one person ever saying *I love you* to him before. His heart had lapped up every single syllable. Keyes remembered in vivid detail the way Alec moved inside him, owning him body and soul as he spoke softly. Closing his eyes, he could hear the exact tone of Alec's voice, the haggard whisper against his ear when he'd confessed his love. The shudder that had gone through

Alec's body as he'd held him so tight as if Alec's life depended on Keyes staying right there by his side... He'd have that moment etched in his heart forever.

Keyes hadn't said anything in return, but he'd fucking wanted to, so damn bad. He'd been a foolish coward. Alec needed to hear his feelings. Even after having too much to drink, his lifelong survival skill of self-preservation kept him quiet. The sweet and generous Alec had pushed and pushed, fighting to keep them together from the very first day they had met. Even knowing that, Keyes had still held his tongue, refusing to give anything back to this extraordinary man, because ultimately, Alec deserved someone better than Keyes.

He was a self-centered ass.

What the fuck was he doing?

The headache from too much drinking last night compounded with all his overthinking this morning started creeping in as an overwhelming sadness took over his heart. Keyes had let things go too far between them. This whole deal was supposed to be him taking advantage of a rich guy who liked to slum it—end of story. Now they were six or so months in, and he was spending at least two nights every week in Alec's bed, and Alec was fucking him—which he liked a whole damn lot—and now whispering words of love—which he liked a whole lot too.

Keyes had set himself up to fail. He was living a dangerous life that had him straddling two worlds. One where he belonged, body and soul, and another where, no matter what he did, he would never fit in.

Alec's father was a high-ranking American politician.

Keyes's father was no-good trash, a sorry son of a bitch.

Alec worked for the Dallas district attorney who had a hard-on for bringing Keyes's motorcycle club to their knees.

Keyes changed tires for a living.

Alec was the shiny part of life. He was goodness and kindness. Everything Keyes wasn't.

Keyes had watched his mother overdose and die when he was a young boy. Alec had vacationed in the Hamptons—wherever the fuck that was.

They came from two different worlds.

Fuck. Keyes's eyes closed as the illusion that they'd somehow found their balance began to shatter. The pain in his chest grew, hurting on a level he couldn't quite absorb, and that said a lot since his parents had really done a number on him as a kid.

He had seen enough about the world to know words like *I love you* were a conditional misconception, something said by people who didn't understand what life was about. Keyes was never going to be good enough for Alec's world, and at some point, Alec would get tired of isolating himself inside this house. Keyes couldn't even imagine a time they could ever go out in public together. If for some unseen reason that time came, what the fuck would they do?

If the situation wasn't so damned dire, he'd laugh at the mental image of Alec at a club barbecue. Club whores hanging out with Alec Pierce... What a fucking joke. His brothers would never understand whatever this was between him and the attorney.

Resentment and anger slithered up his spine and coiled around his heart. Fuck if he wasn't so much more comfortable with those emotions.

Nothing had changed between them. They were a good time, nothing more. Fuck his heart's vehement denial. Where his heart and his head completely agreed was that there was no way a good guy like Alec would continue to love him if he ever found out the truth of everything Keyes had done in his life. Hell, he'd been on a drug run less than a week ago. Alec wouldn't understand why he did the things he had.

No matter what happened right now, their end didn't change. They didn't fit no matter how much he wished they did. White hot pain lanced through the useless organ in his chest. It hurt so fucking bad to think of Alec leaving him.

"Babe, your heart's pounding," Alec murmured, laying a warm hand dead center on his chest. Whatever Alec felt caused him to lift his head and open his eyes wider. "What's going on? Are you okay?"

This was too much. How could he have let hope, of all things, cloud his reality? Hope and fairytales went hand in hand, both big fucking wastes of mind-space. He wanted to cry, which pissed him off even more. Thank God for the burst of anger, because now the bullshit pain wasn't the only thing driving him. Keyes bucked his body out from underneath Alec's and flipped the covers off, sending his phone flying. He literally jumped out of bed, making a beeline for his jeans draped over the bedroom chair. He shoved his feet in the legs of his jeans, forgoing his underwear. He needed out of this house. He couldn't fucking breathe. He needed to be back in his world, back to what he knew, and never venture out again.

Luckily, Alec had removed his jeans in such a way that his keys, wallet, and belt were still in place. Keyes shoved his dick inside and zipped himself up as the memory of the unspoken need darkening Alec's eyes when he'd arrived sent his rage skyrocketing. He didn't get the jeans much more than zipped when he dropped down in the chair and started to shove his sockless feet inside his dirty work boots.

"What's happened, Key?" Alec asked, his tone even but on the controlled edge of panic. Keyes looked up to catch Alec pulling on his athletic shorts which spoke volumes to the gravity of the situation. Alec rarely wore clothes around him.

Letting his anger fuel him, Keyes pushed to his feet, leaving the boots untied as he left the room, gathering his hair to tie in a knot at the base of his head. The fucking hair band he always kept at his wrist wasn't there.

"Goddammit!" he yelled as he jerked his T-shirt off the kitchen stool and pulled it over his head while leaving the house. He never broke stride as he bent to sweep up his hair tie off the back porch where it had fallen last night and stalked toward his motorcycle.

"Keyes, stop. Don't go. You're just freaked out," Alec said in his attorney-like listen-to-me voice.

The lawyer had gotten it completely wrong. Keyes wasn't freaked out. He was absolutely aware of how badly he was losing his mind. He knew exactly what he was doing and that was getting the fuck out of Dodge. He had to get away from all the realizations threatening to suffocate him. The sooner he left, the faster he could try to move past this huge lapse in judgment. Fairytales were for children's books, and he sure as hell didn't live in a damn book. He ignored Alec's pleas as he grabbed his helmet and shoved it on his head before jumping on the bike and pushing the key in the ignition.

"Your phone, Key," Alec yelled.

He glared at Alec as he purposefully drowned him out by revving the engine. He kicked the bike into gear and whipped a circle around Alec who stood in the middle of his driveway. Alec could keep the damn phone. He didn't need it.

What a fool. He'd been stupid enough to hope for something more, something that couldn't be. Hope was nothing more than prolonged torture. The crushing pain that tried its best to paralyze him right this fucking minute was proof of that. Fuck it all. His heart shattered at his overwhelming loss.

Fuck hope. Fuck happiness.

All his life he'd kept his head down, his heart and feelings hidden.

Alec had opened him, changed him, made him want more.

Fuck his old man. Fuck being afraid.

CHAPTER 2

Alec stared after Key as he tore down the long drive on his bike. He walked the length of the back portion of the driveway and stood there as understanding set in—his love had left him. Overwhelming pain followed. He had messed up, miscalculated, and let all his emotions get the best of him.

They couldn't end this way. Alec pivoted on his heels, heading for the house. He needed to go after Key and apologize and assure Key everything was going to be all right. He'd take back the words. That made Alec stop at the threshold of his backdoor. He actually stumbled over his feet as his heart screamed not to ever take away the truth of those words. He loved Key. He loved him with every ounce of his being.

Yes, he got that times were difficult for the both of them.

No, he couldn't see how their future might work out, but a solution surely had to present itself, and he would wait for however long it took. He loved Key. Simple as that.

Alec sighed. He saw no other choice but to go to the tire shop. He had to. He'd figure out what to say on the way, he just needed to see Key's face, talk with him while reading his facial expressions. Alec started for his bedroom when he heard the distinctive rumble of Key's motorcycle. He rushed to the kitchen window above the sink, keeping hold of his internal panic as he watched Key drive past. Alec sprinted toward the back door, throwing it open as his biker parked in the center of the driveway. Key left the engine running as he slung his leg over the bike and ripped off his helmet. He carelessly let it fall as he stalked forward. Alec stopped dead in his tracks as Key took long strides toward him with the most determined look covering that extraordinarily handsome face.

He couldn't help the step backward as Key reached for him. In the three seconds it took for Key's arm to lock around his waist and the other to lock around his neck, Alec was struck by the intensity Key commanded. He was a mighty force in the world, intimidating in both his size and strength, but that rush of sudden anxiety fled as the biker drew him against that hard body and drove his tongue deep inside Alec's mouth. Nothing tasted as sweet as his biker's kiss. Alec met the move with one of his own. He dropped the cell phone still clutched in his hand as he wrapped himself around Key, holding on with a strength that only desperation could create.

The passionate soul-searing kiss continued until Key jerked free, but Alec followed, tightening his hold as he reached for Key's mouth. He never wanted this to end. Not ever. He'd found his perfect match on a deserted road in the middle of nowhere Texas. He was so ready for this. They would absolutely find a way to be together. The universe wouldn't have put this man in Alec's path and not let him have every part of him.

"Let go," Key mumbled against his lips as strong fingers gripped Alec's biceps. He locked his arms in place, ignoring Key's request.

"No. I'll never let you go."

Key fought him while dropping to his knees. Alec tried to follow until insistent hands tugged at his shorts. Even then, Alec still couldn't let Key go. He grabbed for Key's head, gripping his long hair as Key curled a warm hand around his suddenly rigid length, taking him directly into his mouth. Alec's eyes slid closed, certain he'd never felt anything quite so good in his life.

Key sucked him with three or four orgasm-teasing pulls before popping Alec out of his mouth.

"Key?" He opened his eyes and glanced at the man on his knees.

Key's eyes lifted to meet his. The conflict was back, reflected in the depths of Key's stare. Alec loosened the tight hold he had on Key's hair and tenderly caressed down his cheek to his jaw, instinctively wanting to give comfort.

"I take care of me." Key poked himself in the chest to help drive his point home. "I've never been scared of anything. Nothin'. Until I met you." Flashes of raw pain, determination, and fear mixed with what Alec hoped was love in Key's tortured expression. He tried to drop to Key's level. He wanted to hold him, tell him everything was going to be okay, but Key wrapped his strong arm around Alec's legs, keeping him upright.

"Don't be afraid. I'll never hurt you." Alec's feelings rushed out in his words as he made that promise.

"I can't say it. I can't. I want to. I want to so fuckin' bad. And I will. I'll work out my fuckin' head issues." There was a storm behind those light colored eyes. He couldn't miss the confusion or deep sadness troubling his lover who had just given Alec the world by way of his confession. Key looked tormented as he spoke again. "I feel that same thing. I do."

Key's brows squeezed together and his shoulders slumped in defeat. He was broken, but trying, and that was all Alec could ask. There was so much sincerity woven through Key's words, so much declaration in his gaze.

"Baby, I believe you. That's enough, Key."

Key nodded, relief easing his tense features. Alec may have even seen tears forming in this fine man's eyes. Things had changed again for them. The commitment was real, even if left unspoken.

Key gripped his waning dick, and again, gave him a tug before swallowing him whole.

Alec's cock tasted so fucking right against his tongue. He ignored his own cock as it pressed annoyingly against the front of his jeans. He licked up Alec's thick shaft, taking his time, letting the salty flesh entice his senses. He wanted to show Alec how much he needed him.

Keyes moaned as Alec grew thicker with every pass of his tongue. How stupid he'd been to think he could so easily walk away from this man. Was he a fool to want a future with Alec? Alec's scent surrounded him, unleashing every one of his predatory instincts.

No. Alec was his. He sucked Alec deeper into his mouth, cupping his lover's heavy sac in his palm as he swallowed around him, allowing Alec deeper in his throat. He rolled the soft skin, squeezing and teasing his man.

"Oh, baby, that's good." Alec's words brought a smile to his lips. The weight of Alec's hands on his head, fingers curling in his hair kept him from floating away as he put all he had into worshiping the man in front of him.

He released Alec's balls to smooth a hand up the back of Alec's thigh to the curve of his ass, digging his fingers into one meaty globe. With the other, he held the lower part of his lover's shaft as he bobbed his head, taking more of Alec down his throat.

Fingernails scraped against his scalp, and motherfucker, he loved the sting. He loved everything about this man and desperately wanted to show Alec how much he truly meant to him. No one except Alec had ever made him feel valued. No one.

Keyes pressed his nose to Alec's groin and swallowed as he again cupped his lover, rolling Alec's balls in his palm. He used his grip to tease sounds from Alec's lips before pulling back and mouthing just the tip of Alec's thick length, dipping his tongue into the slit to tease the precome from his man. He traced the ridge around the head, then followed the thick vein up the underside and back down again.

He nibbled then sucked Alec's balls, taking his time to mouth him thoroughly. He enjoyed every moment.

Keyes used his hand on Alec's firm ass to pull him closer. He slid his mouth over heated flesh to take his entire length back into his mouth, forcing Alec deeper and deeper until the spongy head nudged the back of his throat.

He opened his jaw and encouraged Alec to fuck his face.

"I love your mouth. So fucking sinful." Alec's praises only made him work his man harder.

Keyes kept his mouth open, jaw slack as Alec pushed in and out, ravishing his mouth with every thrust of his hips growing faster until the sweet taste of Alec's come hit his tongue.

=♥=

Sated and wobbly on his feet, Alec grasped Key's shoulders to help steady himself. Love and contentment had him melting into Key. Key wrapped strong arms tightly around him, keeping him upright, and pinned solidly against his biker's chest while Alec rode the high of the intense orgasm.

Key's strong, insistent fingers pressed underneath his chin and tilted his head. Alec grinned even if he couldn't muster the strength to open his eyes as Key's calloused palm tenderly caressed his face as if memorizing him with his fingertips. Say what Key might, the guy was as much of a romantic as Alec.

Still basking in the afterglow of his orgasm, Alec finally lifted his eyelids, meeting Key's gaze. No words were necessary, their strong connection lingered. Key's eyes said exactly what Alec's heart needed to hear. Devotion and determination ignited the promise of a long future for their great love affair.

"I've gotta go right now. I'll be back tonight," Key said, pressing his lips to Alec's in a soft kiss.

"Give me your word that you'll come back to me, even after you've had time to think about all this again. Promise me and I'll believe you." Alec tightened his grip again, wrapping both arms securely around Key's broad shoulders, holding him there against him.

Key smiled. He leaned forward again, pressing his lips to Alec's. "I'm sorry about all that earlier. Stay patient with me."

"I'm taking that as a promise you're coming back," Alec replied, raising his brow and nodding. That seemed to lighten the moment. Key just shook his head, grinning broadly, and slowly extricated himself from Alec.

Alec made himself let go. Key reached down to grab his cell phone Alec had dropped, before leaving Alec standing there, yanking up his shorts. Key tugged his helmet on, staring at Alec. The biker grinned, stealing away the remnants of Alec's heart that hadn't already been given to Key.

"I'll see you tonight," Key yelled over the rumble as he centered the bike and knocked up the kickstand.

Alec watched him leave as it occurred to him the bike had continued running the whole time. He bet his neighbors were fit to be tied, already calling to report him. His homeowners' association would surely be knocking on his door by the end of the day. That was okay. He'd again pay the twenty-five dollar noise violation charge and listen to the lecture about being considerate of his neighbors. Hell, he should just give the HOA a retainer to pull from, because no matter what, Alec never wanted this to end.

CHAPTER 3

Alec pushed through the exit door into the private parking lot of the Henry Wade Juvenile Justice Center with renewed pep in his step. He'd been on his A-game today. He'd convinced the court to not only terminate Donald Cummings's parental rights, but to also keep the habitual offender locked away while awaiting his criminal trial. He owed a lot of his success of the day to Janice, his good friend and colleague. She had worked steadily by his side for nothing more than an appreciative pat on the back, but at least for now, little Keely Cummings, Donald's young daughter, and her always vigilant grandmother wouldn't have to worry about Donald getting out of jail and coming for his daughter. The DA's office still had their work cut out for them. Hopefully, a criminal attorney would be assigned to the case soon. Until then, Alec had done his part, and he might not have ever felt more accomplished in his life.

This latest wave of good fortune was like the icing on his already perfect cake. Three days had passed since that fateful morning where he'd thought he'd lost everything…and three nights of Key returning to his house every evening after work to spend the night and start the next day with him. Everything had changed. No, his biker hadn't said the words back to him, but every one of Key's actions proved his love. Key was more attentive than ever before, and that said a lot, because when they were together, they were so in sync it was hard to know where one began and the other ended.

He might be able to pin his giant grin to the toe-curling pleasure he'd woken to this morning. His big sexy man had nuzzled against his neck, marking him in the sweetest of ways while taking care of his morning wood. By Alec's estimation, there wasn't a better way to start a day. God, he was a fortunate man. All these years—hell, all of his life— he'd been searching for something unknown, and that unknown rested in the hands of one badass biker. His badass biker. Alec couldn't be happier.

His phone vibrated in the front breast pocket of his suit jacket, drawing him from his go-to Key-infused musings. The ones that assailed him anytime he got a moment's mental break. He reached in his slacks pocket for his Bluetooth earpiece, added it to his ear as he approached his vehicle, hearing the doors automatically unlock as he drew closer. With a press of the button, he answered the phone without checking caller ID.

"Alec Pierce."

"Alec Pierce." Blaine, his longtime grade school buddy, mimicked him in a mocking professional tone.

"I don't sound like that," he said, dropping down into his seat.

"And you don't call anymore. I have a new best friend," Blaine quipped, never missing a beat in getting to his point.

"You do?" Alec shook his head and resisted saying he had a new best friend too. Instead, he tried to give his voice a concerned edge as he pressed the button to start the engine.

"Yep. You're replaced," Blaine said with all certainty.

"What do you want me to ask next? By whom? Is that the right direction?" Alec retorted, playing along, looking in the rearview mirror as he backed out of his spot and started toward the exit.

"The only hint you'll get is his family owns a large hotel chain and his last name begins with an H."

Alec's grin, which was already so big, grew. He racked his brain, trying to come up with anything except the obvious answer. "Who owns the Holiday Inn?"

"Har, har, har. Humor's never been your strong suit. You should leave the jokes to me," Blaine said drolly. "How's working life?"

"Fulfilling," Alec answered honestly as he pulled into the far-right lane, taking his place in the long line of traffic approaching the red light.

An idea came to mind causing Alec to look around, trying to get his bearings for the area. This had to be close to Key's tire shop. He just didn't know enough about the area to know for sure.

"How's the judgeship coming?" Blaine asked as Alec used his GPS to find Key's shop.

"I've decided to let that opportunity pass me by," Alec said distractedly as a honk came from behind. He punched the gas, moving up several car lengths while the GPS searched then found Key's shop. It was only a few miles away. Did he dare do a drive-by?

"Hmm. Have you told your parents?" Blaine knew him too well. Both his and Blaine's families were longtime elitists of the New England area. Alec's family had purchased but never lived on a tract of land in far south Ellis

County to help build a political stronghold in the state of Texas. From that standpoint, Alec was the only Pierce to ever make Texas his permanent home. Thank God he had or he would have never met Key, and there he was again, back in the forefront of Alec's thoughts. Wow, Key even lessened the normal sickening in Alec's gut at the thought of talking to his overly politically motivated family about his decision to end this judgeship farce.

"That's coming," Alec finally answered. This conversation helped him understand another layer to his relationship with Key. The painful past his terrible family had forced him to endure in their attempt to distance themselves from Alec's sexual orientation was beginning to heal with Key's help. It didn't matter that he hadn't told his family. Those decisions were made, so end of that story. Alec quickly changed lanes, taking the route to Key's shop. Maybe he could get a quick peek at his guy—a reward for his good job in court today.

"When the time comes, I'm here if you need me." His normally animated friend became serious. "How's the biker?"

Alec went silent as he turned, following the GPS's automated directive. He hadn't shared the details of his relationship with Key with anyone. Blaine only knew of Key because he'd been there the night his tires had blown. Key had rescued them, saving the day by changing the two flats and sealing his and Key's inevitable fate. Key was far too special for the jaded and cynical Blaine to understand.

"You can't be serious?" Blaine asked, his tone dripping with condescension when Alec made no reply.

Alec contemplated hanging up on Blaine. It was one thing not to understand the complete one-eighty Alec had done since meeting and building a forbidden relationship with Key, another altogether different thing to mock the special bond they shared. Blaine had been his best friend and daily companion since grade school. The two of them had had a hell of a good time together, thumbing their noses at their pretentious families. But Blaine refused to accept that lifestyle had grown old years ago. Alec had begun distancing himself from the constant party back in law school.

"What?" he finally said.

"Are you still seeing him?"

Alec's back got up, his spine stiffening to ramrod straight in defense of his relationship while he wove through the congested traffic. "Hell yeah, I am. Why?"

"What in the world do you two have to talk about?" Blaine asked incredulously.

"We talk about everything."

"Politics?"

What a dumb question, of course they didn't speak of politics. As an inducted, patched member of the notorious biker club, Disciples of Havoc, Key was a tried and true anarchist. He and Key didn't speak of politics or religion. Those things held no interest for Key and, honestly, little interest to Alec anymore.

"How about fashion week or geography or maybe civil disorder around the world? All serious interests of yours."

"You're pissing me off. Stop trying to rain on my parade," Alec said, his brows snapping together.

"So it's the size of his dick?"

That eased some of his sudden burst of frustration as Alec gave a noncommittal shrug, letting his thoughts be redirected. He didn't want to ever pare Key down to just sex. They'd proven over and over again it was more than the sexual quest they had started with, but he couldn't deny Key did have a nice cock. A very nice and pleasurable cock. His body stirred, thinking of a fully naked Key. Alec bit his lip, lost in the instant mental image of a nude Key and blew through a yellow light as it turned red, lost in the distraction.

"You two together? I can't see it." Blaine would shit if he knew the truth. This conversation with Blaine proved how unaccepting his friends and family would be toward Key. When the time came for them to be a true out couple, Alec would willingly leave that life behind and forge this new one with his biker.

"Who the fuck cares what you see? He likes me. I like him. And he thinks I'm the hottest guy on this planet." The smile was back on his face. Alec had been told countless times he was easy on the eyes, but because Key had said those exact words, it made Alec feel so special.

"Shows how little of the world he's seen. You're not the hottest guy on the planet," Blaine said with all authority.

"Thanks. You know, you should consider fucking inspirational speaking as possible employment," Alec quipped, increasing his speed, mentally running Blaine over in the process.

Blaine completely ignored him. "Clearly, you're spending lots of time with him. The biker's coming out in you."

Since Janice had mentioned his frequent use of more colorful language, he suspected that was probably true. Key used the word fuck as a verb, noun, adjective, and adverb, sometimes all in the same sentence.

"So if his club gets taken down by the feds, are you an accomplice?"

"You're a douche. I'm hanging up."

He didn't have to justify his decisions to Blaine or to anyone. Alec reached to end the call.

"Because, honestly, I don't think orange should be your new black."

Alec hung up while laughing at his friend's absurdity. Blaine never quit and had always been there for him when needed. He honestly didn't see that changing, but one thing was for sure, Blaine needed to get used to Key being in his life.

As Alec turned on West Davis Street, he thought about calling Rosa Daly to let her know of his success this morning, but decided to wait as he saw the approaching tire shop. His heart picked up a beat, staring at the sign in the distance as he came to another red light. In all their time together, Alec hadn't gone back to the tire shop, not since he'd had his tires changed the day after meeting Key.

This seemed like a breach of his and Key's vow to stay hidden. Maybe he shouldn't do this.

No, driving down a street was a normal act. Hell, he could be having lunch in the Bishop Arts district. That was something he'd wanted to do since he'd driven there his first time.

The light turned green as his phone rang again. He looked down for a second to see Janice's name appear on the screen. He answered while slowing his speed on the approach to the tire shop.

"Hey, can you have lunch today?" Janice asked.

"Sure, I'm in the Bishop Arts area. Come here?" Alec asked.

"Oh, good choice. How about Gloria's? I'm fifteen minutes away."

"See you then." Alec ended the call as he slowly drove past Tires. To his relief, Key was outside, standing in the partially filled parking lot. Alec's gaze locked on Key, who became the only thing he saw. His heart leaped at the sight of his man and the innate connection they shared seemed to hold as Key looked over at the street as he passed by. For a brief few seconds, Alec was filled with unbelievable joy that instantly faded as Key left his view. Alec took a deep breath, absorbing the sudden rush of such a high, then the immediate low as the shop disappeared behind him. That was all right. He got his fix. That would be enough for now.

=♥=

Hound, a patched brother of the Disciples of Havoc, came to a stop directly in front of Keyes. He then took a half step to the left, purposefully blocking Keyes's view of his father who sat dutifully in the passenger side of a club-owned tow truck with a car loaded in the rear. Keyes gave Hound props for trying to shield him from his old man, but he should have rolled up the truck's windows because nothing could drown out the vitriol spewing from his father's hateful mouth.

"Ignore him," Hound said, hooking a thumb over his shoulder toward the tow truck. "We're slammed today. I got another tow waitin'. I didn't have a choice but to bring him along. I told him to keep his fuckin' mouth shut. You see how that worked out."

Keyes nodded, knowing even though he tuned his old man out, his current customers waiting in the parking lot for their tire changes could certainly hear every disparaging word coming from the cab of the truck. Whatever Hound wanted, it needed to get done as fast as humanly possible.

"Mack asked if you could get these tires changed. It's all the customer needs. He'll handle the payment."

"Sure," he said, and with a cock of his head, he nodded Hound toward the truck. As he started them that direction, a weird tug at his heart made Keyes slow. The feeling was instinctual more than anything tangible. Whatever it was had him turning toward the road. Keyes's heart skipped a beat when the shiny flash of red and chrome caught his attention. His forward steps halted as he recognized Alec's sports car rolling past. In that ten or so seconds, everything faded away. Keyes's anxiety eased, his face softened, and a smile pulled at the corners of his lips. He didn't know what Alec was doing on this side of town and didn't care. He had needed the mental boost Alec always brought. Keyes had to check his urge to lift his hand in greeting.

As quickly as Alec had come, he left, and Keyes's world rushed back in around him. Keyes's gaze swept the parking lot, watching his staff dart around like a seasoned pit crew. The sounds of impact wrenches and his father's shouted insults filled the peaceful place Alec had momentarily created. He turned toward the tow truck to see Hound several steps ahead of him, staring at him as if he lost his mind. Technically, he probably had, but he finished his steps and his thought as he headed around the rear of the truck.

"Umm. Yeah. I'll help get the car off the truck. He's gotta go before he fuckin' freaks out my customers."

"Prez says for you to stop by this afternoon," Hound's gravelly voice called out from the other side of the truck.

Keyes nodded, knowing that was code for another drug run. They were growing in frequency, which was risky as hell with the way the Dallas district attorney still breathed down their backs, but the prez knew what he was doing. He could trust that. Besides, Keyes was banking and socking that bonus cash away, so he'd count it as a win-win for everyone.

"He also called everybody to church tomorrow afternoon."

Keyes paused in loosening the chain holding the back of the vehicle in place. A club meeting would mean two nights in a row he'd have to stay on this side of town. Technically, that wasn't abnormal except he'd been going over to Alec's every night this week, and he liked it. Alec seemed to like him there too.

"Smoke's declinin'. They told me not to say anything, but I thought you should know," Hound said, leaning toward Keyes, angling his body across the back of the truck bed. They made eye contact, and it held as Hound nodded toward his father. Honestly, Keyes didn't want to know how or why his old man might have taken a turn for the worse. It was out of his control. No matter how hard he'd tried in the past to build a relationship with his father, it wasn't ever going to happen. The man hated him, and there was no love lost on his end either, so it was best if they stayed out of each other's way.

He didn't say a word. Instead, he moved to the front of the loaded car to help lower the vehicle. As he worked, his father hit the outer side panel of the truck, drawing Keyes's attention that direction. He caught his old man's reflection in the side mirror. His father looked much thinner than the last time he'd seen him, and that couldn't have been more than a month ago.

"You're a fuckin' pussy," his father drawled with venom in his voice that didn't match the sickly shell of the man he'd become. His father held his gaze in the side mirror then lifted his hand, pointing at him, making a pistol out of his forefinger and thumb. He fired at Keyes through the mirror. "It's gonna fuckin' happen, pussy."

Keyes made a show of rolling his eyes then lifted his middle finger at his father before turning back to the car, refusing to engage no matter how badly he wanted to shove his fist into his father's gaunt face for threatening him like that. He'd leveled far bigger and badder men than his father for much less of an insult.

When the car settled on the pavement, his father unlatched the passenger side door. Keyes whipped his head that direction. There were maybe ten feet and that damn door separating him from his old man.

"Don't you get out of that fuckin' truck, old man," he warned.

From the side mirror, he watched his father remove the oxygen tube from his nose and an arm shoved the door open wider with a dirty jean-clad leg following. His father's work boot hit the pavement as he lifted his middle finger at Keyes. "What you gonna do, fuckin' queer?"

Keyes saw red. Lost to the burst of anger, he went straight for his old man even as he heard Hound scurrying around the back of the truck. "I got it, bro. Key, stay back."

The hate they had for one another was legendary. His father had been viciously cruel to him for as long as he could remember, but when he had found out about Keyes's sexual preferences, shit became unbearable. His father's deep-seated contempt for him caused problems throughout every layer of the motorcycle club. Keyes was done being so damned disrespected.

"You ain't shit. What you gonna do? Every time anything happens, you coward away," his father snarled, stepping fully out of the truck. "This is my business, and I'm takin' it back. Nobody's gonna wanna do business here if they find out you're a fuckin' queer."

Not the first time he and his old man would come to blows. His whole life, he'd been nothing more than his father's regular punching bag. Not once had Keyes ever truly fought back, until now. He been tortured, abused, and humiliated at this man's hand for far too many years. Keyes stalked forward, remembering this scum's hate-filled text messages that had almost caused him to ruin the best thing that had ever happened to him.

Against the fire brewing inside him, Keyes's balled fists relaxed as he barreled down on his old man. He was skin and bones, looked sickly as hell and shaky on his feet. Yeah, there was something really wrong with the man. His dire health kept Keyes's fist from making contact, but that was it. As his father got into fight mode, he took a swing. Keyes ducked and dodged the hit as he reached out for his father, manhandling him back inside the truck. He wasn't careful as he shoved his old man through the open door with Hound on his ass, trying to grab him from behind.

"Get the fuck off me, Hound," he growled, easily breaking any hold Hound managed as he reached for the door, slamming it shut on his loudly cursing father.

"Stay the fuck away from me," Keyes warned his old man. His jaw clenched tightly closed, the need to level this hateful man eating at him. The finger he pointed at his old man curled into his fist again. It would be so easy to knock the son of a bitch out right where he sat.

His father started beating up the interior of the truck, his breathing labored, but he didn't open the door again. "You're the fuckin' embarrassment of my life."

That was it. Fuck frail. He wasn't going to let his father die without cold-cocking him at least once. Keyes again started for his father, but he should have known better. He got within range and his father spit at him. A thick wet wad landed on his chest. Keyes leaped for the truck, but Hound bravely, if not stupidly, slid between the two of them. His big hands landed on Keyes's chest.

"Let it go, Key. It's not worth it. Everybody's watchin'."

He didn't fucking care who watched, let Jesus Christ himself watch him make that sorry old man eat his words. The exertion proved too much for his father as he collapsed into a horrible coughing fit, which helped Keyes clear his single-minded tunnel vision bent on destruction. He looked over to see his customers and employees staring at the tow truck. Thank God they couldn't get the full visual.

Keyes took a mental step back.

"See? Fuckin' coward," his father managed to say between bouts of coughing.

Keyes followed the mental step with a physical step backward. He turned away, the tic in his jaw double-timing in his anger. He rolled the T-shirt from the hem up until he covered the spit wad, then pulled his shirt over his head. Keyes didn't look back as he started for the shop and the change of clothes he kept in the back office.

No one said a word as he stalked up the steps and disappeared inside.

CHAPTER 4

Alec followed the sidewalk leading to the entrance of Gloria's. The food smelled amazing, and as he made his way through the outside seating area toward the front doors of the restaurant, he spotted several delicious looking dishes on the tables as he approached the hostess stand. He waited in line for his turn to be seated and grabbed a menu, giving it a quick glance. Like he found himself doing all the time, he easily ticked off several appetizers he wanted to try then rescanned the selections, picking the ones he thought Key might like. He wished there was a way to place a to-go order and have it delivered to Key. He just wasn't sure how to make it happen without leaving, at the very least, a paper trail leading back to him.

"Just one?"

Alec looked up to see a handsome young waiter standing in front of him.

"No, two. Can we eat outside?"

"Sure. Come this way." The guy grabbed silverware and another menu, leading Alec back the way he'd come to one of the tables with a large open umbrella. It was a beautiful day outside, the wind was light with a soft alluring breeze and the temperature was easing off from the intense summer heat. Alec again felt the good fortune of the great moment he experienced—he loved looking at life in this way. He also gave Key props for helping change his perspective.

Alec hiked a leg over the bench seat and sat at the table as a cocktail napkin and the silverware were placed in front of him. "Can I get you a drink?"

"I think I'll stick with iced tea," Alec said and pointed to the order of loaded nachos on the menu. "I'm starving. How do these rate?"

The waiter grinned knowingly. "They're good. One of the most ordered items on the menu."

"Bring me that while I wait," he said, his mouth already watering. He had a newfound hang-up for anything hot and spicy since meeting Key. It was his mister's first choice every time they ordered anything together.

"Sweet or unsweet iced tea?"

Just when Alec thought he'd been fully indoctrinated into the Southern culture, he had forgotten something so basically engrained as how iced tea should be sweetened.

"Let's do a half and half. Have any mango or pineapple flavoring for the tea?" Alec asked, releasing the buttons at his wrists and carefully rolling up his sleeves.

"Pineapple—it's a fresh puree." The guy grinned, maybe with a hint of interest gleaming in his eye. Funny, there was a time that would have been all he needed, but not anymore. Not since Key, and Alec recognized the absurdity of how many times he'd considered his boyfriend in the last two minutes. He was ridiculously in love with that man.

"Perfect."

The waiter left as Alec heard an alerting chirp from his phone. He fished the phone out of his pocket, happy to see Key's name in the corner of the screen. With a finger swipe, he opened the text to read.

"*that u?*" The text brought another silly grin to his face.

"*It was. Did I risk anything?*" he typed back. Luckily, he didn't have to wait long for a reply.

"*good timing.*" Hmm. Why good timing? Alec's brows slid together as he typed.

"*That doesn't sound good.*"

"*My old man.*" Key didn't need to say anything more. Although he rarely discussed his life, he'd let out enough to know he and his father didn't have a good relationship. Alec didn't press him for more—he wanted to, but didn't—and just went to the important part.

"*Are you good? Do you need me? I'm having lunch down the street. I'm close.*"

"*u helped,*" Key replied.

Then it was a good decision to do an impromptu drive-by today. He'd noticed how connected he seemed to be to Key, sort of an otherworldly telepathic bond that sent glorious chills down his spine. Something he'd never experienced with anyone before. Maybe that was what had him deciding today was the day he should venture into the biker's neck of the woods.

Another text came through as he sat there contemplating the possible psychic side to their relationship. "*Have lunch. I got work.*"

He could sense the turmoil in his lover. Alec hated that for him. Key was such a good man.

"Hey you," Janice said, coming to the table. Alec lifted his gaze to her as his iced tea and large platter of nachos were placed on the table.

"Great place," he said, lifting the tea, taking a sip, giving a thumbs-up to the waiter. The pineapple puree was an incredible touch, one he needed to remember. Janice took her seat and placed a red file folder on the table between them, making Alec cock his head as he drank from the straw to see his name scrawled out in a pretty penmanship across the tab.

"What can I get you?" the waiter asked Janice.

"I'll have a glass of pinot grigio."

Oh, okay. So they were having a drinking lunch. An idea Alec absolutely agreed with and seconded that decision to the waiter. "Make that two."

His phone vibrated again in his hand, and he looked down to see another message from Key. "*club biz tonight and tomorrow. See u Saturday.*"

No! Alec's heart sank, and the day took an unfortunate turn. He forgot everything around him as he typed back quickly. "*Come over when you're done.*" He felt selfish for asking Key to drive all that way to spend five or six hours sleeping with him only to turn around and fight the rush hour traffic back the following morning. His thumb paused over the send button. He shouldn't send this message and put that pressure on Key.

"I think we lost him," Janice said. Alec looked up to see Janice and the waiter staring at him.

"What did I miss?" he asked, turning back to the phone in his hands. How should he reply?

"Are you ready to order?" Janice asked, laughingly.

"Enchiladas, the chicken enchiladas," he said, glancing at the top of the menu to make sure he got the name of the dish correct before his eyes went back to the phone in his hand. He erased his words and decided to go more generic, not to put undue pressure on Key. "*If it's not too late, and you feel like driving, come home.*" Alec liked the use of the term home for Key. It felt natural and right, and what he wanted his lover to think when he thought of Alec, so he kept it there and continued. *"Be safe in whatever you're doing. Now, I'm very glad I did a drive-by. At least I got to see you."* Alec pushed send and started to put the phone in his back pocket when he looked up to see Janice staring at him with a big giant grin. "What?"

"Who is he?" she asked, knowingly.

Alec didn't even try to hide his infatuation. He was smitten, head over heels in love, and if he could shout it from the rooftops, he would. Instead, he went with a more sedate, "No one you know," while reaching for a gooey cheese-covered chip to put on his plate, pushing the full platter toward Janice.

"But it's serious?" she asked, reaching for the plate.

"Oh yeah." Alec grinned, leaving it right there as he scooped the fallen toppings with his cheese-laden chip, putting it in his mouth. Oh man, he wasn't disappointed. With his mouth full and a second bite prepared, he nodded toward the folder she'd brought. "What's that?"

Her face went from excited to solemn in an instant as she opened the folder. "I know you won in court today, but I kept digging around on Donald Cummings. He's got so much that just didn't add up or connect."

Alec lifted his eyes to hers as she grew silent for a moment then shook her head.

"I know I'm not making sense. I found something that's a bit alarming, and the best I can tell, no one knows. I'm unsure what I should do with the information. I'm genuinely torn."

"Okay," Alec said, watching Janice turn several sheets of paper in the folder until she pulled out one page and slid it across the table to him. Alec quickly added a third bite of cheesy goodness to his mouth then reached for his napkin, wiping his hands before he took the sheet.

"I'm sending all this with you. It's got everything the criminal side will need when they prosecute this guy. I was as thorough as I could be and decided I'll stick with the case if they allow me to."

Alec scanned down the page, looking for anything obvious before starting from the top as the waiter placed a wine glass in front of him. This looked like a poorly scanned handwritten police report from one of the several times Camille Doreen Cummings, Donald's wife and Rosa Daly's daughter, had called the police on her abusive husband. The penmanship made it hard to read, but Alec's eyes narrowed when he came to a line stating Donald had been spending significant time with the Disciples of Havoc motorcycle club. Per the officer, Camille said he'd become a prospect for the gang.

To quote Key... *Motherfucker*.

Alec lifted his concerned gaze to Janice. "Who knows this?"

"As far as I can tell, me, you, the arresting police officer, and Keely's mother who's still on the run. This was never connected to any official police report against Cummings. I stumbled on it only by accident, but it makes lots of sense. Cummings behaves like a gang member," she explained, crossing her arms at the edge of the table. Alec's mind raced over the possibilities. "I'm torn, Alec. My first thought was this guy's dangerous to his child."

Alec nodded. That was an understatement. He continued reading, making sure he didn't miss anything more in the report.

"If I make this known, I can see Twiford offering Cummings a plea deal or worse for information on the club."

"Exactly my thought. She'd grant him immunity on unrelated crimes to get him talking. He'll terrorize his daughter and her grandmother."

"Right." Her hand moved papers around on the table until she lifted another one. "With this rap sheet, if Cummings gets immunity, I can't imagine what he'd do."

Alec took the multi-page stapled document Janice handed over. He'd seen a lot of this information before, but this particular form listed each offense, one right after the other. Dammit. He'd met Keely and her grandmother on several different occasions now. They were fresh and honest...and very frightened. Rosa and Keely played a large role in doing what it took to keep Donald behind bars until his criminal trial, and Donald's ugly outburst in court today, stating clearly his intention to exact revenge on Rosa, didn't hurt their case either.

His mind reeled as the metaphorical gate swung shut, possibly locking him into this unwanted job. With this case complete—at least Alec's portion had been wrapped up in a nice bow—Alec had been free to tender his resignation with the DA's office and implement his plans to remove the obstacles keeping him and Key hidden.

Alec let a defeated sigh slip free. What were his options now? His mind raced as he looked for any out he could find. "Give me some time before you say anything, will you? I want to go through this information. When I get back into the office, I'll call Rosa, Keely's grandmother, see what she knows."

"I'll help you, Alec, any way I can, but if Twiford finds out we're holding this..." Janice shook her head, and he completely understood her concern. The DA had such a single-minded focus to bring down the Havoc bike club both he and Janice would immediately be on the chopping block for failure to disclose this valuable information.

"I'll take responsibility—" Alec started, but Janice cut him off.

"My prints are all over this, so to speak. My log-in pulled the information," she explained, showing the depth of her concern.

"But you pulled it for me and never read it—it's that simple. Just give me a little bit of time," he said, meeting Janice's worried stare, and nodded. Janice was slower, but she did finally nod her agreement.

"That was pretty much my plan from the beginning. That's why we're here and not the office. Just be careful, Alec. That club's something else," Janice said, reaching across the table to squeeze his forearm. He appreciated the sentiment, and of course, his emotions were all over the place about Key's club. It was hard to reconcile the kind, generous lover he'd grown to adore with the awful allegations spouted by a vicious, manipulative district attorney who seemed as horrible and calculating as the club she'd sworn to take down.

Ultimately, though, Alec didn't care about any of that. His concern rested with the safety of a little girl and with the man he loved. Nothing more.

"Does it say who sponsored him in the club?" Alec asked absently, placing the sheet back on the stack of papers in the folder. The best Alec could remember, Key had only mentioned one or two of his brothers by their nicknames. The likelihood of Alec recognizing the name of the sponsor was slim.

"Yeah, I went ahead and pulled his record too. He's a long-time member." She reached for the folder, thumbing through several pages, before handing one to him with the name Paul "Smoke" Dixon at the top. Alec's heart dropped. No fucking way. "He has a long, sordid past. He's been arrested many times, most recently in the raid a few months back. Dixon's also very familiar with CPS. From the early nineties on, he was regularly investigated. His child was taken from him and his wife, and it looks like the club attorney fought to bring him back. Not a good mentor for Cummings. Alec, this club's bad news," she said again in warning.

The information in the folder just grew more important. The ugly demon tattoo on Key's chest came to mind, clouding these murky waters even more. Alec laid his papers inside the file and closed the folder before setting it to the side. He needed to be in the privacy of his home office to explore Key's past. The thought made his stomach turn. Alec reached for his wine, draining the glass in a couple of long gulps as he heard the distant rumble of the pipes. He turned, hoping to see Key. His gaze locked on the familiar Harley and the very man he'd hoped to find. The biker was sexy, his long muscular body relaxed as he cruised by. His eyes landed on the black boots Key had shoved on this morning then followed a line up his jean-covered leg to his muscular thigh. Alec was instantly jealous of the bike, because he knew exactly how hard those thick thighs could squeeze. His mister wasn't wearing his helmet—he'd have to talk to him about that later—but damn Key was a tempting sight. His dick plumped, wanting Key's attention. Key wore his leather vest—his patch—something Alec couldn't remember seeing on Key before and a pair of aviator sunglasses. His long hair whipped behind him. His lover did glance over at the restaurant, the heat so intense Alec swore Key had seen him.

"That's one of them. Their hangout's over here somewhere," Janice stated, and Alec turned back when Key was out of view. He did everything he could to school his facial features and act neutral even with the chaos spinning rampant inside him.

"Hmm," he said noncommittally, then with more determination, added, "You're going to have to give me time."

"I will, but if I found this, someone else will. They're combing everything, Alec. Work this as fast as you can. Get the family protection, do whatever you do, because I promise you, this isn't good," she said, pointing to the folder.

Alec nodded as the waiter placed his plate of food in front of him. His appetite had waned, worry taking its place. He looked down at the file folder, knowing the information inside was most likely going to rip his heart out.

CHAPTER 5

Keyes parked the tire shop's service truck next to his best friend Devilman's motorcycle in the parking lot of Chain Metal, a seedy little hole-in-the-wall dive bar. As teenagers, he and Dev had snuck into this place more times than he could count. He couldn't figure out for the life of him why Dev had gone to the bar tonight. Keyes cut the engine and was out the door, pocketing his keys as he headed for the entrance.

Dev was apparently trashed per the bartender who had taken his keys away over an hour ago. Keyes had been halfway to Alec's place—because he was such a fucking pussy; he'd missed Alec and planned to surprise him even at this late hour—when he'd gotten the call to come get his boy.

He guessed Dev's pretty new girlfriend, who'd had him taking responsibility seriously, was wearing off. They were back to the future, or maybe it was better said that they were back to the past. Either way, Keyes was always Dev's designated driver, meaning he wouldn't be sleeping next to Alec tonight.

He pushed through the bar's front door. The place was dark. It usually took time for his eyes to adjust, but he didn't need them tonight. Dev was loud, and it was late, already close to midnight, only the barflies and stragglers were left behind. Keyes started toward Dev's loud mouth, walking past the bartender who dangled Dev's keys his direction. He shook his head, "Hound'll be by in a minute to grab his bike."

"My brother," Dev called out, Keyes's voice enough to gain all Dev's attention. Dev jumped up, knocking his chair backward, staggering as he came forward, his arms wide falling into Keyes while trying to give him a hug. "Where you come from?"

"I came to take you home," he said, chuckling at the exuberance of the hug.

"Nah, man! Have a drink with me," Dev insisted, not letting Keyes go. Dev's arms tightened around him, causing Keyes's brow to furrow. He angled his head, trying to see what was going on with his friend to cause this extended hold.

"You okay?" he asked and grabbed Dev's biceps, moving him back several inches to look in his face.

Dev's mocking grin was instant, and he pointed a finger in Keyes's face. "I drank too much tonight. Did you know?"

Any worry eased, and Keyes laughed at the certainty of Dev's slurred tone. "Yup, that's what I heard."

When Dev took a step to the right then another step to help keep himself upright, Keyes anchored an arm around his best friend's waist, moving to help carry/walk him out of the bar. "I gotta get us home. Come on."

"Best friend a person could have," Dev called out to the whole bar as he pulled from his hold. He did a twirl, pointing to Keyes so everyone could see. That forced Keyes to bust a quick move to catch Dev before he completely lost his footing and face-planted on the concrete floor.

"Come on." Keyes struggled to keep Dev focused on leaving even as he got them through the bar and out into the parking lot.

"I miss you, man. We were together all the time," Dev said as he missed the sidebar to Keyes's truck, falling face-first into the seat.

After missing the sidebar again, Keyes had to partially lift Dev into the seat to get him inside the cab.

"See all that fuckin' meth tonight? My old man fuckin' killed it. I could use a bump, brother." Dev's head slumped forward, and he passed out as Keyes tucked him in then climbed over Dev to lock his seatbelt in place. He went around the truck to the driver's side and climbed in to a long, sinus-filled snore from his passenger.

So many things were wrong with what Dev had just said. Shit was getting harder to ignore where his buddy was concerned, specifically his growing fixation on crystal meth. Keyes had only tried it a couple of times. He didn't like the chaos it created in his head when his body sped up that way, nor did he like the way it wrecked him when he came down. He also didn't like the fire-breathing dragons his parents had become when coming off their highs. He never wanted to be like that. Dev, on the other hand, struggled to stay away—the drug had fucked up everything for his friend when they were in their late teens and early twenties. Keyes prayed he wasn't using again.

He started the engine. The rumble jerked Dev awake, and he raised his head, looking around, surprise showing on his face when his gaze landed on Keyes. "You came."

Keyes grinned and started to back out of the parking space. "Yeah."

"Best fuckin' friend a guy…" Dev didn't finish. He was back asleep, this time with his head falling back against the headrest.

Months had passed since he'd been to Dev's new apartment complex. Keyes took a turn or two wrong, but eventually found the place. He rolled his diesel engine through the quiet complex, trying to remember the apartment number. Only because of Alec's quiet neighborhood did he even consider that every vehicle he owned should come with a noise warning.

He cut the engine, staring at the dark building. A corner window showed a light turning on. By the time he got Dev out of the truck, Holly was standing on the porch with the porch light on, a pretty little robe wrapped around her, both worry and relief clear on her face.

"Babe," Dev said, slurring his words as he tried and failed to pull free of Keyes's hold. With as much as he had to carry Dev to keep him on his feet, Keyes didn't think it was wise to let him go. "You're home."

"I came home early, but you weren't here," she said, worry and confusion etched on her pretty face as she took in everything she was seeing. By her reaction, this might be a first for her, which spoke volumes for how much Dev must care for her.

"Didn't wanna be here without you," Dev managed to say before slumping in Keyes's arms, requiring him to carry Dev the rest of the way inside. Together, they knocked through the front door then down the hall, Holly shimmying past to lead the way to their bedroom where Keyes laid Dev out across the bed.

"Want me to get his clothes off?" he asked, tugging off one of Dev's boots then the other. He placed those on the floor beside the bed.

"No. That's enough. Thank you for getting him home. He's been drinking quite a bit more, but I haven't seen him like this," she said, her worried gaze focused on Dev as she wrapped her arms around her waist.

He'd have to give that topic a hard pass. Keyes didn't want to know their problems and certainly didn't want to talk to her about them. He immediately started for the bedroom door. "I'll be by in the mornin' to take him to work."

"I can take him. I don't have to work and the girls are gone this week," she said, following behind him back toward the front door.

"You sure? I don't mind," he asked, his only real focus was on making his way out of the house as quickly as possible.

"No, I got it. Do you have his keys?"

He only slowed from his quick getaway to turn while walking over the threshold of the front door. "Tell him Hound's got 'em."

Keyes hightailed it back to the truck, jumping in and shoving the keys in the ignition, starting the engine within a couple of minutes of tugging off Dev's boots. He put the truck in reverse and paused to pull his phone from his pocket to check the time. Solidly past midnight. Alec was probably sleeping. He shouldn't text. He sighed. With that decision made, he pressed on the gas, looking over his shoulder to back out of the parking space.

Alec dropped Paul Dixon's record on his desk and had to fight the bile rising in his throat. The story of Key's tragic childhood unfolded in the long list of complaints and charges filed against his father. How in the world had Key turned into such a fine man growing up under the influence of that horrible human being? Alec shuffled the pages now spread across his desk to find the photo of Paul Dixon. The image led to another glaringly obvious question: how was this man Key's father? He was short with a stocky build and jet black hair. Alec wished he had a photo of Key's mother.

He pushed back in his office chair, his chin resting between his forefinger and thumb as he stared unseeingly at the scattered sheets, thinking about Harmony Carter Dixon. Based on the words painting the picture of Key's mother, she seemed like a train wreck, and that was putting it nicely. What had that life been like for such a young boy?

Alec leaned back in his chair, dropping his head back on the headrest. This was exactly why CPS was wrong for him. His heart ached for Key and his heart feared for Keely. He'd gotten lost for hours, trying to piece together the timeline of Key's abusive life. Janice had only presented him with the facts, very few in-depth details, and those were only from the time Key landed in CPS custody. Key had run away from foster care several times, gotten arrested as a teenager, and dropped out of school by the middle of tenth grade. If Keely was subjected to this lifestyle, would the same happen to her?

Alec searched the papers for the reference to the man who'd posted bail for Key when he'd been eighteen years old. Clyde Carter. He must be Key's uncle.

Key wouldn't like Alec knowing all this. He was too proud of a man.

How did Key not have a million trust issues?

Of course, his biker couldn't say *I love you*. He might not ever be able to say those words aloud.

Moreover, their differences just became more clearly defined. He didn't really know Key—not all of him. What had Alec hoped to accomplish by insisting an outlaw biker blend into his life? Key was so grounded, at ease with his decisions. He navigated a world that Alec had very little knowledge of. The man hadn't let his environment consume him. It flowed around him but never swallowed him. Alec envied that.

Alec's life hadn't been perfect, but the show his father put on for the world would easily convince anyone otherwise. Alec had grown accustomed to the cold, distant acknowledgement whenever he came around. His family continually rejected him. No, he hadn't been physically injured like Key, but emotionally, he'd been hurt. Abuse wore many faces, and Alec had no doubt his parents' public life had probably been the only reason their disgust hadn't manifested into a physical form. The marks left by his and Key's pasts made them the men they were today.

Somehow, he had been able to develop a strong sense of self—perhaps Key had too. Alec would always have to remember to rein in his natural pushy tendencies and allow Key room to be comfortable. It was a lot for Alec to take on, and he let out a long, deep sigh, resting back in the seat again.

"Why all the doom and gloom, Pierce? Nothing's changed," he said to the empty room, trying to pick himself up, shake off some of this sadness plaguing him since reading all this terrible information.

"Except, everything's changed."

What was he doing?

Hell, if this relationship ended, Key could be hurt, but as fast and loose as Alec had been with his heart, Alec would be destroyed.

Building resolve, Alec knew he must guard against ever hurting Key—he'd been through too much in his life. Alec must always be open and honest with Key. On this point, there was no room for failure.

The image of Key on his knees, begging Alec for time, soared to life. Key had never been afraid of anything until Alec. The true understanding of what that meant nearly crushed his soul.

Alec's phone chirped, and he looked to where his phone rested on the desk, thankful for the interruption of his downward spiraling thoughts. Alec reached over, expecting to see some partying photo from Blaine. His buddy had been sending them all night, taunting Alec with the good time he and his new best friend were having. Instead of Blaine's name, he saw Key's.

It was insane how much his heart needed to hear from his guy tonight. No doubt, Key had overcome his upbringing, but Alec seemed to be the one needing comfort as he imagined the life Key had once endured. Alec swiped a thumb across the screen to one of Key's longest messages ever.

"*Goodnight sorry I did not call before now. Tried to make it over got tied up.*" The simple words were read as if Key had caressed his heart. Instead of texting, Alec pushed the phone option, calling Key as he rose from his office chair, pulling the chain to his desk lamp.

"Did I wake you?" Key asked in lieu of a greeting. "I didn't think I should text."

"Not at all. I'm awake. I've been working. I've got a case that's bothering me." Alec rolled his eyes at the extreme understatement as he left the office. The lights behind him dimmed as he started down the hall, his newest smart home feature.

"Have I been comin' over too much?"

Alec ducked his head, chin to chest, watching his feet move and smiled. Key always worried he was an imposition. Alec's heart warmed. He couldn't change Key's life up until the time they'd met, but he could do his part to give Key a better life now. He just had to figure their way out.

"Not at all. I want you here. Maybe a more honest explanation as to why I'm still awake is that I don't sleep as well without you here. I seem to think you belong here with me," Alec mused, knowing he'd never spoken truer words.

"Hmm..." Key's voice turned husky and deep—his sexy-time voice. Next came a yawn that slipped out and dented the mental image Alec had drawn of his guy readying for sex. Key was more likely readying for bed, but that was okay too. "You've never told me that before."

"You know I'd rather you be here. I've made that clear." Alec put the phone on speaker mode, placing it on the sink counter in his bathroom. He dropped his shorts, and immediately bent down, reaching for them to fold. That was the-always-clean Key coming out in him.

"You could do better. I'm a freak show. If you knew what I was thinkin' half the time..."

"Like what?" Alec interrupted when Key gave another yawn. There were all these imaginary lines he and Key never crossed. They only spoke of what the other was willing to say and never prodded for more. That needed to change. Alec wanted to be Key's anchor, which required trust and honesty to achieve.

"I watched a gay couple once at a dance club..." That had Alec picking up the phone as he interrupted again.

"You go to dance clubs?" Alec shook his head, thinking about his very reserved, not overly outgoing Key in a techno music blaring club with bright lights flashing... Yeah, Key wasn't a dance club type.

"As a wallflower. So these guys were clearly together and trashed and all over each other." Key gave another deeper, much longer yawn. Alec tossed his shorts on the built-in dresser, forgoing the brushing of his teeth to keep Key on the phone and talking. "The guys ended up doin' it in the parkin' lot. I mean right there, close to my bike, on the pavement. I don't know if anyone else saw. It was late and dark, but they were fuckin' hot. I wanted in on that shit, wished I was bolder. I'm a freak."

Oh, that took an unexpected turn.

"Then I'm your kind of freak. I'd watch too." Alec turned down the bed before crawling under the sheets. "Alexa, turn off my bedroom lights," he said to his Amazon Echo. The lights slowly dimmed as he settled into place. "I was at a club once with my friends and walked out to my car to find my friends had moved their good time from the cab of their pickup to the pavement of the parking lot. Later, I found out they claimed they needed more room. It's hot. I snapped a picture. Until I met you, I haven't ever been so overcome that I couldn't wait to get somewhere more private, but it's hot as hell to think about doing you at a dance club."

"Hmm..." Now that tone was most definitely lust-infused, and Alec perked right up. "I don't know, I'm pretty possessive over you. I'm not sure I want everybody to see what you got. I'd be fightin' every motherfucker off you..." Key paused, giving a throaty chuckle before adding, "Not that we could even go out."

"At least not right now. Are you in bed? Want me to get you off before you fall asleep?" Alec asked, watching his blanket tent.

"I'm hard as stone. Your voice does it for me." Key's voice deepened, suggesting he'd already started without Alec.

"Exactly the same for me. Are you touching yourself? I want you to touch yourself and think of me. It's my hand there on you," Alec said, whipping the blankets off.

"Hmm…" Oh yeah, that was a good sound, and Alec curled his fingers around his cock, giving a solid tug.

"Key, it's not gonna take me long. Be there with me." Alec stroked himself. Maybe they could switch to video. His hips eagerly rolled into his palm at the prospect. As Alec started to make the suggestion, he heard a heavy exhale that didn't scream extreme lust. It was too thick and lazy. He listened closer as a deep inhale came next.

"Key, baby, you there?"

He listened closer and got nothing. Alec looked over at the clock on the nightstand. It was a little after one in the morning, which meant Key had been awake twenty hours. Of course he'd be exhausted. Not even disappointed, Alec laid the phone on the pillow next to him. It was a silly move, but he rested back in his spot and listened to the sounds of Key's breathing while he finished himself off.

He had needed this tonight. His heart had somehow managed to reconcile the pain and suffering of Key's life to the love he wanted to give this man. And Alec would love Key, or at the very least, he'd try. If patience and an open heart were necessary to accomplish his goals, he had an abundant supply where Key was concerned.

Alec reached for tissues to clean himself up. Once done, he whispered his love to Key as he tugged the blankets around him and left his phone on the pillow, still connected to the call. He closed his eyes, listening to Key's soft snores. They easily lulled him to sleep.

CHAPTER 6

Keyes pulled out a chair at the conference room table tucked inside a backroom they called the church in the club's private clubhouse. A sacred place designated only for the patched members of the Disciples of Havoc, a place where he and his brothers regularly gathered to talk confidential club business.

For all the years Keyes had been with the club, he'd never had an experience like this one before. He and Fox, the club's prez, were behind closed doors all alone. Even more different than normal, an eerie quiet descended over them. The only sounds came from the chair legs scraping across the floor before he took his seat.

Fox sat in his normal seat at the head of the table with a stack of papers in front of him, seemingly not paying any attention to Keyes's entrance. Keyes leaned back in his seat, crossing his arms over his chest and waited.

"Thanks for comin' in early," Fox said, not lifting his head from the pages he worked with.

Keyes didn't respond. He was growing too freaked out and tightened the cross of his arms at his chest. He stared at the top of Fox's head as he diligently kept working and ignoring him. Maybe as much as five minutes passed before Fox placed his pen on the table. The prez still didn't look at him, but did scoot a wrapped bundle across the table toward him before gathering his paperwork and stuffing it inside a well-used file folder. Keyes knew what the envelope held and reached for it, stuffing it in the front pocket of his cut.

"I wanna talk to you privately about your old man," Fox said, and for the first time, his weary gaze lifted, looking Keyes straight in the eyes. Okay, that wasn't the worst thing Fox could have said but still terrible in its own right. "I know shit's real fucked up with you two, and I know it's the reason you're stayin' away. I also know I haven't handled this shit right with you and him and the club, but it's just so fucked up. Your old man never fuckin' quits. And there's no fuckin' common ground between you two, and that's completely Smoke's fault."

Huge understatement, but Keyes kept that to himself for now. Fox reclined in his chair, scrubbing his hands over his face. He looked tired, haggard, and old. That was a mind-blower. Keyes had never thought of Fox as old until right this minute.

"We've got some shit goin' down. Real fuckin' problems. The Serpent club's growin', doubling in size, while we're fuckin' stagnant because of that bitch DA. Our prospect pool is shit, and your goddamn father's recruitin' is a fuckin' joke. He's bringin' in trash."

Keyes didn't need to respond to those statements either. He agreed completely. The Serpent motorcycle club was their oldest rival. The beef between the two clubs was legendary. Of course, it wouldn't sit well with any of his brothers that those sorry sons of bitches were building so quickly. Keyes also agreed that, since they'd named his father head of recruiting—an honorary title to give him something to do after his motorcycle accident—his old man had brought in nothing but shitty trash as potential prospects. A bunch of sorry thugs whose vision was to take the club back thirty years to their outlaw roots. Keyes would never vote any of those guys in as prospects much less for their full member patch.

"Here's my problem right now," Fox said, shifting his chair to a sitting position, leaning forward to where he rested his elbows on his knees. "Mack and I decided to keep shit from you. I don't know if it was the right thing to do or not, but I heard about yesterday. Your old man threatened you, and I don't fuckin' like it at all. And I don't like the revenge you'll be forced to take if he tries to follow through."

Fox went silent as he cocked his head, staring at Keyes with disgust written all over his weathered face. Keyes said nothing because Fox was correct—there had been a clear threat when his old man made of show of pretending to shoot him in the side mirror. Keyes's chest swelled again with the indignation of it all. His old man would get one fucking shot before Keyes would wipe the floor with him, most likely spending the rest of his life in prison for killing his father.

"Your old man's dyin'."

Good. Of course, he was dying a slow miserable death. A person couldn't ram their motorcycle into a moving pickup truck in a fit of road rage anger and walk away unscathed. The bigger problem seemed that his old man hadn't died fast enough from his stupidity.

Fox's weary gaze stayed glued on him, and Keyes had no idea what he wanted from him.

"You don't care," Fox finally said with a certain single nod before he sat up, placing his elbows on the table, threading his fingers together. "Here's our official take—we don't consider this your problem anymore. I appreciate what you did for him after the accident, we all do, and he was a thankless bastard to you. He's got stage four lung cancer and won't make the year. He's in denial, actin' tough and badass. You don't need to worry. He can't act on his threats. We're tellin' the brothers tonight, but I wanted you to know first."

Keyes's body went numb. He clamped his mouth together to keep from asking for any details. He didn't give a shit about that old man. How could he? His father was the fucking devil and needed to get his ass back to hell where he belonged.

"I know you're holdin' your tongue, Keyes, but I know you too well. This is gonna eat at you. There's a lot you don't know. I've warred with myself about how much to say for years. I still don't know what's right." This time, Fox clamped his mouth together then shook his head, staring down at the table while growing visibly frustrated. "Look, you have to know, the likelihood of you bein' his biological son is highly unlikely. There's no easy way to say this, but dammit, things were different back then. It was almost thirty years ago. This newfound consciousness we do things with wasn't around back then. You know that. Your mother was a club whore. She just was. We all fuckin' passed her around. I suspect your real old man was probably Bigun. She had a thing for him. Destroyed her when he died. Smoke was fuckin' obsessed with her, but she never gave a shit about him and that drove him batshit crazy."

Keyes jaw ticced at his frustration over the trip down memory lane. That shit needed to stay in the past. No good would come from reliving one single day of his history.

"Suppose you'd've had a better life had he lived, but Smoke ended up marryin' your mother when she found out she was pregnant. I'm only tellin' you this to say, give me time. You need to keep your distance. I know it's askin' a lot. You're as much a member of this club as your old man, but he's sick, his days are numbered, and he's my brother just like you're a son to me. I'm askin' too much, Keyes, I swear to God I am, but hang on for me. I depend on you. I need you to help lead this club for the next generation. Give me time." Fox's tormented gaze finally lifted to Keyes's.

He was essentially being banished. Any other member would have demanded more respect but that never seemed to apply to Keyes. He immediately squelched those thoughts, pushed them way down like he always did. Keyes understood what Fox meant and where all of this was headed. Once again, he accepted the decision, and agreed to distance himself to help save the balance in the club. He guessed this was Fox's way of appreciating his efforts and asking for him to continue a little while longer.

"I've never asked for anything to be different than it is. I get it."

"You sure about that? You're always quiet, but more so now," Fox said, scanning Keyes's face. He had no idea what to say to that. Maybe there was a time this conversation would have upset him, proven to him that he never truly fit with the club members he called family, but not now. Fox had given him a free pass to keep his distance a little while longer.

"My old man can have his final days however y'all see fit. I'll be around when you need me. I think the tire shop's pullin' in its share of the cash. I'm good. You know how to find me. I'm loyal to you, you know that," Keyes declared and gave his standard single nod, driving his point home.

"You've always been a top earner for us. It's more that I feel like I've failed you," Fox said, again pushing back in the seat. Keyes busted out with an honest laugh as he rose to his feet. It was the mood lightener they both seemed to need.

"I don't feel that way at all. I'm fine. Don't worry about me." The honesty of those words had Keyes reaching for the back of the chair, pushing it underneath the table. "So, I'm guessin' I don't need to be here tonight?"

"No, you don't. Your old man's movin' into the clubhouse tonight, so we can watch him until we can't anymore. He'll be livin' here. It's where he wants to be."

Keyes nodded and still refused to ask any of the half-dozen questions he had about the diagnosis or about how much time he had left.

"I'll tell the guys you're keepin' distance for him. They'll understand."

"Thanks for this," he said, patting his breast pocket as he started for the door.

"You earned it. I heard you picked up Dev last night," Fox said about his son, Devilman, as he got to his feet.

"Word gets around," he replied, pulling open the door.

"Hold up, Keyes."

He turned back to Fox as he walked up to him with outstretched arms. He enveloped Keyes in a rare fatherly hug that ended with a solid pat on his back. "He never deserved you. You watched out for him, took care of him. It's all any of us can hope for from our children."

It took a second for Keyes to finally hug him back then he avoided eye contact as he turned to leave church. He wasn't certain he was worthy of Fox's praise.

Mack and Ace were there, Mack sitting at one of the many tables scattered in the bar area of the clubhouse. Ace, their resident bartender, stood behind the bar where he was just about every night of the week. Both his brothers looked worried as they eyed him closely. Ace and Mack were trusted advisors to the prez, Mack was next in line to be the club president if anything happened to Fox. Of course they had been the ones Fox had come to all these decisions with.

Mack gave him a fist bump as he passed by the table heading for the front doors. "Stay for a drink?"

"I gotta get back to the shop." Which was a lie, he needed to ride to help process everything he'd just heard, because no doubt, if there was a way to have guilt in his deal, he'd find it at the worst possible time.

He pulled his phone, checking the time. Two thirty in the afternoon. He could drop this cash off by his Uncle Clyde's place south of Dallas then take a spin, maybe take a super long out-of-the-way ride to Alec's house. He lifted a hand to Ace before he left the building. Keyes started for his bike, cocking his head at the prospects loitering around the place. He was glad he wasn't the only one who thought they were unworthy of a Havoc patch. On that note, he dialed Louis at the tire shop

"Yep, boss man?"

"Can you close up tonight?" he asked.

"Sure thing." Louis never hesitated. He was a fucking work horse, and Keyes knew he could count on him.

"I'll be back in the mornin'." He ended the call and looked at the time while settling his sunglasses in place. If he hightailed it to Clyde's, maybe he could make it to Alec's before he got off work. A grin split his face as he realized the gift Fox had given him. He'd be spending more time at Alec's house with no guilt or worry about being gone so much.

As for his old man? It wasn't a surprise he wasn't his father's biological kid. The *reason* for all the years of Smoke's hate still didn't lessen the impact of the way he'd treated Keyes. A child should never have to grow up like he had.

Was it wrong to wish a slow, painful death on someone? Keyes mounted his bike, knowing full well good people like Alec didn't wish for those things, but he kind of did.

Late seemed to be the word of the day—Alec's day specifically. He came off the elevator to see Rosa Daly and her granddaughter, Keely Cummings, waiting on a bench next to the bank of elevators. Rosa looked to be in her regular state of anxiousness as her gaze landed on Alec. In stark contrast, Keely played with her doll in the seat next to her, lost in the make-believe world she played within. Jacob, his assistant came into the small waiting area from the opposite direction of Alec, and without saying a word, he took a seat next to Keely. He had agreed to sit with the little girl while Rosa met with Alec.

"Thank you for coming," Alec said, stopping directly in front of Rosa as she got to her feet. He stuck out his hand, and she followed, clasping his tightly. "I'm sorry I'm late. It's been a day."

"Is she okay out here?" Rosa asked, turning toward her granddaughter. Keely's head lifted, her eyes rising to meet Alec's. Much like the first time he'd met Keely, he was taken aback by the maturity staring at him from such a young child, proving she hadn't been so lost in play after all.

"Jacob's going to sit with her, and you'll be able to see her the whole time. We won't be long." Alec nodded toward the secluded sitting area and led the way. He shut the door behind Rosa to help give them more privacy, offering her the seat closest to the large window overlooking Keely and Jacob.

Rosa was incredibly territorial where Keely was concerned, and as far as he could see, she had every right to be. What happened to Keely played a large role in his success at keeping Donald locked away. Keely had been in the vehicle when both her mother and father were arrested. The authorities found a sizable amount of methamphetamines in the backseat where Keely sat holding a firearm in her hands that she had accidentally discharged during the traffic stop. The little girl was lucky to be alive today.

"We had a win yesterday. Did you get my message?" Alec asked, taking his seat across the small table from Rosa.

"I did. I was working, but it made everything better. I've been worried," she said, her gaze shifting from Keely to Alec. The relief didn't quite reach her eyes.

"It was a great day for me as well. I'm going to keep doing everything in my power to keep him locked away, I assure you. I've worked with the criminal division extensively, and I feel confident you'll be assigned an attorney soon," he said, which wasn't necessarily the truth, but he sure hoped it worked out like that. Alec opened a much more condensed version of the packet of information Janice had supplied him with yesterday. "I've stumbled on something that I need clarification on. That's why I asked if you could stop by."

"I've told y'all everything I know," she started. He could see the anxiety building and interrupted her by lifting a hand to stop her flat denial.

"I know, but we've found something from an old police report. Something your daughter told a police officer almost three years ago about the Disciples of Havoc Motorcycle

Club," Alec explained, reaching for the report inside the folder. "I'm wondering if you remember anything about Donald's time with the club."

"Oh no, they're a real gang," she said immediately, insistently nodding with all her certainty. "Donald always bragged that they were a gang. He liked things a little rough, but when he met one of their members, everything changed for the worse. He became obsessed with them and my daughter changed too. She'd follow him over to their parties. They're no joke."

"Talk more about how things changed after he got involved with Havoc," Alec asked, dread coiling in his gut as he picked up his pen, prepared to take notes.

"My daughter would complain that Donald started staying out all hours of the night. When he did come home, he was drunk and high. All he could talk about was earning his jacket—I think that's what he called it. Soon after that, my daughter started joining him and hanging out up there all the time. That became their whole world. The robberies started because Donald couldn't make ends meet and stay at the club all the time, so he started stealing, and my daughter was right there with him. I sure hate to say that," Rosa said, her shame-filled gaze lowering in what Alec suspected was embarrassment.

Alec gave her the second she needed as he scribbled unneeded words on to the blank pad of paper inside his portfolio. Her clear memory about the club was exactly the concern Alec had. The small ray of hope Alec had that the police report would go unsubstantiated by a third party died a dismal death with Rosa's instant and detailed recall of the events. Donald would in fact be of great value to the DA if his connections were discovered. He paled, thinking about the chaos Donald would bring to Rosa and Keely if he had a get-out-of-jail-free card, and free rein at doing whatever to help DA Twiford infiltrate the club.

"Have you heard anything from your daughter?" Alec asked. Keely's mother had skipped bail months ago.

"Nothing. She knows better than to call me," Rosa said sternly.

Maybe as much as a minute later, he pulled a picture of Key's father out of the file folder and slid it across the small table toward Rosa. "Did you ever see this man with Donald?"

"No, I never saw any of 'em. They scared me," she said, looking over the photo and shaking her head. She pushed back in her seat as if the picture were evil in its own right. "This isn't going to jeopardize Keely, is it?"

"No, not at all. I made sure of that yesterday," Alec said, knowing even with losing parental rights and Rosa having full custody, there would be little hope for either of them if Twiford found this information and freed Donald. Back on the streets, he'd have ample opportunity to terrorize his daughter. Alec forced a reassuring smile while tucking the photo back inside the folder. Her anxiety didn't leave her face, and he feared his poker face might be showing some cracks, exposing his increasing tension.

"Why did you ask all this if it's not important?"

"I'm combing through everything, Mrs. Daly. This won't be the only question that arises as we get through this process. I need you to be honest with me, and I'll always be honest with you. If I see any new developments, I assure you that you'll be the first to know," Alec said, getting to his feet.

He managed a small, hopefully reassuring smile, and she seemed to take it at face value. She gave one back to him. That wasn't necessarily a lie, but what was becoming increasingly more concerning was Alec wasn't finding his way out of this job. He would have to stay to watch this case. These two needed him…and so did Key. What could Donald expose about the Disciples, and how would that affect Key? Damn.

CHAPTER 7

Alec rounded the curve of his driveway, confused when he saw Key's motorcycle parked in his normal spot. For much of the ride home, Alec found that not even the Cummings case took his mind off his pout since Key hadn't returned any of his text messages this afternoon. Just when Alec had decided to go full-on self-pity mode, knowing he'd be spending the night alone again tonight, he turned the corner of his driveway, pressing the garage door remote when there was Key sitting at the patio table on his back porch right off the kitchen. His large frame made the small table and chair set appear even smaller. Alec's gaze roamed over Key as excitement rushed through his veins. That meant somehow Key had managed to break free of his club responsibilities and come to him this evening.

Alec parked his car in the open garage, and didn't bother closing the overhead door. He walked out of the garage directly toward Key who rose and headed straight for him. "I'm glad to see you."

Key's eyes slid down the length of his body and any lingering thoughts from his earlier pity-party mood immediately lifted. The weight of Key's gaze had Alec's dick pushing at his zipper. Those light eyes lifted to his, then lowered to Alec's lips. Key's uncanny way with non-verbal communication spoke clearly, giving Alec everything he needed to know.

Alec didn't say another word. He lifted his arms, slipping them around Key's neck, and pressed himself against the firm wall of muscle. Alec opened his mouth, meeting this sexy man halfway. The kiss was erotic as hell, something next-level perfect just like everything they'd done since Alec had confessed his love. Hot as hell and full of carnal pleasure, Key pushed his big hands through the opening of his suit coat to draw Alec tighter against his body. And the pounding in his handsome biker's chest matched that of his own.

Only the need to breathe had him pulling back from the other man and drawing air into his lungs. He tilted his head back, encouraging Key's warm kisses along his jaw and neck. Key's mouth felt so damn good on him, and he wished he'd taken off his tie before he'd gotten out of the car. "This is a nice surprise."

"I can't think of anywhere else I'd rather be." Key's husky voice cracked with need.

Alec lowered his chin to whisper directly into Key's ear. "Me neither. Just you. Being with you," he said breathily, reaching the desired effect when a quiver made Key tighten his hold around Alec.

At the same time, Key's large hand cupped the back of Alec's head. Key's hot breath tickled his ear as his lover traced the shell with his tongue. Such a sexy move it made his knees weak.

"Let's go inside," Alec muttered, giving in to his own shiver as it raced up his spine. Key's answer was to settle his lips on Alec's. Everything right in the world came from that mouth moving over his. Before he completely lost himself, Alec managed to break from the kiss, drawing back from Key's insistent lips to whisper, "Inside, baby."

"I wasn't gonna do this. I wasn't." Key sounded tortured. His words were in direct opposition to his seeking lips trying to continue the kiss.

"Do what?" Alec asked, concerned with the ragged emotion he heard in Key's voice. Key gave him nothing to help understand, his mouth angling back to Alec's neck, forcing him to cradle Key's handsome face to keep him from looking away. "Babe, what are you saying?"

Key tried to fight the hold, reaching for Alec's mouth. He held on tight, dodging the move even as Key's brows slid together in frustration and his hips rolled, grinding that hard cock into him. "Alec…"

Alec just shook his head no, encouraging Key to answer. His voice came out in a hoarse whispered command, "Tell me."

"I rode this afternoon. I think best on an open road. I tried to convince myself it was just sex with you." Key readjusted his hold and pulled Alec tighter to him. Key's firm, thick body pressed heavily against his. Fuck, he smelled so intoxicating. Alec inhaled deeper, drawing his biker's wild woodsy scent into his lungs. Key moaned, and his tongue swept forward, dominating Alec to where his only choice was to open, allowing entry. Frantic hands slid down his sides and tugged his shirttails free of his slacks. Key ran calloused hands underneath the material, across his back, and Alec tried his best to crawl up this beautiful man to get as close as he possibly could. Alec shrugged from his suit coat, letting it fall to the pavement, before reaching for Key's T-shirt, trying to pull it over his head.

Unfortunately, Alec had to break from the kiss to accomplish the task, and he tangled Key's hair in the process. When Key withdrew his hands to help, Alec felt their physical loss.

"What's just sex?" Alec wasn't even sure why he asked that question or where it came from as his hands aimed lower, going for the belt circling Key's waist.

"Us. What you said, but I really like it even though it scared me." Key's hands came to Alec's face. His eyes searched Alec's, taking in everything, memorizing it all.

"Baby, I'm so lost. I just can't decide if I need clarification before or after you fuck me," Alec said, opening Key's jeans button, skimming the head of his hard dick with his fingertips.

"Or you fuck me," Key suggested, gripping Alec's ass cheeks and rocking his erection against him.

"After." He loosened the tie at his neck, unbuttoned the top buttons, and pulled off his shirt while lifting his mouth to plaster his lips to Key's. This moment held the same urgency and untamable frenzy as the first time they were together. He shoved Key toward the back door, and the man's hands were all over him, undressing, caressing and teasing him. As he shuffled across the tile of the kitchen floor, his slacks tangled at his feet while Key stroked him and Alec worked at freeing Key of his tight-fitting jeans.

Shedding clothing as they went, Alec made it a few feet inside the bedroom door before Key pulled him down to the thick carpet, their naked bodies slotting perfectly together as they kissed. Neither bothered to move to the bed, need overriding all of their senses as Key ravished his mouth.

He was being consumed, and if something didn't happen soon, he'd self-combust right there. Alec inched his hand lower, past Key's stomach muscles, and wrapped his fingers around that hard, swollen cock.

Key watched him, his face etched with need before he screwed his eyes closed and leaned into Alec as he squeezed tighter. Alec traced the shell of Key's ear before sliding his tongue inside and breathing heavily. Alec nosed Key's hair as he bucked into his hand.

"Motherfucker, I need you inside me." Key yanked free of the hold and crawled to the nightstand, but quickly returned, giving him another toe-curling kiss as Alec again reached for Key's erection. He pushed a cold bottle and a packet between their bodies. Lube and a condom. Right. His guy thought of everything. Alec took the items with his free hand while Key's cock pushed in and out of his fist. His lover's strong thighs shook under the intensity of his need, causing Alec to gentle his grip and ease off, releasing Key before settling back on his heels.

"Let me show you how much you mean to me," Alec whispered, enjoying the sight before him of this man's big body straining for control.

"Show me, but I want you to fuck me," Key commanded and maneuvered to all fours. He braced his hands on the thick carpet then turned to look over his shoulder. Alec's heart sped up at the encouraging grin Key gave him.

"Someone's impatient," Alec teased and gave his pushy biker a wink as he got into position behind Key. He slid his hand up Key's back and pressed between his shoulder blades to urge him down, chest to rug, before tracing a path with his fingertips from the top of Key's spine all the way down to his ass.

Alec quickly unrolled the condom, sheathing his dick, before he popped the top of the bottle, adding a generous amount of lube to his fingers and cock. He tossed the lube to the side then rubbed his slick fingers around Key's perfect hole. With his other hand, he spread Key's ass to get a more intimate look. This man was beautiful, exceptional in every way.

The sight of his thumb as it easily disappeared into Key's pliant body mesmerized Alec. His cock leaked into the latex as he fucked Key with his digits. Key's hips responded to the onslaught of pleasure, arching and pushing their bodies together. He ground his ass impatiently against Alec's groin as he growled, "Get on with it."

With a chuckle, Alec positioned his cock and pushed forward into Key. A delicious warmth squeezed him, and pleasure buzzed in his balls, electrifying every nerve ending in his body.

Both men cried out when Alec buried himself to the hilt. Alec screwed his eyes closed, his body wound up so tightly, he might not last. Heat swamped him as his breath took root in his throat. He fought the urge to grip Key's hips and pound into his man.

"So perfect." Key's body rippled around him, urged him in deeper. He pulled back slightly then slowly nudged into all that heat again. Key's body molded hotly around him as if he were made especially for Alec. It didn't take long to build a steady rhythm that had both of them grunting and panting, every thrust of his hips leading them closer to their release.

Keyes's eyes slowly slid closed. His body heated in the most delicious way as Alec gave him exactly what he wanted. He curled his fingers into the plush rug, lifting his hips to meet Alec as he pulled out then pushed back inside him again. The decadent burn of being stretched so fully gave over to mind-blowing pleasure as Alec's hips snapped harder and faster.

Hell fucking yeah. His knees and ass burned, and heat swirled in his balls.

Alec had always taken him with measured control, but he didn't want that this time. He gripped the thick rug, hanging on as his muscles strained in carnal indulgence that had him soaring. He worked at keeping Alec's pace, pumping and thrusting, matching every single move Alec made until his guy pulled out of him and flipped him to his back then pressed between his thighs. Alec hooked a knee over his strong arm and pushed back into him. Fuck, it felt so damn good to have Alec filling him so deeply again. Keyes rolled his hips, forcing Alec to thrust harder and faster while he adjusted Alec's hold, wrapping his legs around Alec's back, and digging his heels into Alec's flexing ass, keeping that cock moving so enticingly inside him. No way would he last much longer, not with the way the gorgeous Alec was driving into him, nailing his prostate with every thrust.

"Oh fuck, you feel good," Alec said, bending to reach his mouth. Alec's tongue slipped through his parted lips as his soft moans urged Alec faster. His guy reached between their bodies, touching his neglected dick, and that was all it took. He clawed at the plush carpet seconds before his body arched from the rush of his orgasm.

Alec's hips faltered, his rhythm becoming erratic as he pushed Keyes's thighs to his chest and held him down.

"Your body's squeezing my cock so good," Alec rasped. Keyes was so fucked in more ways than one. His sated haze threatened to block his view from what he loved the most—Alec. His lover's face crinkled, his eyes sliding shut, and Alec's eager body slowed as he continued fucking

Keyes through his release. Alec collapsed on him, freeing Keyes of the visual hold as he absorbed Alec's weight and closed his eyes.

CHAPTER 8

With extreme effort, Keyes bucked Alec off to land with a thump on the thick carpeted floor next to him. That move allowed Keyes to fully collapse beside Alec, stretching his body out as he panted, much like the man lying beside him. At least for Keyes, a satisfied grin curled his lips as he absorbed the sweet ache in his ass.

Man, he loved that feeling.

"Who'd've thought you'd be a power bottom?" Alec's voice dripped with satisfaction. Keyes turned his head, studying Alec's handsome profile. His guy's face held the exact same blissed out expression he felt. Alec's skin was flushed and his blond hair damp from exertion.

"I learned from the best," he drawled, lifting an arm and draping it over his eyes. Yeah, he'd thought about a lot while out on his ride this afternoon. Love and lust were confusing things, but their sex was always off the charts good. He completely saw how he could be over the moon in love with Alec, but he had absolutely nothing to offer in return. Now, if he were a doctor, lawyer, or even had a lot of money like Alec, then he'd better understand how Alec could have seriously fallen for him. The only logical explanation to all this talk of love had to be Alec confusing love and lust.

That made more sense than anything else, and Keyes agreed, their sex was fucking amazing. As long as he kept his perspective, he was fine continuing just like this, living in the fantasy of what could be, pretending some magnificent dude like Alec loved him and only him while knowing deep down it was nothing more than a pipe dream.

He dropped his arm to his side and stared at the ceiling. What a day. He'd needed that ride this afternoon more than he realized. Before he'd started hanging out with Alec in all his free time, he would take a few hours off, at least once a week, and just go wherever his bike led. Keyes needed to find a way to reinsert that back into his week.

The warmth radiating off Alec's body lulled him, his eyelids grew heavy and slid closed. Alec's throaty chuckle came with movement, probably removing the condom.

He was completely unprepared for the hard body to land on his. Alec crawled up him, his head coming to rest on Keyes's pec. Keyes might not have planned the embrace, but he sure did participate. He adjusted, tangling his hand in Alec's still sweat-damp hair, the other resting on Alec's shoulder, keeping him pinned there.

"We have great sex."

"I prefer the term making love," Alec murmured, and those perfectly pouty lips pressed against his chest.

There was a small lancing sting to his heart. Maybe some small part of him had truly wanted to believe Alec might love him, but that was all right too. He'd learned how to absorb blows to the heart a long time ago. Even gotten to the point where his heart had stopped feeling anything until he had met Alec. He'd get back there again when the time came for this to end. Instead of dwelling on the inevitable ending, he went the other direction, celebrating a victory of his rightness of the meaning behind their relationship and chuckled. A rumble that erupted in his chest and caused Alec to lift his head to look at him.

"What? You don't like my choice of words?" Alec asked cheekily, resting his chin on the back of his hand placed over Keyes's heart.

"We're too different," Keyes responded, lifting his head enough to look in Alec's eyes.

"And?" Something speculative crossed Alec's handsome brow. Alec had told him often enough that he was hard to read, and this same look happened right before they started to play the twenty questions game Alec seemed to like so much.

"You're confusin' great sex with somethin' more meaningful," he explained, waiting for the next question. Seconds passed before Alec's weight abruptly lifted off him. Keyes fought the sudden move. When that failed, he reached out, grabbing Alec's arm. He wasn't ready to lose Alec's warmth or those heart-pleasing, light soothing caresses. He watched Alec's back go ramrod straight and his jaw clench shut. "It's okay. It's really great sex."

"Don't belittle my feelings, Keyes. I meant the words I've said. It didn't just slip out unexpectedly." Alec yanked his arm free while rising to his feet.

Keyes sat up, resisting the urge to knock himself in the head. No talking was the best talking. Why couldn't he keep his thoughts to himself like he always fucking did?

"You're mad," he said half-accusingly.

"No shit." Alec left him there and stomped toward the bathroom. The pictures rattled on the walls as the bathroom door slammed shut. Keyes shifted, his overexerted body protesting as he pushed to his feet. He wandered through the house then out to the patio, gathering their discarded clothing before going back to the bedroom, his whole focus locked on that still shut bathroom door. He tossed the clothes on the bed, dropped his boots by the nightstand, and carefully placed Alec's expensive shoes next to his. He manned up and padded across the floor to gently knock on the bathroom door.

"I'm sorry I made you mad," he said through the closed door and waited. There was no response, and he couldn't hear anything from the other side of the door. After a minute or so, he tested the doorknob. It turned, and he pushed it open a few inches, peering inside through the crack he'd made. Alec was naked, his bare ass propped against the sink counter, his arms and ankles crossed defiantly. Alec lifted his gaze, keeping his head bent as he stared at Keyes. He had only seen Alec mad once or twice before, but he was fierce. Where most people didn't cross Keyes due to his size, in the moment, Alec became the bigger threat, so he tried again. "I'm sorry."

"For what?" Alec asked, his tone clipped and sharp. No unnecessary words, which was weird for the usually talkative lawyer.

"For makin' you mad," he replied, because until right that second, he hadn't considered why he was sorry, other than he wished he hadn't said what had made Alec so upset.

"I know my feelings. I'm pretty self-aware and open to whatever happens between us." Okay, maybe this was the first time he'd seen Alec truly angry. His mister was severely serious and intently focused, those icy eyes staring a hole right through him. Alec's tone was hard and unyielding and left no room for doubt.

"Okay, agreed," he said, still stuck in that weird position with the door only open a few inches. Should he push the door completely open and walk in or should he just close the door and let Alec have his privacy? He truly had no idea what to do next. He just wanted Alec to stop being so angry.

"So why in the world would you think I'm lost in all the sex we're having?"

Oh, hell no. That was a landmine kind of a question. One of those fuck-with-your-head questions where there was no right answer.

"Do you want me to leave?" he asked.

Alec's jaw firmed, his eyes narrowing, making it clear he didn't like that question at all. "Of course I don't want you to leave. I was elated to see you here. Even if you come here every night, that wouldn't be enough time spent with you—and before you think it, my wanting you here has very little to do with our sex. You're great company."

Okay, that was something Keyes wasn't, but before he balked at the obvious dramatization, he said, "Then I'm sorry."

Alec just lifted a hand to run through his stylish, hardly ever out of place blond hair and let out a deep sigh, shaking his head while his intense stare never wavered. Keyes finally pushed the door open all the way, remaining on the threshold, giving Alec his distance, but staying close.

"What can I do to make this better?"

"Take me riding on your bike."

Keyes wanted nothing more than to have Alec with him on the open road, his lover's body wrapped around him as they disappeared into the sunset, but that fell strongly in the fantasy portion of their relationship.

"You know I can't do that," he said, breaking through the invisible barrier, stepping closer to Alec. He counted it a win when Alec didn't move away as Keyes reached for his arms. He wasn't entirely sure what to do once he had Alec. He wanted to soothe away the frustration, so he caressed him, shoulder to elbow, because of Alec's still crossed arms.

"I want a promise of someday. Someday, I'll ride on the back of your bike. Someday, we can go to dinner together. Someday, you'll travel with me," Alec said, his light-colored eyes full of determined intensity.

He chose to nod, to pacify Alec for now, not ever seeing it as a real possibility for them as long as he was a member of his club. If and when it did happen, that would be years down the line. So many years Keyes couldn't imagine Alec waiting for him.

"And do not trivialize my feelings for you. That makes me angry as hell. I see everything about us clearly, even if you don't, but do not mistake the lengths I'll go to keep loving you." Alec wasn't giving one single inch. Keyes only nodded again, wishing more than anything that he'd never opened his big mouth.

Alec nodded too. A firm single dip of his chin, driving his point home. After a second of continued staring, Alec lifted his arms, running those smooth, warm palms up Keyes's chest and around his neck. "Are you staying tonight?"

"I thought so. Louis needs more hours. He closed for me tonight."

"And Louis is your trusted right-hand guy. He's been with you awhile, right?"

Keyes nodded, moving his hands to Alec's waist, drawing him closer.

"And your father still hasn't come around?"

It took a second for Keyes to understand. He confused the question about his father not being around with his intended plan to tell Alec about his father's diagnosis. On the ride, he had decided to tell Alec everything, all his old man's vengeful text messages, their heated exchange yesterday, and about his conversation with Fox this afternoon, but after the last few minutes, he felt it was wiser to hold off. Clearly, communication wasn't his strong suit. He was shit at reading what made people angry, and he didn't want to risk Alec growing more frustrated with him tonight—not now, maybe not ever. He'd deal with it all on his own.

Alec broke from the hold, his emotions back to a happier place again. With effort, he had quickly reconciled his time alone with his biker was too precious to waste, so he reached out and slapped Key's bare ass with his open palm, hoping to lighten the mood. "It only took five months to get you comfortable enough to lose the clothes."

From the corner of his eye, he caught Key's reflection as he looked down, almost acting surprised he wasn't wearing clothes. Alec laughed, drawing Key's attention to him, giving him a wink. He walked through the bedroom toward his walk-in closet and pulled out two pair of athletic shorts for them to wear.

"Here," he called out since Key had remained standing at the door of the bathroom.

Now, this felt right. When they were together, all parts of the outside world melted away. That was what he could never make Blaine understand. Hell, he had even been doubtful this kind of connection and love was possible. Politics, religion, education, or whatever else held society in a combative stranglehold no longer mattered when it came down to the way he was drawn to this man.

"You should bring some clothes over. Have them here when you need them," Alec suggested, watching as Key stepped forward to take the shorts.

"I live light. I don't have much that won't fit in my duffel bag," Key said, following Alec's lead and putting the shorts on.

"That doesn't surprise me. I'm pretty sure that's the same hair tie on your wrist." He nodded at the black band circling his lover's wrist.

"I wish. They lose the stretchiness after a couple of months," Key said, touching the always there hair tie.

"I have some for you in the bathroom. You know that, right?" Alec asked, leading them out of the bedroom, going to the kitchen.

"I do," Key mumbled behind him.

Dammit, maybe his emotions weren't solidly back to happy. More than anything, maybe even more so now after Key had doubted the validity of his feelings, Alec wished Key would use the hair ties he had purchased. The need to provide and take care of Key was growing stronger. Even the shorts his biker now wore were purchased specifically for the man. Alec just couldn't say those words due to the I-take-care-of-myself code Key lived by.

Alec glanced over at the kitchen clock. Nearly six thirty. Time flew when Key was around. He opened the refrigerator door and pulled out a cold Bud Light, handing it back over his shoulder to Key who plucked it out of his hand in the most natural of moves. Alec opted for a glass of chilled wine then moved a step over to the wine cooler also handing the unopened bottle back to Key who took both then headed for the drawer housing the bottle opener.

"Too hot for dinner outside?" Alec asked, having heard the temperature had topped out at a hundred and one degrees this afternoon. Back at the refrigerator, he lifted a covered dish, seeing the fajita meat he'd had his housekeeper Olivia pick up from a little hole-in-the-wall butcher in Lewisville.

"Not for me," Key said. Alec heard the distinct pop of the wine cork as he reached for the pre-sliced vegetable tray. He also saw a nice-sized bowl of frijoles, his housekeeper's secret recipe. She most definitely deserved a raise. She'd thought of everything he needed to pull this dinner off in style.

Key left the kitchen with the wine bottle in hand. Alec smiled. Either the guy was going to chug the bottle under all the stress Alec had added to their evening or he was going for a wine glass. Alec washed his hands in the sink. This whole scene seemed very domesticated to him. They were in sync, and Alec had to admit he really enjoyed spending his time with Key.

Alec shook the excess water off his hands and reached for the hand towel as a glass was placed on the counter beside him. Key's strong arms wrapped around his waist, and Alec took the miniscule step backward into the warm, welcoming embrace. His biker's beard tickled as Key nuzzled into the crook of his neck.

"Thank you for gettin' over your pissed off so easy. Nobody in my life gets over anything that easy," Key whispered, his lips pressing against Alec's skin.

Alec stared at the sink and chose his response carefully. "I wasn't angry at you. I was concerned at what I had done to cause your response."

Key's palms slid over his belly as he ran his nose up the length of his neck and reached out to playfully nip at his earlobe. God, he loved that move. Alec rested against Key's chest, content to stay like that forever. He dropped his head to his lover's shoulder and smoothed his arms along Key's to keep him right there.

"You seemed happy when you got home today. Why?" Key asked.

"You were here," he answered, staring absently out the kitchen window above the sink, loving the way Key tightened his hold at his response.

"It was more."

For Alec, there truly wasn't anything more to say. His happiness seemed contingent on Key. Having the surprise of Key magically showing up could change even his most dismal of days. Instead of saying that, Alec chose a different tactic, not wanting to give Key any room to doubt the intensity of his feelings again. "I have a case and things have somewhat gone my way. At least for right now I was able to keep the defendant incarcerated a while longer. There's been some new developments that concern me, but all in all, he's locked up for the time being, and it's exactly where he needs to be."

"You've mentioned him before, right?"

"Yeah. It's the little girl with big blue eyes who reminds me of someone else I know with the same color. She's older than her young age. I suspect you were very much like her as a child," Alec explained, trying to remain passive and neutral. His recent findings were too fresh in his mind. He needed time to find the best way to tell the very private Key that he'd seen glimpses of his past.

"You're incredible. I bet that little girl's mom's relieved," Key said, turning Alec to face him.

"I doubt it, but I think her grandmother most certainly is. I need to learn how to distance myself from my job. I'm working on it, but it hasn't come easy for me. This particular case has wormed its way into my heart." Alec wrapped both his arms around Key's waist, keeping them locked there together.

"Mmm," Key said, placing a sweet chaste kiss on his lips.

"Blaine told me he could hear the biker coming out in me. My vocabulary's apparently changing," he said to divert the current course of the conversation.

Key's expression unexpectedly shifted, his body tensed, and his arms tightened around Alec. A territorial move that caused Alec to do a double take. Key's possessive intentions showed on his suddenly easy to read face, causing Alec to chuckle then lift a finger to trace the skin of his severely creased brow. Say what he would, this right here proved that Key knew they were more than great sex. Lust didn't provoke such primal jealousy, and Alec called him out.

"You're jealous."

"I ain't jealous." Key scoffed as if that were the most absurd suggestion. He abruptly released Alec, turning away as he reached for the tray of fajita meat.

Alec stole Key's earlier move, coming in behind to embrace him, lifting on his tiptoes to whisper in his ear. "Then what are you?"

"I told you I don't like him. He left you out there on the road like that," Key said, looking over his shoulder. Alec kissed his cheek, knowing Key always got stuck right there. He had never let it go that Blaine had left him on the dark roadside alone the first night he and Key met.

"But you took care of me," Alec reminded Key. Alec understood the dangers that had been involved, but he'd always considered the whole night a big win for him. If it hadn't all gone down exactly the way it had, he might not have this man in his house right now.

"What if somethin' had happened to you?" Key challenged.

"I'm certain you would have handled the situation upon your return. Anyone stupid enough to confront you would get what they deserved. Besides, I'm not a weakling. I can handle myself. If I remembered correctly, at the time, I brought up the hours of defense training courses I've watched on Viceland." Alec got the desired effect as the brooding biker smiled and shook his head at Alec's silliness, returning to the tray, stacking the veggies on top, and balancing the bowl of beans with the other hand.

"You're butterin' me up for somethin'." Key's sudden shift in thoughts confused Alec, and he watched Key's ass bounce toward the back door. Alec bit his lip, proud of his purchase. He'd gotten it right. He'd suspected those shorts might help accentuate that bubble butt perfectly. "Grab my beer?"

He wasn't even embarrassed that Key caught him appreciating the view. Alec grabbed the beer bottle and his wine glass then started for the back door. Resolve struck. He had to show Key he meant what he said, not with words, but with actions. All Key's impenetrable barriers were nothing more than big gray sheets of glass waiting for Alec to shatter.

There were some holes in that theory. His father was the Speaker of the House for the United States Congress. That would never change no matter how estranged they were. Various images of the club members came to mind. Key was extraordinary, beautiful in every way. The others...not so much. His mind jumped straight to a scene out of the movie *Deliverance*, with burly mountain men saying, "He got a real pretty mouth, ain't he?"

Alec shivered at the thought then shook his head. How in the hell had the bikers in his head suddenly morphed into backwoods hillbillies? Probably remnants of Key's father's rap sheet bouncing around in his head. Key might be in self-preservation mode, but his guy needed to know how badly Alec wanted him on all levels, not just a sexual one. A challenge he looked forward to winning. And he would win. No question.

CHAPTER 9

Four days later

Keyes's gaze stayed fixed on Alec's swaying ass as he walked through the house in a pair of barely there workout shorts. His arms rested on the kitchen bar countertop, an ice-cold beer nearby, and he was tired as hell. He had come to Alec's place every night after work, which required he leave each morning at the crack of dawn to fight the hellacious traffic all the way back into downtown Dallas. Adding to the misery, it was hot as hell outside, the temperature boiling, making the ride that much more unpleasant.

Now, he was there, butt-ass tired, and Alec was ignoring him. Keyes sighed. Alec wasn't really ignoring him. They'd fallen into this weird routine of dinner, some sort of entertainment that usually included swimming or television, then bed. Strangely enough, for four long nights they hadn't had sex. Alec "the toucher" wasn't truly touching him anymore. Which was confusing as hell. He got a kiss goodnight and a kiss goodbye the next morning. A simple peck with barely any tongue and definitely nothing more. He didn't like that shit one little bit.

Tonight, Alec's thin shorts mocked him. He drank his beer while staring at that perfect ass until Alec turned and lifted a cold brew from the refrigerator. Keyes nodded, draining the one he had as Alec slid the new one across the bar to him.

"What day are you off this weekend?" Alec asked, leaning against the kitchen sink, twisting the top off his bottle of beer.

"Probably Sunday," he answered, tracking everything about Alec, trying to understand what had happened between them.

"A friend of mine from work's having a get-together at her place tomorrow evening. I thought I'd go. She's announcing her engagement," Alec explained, pushing off the counter and rounding the bar to take the barstool next to his.

"Go," Keyes encouraged, turning to face Alec as he took the seat. "I can stay on my side of town tomorrow night."

Alec took a drink of the beer, before reaching for Keyes's hand. He gave a squeeze, and that gentle smile that Keyes loved so much tugged at the corner of Alec's lips.

"I'll swing by for a few minutes then come home. I'd rather spend time with you."

Keyes scanned Alec's face. The lawyer seemed completely unaffected by his presence, which was in direct contrast to the raging hard-on pulsating behind the zipper of Keyes's suddenly too tight jeans. Was Alec intent on driving him mad?

"Are we still good?" Keyes asked, his voice softer than normal, uncertainty had his hand twisting in Alec's, threading their fingers together.

"Absolutely," Alec said, looking as if the question were ridiculous. "I've loved you being here so much."

"All right. And you'll tell me when it's not good for you anymore?" He asked the words that hurt his heart to say.

"I'll always be honest with you."

Keyes nodded, watching Alec take a swig from his bottle.

"Your hair's an incredible color now."

"The sun bleaches it and the beard." It was this right here—Alec mentioned his hair without reaching out and touching it. Something had changed. They were weird now. Right when Keyes had decided to ask what the hell was going on, the doorbell rang. Alec turned away, sliding off the stool, and grabbed his money clip off the counter. He came back a few minutes later with a box of pizza. That was new too. Alec always texted him to ask what he wanted for dinner. They had grown into a habit of cooking together. It was rare to even order out anymore.

"I ordered while I was running. I hope it's okay. I ordered you a meat lover's supreme, right?" Alec asked, absently tossing the pizza box on the counter while going to the cabinet for the plates and napkins.

"Yeah, sure," he said, tracking every one of Alec's moves. He grabbed two water bottles from the refrigerator, placing those on top of the plates and napkins then started for the back door. "Grab the pizza and come on. You like the patio better." Alec left him there, walking outside, managing the door while Keyes carried the pizza and both their beer bottles.

"Alexa, play If Our Love Is Wrong by Calum Scott," Alec called out, reaching to shut the door behind him. Keyes stopped in the middle of the doorframe, crowding Alec.

"Are you sure we're okay?" He tried again, staring intently at Alec, needing to find the answers to all the questioning nagging at his heart.

"I haven't been happier. Just tired. My legs feel like noodles. I've been bad on my workout." Alec lifted to kiss him. Keyes wrapped his arm around Alec, wanting to believe Alec and needing the moment to help ease his worried heart. Alec grinned up at him, gave his normal wink, but left his hold almost immediately. Keyes watched Alec go straight to the patio table, setting the plates in each of their spots. He didn't scoot their chairs closer together like he normally did.

Something was off between them.

CHAPTER 10

Saturday Night

Alec couldn't lift another weight or run another mile. His body fucking hurt. Dammit if the curse words weren't streaming in vivid clarity through his mind, damning his traitorous dick. He wanted Key so badly. Sure, he'd gone weeks without sex before, usually a hand job had done the trick. Yet, now, Alec couldn't seem to jack himself enough to calm his greedy dick, and Keyes Dixon wasn't helping matters at all.

Of course, he'd been overly attracted to Key's whole look the moment he laid eyes on him—Alec had never pretended otherwise—but something had changed, and now only this specific bad boy did it for him. The sexy head of hair and beard that had turned every shade of color between honey and blond... Oh man, his biker was one hot guy. Even Key's long eyelashes were multi-colored wisps of sexy.

They rarely spoke about Key's work except to say business had gotten better and he'd struck a deal with his right-hand man to close the shop in the evenings, letting him get on the road to Alec's place a little earlier. By the look of his biker's hard body, with all those toned and defined stomach muscles, Key did a lot of the physical labor himself. And dammit, Key had gotten used to going shirtless around Alec's house. The mental image of Key's hard chest caused Alec to trip over his feet in the cool-down portion of his treadmill run. Luckily, he caught himself the exact same moment his home security system alerted him of the backdoor opening. Shit, Key was already home. Alec was past the point of exhaustion, yet his dick tented in his shorts, jutting straight out like a fucking heat-seeking missile.

"Alec?" Key called from the bottom of the stairs.

"Yeah," his voice croaked as he mashed the heel of his palm against the hard as steel shaft in his shorts. Even Key's voice caused his dick to twitch. "I'll be down in a minute."

What the hell was he going to do? Sex was a fucking natural part of life. Alec should be up for sainthood for having Key in his bed every night and not fucking the guy senseless. How long did he have to wait? What was an appropriate amount of time to legitimize all these feelings so his biker knew what they had was more than just sex?

Alec went to his upstairs bathroom and shoved his overly excited cock under a stream of cold water. Hopefully, he'd calmed the damn thing down enough to at least get downstairs, say hello, then run take a quick cold shower.

He trotted down the stairs, rolling the tight muscles in his shoulders as he hit the bottom step, barely turning the corner before running smack into Key. Alec stopped short, took an immediate step backward, and looked at the guy from top to bottom. Key had on new jeans, new boots—more designer than work—and a button-down the color of his striking blue eyes, both sleeves rolled a couple of times. He'd left his hair loose, and the silky strands tempted Alec's eager fingers. Key's beard had been trimmed, and he wore jewelry—skulls, chains, and sexy leather straps. They fit this man perfectly.

Oh hell. Key had always been mouthwatering, but this… "You're handsome."

Key chuckled. "Surprised about that?"

"No…"

His lover outright laughed at him this time. Alec was never at a loss for words, not ever. He could talk his way out of a box and had before, but this was such a surprise.

Key ran his hands down the length of his pressed shirt. His Adam's apple bobbed, and his eyes followed his hands roaming over his clothing. "Bad choice? I got others."

Alec forced himself to move before he dropped to his knees to show Key exactly what he thought about his look. Instead, he puckered for the one welcome-home kiss he'd allow himself to have. Against his will, Alec's lips lingered. His entire body tightened, and he clenched his fists, forcing himself to break away, settling back on his heels as he looked up into Key's bright eyes. "You're stunning, and you smell amazing. Your hair's even different."

"That woman who fixed me up before used the hairdryer. She called someone in the mall who hooked me up with the rest." Oh hell, Key had done all this for him.

Alec couldn't help his lift of the chin for another kiss. As handsome as Key was with the clothes on, all Alec wanted to do was peel him out of them.

"You surprised me. I've always thought of you as handsome, but you clean up really well. Let me run and shower and throw on a change of clothes. I thought we could run up to Whole Foods," Alec said and bypassed Key to head for the seclusion of the master bathroom.

"We can't go to the grocery store together," Key said from behind him as if Alec had lost his mind.

"Key, we're going on six months. No one's seen us. Give me a few minutes, and we'll continue this conversation." Alec didn't turn back as he jogged for his bedroom. He rarely shut the door on Key, but he did this time and locked the bathroom door behind him. Alec gripped the counter, pressing against the granite as sweat dripped off his face.

What the fuck had just happened out there? Key was male model material. He should be donning those clothes on the covers of magazines.

"It's working," Alec muttered almost silently, looking up in the mirror at himself. "It's working." Key thought Alec was caught up in their sex, so he was proving those words wrong, and it was working. Five days into his promise to show Key how much he meant to him, and Key had walked into this house with confidence, looking like a new man, enticing Alec with every stitch of his new clothing. "He bought new clothes for me."

That heady realization made Alec stretch to his full height. This was Saturday night. They had all day tomorrow together. He would make love to Key tomorrow. He could wait. Until then, he'd jerk off in the shower and dress for Key like his biker had dressed for him. And they were going to the store together. That was going to happen. He loved that man, and no, he couldn't yet be open with the world, but they could walk into a grocery store and pick out their dinners together. Hell, friends did things like that all the time. Set in his resolve, Alec went for the shower, dropping his shorts, and palming his dick. He could do this. He could. He had a point to prove.

Instead of sitting outside, letting sweat create pit stains in his new shirt, Keyes sat on one of the barstools, staring at the entrance to the hall leading to Alec's bedroom. His elbows rested on his knees as his gaze stayed fixed on the reflection of the walls, waiting for Alec's shadow to appear. There was hesitation and insecurity in him. This time might even be worse than the last. Alec had been weird about his clothes. Of course, he'd been weird. He liked the grungy biker, not the cleaned-up biker, and that had Keyes clasping his hands together, looking down at his feet, feeling like a dumbass.

They weren't right. There was a butt-load of tension between them. Every morning Alec asked him to come back in the evening, and every night, he did, but it wasn't right. That fluid way they were together seemed strained, and he didn't know how to fix it. Alec wasn't having sex with him, but he wasn't pushing him away either.

From his position, Keyes could see enough to take in several stacks of legal looking documents scattered across the living room floor. Maybe ten different piles of various sizes. The television was on, but muted. His gaze moved back to the hall when he heard the bedroom door open. He waited, letting his hair fall forward, an old defense mechanism he'd developed as a child, and he watched Alec round the corner. He was dressed casually, but put together, gorgeous as always. He'd matched Keyes's style, except Alec wore his clothes far better. He fixed his blond hair, that longer on top bit flipped back perfectly, and he wore jewelry too. He looked like a million bucks, which might be close to the cost of the jewelry, and Alec smiled when he spotted him.

"I pale in comparison, but I tried." The perfect ice-breaker. Keyes laughed, leaning back in the seat as Alec came to stand in front of him.

"If that means you're hot, then you're right," he added.

"So the grocery store—"

That made his smile vanish as he quickly cut Alec off. "Is not a good idea." Keyes shook his head as Alec nodded.

"Sure, it is. I promise the members of your club aren't hanging out in the grocery store in McKinney, Texas."

"I'm here," Keyes stated the obvious as Alec went for his key fob.

"And the way my HOA freaks out with every rumble of the pipes, I'm certain they've never seen the members here before," Alec said, going for the door separating them from the garage. Keyes heard the outer garage door lifting.

"What's that mean?" he asked, not moving a single muscle to follow.

"I'll explain in the car." Alec's head cocked toward the garage in a clear get your ass up and come on.

"Alec..." He still didn't budge. He might agree that no one would see them in the grocery store, but this broke a major rule. First this, then what?

"We won't touch. We'll walk in, go to the meat counter. I'd like a salad of some sort..." Alec patted his belly, grinning at him. "I've been trying hard to tone this back up."

"You're toned," he said and finally rose to his feet. When had he lost his balls? Alec had him so whipped.

"You're biased. We'll pay and leave and come back here. No one the wiser." Alec walked into the garage, saying, "Alexa, we're leaving." When Keyes still didn't follow, Alec came back through the door. "We have twenty seconds. Whatever that look on your face means, you'll have to tell me in the car."

Keyes gave up and followed his pushy lawyer-man. Alec's whole setup was planned to the second, and the car was already out of the garage, idling, waiting for Keyes. He barely got outside before the garage door lowered and the alarm stated clearly it was initiating.

He went to the driver's side window, motioning for Alec to roll the window down. "Alec, if they see us together, they'll find out who you are and jump to conclusions. They won't ask questions, and your body won't be found."

"That's very dramatic. We'll talk in the car." Alec's window rolled up in his face.

Man, he didn't want to do this. This was risking so much. He slowly went around the hood and slid into the passenger side. It smelled like rich leather, things he couldn't afford, secrets he couldn't reveal, and hopes he should walk away from.

"Babe, you need to listen to what I'm sayin'. They'd fuck me up, but they'd kill you. They hate your boss."

"We're not going to be seen. You leave the car after me. Whatever. I'm confident we're a world apart from your biker brothers," Alec said, pushing the remote as he pulled out into the street. "I was also thinking we could go to the movies together."

"Have you lost your fuckin' mind?" Keyes asked as he swung his head Alec's direction.

"No. Just hear me out. We meet inside the movie. No one will know. It's dark in there—we sit together once it's darkened. It's perfect…"

Keyes was pretty damn sure that was the exact opposite of perfect.

"This whole week's been fucked up. What's wrong with you?" he asked, finally growing enough balls to ask his lover, hopefully getting to the root of the problem between them. Alec gave him a confused indulgent smile as he reached over, taking Keyes's hand in his, bringing their joined hands to the gearshift.

"I'm showing you we're not just sex. We're more than that. And we are more than that, Key," Alec stressed, splitting his attention between Keyes and the road.

"All this"—he couldn't find the words, so he used his hand, motioning between the two of them—"is that?"

"Of course. You need to know you're special to me. I wanted you to see we don't have to have sex. We're supposed to be happy with each other's efforts in making this real between us. I'm happy with yours. You look incredible. You're so handsome."

Keyes was officially freaked out and stared out the side window, looking at every single car they passed. This whole week had left him second-guessing himself, and here they were in Alec's fancy sports car for the world to see. Keyes's heart drummed in his chest.

"I'd guess she used a flat iron on your hair."

This whole week had been Alec's attempt to show him they weren't just sex... How had that never occurred to him?

"She did," he finally answered after a long pause. "I felt like a fool with all those women watchin' me." He watched Alec pull into the parking lot of the store, parking in an unlit section to the side of the store.

"Are we walking in there together?" Alec asked.

Oh man, Keyes didn't want to be there. He pushed open the door, got out, and carefully shut it behind him. He scanned the entire parking lot then did it again as Alec left the vehicle. Keyes tucked his fingers in the front pockets of his jeans and walked alongside Alec toward the front of the building. There was no question in his mind, he'd fight his brothers to the death to protect Alec. He just knew that wouldn't be enough to stop them. Why had he come?

=♥=

"They have a big steak section and a huge salad bar. They also have lobster. We haven't had lobster before," Alec explained, feeling as internally freaked out as Key looked. That badass bike club coming after them was an alarming thought, more so than he had considered when suggesting this grocery store run, but he did his best to hide his sudden fear.

"Whatever you want," Key said, walking about three feet away from him.

Normally Alec would pause, let Key go first. He didn't this time. He walked straight through the front doors, and thankfully, as suspected, the grocery store was close to empty. He saw a few employees, who did turn their way, but they were women and only seemed to have eyes for Key. Alec got it. There was something forbidden about the guy. The biker had swagger and sex appeal down to an art form, and Key put out an air of being off limits. And he *was* off limits. He belonged to Alec.

All those primal instincts kicked in, pushing him to remember his plan of attack. He was showing Key they were more than sex. They were a couple. He grabbed a small basket before starting for the meat counter with a renewed commitment in his heart.

"This way." Alec pointed toward the far side of the store. "You look angry."

"I am angry," Key muttered, disgust in his voice.

Alec burst out in a sudden laugh and reduced the space separating them, bumping Key in the shoulder. "Lighten up. Act normal. How was your day?"

His biker didn't respond.

"Okay, well that didn't give me much to work with to start a conversation."

The deep sigh, made louder to ensure Alec heard his irritation, had him grinning. Alec imagined Key rolled his eyes like a spoiled child before he spoke.

"I bought some things to leave at your place," Key said so casually it took Alec maybe as long as two seconds to jerk his gaze toward his lover and slow his stride. That was a big step in the right direction of Alec's goals.

"Did you bring your duffel bag?" Alec asked seriously. Did that mean Key planned to move in? Alec's heart pounded wildly at the possibility. Was he even ready for such a commitment? Hell yes, he was. Right? Big step, yes, but he wanted everything with Key.

"You makin' fun of me?" The corners of Key's mouth inched up, but he never looked over at Alec as they reached the meat counter.

"Why would I make fun of you?" Alec asked in the way he did when his lover threw him a curve ball in the middle of a discussion.

"You know," Key said and left him standing there. The biker walked along the curve of the display, looking at the selections as a woman came to the counter in front of Alec, drawing his attention her way.

"Can I help you?"

Alec opened his mouth and nothing came out. His thoughts were too focused on everything Key had casually tossed out like it wasn't the biggest deal in the whole world. All Alec could do was turn toward Key and say, "Help him. I'm doing the salad bar."

It took five minutes for Alec to pick his salad ingredients, because every fifteen seconds, he lifted his gaze to Key and studied his guy, wondering over the possibilities. Key chose a meat and potato before they were heading back toward the cash registers. Alec held his tongue, not asking any of the dozens of questions he want to, forcing himself to wait until they were alone again.

On the way to the front, Key picked some cheese, a small fruit tray, and fresh baked bread. As always, Key was efficient in his choices. He didn't peruse the selections, waffle back and forth on what to buy. He took what he wanted, barely breaking stride as he passed by.

"Do you like coffee cake?" Key asked from a few feet away as Alec unloaded the basket onto the conveyor belt.

"Get what you want," Alec said, so he did, picking a cinnamon cake. When the cashier, who had ogled Key before, finished scanning the groceries and gave them the total, he and his boyfriend had a first. Key reached for his wallet at the same time Alec did. Key had a wallet full of cash, but Alec was faster, pushing his card into the chip reader while his biker counted out his bills.

Since Alec was the winner, he reached for the bags, watching as Key and the cashier got confused when the purchase completed while cash changed hands. Alec was already walking toward the doors, chuckling at the absurdity of the moment, before Key caught up with him, reaching for the grocery sacks. "I can pay. I have money."

The struggle was real until Alec just gave in and handed Key a grocery bag so he could lift the hatch to his car. "I know you can." He listened for the locking system to release as he got closer and opened the back, placing the grocery bags inside.

"Then why did you laugh?"

"Because she was all about my guy and hadn't noticed I paid. That look of startled confusion as she tried to understand why her drawer didn't open made me laugh," he said, rounding the car. He opened his door, dropping down to the seat, leaving Key still standing at the back of the car.

"She wasn't into me. I get that same look everywhere. People watch me, because they tag me as a threat," Key said once inside the car.

"Yeah, keep telling yourself that." Alec pushed the ignition button and the car roared to life.

Key's whole attention remained focused on Alec, the club and their outing seemingly forgotten in favor of the conversation they were having.

"It's true."

"So back to the meat counter. How was I making fun of you over the duffel bag?"

That had Key rolling his eyes, turning away from Alec, and staying silent. Key pointed him toward the street, a gesture Alec took to mean he needed to get moving.

"No, don't go silent. Talk to me. I'm not driving until you do."

"All my stuff fits inside a duffel," Key said and rolled his eyes again with dramatic flair this time as if that explained anything. Key again pointed him toward the street. "Not anymore though. I got a shit load of crap tied on the back of my bike. That woman sold me too much."

Alec narrowed his eyes and tried to work out how Key thought he'd been making fun of him. He did start for the street, thinking over the possibility, and he couldn't figure it out. Nothing he came up with made sense. "I asked about your duffel, because if you brought it over, then I assumed you'd be moving in, which I'd love to have happen."

Key flipped his head Alec's direction, so horrified he made Alec laugh as he merged into traffic.

"Stop. We're building a relationship. It seems a natural progression, and you spend quite a bit of time over here already."

Key's full attention was back on Alec as he lifted a hand, using his fingers to tick off the obvious point about each of them. "I'm a biker. You're an ADA. My club…"

"Stop with the doom and gloom. We're safe, and we'll continue to be, but my decisions are made. I'm not planning to be with the DA's office for too much longer," Alec explained, taking the curve into his neighborhood. "So what are you leaving at my place?"

"What? You're leavin' the DA's office?" Key asked, sounding surprised. "When did that decision get made?"

"My questions first," Alec insisted, just now realizing he'd let his plans accidently slip out. That didn't happen too often with Alec. He did talk a lot, but he was always aware of what he was saying. He was truly comfortable with Key.

"Clothes. What else would I leave at your house?" Key asked, again like that was the most obvious answer in the world. Alec reached for his gate's remote, slowing as the gate started the process of opening.

Alec's pushy side rejected the mental lecture he gave himself to let that be enough for now. He tried to convince himself it was purely economics that drove him to say, "It seems silly to keep paying for an apartment you aren't using."

It was dark outside, made darker on the unlit portion of his drive, but he still could feel the weight of Key's stare on him as if he'd lost his mind. An expression he'd grown accustomed to this week. "I've got months on a lease. You've freaked my shit out tonight, Alec. Stop. I'll give."

The problem, Alec was officially freaked too, but in a weirdly satisfying way.

CHAPTER 11

Keyes stood in the entrance of the small hall leading into the living room, the bulk of his weight resting against the wall, a cocktail glass in hand. He stared at Alec who was deep in thought, working on the piles of paperwork he had tried to explain to Keyes over dinner. Honestly, he hadn't retained much of what Alec had said. Instead, he had focused on the way Alec's eyes twinkled when he became excited and animated over his explanation. The way Alec used his hands to speak, or in this particular case, the fork and knife became instruments to guiding his talking points. Alec had whipped the utensils in the air as he spoke, pointing as if he were seeing a whiteboard in front of him. The lawyer commanded his attention.

As far as Keyes was concerned, Alec could talk all day long and he'd never get bored. He loved that the deep tenor rolled down his spine, soothed, and calmed him. Keyes relaxed, feeling safe and secure.

That was the odd part, the safety aspect. He'd managed his life all by himself and had somehow come out on top. He wasn't scared of anything—he truly wasn't—so to feel safe touched a deeper part of him. A part he hadn't known was there. A piece of him that belonged only to Alec.

Keyes loved Alec.

Yup. Love.

Love had been an empty word, devoid of substance, until Alec Pierce gave it meaning.

He sipped at the watered-down Crown in his hand. Keyes was comfortable here. Not only did he feel he belonged, and he'd never belonged anywhere before, but Alec made him feel wanted as if he genuinely enjoyed having Keyes around. Alec had this great big house, but they stayed in these three rooms—the kitchen, living room, and Alec's bedroom.

He again lifted the glass, sucking down more of the smooth whiskey as he stared at the gorgeous man who sat on a rug in the middle of the living room floor, bent over the paperwork. Keyes hadn't seen Alec nude all week, which was weird. Alec didn't believe in clothing, especially pants, yet tonight, he had on a T-shirt and a pair of loose-fitting shorts. He had one leg drawn to his chest with an arm wrapped around his knee. The other stretched out on the plush rug. The papers spread all around him.

"Did you get your things put away? Have enough room?" Alec asked, never looking up from the page he studied. His mister was funny. Alec had cleared half his closet and given Keyes a whole set of dresser drawers for his four new shirts, two pair of new jeans, and packs of unopened underwear, undershirts, and socks. Yeah, he had enough room.

"I did."

"Rain's coming again. Did you get your bike in the garage?" Alec asked, keeping his gaze lowered.

"I did." Keyes left his spot and went for the wine bucket near Alec. He refilled Alec's near empty glass. That time, Alec did acknowledge him, looking up to give a soft, pleased smile, and murmured a quiet thank-you. He lifted the glass and took a long drink before turning back to the documents.

Keyes stood there, staring down at the lawyer who continued to ignore him. Keyes's dick was hard just from watching the man, which was technically nothing new. Alec was intense to say the least, with loads of sex appeal. He would always want this man. He had warred with the best way to fix their problem, and ultimately decided it might be too crude to shove his dick inside Alec's magnificent mouth like he wanted to do. Instead, he placed his almost empty glass on the coffee table, took out the bottle of lube and condom packets he had in his back pocket then dropped his pants where he stood. They pooled at his feet as he tugged his shirt over his head, carelessly discarding it on the floor.

Keyes dropped to the floor and scooted in directly behind Alec, his hard dick slotting between their bodies, pressing against Alec's back as he wrapped his legs around his man.

Of course, he could feel the weight in the room as Key hovered nearby. If Key was within a mile's radius, Alec instinctively knew. The warmth of Key's bare legs alongside his confused him at first. Key had been wearing pants when he walked toward him. Key was a sexual being, so the rock-hard dick pressed against his ass and lower back shouldn't have been a surprise either.

Key's big body was warm and inviting as his lover wrapped himself around Alec. His own body overrode his head, wanting him to surrender to such a blatant invitation. Alec had already planned for tomorrow to be their day together. The rain was coming and expected to last throughout the day. It had been too long since he'd been with Key, and he planned to take full advantage of the lazy day. It seemed a perfect opportunity to enjoy one another physically. Then Alec planned to wait another six days and do it all over again. Something he hated doing, but he needed to prove a point, even if it was killing him.

"Would you call your skin tone olive?" Key asked, and Alec looked down at their legs, Key's tan was coming along nicely for a man who didn't usually wear shorts, but Alec's skin had turned a deep bronze, something that happened regularly when he spent his summer months in the sun.

Key's strong hands went to his belly, first sliding over the worn cotton of his T-shirt then lifting underneath the hem. His biker's skilled fingertips skimmed the barely there indentions of his abs.

"I can feel the difference in all that workin' out you've been doin'," Key murmured huskily against his ear.

How crazy that Key actually believed the workout lie. Alec had spent those hours in his home gym running and lifting to keep from jumping his sexy man the minute he walked inside the door. Even the papers at his feet were a means to keep him from caving. Busy work to keep his mind off what his body craved the most. Alec closed his eyes and willed himself to move away.

"Tell me again what all this is?" Key's lips pressed into the juncture between his neck and his shoulder. The hair of

Key's mustache prickled his skin. His lover's warm tongue licked up the side of his neck.

Alec shivered and dropped his head, chin to chest, his body threatening to spontaneously combust. "I told you it's a project my grandfather started..." Alec kept talking, didn't even know what he was saying, his whole focus rested on Key's palms, sliding upward to his pecs. Those skilled fingers pinched the tight bud of his nipples at the same moment Key's lips parted and he sank his teeth in Alec's neck.

His train of thought vanished when Key pulled him back against his broad chest as he skimmed his nose across Alec's neck and into his hair then breathed him in. Key's lips brushed across his ear. Alec craned his neck to give Key better access. He nibbled there then whispered, his hot breath dancing over the damp skin. "Is that a new cologne?"

Dammit, the man wasn't playing fair. Key's hands were everywhere, burning a path in their wake and setting his flesh ablaze. His guy stroked his arousal through the thin material of his shorts. Alec's breath caught as a rush of goose bumps sprang up across his flesh, and his dick twitched from his lover's ministrations. Key shoved one hand inside Alec's shorts and Alec's hips rolled to meet his fingers, his dick pushing past the jockstrap designed to help hide the constant hard-on he sported around this very sexy man. Key had learned how to please him, no question there. His palm grazed Alec's aching length, his long hot fingers pushed the bothersome material down before circling his needy cock.

Key's legs crossed under his as he was pulled higher on his lover's lap. The move helped support Alec's upper body, and he rested against Key's shoulder. Alec leaned into the circle of Key's arms, turning enough for an awkward but slow burning kiss. Alec lifted a hand, threading his fingers through Key's hair, keeping him right there while he licked his way around those fleshy lips before sliding his tongue deep inside to do it all again. He wanted more, needed to feel Key moving inside him.

The exploration was slow yet thorough, and Key matched the urgency of the kiss by sliding one hand down to Alec's balls. Key's hand was so strong and felt so hot holding him. He let his thighs drop open as he shifted his weight.

Key got the hint. He quickly sucked his fingers, getting them wet before snaking them into the leg of his workout shorts and pressing against his hole. The assault was almost too much. Key's thick finger pushed inside him, easily finding his gland. The other hand gripped and tightened around his dick, moving with purpose. Key leisurely circled his broad head, coaxing small beads of moisture from Alec's tip. That thick finger sliding in and out of him felt so fucking good. He needed more, had to feel Key moving in him.

Somehow, Key managed to tighten his body around Alec, pulling him closer by maneuvering Alec more completely in his hold. Key rolled his hips into Alec, probably creating a delicious friction for Key's cock stuck between them.

"Make love to me… Don't give any excuses. Just turn around and make love to me…" Key's choice of words sent a tingle sliding down his spine. Fuck all those best laid plans. He wanted his man, and Key needed him as much as he needed Key.

Alec didn't say a word as he eagerly turned to face Key, deftly shedding his shorts and jock before straddling his biker's thighs so they faced one another. Overwhelming need raced throughout him as he took in his lover's heaving chest and lust-filled gaze. Alec crushed their mouths together. He drove his tongue past Key's fleshy, parted lips. How he'd ever lived without this man in his life was beyond him. Alec's world had grown smaller, his needs more singular, and every bit of his newfound world rested in Key's caring hands. Alec deepened the kiss.

Key's wicked tongue slid forward, dancing against his, ravishing his mouth. This was heaven, his dreams come true. He could never go back to his life before, he was so deeply in love with Key.

Alec tore from the kiss, staying within inches of Key's face, staring him straight in the eyes, and growled, "How do you want me?"

The smile that touched Alec's lips brought joy to Keyes's heart. He grabbed the bottle of lube and condoms off the corner of the table, dropping them on the oversized rug beside Alec's scattered folders.

"Hands and knees. I need you." His voice was deep, his body already vibrating from excitement as he nudged Alec's hip with his knee.

"Bossy," Alec murmured and rolled over. Keyes covered Alec, running his palms from the base of Alec's back, all the way up to his shoulders as he rested his weight along Alec's body.

Keyes bent to Alec's ear, running his nose across his hair and along his ear and neck as he spoke quietly from his heart. "I've missed you this way. I know you're tryin' to show me how much you love me, but I need to make love to you. I don't want to be without you this way. I'm always aroused by you. Always."

When Alec shuddered, Keyes pushed himself back to his knees. Staring at Alec's delicious ass, he grabbed the lube from beside his knee and spread Alec wide. He poured a generous amount right in his crack, chuckling when Alec wiggled in an attempt to escape the cold liquid. Keyes gripped his hip, keeping him in place as he slid his fingers through the cool lube.

Keyes took time to slowly and methodically relax Alec, opening him. Carefully, he inserted one finger past the rim, searching and finding the exact spot his Alec loved. "Is this what you like?"

"Mmm…" Alec's ass pushed back into his hand. "Please, babe… *Yes*." Alec started to rise up on his elbows, but Keyes pressed his palm between his shoulder blades to push him back to the floor.

"No. Stay there," Keyes said and added another finger, pressing deeply, crooking it, massaging as he worked his fingers to give Alec pleasure. "I can feel you're ready for my cock." He knew how much Alec liked words, so he tried. Fuck, it didn't come easy for him.

"Yes." Alec squirmed, his ass clasping tightly around the invading fingers and his breath heaving as he spoke. "Need you."

"I wasn't sure where I stood, I didn't…"

"You're everything to me." Alec panted and rolled his hips while Keyes's fingers teased and toyed, pressing deeper into Alec's heat.

"Everything?" Keyes asked, watching Alec's body move against his hand.

"Everything." His lover's voice sent shivers through his soul.

"I've wanted you so bad, Alec… I'm so fuckin' hard for you. I can't wait to be inside you." He had never spoken truer words in his life. Keyes gripped himself, adding the condom before positioning his eager cock. He slid forward in one deep, satisfying thrust.

Motherfucker, Alec felt good as his body clenched around him.

He ground his teeth as he closed his eyes and steeled his spine. Keyes had learned how best to seduce Alec; he just had to hang on long enough to do it right.

"Oh God, yes… That's it, baby," Alec cried. Keyes pulled himself out, massaging Alec back open with his broad head. His body tensed and tightened, the tendons in his neck bulged under his restraint, and his breath panted from his lips.

"I wanna be with you always, like this, always." His breath hitched as a deep growl built in his chest. No more words could form in his head. He tried to force himself to take it slow, but fuck, Alec was so tight and so welcoming. He pushed forward, gripping Alec's hips, digging his fingers hard into his man's skin.

"That's it. Fuck me, Key," Alec implored and pressed against him, bucking his hips, urging him on, harder and deeper. It felt so good. Keyes bucked, grabbing Alec's shoulder, trying to hold him in place as he answered Alec's call, pounding him harder. He filled Alec completely with every thrust.

His panting deepened, his thighs burned, and he ran his nose along Alec's neck, licking at the trickle of sweat beading there before he whispered, "Feel me claiming you? You're mine, Alec Pierce. Only mine."

Those were promises he intended to keep. Sweat rolled down his chest as he bucked harder.

Alec gripped the rug beneath him, his knuckles white as he strained to keep Key's delicious momentum from pushing him forward. It had been way too long, and he was afraid it might end way too soon, because Key knew his body too well. Alec rose higher on his knees, trying to find that perfect position as Key pounded into him. Key's body moving in and out of his made him crazy, but he had to hold back, and Key wasn't playing fair. His biker seemed determined to be last in receiving pleasure. A trait he normally loved about Key except he was just that determined to bring Key to his release first. But he had a problem with that plan—Jesus, Key's need turned Alec the fuck on.

Alec had to think of something other than the sensation of that perfect cock sliding in and out of him, brushing against that spot inside him that made his body want to rush to the finish line. He also had to think of anything other than the sound of his lover's body slapping against his.

Fuck, he was going to come....

No! Don't think about the low sexy growls huffing just above him.

Think boring...

Code of criminal procedure...

Plaintiffs, plea bargains, due process, investigations...

Wiretapping...oh God, tap that ass... Alec groaned. He desperately needed a distraction. Baseball...no...no balls. God, his balls were tightening with his need. This wasn't helping at all. The drag of Key's cock sliding against his prostate sent stars shooting behind his tightly shut eyes.

Alec released the carpet scrambling for a better grip, he braced his arms above his head as one vigorous thrust threatened to send him tumbling forward. Fuck! Being with Key felt too good, too right.

Do.

Not.

Come.

Think…Einstein.

$E = mc^2$ Energy and mass are equivalent and transmutable.

He had to make this feeling last. If he could just recite Einstein's theories over and over in his head… What was it again?

Special principles of relativity. Oh…God… His body pulsed and tightened around Key. Key's cock igniting every nerve ending along his channel as his lover shoved deeper. He was going to lose it. Key lifted, changing his position, deepening his thrusts. Pleasure found his prostate with each snap of his biker's hips.

Alec…think about…Einstein. What does the principle state? Something about relation, physical, moving in…fuck. No matter how innocuous, the words painted vulgar images in his mind. Sweat rolled down his face as he fought to keep his release at bay. Holy hell, as much as he hated this shit in school, it seemed Einstein's theory only made him hotter, who knew? The words conjured vivid and crude images in his mind. For a split-second, his determination wobbled.

Alec braced himself, pushing his hips back against Key's, forcing his lover onto his heels. Key's thrust didn't falter as those big arms surrounded him pulling him upright too. His back rubbed against Key's impressive chest; the friction from the position threatening to shatter his resolve. Key embraced him, holding tightly around Alec's waist.

"Stop fightin' it," Key whispered with a husky breath, hips rolled against his sending Key deeply into him. "I know you're close." Key's tongue traced a heated path along his neck, dipping into his ear as he slid a hand slowly down Alec's hip before thick fingers closed around his shaft.

"Stop," he croaked, just managing to get the words out before it was too late.

Key's hand stilled, and the mind-numbing movement of those hips stopped. Heavy pants accompanied Key's words as the fragments of reason fell back into place.

"You okay?" There was such concern in Key's voice it caught him off guard.

"Yes. I didn't want to come. I do. Just not first."

"Competitive much?" Key chuckled against his ear.

Alec laughed and let his head rest back against Key's shoulder using the moment to gather his wits before easing away from his lover and turning to face him. Alec took Key's mouth with his in a sweet and tender kiss. He couldn't help himself when he saw the disbelieving look on Key's face.

"I like to win." Alec placed both palms on Key's chest, and shoved, pushing Key to his back, scrambling quickly to take advantage of the situation. The hairs on Key's legs rasped against his inner thighs, making him groan as he settled on his lover's body.

Alec wiggled his ass, grinning at the sharp intake of breath below him as he straddled Key's waist.

"I should have known a DA wouldn't play fair." Key tried to move, but Alec anticipated the action and pressed firmly against that thick wall of chest muscle to keep him down.

"Says the outlaw biker."

His lover might be posturing for show, but based on the rigid length pressed against his ass, Key was all-in with this scenario. Key's fingertips moved lightly up and down the outside Alec's thigh, before tracing heated paths over his hips.

"I love your hands on me," he said, lifting enough to position himself, placing Key's tip at his entrance. Key's teeth tugged at his bottom lip, his pupil's wide with passion. Firm fingers closed around Alec's arousal as he sank down on top of Key, moaning as Key's thick length impaled him, inch by inch. He loved the power he felt when Key's sexy growl echoed along his body. He craved this closeness, loving every single way Key filled him.

The look of sheer bliss on Key's face had his resolve strengthening. Alec slowly rolled his hips, the move forcing his own hardness deeper into Key's fist over and over again.

Key closed his eyes, arching his long back, rolling his stomach muscle to keep rhythm with Alec. He batted Key's hand away and dropped forward, bracing himself with his hands as he quickened the pace. He closed his eyes in ecstasy as he rode Key.

Key's fingers dug deep in his thighs, causing a hiss to escape his lips. He opened his eyes, easily losing himself in the sight of Key. "Oh God, yes…Key. I love you…"

Key writhed beneath him, mumbling his name as he moved in him. Alec's leaking cock, trapped between their bodies, rubbed deliciously against sweat-slicked skin as he held his face mere inches from his lover's. Alec was held hostage by a gaze so captivating he swore the intensity caressed his soul. In this moment, they were on the exact same page in the exact same place. It was there he saw everything he'd hoped for reflected in those blue depths.

Key's face tightened in pleasure. Alec loved watching Key's expression, especially when he was so close.

The erotic pressure built with every grunt and thrust until its explosive heat rolled over him with little warning. "Come with me," he panted. Pleasure bubbled hotly in his balls, sending waves of bliss through his body as he said the words.

Key bucked up into him, his grip tightening, stroking him faster, keeping in rhythm with their thrusts. Then that grip faltered as his lover stiffened and thickened.

A motherfucker of an orgasm raced down his spine, pleasure zinging through him as if a million electrical currents flowed back and forth, branching out like fingers to caress every nerve pathway in his body. Heat burned the tips of his ears and his toes curled at the shocking intensity strumming through his body in the sweetest way. His breath escaped his lungs on a moan as he tried to prolong the inevitable. It was useless. He couldn't hold back any longer. He was about to lose the game. Key was going to win this round after all. Everything amplified as his body surrendered and his orgasm sent him over the edge.

Alec's release hit him hard, shooting from him in hot bursts, spilling onto Key's stomach and chest as he fought to maintain consciousness. He collapsed completely on top of Key, his body as sated and spent and limp as Key's.

His breathing slowed, his mind and body settling as he lay on top of Key. Cocooned completely in his lover's arms, he could feel their hearts thumping in unison. A perfect beat all their own.

No question they were explosive together, and he was determined to make up for lost time. He wanted more, just as soon as he could think coherently again.

"I belong to you," Alec said and pressed his lips to Key's chest before he forced himself up, the lightheadedness making him wobbly. They had fallen on his papers, wrinkled and displaced his stacks, and he didn't care in the least. Instead, he reached to pick up Key's hand, and tugged. Key only laughed at him, keeping his eyes closed and refusing to budge. "Did you hear me?"

"I thought you were already mine," Key said, taking his other arm and draping it over his closed eyes, letting out a lengthy yawn.

"Just a reminder." Alec dropped Key's hand and reached for his wineglass, downing the rest before he started for the bedroom. "Come on. Shower, bed, sex—in that order. You've got a lot to make up for."

"What? Why do I have a lot to make up for?"

Alec grinned. He'd gotten the desired result. Key rose to a sitting position, letting out an oomph as he attempted to stand and tumbled back to his ass. "I wasn't the one withholdin' sex. No more of that bullshit. Understood?"

"We'll talk about that too. Come on," Alec said, stopping at the edge of the sofa, wanting Key to come with him.

"Why do we have to talk so much? Just agree," Key said, finally making it to his feet, before slowly heading his way. "And why can't we rest here for a few minutes?"

Thunder clapped, rattling the windows near them. Evidently the weatherman had been right this time as the forecasted storm rolled in, making the lights flicker.

"Stop whining and come on before we lose power." Alec left Key to trail behind him, letting a smile touch his face. He was happy. Seriously, very happy.

CHAPTER 12

Three months later

Alec stood in front of the bathroom mirror, knotting his silk tie while listening to Alexa play Key's preferred morning playlist. This song was by Five Finger Death Punch, a favorite of Key's which somehow made it a favorite of Alec's, the only reason it still continued to play even though Key had left well over an hour ago. Alec cast an appreciative glance at the second sink in his bathroom. The one that been unused for all the months he'd lived there alone. That was no longer the case. It was Key's sink now, his few toiletries left out for easy reach and his toothbrush securely in the holder right next to Alec's.

No, Key hadn't "officially" moved in. He still considered himself a guest in Alec's home, and much to his heart's dismay, his mister still hadn't said those three little words, but Alec had easily justified the lapse by remembering words weren't Key's strong suit. Key's actions spoke louder. What Key excelled at was showing him every single day how loved he truly was. No one had ever made him feel more valued or secure. Key slept over most nights. Only when club business called was the man absent from his dinner table or his bed. Alec had grown more resentful of the club now that he realized how much it controlled their lives.

On that note, he steeled his spine and grabbed his suit jacket before heading toward his home office. He might resent the club, but he was filled with contempt when it came to his own pretentious family. Key had shown him his value, made Alec believe he was worthy of someone's time and attention...

Stop, justifying, Pierce. You know what needs to be done.

Key could continue the life he had, do whatever he felt obligated to do, but no more of that for Alec. He was done with his old life. Alec had purpose now and an overwhelming need to care for Key which ultimately gave him the strength to act. Starting today, he planned to live as genuinely as possible.

"Good morning, Mr. Alec."

Shit! Alec jumped. He'd been so caught up in his self-motivational pep talk he hadn't heard Olivia, his housekeeper, enter the house. With a hand over his pounding heart, he took a calming breath and grinned at her. "You scared me. I didn't hear you come in. Good morning." Then he turned to his Echo. "Alexa, stop the music."

"I found these on the kitchen counter." She extended her hand, giving him a pocket tire pressure tool and Key's frayed hair tie. He took both, smiling as he imagined the fit his big, sexy biker might throw when he realized he didn't have the hair tie on his wrist.

"Thank you." Alec started down the hall toward his home office when he pivoted around, remembering Key's suggestions last night for his flower beds. "Also, will you speak to your husband about adding more mums to the front and back yards. The colorful variegated ones, orange to yellow, and maybe some red or plum colors too." His household team consisted of Olivia who took care of the interior, her husband who acted as the gardener and mechanic for his two vintage automobiles, and her sister, Gabrielle, who ran his errands, stocked the refrigerator, and handled many of the odds and ends of his day to day life. "Also, I'd like to add some cactus plants. Maybe the ones without the thorns?"

She nodded. "Variegated mums and cactus, no thorns."

"Thank you," he said, turning back toward his office.

Key had confessed that fall was his favorite time of the year. Apparently, he loved mums and cactus plants. Who knew? Key's birthday fell on Halloween—information that had taken quite a bit of prodding to acquire. But Alec couldn't be happier. Halloween happened to be Alec's favorite holiday. They still had a few weeks to go, and if Alec played his cards right, they might actually have their first official date, almost nine months from the first day they met. He shook his head, biting back a grin at the thought. Their first date. Regardless, he envisioned dressing up from head to toe and going out as long as he could find suitable costumes this late in the game. Janice had invited them to a masquerade party at a bar she and her fiancé regularly frequented, and honestly, if he could find something to conceal their identities, there shouldn't be any problem with them attending. With the way things were going, maybe next Halloween could be their second official date.

Alec rounded the corner toward his office, reaching in his pocket for his cell phone. He hung his suit coat on the hanger by the door before texting Key.

"*You left your hair tie here and a tire pressure tool.*" Alec had barely gotten seated behind his desk when the phone dinged.

"*Tool 4 ur car & new tie.*"

Short and sweet, and the idea the tire pressure gauge was a gift warmed his heart like only Key could. Instead of getting all mushy, as his biker called it, he went for the humor.

"*Afraid I might call you needing a tire change?*" he teased, and Key responded right back.

"*More like afraid of the places u get stranded.*"

Alec read the words and laughed. Key had a point. He stared at the hair tie he'd placed on the desk. It had lost its elasticity and was a frayed, used up thing. His sisters had long hair—really the only other people Alec knew with hair long enough to tie back—and they seemed to use a new ponytail holder an hour and not think twice about it.

"*Thank you for my gift. Have a good day,*" he typed. The inevitable teasing from Key about his sentimental text would come. He'd be merciless with his ribbing, but then his guy would go out of his way to bring Alec another gift, something more meaningful, because at the end of the day, Key wanted him happy.

He pushed send, and Key sent back a fist bump emoji, causing Alec to laugh again. It seemed everything the man did made him insanely happy. Their connection had only grown stronger over the past months. Alec tossed the phone on his desk and reached for the computer's mouse to bring the screen to life. He entered his password and took a deep breath as he clicked on his email program, opting for his personal account to send this very personal message. The sound of the vacuum cleaner droning in another part of the house had Alec rising from his desk and shutting his office door to silence the extra noise.

He dropped back down in his office chair, letting out a long, cleansing exhale as he thought about his future. He hadn't made a rushed decision. Alec had known Key almost a year, and no matter what happened between them or how this ended, he was forever a changed man. He had been shown the meaning to the words happiness and love. Only one person mattered now and that was Key Dixon. Alec reached for his cell phone and searched his locked photo gallery until he found his favorite picture of Key. He was in the swimming pool, man bun securing his hair and sunglasses in place. His hard muscular chest was bare while he floated on the swan-shaped raft. Alec smiled, touching Key's face with his finger, remembering their leisurely day spent together.

Alec positioned the phone where Key's picture faced him, giving him courage as he composed a long overdue message. Alec started typing, but stopped, lifting his fingers off the keyboard. Emailing was the coward's way out. Alec was done being used, neglected, and shamed based on how the Pierce family fared in the voter polls or whatever latest market research effort they'd engaged in. He'd rather be condemned by honest feelings than by a hypocritical religious jackass with a voter's registration card threatening not to vote for Ryan Pierce because of his son. Hell, if asked, he could supply a lengthy list of far better reasons not to vote for his old man…

Stop. Don't think about it. It's destructive and puts you on the defensive. Be done so you can move forward.

Alec looked down at the phone in his hand as he pulled up his father's personal cell number. Before connecting the call, he glanced at the time. It was early. Key naturally woke super early. Seven thirty Dallas time meant eight thirty in DC. Maybe he could catch his father before his first meeting of the day. He cocked a speculative brow and gave a single nod at an even better option, maybe his father was already in a meeting and wouldn't answer at all, allowing him to leave a voice mail. Again, the coward's way out, but he couldn't control another person's availability. And surely leaving a message amounted to less cowardice than an email.

Alec closed his eyes, took a deep centering breath, and gained strength from his list of newfound priorities. And as always, his analytic mind began listing those reasons.

One—Key Dixon was his entire world, which only solidified with each passing day.

Two—Key's happiness surpassed the need for his own. Hell, the man's life meant more to him than his own. Alec was certain Key was his future and had been from the moment he'd seen that stunning man staring down at him with concern over the condition of his tires.

Three—he had had a weird mental paradigm shift over the last few months. He blamed Key's hard work ethic for rubbing off on him. He desperately wanted to support and spoil Key in the worst way. That was never going to happen with the meager salary he earned working for the Dallas County District Attorney's office.

He wanted to downsize the house only because they lived in three rooms and the backyard. He liked the idea of sharing a more intimate home with Key. They'd need a secure place for his cars and Key's bikes, and some wooded acreage so his biker would have a place to just be outside like he preferred.

Alec wanted to put this house on the market and build something more suitable to fit both their personalities. He smiled as he thought about marriage and the possibility of children. The image of a beautiful little chestnut to blond-headed baby warmed his heart. He'd thought about starting a family with Key. Of course, he hadn't mentioned anything, and it wasn't a deal breaker if Key didn't want children. If everything worked out like he hoped, maybe someday they could expand their family. He was certain Key's gentle caring nature would make him an attentive, kind, and loving father.

He sat back in his seat and marveled at how none of those thoughts freaked him out.

Focus on the here and now, Pierce. One step at a time.

Four—which might actually move to number one— Alec wanted to explore a traditional relationship with Key. Dinner out, traveling, shopping, movies, musicals, house parties, leisurely drives together whether it be by motorcycle or in one of his automobiles. With Key, he just wanted to do everything couples did together.

Five—he wanted Key away from that unforgiving world. Yeah, that one seemed selfish on his part. It did. Key never indicated anything other than those badass bikers being his family. Wouldn't consider anything else and Alec didn't try to persuade him differently. He listened to the things Key said and didn't say, letting Key's silence speak for itself. Key's outlaw biker father didn't accept Key any more than Alec's family accepted him.

They were from such different backgrounds, yet their families regarded them in the same manner. Alec suspected the club used Key for his loyalty, strength, and reasonable nature, but they didn't understand him or truly include him inside their inner circle—no way possible they truly accepted Key, not with as much time as he and Key spent together.

Whatever current situation Key found himself in with his club seemed to be leaving lasting scars. His lover wouldn't discuss it, claiming vows and oaths prohibited him from talking club business, but Alec saw the fine lines of anxiety etching the corners of Key's eyes and mouth, and maybe a distant sadness clouding those light-colored eyes any time Alec broached the subject.

The exception seemed to be with Dev. And that was Alec's number six.

Six—Alec wanted to know Devilman. He also wanted to meet the rarely mentioned uncle. They were both kind, helpful, and unconditional in their acceptance, or so Key thought, but for some reason, Key kept Alec from them when all he wanted was to shake their hands.

Ultimately, Alec held all the power to change their lives. He'd only been sticking around the DA's office for two reasons. The weakest of which was his father, but he was well past that obstacle. The real reason he'd stayed had been the Cummings case. The federal seat nomination and telling his father about his decisions had only been pushed back because he was vested in the welfare of that little girl.

The case grew more complicated with each passing day. Keely Cummings had touched Alec's heart, but more so, Key's unexpected tie to the case had sent his protective urges skyrocketing. Getting a clear picture from his father's detailed rap sheet charges and how Key's life ran almost parallel to the young girl's had almost gutted Alec. That kind, gentle, sweet man had had a hell of a life.

Once Alec had digested Key's father's sordid life, he'd asked Janice to quietly pull Key's CPS reports. That information was still sitting untouched on his desk. He was certain he wouldn't like the information inside and wished he'd never asked for it in the first place.

Honestly though, Alec had stuck with the district attorney's office to keep an eye on Keely Cummings's father. After months of lengthy consideration, Alec's personal concerns appeared to be just that. Months had passed and no one else had stumbled across the connection of Donald Cummings to the Disciples of Havoc. If that did happen, Alec would be honest with Key, give him the heads-up that Cummings might rat them out.

It was time to end this ridiculous farce with his family, though. He needed to end his nomination then his employment. He couldn't change his heritage, but he could put distance between himself and his family—hell, it was already there. He hadn't spoken to anyone but his father in well over six months.

On that note, he tapped his father's number and lifted the phone to his ear. He stayed tense and listened to the fourth and final ring, a little relieved at the idea of leaving a voice mail.

"Yes," his father answered, clipped and obviously stressed. *Shit.*

"Father?" Alec asked and closed his eyes. Why was he always reduced to the little boy so afraid and uncertain of what his father's hateful tone might mean?

"I said yes." Well, okay, that helped relieve some of his worry. Alec sat with his eyes closed as he took a deep breath and gathered his will. His father's irritable attitude helped steel Alec's spine.

This was his chance to take control of his life.

"Listen, I'm not going to keep you. I'm calling to tell you I'm pulling my nomination and leaving the DA's office. I should have never—"

"You're doing what?" his father bellowed, causing Alec to pull the phone away from his ear. Fuck, he hated when his father did that. That tone was like a blade driving straight into his brain. With his heart pounding, he winced at the sudden headache brought on by the pitch of his father's voice.

Alec was now pissed off and knew how to push his father's buttons so he repeated the words he'd used before, word for word, knowing his response would send his father's anger to the next level. "I'm pulling my nomination…"

"You think I didn't hear you? Do you know we're three weeks before election? The public sees me as tolerant in a goddamn time the voters want tolerant." His father's tone and volume hadn't decreased. Alec held the phone out to put some distance between his ear and the screaming coming from the other end.

Sure, he understood the timing left much to be desired. He should have done this months ago, but he hadn't. What he had done, though, was notice he hadn't been included in any of the pre-election family gatherings with the exception of having his name tossed around when needed. Before living in North Texas, he'd never seen the Dallas local news, so Alec wasn't aware he hadn't been invited to the photo opportunities. Now the evening news was his glaring reminder of their continued indifference.

He and Key sometimes watched the nightly news together. His mister never acknowledged Alec's absence when his family's campaigning made the news—

"Is this some sort of ploy to increase your allowance?"

"You've never given me an allowance," he informed his father, letting his tone turn incensed.

"Of course I have."

Alec remained silent at that reply. New parts of their family dynamic came to life like the sun rising over a ridge. Shocked he'd never considered it before, the excluded hurt little boy in him now wondered how much money his parents gave his worthless siblings while giving none to him.

Not the point, Pierce. You take care of you.

"You can't do this. It would be political suicide. Goddammit, Alec. You always pull this shit. You're about as dependable as tits on a boar hog."

What the hell? Alec stared down at the phone in his hand. His father sure took on a solid Texan twang during election season. There were no boar hog tits anywhere near his father.

"Your brother's decided to run for office. Your selfishness hurts all our chances. The answer's no. You will continue like we planned," his father commanded.

"I wasn't asking, and honestly, you don't want me in office. I'll work cases in such a way I'll embarrass you even further."

His father went silent. All Alec could hear were the deep breaths of fury blasting through the phone's microphone.

"Okay…" *No, don't say it.* Why did Alec take on everyone else's problems? His father was nothing more than a more civilized version of Key's father. *Don't say it, Alec.* End the call. End. The. Call. "I'll concede this. I'll give you through the election before I formally pull my name." His disappointment in himself was immediate.

"After all I've done for you. I put my neck out for you. You're an ungrateful little—"

"Father, don't say something you'll regret." Alec quickly cut off whatever insult was planned. "That may certainly be the case, and you're right, I shouldn't have ever gotten involved in any of this with you—"

The phone went dead. His father's sign that he was truly angry. Alec tossed the phone on his desk, and his shoulders slumped as he let out his own heavy exhale. That had been harder than he'd thought. His head was pounding and his heart was still racing as fast as Key's sexy black crotch rocket.

Alec's eyes were drawn down to the cell phone rattling on his desk. It stopped, only to start again then again. Hesitantly, he reached for the phone, worried his father had taken to texting. Those were always brutal messages to read.

He should have blocked his father's number when the call ended. Alec swiped a finger over the screen and opened the messages icon. His grin was instantaneous at seeing the alerts were from Key.

"Sorry, changed tires. Have a god day."

The next text message read, *"Shit. Sorry. Have a good gay."*

The next message read, *"Motherducker."*

Alec's headache eased as he laughed at the screen and the phone vibrated again. *"Bue."*

Oh man, anything surrounding Key was like a magic healing balm, instantly easing his burdens. He had done the right thing for the right person, no question at all.

Alec pushed back in his office chair, staring at all the misspelled words, knowing how much Key hated to text message, but his mister loved him, so he tried. Right now though, he wished he was at the tire shop to witness firsthand the fit his sexy biker was inevitably throwing in frustration. Most certainly, a long colorful string of curse words were being yelled at the poor phone.

His phone vibrated again. *"B y e"*

Alec laughed out loud. He'd needed that bit of comic relief. With a renewed sense of hope, Alec opened Word and quickly crafted a rough draft of his resignation letter to the district attorney's office. He wrote from the heart with the words flying from his fingertips. Minutes later, he sat back in his chair and stared at the three sentences.

He should probably let this sit. Perhaps a rewrite might be in order since he was unsure whether it was wise to call DA Twiford a vicious, selfish-righteous, arrogant bitch. He chuckled at that line. His true indecision came from how much time he should offer to transition his caseload. A month's notice seemed more than sufficient under normal circumstances, but his division's workload was insane.

Maybe he could offer six weeks' notice. Depending on when he tendered his resignation, he could still be out of there by the first of the year.

Since he was in such a strong take-charge-of-his-life mode, Alec switched back to his open email account and typed Reed Kensington's name in the still open new message screen. Reed's email auto-filled the line and Alec composed his email, not even trying to hint at what he needed.

Reed,
Come first of the year, I'll be unemployed. I'm not in a position to relocate right away. If you hear of anything in the DFW area, let me know or please feel free to give my email address or phone number to any possible connections.
As always, I appreciate you,
Alec

Alec pushed send on the email then reached for his phone, looking over at the desk calendar. The day he sent his resignation, he should talk with his department head about the best possible transition of the Cummings case until criminal was ready to take this over. Who would be the family's best hope? Truly any of the attorneys in CPS were qualified. Those people were saints.

Going for his suit coat, Alec shrugged it on, gears already switching to a new topic in his head. Maybe he could dress as Captain America and Key could be the Incredible Hulk. He laughed at the idea of his sexy biker with all that green body paint, because he wouldn't need much more than the mask to pull off the Hulk.

He passed by Oliva who was still vacuuming and lifted a hand in goodbye. Key might need to shave, and Alec didn't want that at all. Putting his Bluetooth to his ear, he dialed Gabrielle to see if she could scout out whatever might still be available this late in the game. He needed to know the costumes available before ever mentioning the idea it to Key. One less hurdle to jump before the negativity Key was sure to hit him with.

CHAPTER 13

Keyes twisted his hair at the base of his skull, executing a perfect quick knot as he stared out over the sea of vehicles currently lining his parking lot. He didn't necessarily have an overwhelming relief at the increase in customers, even though that comfort was there, he just saw a shit load worth of work waiting for him.

Business had seemingly turned around for Tires. Apparently, one news station had aired a small segment early this morning that the feds had finally dropped the bogus charges against his bike club. Customer volume had steadily picked up since then. Hopefully other stations would spread the word, even though dropping charges wasn't nearly as exciting or newsworthy as covering the raid on multiple local businesses.

Keyes walked the length of the SUV he had just serviced and started motioning the customer out of the space while sticking the other hand out to momentarily stop the next car from blocking the SUV. When the new car pulled forward, he waited until the window rolled down, then he bent his head until he caught the driver's eye.

"Wha'd'ya need?"

"I have a slow leak in the back, and I got my tire…"

The rumble of Harley pipes snagged his attention away from the customer. He watched Fox and Mack pull into the crowded parking lot and tracked them as they drove around to the side of the building where they normally went for privacy. Keyes looked over at Louis who had stopped what he was doing to look at him. He did a finger pointing thing, giving silent instruction, and Louis confirmed with a chin-up motion then yelled at one of his guys to take Keyes's car. He never looked back at the customer while grabbing the rag out of his back pocket, wiping his hands as he took long strides toward his brothers.

"What's up?" he asked after Mack cut his engine. Fox knocked his kickstand in place, hiking a leg over the seat. He walked the few feet toward Keyes, removing the distance between them. Fox gave him the same hand slap that he and Dev shared.

"Checkin' on you. Everybody's busier today. See you are too. That's a good thing."

Keyes gave him a firm nod and reached past Fox to fist bump Mack.

"Yeah, heard about the news coverin' the dismissal."

"Cocksuckers." Mack looked up like he'd been caught with his hand in the cookie jar. "No offense. Just sayin', reporters sure shagged their fat asses out to cover the raid but can't say a damn word when the fuckin' shit clears. Fuck 'em." Mack spit disgustedly on the ground.

Keyes gave his own nod to show no offense taken. That was light compared to what his brothers normally said in unguarded moments. Fox pulled an envelope out of his pocket and handed it to Keyes. By the size and weight, this was another sizable bonus, meaning the sale must have been big. He lifted his shirt and made quick work of tucking it in his jeans. Normally the cash exchanges came privately at the club, but it had been at least a month since he'd darkened the doorway of the clubhouse. His old man was a permanent fixture there, and the nearing end of his life hadn't humbled him. He was a surly, hateful asshole. He made everybody uncomfortable when he started in on Keyes, and that usually happened within seconds of him walking over the club's threshold.

"You cool?" Fox asked. "Everybody's askin' about you."

For some reason, he highly doubted that. At best, he saw himself the ridiculed wallflower of the club—ridiculed by his father and an introvert of his own choosing—only paid attention to when they needed his monthly cut of the profits or his brute force or merely another body to increase their sheer numbers when they needed to intimidate…

Wait. Whoa. Okay. Wait. No. He needed to stop that line of thinking. That was Alec's fairness and sense of justice coming out in him. Keyes didn't think that way about the club or his brothers. His brothers were his family. They had tight bonds between them. Whatever happened, Keyes knew his place was with his brothers.

"Yeah, I'm good. Spendin' time waitin' this shit out." His hands went to his hips as he met Fox's eyes, refusing to look away as he asked, "Am I shirkin' my responsibility?"

"Not at all, brother. We're just makin' sure you're good," Mack answered instead, his voice deep and gravelly, but filled with concern.

"Got busy as fuck," he replied, gesturing with an awkward half body turn toward the full parking lot.

"Son, we're here for another reason too."

Keyes's gut twisted at the use of the word son and the hands at his waist closed to fists.

"Your old man's gone into hospice. He's moved back to his place. Got some prospects over there, and they cleaned up that shithole," Fox said, eyes still on him, likely gauging his reaction as he spoke. "He's been there a little over a week, but he's goin' down fast. They're sayin' it won't be long now. They're tryin' to keep him comfortable."

"He ain't been comfortable in months," Mack added and sent another loogie barreling toward the ground in his obvious disgust. Keyes just wasn't sure what made Mack so upset, his old man's pain level, the cancer, or just the whole experience. He chose the last one. Mack and his father had been best friends for well over thirty years. It had to be painful to watch his friend's deterioration, and Keyes cut his gaze back to Fox.

"Dev was supposed to keep you updated, but he told me today he hasn't said shit. He says you don't wanna know. But, Keyes, if you're gonna say goodbye, it's probably gettin' time," Fox said, his head cocked, his gaze staying trained on Keyes, and he used Keyes's whole name.

"How long do you suppose he's got?" he finally asked. His buddy had hit the nail on the head. Keyes was completely devoid of emotion in this situation. There was nothing there—no pain, no hate, just nothing at all.

"Don't know, but not much longer. This weekend we're havin' a fundraiser barbecue for your old man and a thank-fuck-its-over-with-the-feds celebration Saturday night. Come. If he somehow manages to show…" Fox just stopped and shook his head. "Nah, he can't get there. He's in too bad of shape…"

"Yeah, he's frail as fuck," Mack interrupted. "They got him all doped up."

"Dev's bringin' his new lady. Bring anybody you got," Fox suggested maybe as an afterthought, talking over Mack's continued grumbling over the feeble condition of his father.

The way the two men acted like legit blood brothers, interrupting each other and talking over the other didn't go unnoticed, or the abrupt silence Mack gave after Fox's chosen words that he should bring someone—words that had never been uttered aloud before. It seemed almost an olive branch of sorts, maybe hints to what the club might be like once his old man was no longer around. The invitation did its job. It settled some of the divide and discord building inside him against his brothers.

The idea he'd bring a man he was seeing to a club party... Mack's freaked stare showed his brothers still weren't ready for those lines to be crossed. Keyes furrowed his brow. And not just any man, but the actual man he was seeing—Alec—to a club-sponsored event... His thoughts shifted again—Alec Pierce at one of the club's filthy, trashy parties. Yeah, at that mental image a grin broke across his face and the bubble of laughter rumbled from his throat.

"Yeah." Keyes just shook his head, kicking at the dirt at his feet. "No, can you imagine my old man seein' me like that?"

"I got him," Mack said confidently. He looked up to see his brother's chest swell in a kickass fashion, but Keyes just shook his head. That was one thing the club didn't have, any control over his father's hateful mouth.

"Ain't worth the effort. Don't have anyone anyway." That bald-faced lie slid off his tongue easily, but his club prez didn't look like he bought one single word. "Besides, Dev would get drunk, kickin' everybody's ass for sayin' anything." Keyes just shook his head and left the grin on his face, pretending he was okay with it all when his world and his allegiance were shifting in ways he didn't yet fully understand or want to look at too closely. "But I'll be there."

Fox gave in with a nod and reached out to pat then grip his shoulder in a comforting squeeze before turning around, silently motioning his head toward Mack to get ready to ride out.

"Have I missed shit?"

"Nah, but we're expectin' the same response from the city that we got from the feds," Fox said, mounting his bike.

"Fuckin' taxpayers gotta be pissed off with all the resources that cunt's been wastin'. They ain't got shit on us. As a taxpayer, I'm fuckin' pissed," Mack said, mounting his bike.

"You ain't ever paid taxes in your fuckin' life," Fox countered, mocking Mack.

The good-natured ribbing between the two continued. "If I did, I'd really be good and pissed off," Mack added with a toothy grin and winked at Keyes.

"We'll be back up and runnin' by year's end, so have your fun now," Fox said, giving Keyes his own sideways grin and a nod. Fox seemed to know that bit of information for certain. Whatever Fox had up his sleeve, he could only imagine. At least twice a month, Keyes was going on their side deals and those weren't small sales by any stretch of the imagination. With as pissed off as his brothers had been, once they got free of these restraints, he envisioned all kinds of illegal shit going down just to prove they could do it without getting caught.

Keyes gave a nod as Mack's bike rumbled to life, vibrating loudly in the small space between the two buildings and he pushed the bike backward. Fox drove forward, turning around in the back of Keyes's property, then lifting two fingers in a peace sign as he passed by. He stared after them before turning to his bike and locking the cash in the seat. He was torn. Saturday nights were his and Alec's, but he guessed not this weekend. And technically, he was over there every day, so one day didn't necessarily stand out like it used to.

He studied the ground as he walked back to the shop. He had gone on the defensive against his brothers right out of the gate. Most likely because he was getting backed into a corner with no easy way out. Fuck, he lived in the corner. From the beginning, he'd known he was playing with fire. Alec Pierce was a big open flame that he'd gotten too comfortable with.

He'd been coasting, assuming, and waiting for Alec to dump him. The idea of letting Alec go made him want to fist fight this fucking building to keep it from happening. Viciousness gripped his heart, the kind of anger only his father ever provoked inside of him, at the thought of anyone ever trying to come between him and Alec. He clenched his hands at his side. He'd destroy every motherfucker in his club to protect his man.

With effort, Keyes pushed the unprovoked anger down, letting his feelings for Alec smooth over his jagged psyche. If he were to truly acknowledge his feelings, he was relieved this shit with his old man happened like it had. It gave him more time with Alec. He was driving a million miles a week, but he'd been more content than any other time in his life. Keyes had let the club own him because he talked himself into believing it was where he belonged. Alec showed him what true acceptance and commitment meant. If soul mates were real, it truly seemed Alec fit his person. He didn't know why, but it didn't change it either.

Now that his old man had left the clubhouse, Keyes needed to stop by more often, make a few appearances, be a little later getting to Alec's while continuing the month-to-month rent on Dev's apartment. The place gave him good cover until something gave to help him and Alec be together. Maybe with business picking up like it had, he could afford to give Louis a few more dollars an hour to take on more responsibility. He had turned out to be reliable at helping him keep things running around the shop, and the guy wasn't afraid of his brothers. That would give Keyes a chance to cruise out earlier in the day, stop by the club, then head to Alec's place. Seemed reasonable enough. Maybe.

Keyes rounded the corner, looking at his old man's bench still sitting against the building. What did he plan to do about his father?

Nothing.

He had no feeling about it at all.

CHAPTER 14

Keyes pulled to the back of the middle school where his uncle taught, combing the parking lot for Clyde's car. Luckily, it was still there. He pulled the bike into the parking space next to his uncle's and cut the engine. He hadn't told his uncle he was coming and had a fifty/fifty chance that Clyde hadn't left for the day.

As the day wore on, Keyes found he needed to talk, and Clyde was always his go-to guy. He dropped the kickstand in place and scanned the back of the school, wondering if any of the doors were unlocked.

His boots made deep thuds as he headed for the door closest to his uncle's classroom. It had been years since he'd been at the school, though. He tested the door handle. Locked. He reached for his phone to call his uncle, but as he scrolled his contacts, the door pushed open.

"Can I help you?" a janitor asked. His face changed from concern to recognition. "You're Clyde's boy."

He nodded. The last time he'd been here, he'd been younger, maybe seventeen, and Clyde had talked him into finishing his equivalency diploma. He'd barely paid attention to the building then, and he surely didn't remember anyone who had worked there. "I thought I'd surprise him."

The grin was genuine as the janitor pushed the door wider for Keyes to enter. "You were tall back then. You sure kept growing."

"Yeah, I guess," he said, sliding in past the guy who pointed him down the long hall. "His room still there?"

"Yeah, three doors down. He's finishing up tutoring. Go see."

"Thanks." He walked the three classrooms down, looking in each darkened window until he saw Clyde standing at a desk, talking to a student. The best he could see, they looked to be alone. With a rap of his knuckles on the small window in the door, Clyde looked up, clearly in deep thought if the furrow in his brow were anything to go by. His aging face changed when he recognized Keyes, a grin springing to his lips, and he waved him in.

"I don't want to interrupt."

"No, come in. Have a seat. We're almost done." Clyde turned back to the student, falling easily back into teacher mode. "When you solve this system of equations, you get x equals eight and y equals twelve. Do you see?"

"Yeah…" The lightbulb must have blinked on for the teenage girl who sat up straighter and grinned.

"Try that suggestion and email me tonight if you get confused, how about that?" Clyde said.

The same care Clyde had used with him, he had for all of his students. He never got tired of teaching. Keyes looked around the room. A lot of the same math posters were on the walls. The room hadn't changed much at all over the last ten years. Keyes walked the length of the row of desks to a back shelf, spotting a picture of him and Clyde and his Harley XR750. He picked it up, looking down at the young man he used to be. He had gotten his high school equivalency diploma on the sly and the old broken-down Harley had been his gift from Clyde. Next to that picture was the same motorcycle after he finished the rebuild. That was about the time he completed the online mechanics course Clyde had talked him into. His uncle had been so proud of him.

"So, to what do I owe the pleasure?"

Keyes turned to see Clyde shutting the door after the pupil. His uncle felt like home. He hadn't named that feeling before meeting Alec, but he understood it now. He placed the picture back on the shelf and went to the front of the classroom where Clyde leaned against his desk, crossing his arms over his chest.

"I stopped by the shop and you weren't home."

"This is my evening-tutoring day. I try to stay one night a week—you know all that. I haven't seen you too much lately. Everything going okay?" Keyes stopped about a foot and a half from his uncle, crossing his arms over his chest. Of course, he hadn't told Clyde about Alec, and since everything he thought about had Alec in the forefront, he had to get past that before he could go on.

"I'm cool, but my old man's not. I thought you should know," he said, unfolding his arms, sticking his fingers in his front jeans pockets.

"What's going on?" Clyde asked, looking concerned.

"Lung cancer. Sounds like he's in hospice." He gave a single nod to emphasize the dire situation.

"Key, that's terrible." And that was the true reason he was there. He needed Clyde's conscience. Keyes seemed to be missing his reasoning ability lately. It made him nervous at how detached he'd gotten from his father, his illness, his club, even Clyde. "I'm sorry."

"I'm not," he replied honestly, furrowing his brow, tucking his chin to his chest as he re-crossed his arms. He trusted Clyde, and after a moment, he lifted his frustrated gaze, holding Clyde's concerned one, wanting Clyde's true opinions on the distance he had placed on his old man. "I hate that motherfucker."

"Keyes…" Clyde's tone turned scolding.

"I do," he reaffirmed, battling back.

His uncle's stern expression turned into a small smile. "I was scolding you on the language, not the dislike. I've been on this journey with you for a long time. I know why you feel as you do. He's a monster. You know I've wanted you away from him and that club since the moment I found you."

"He should've just given me to you," he said, brought back to the time he had been sitting on the porch, locked out from his parents' house when he saw Clyde's very normal looking car pull to the front of the house. His mom had died by then, and Keyes had been in trouble for whatever reason his old man found. Keyes was good and pissed off when Clyde rounded the hood of the car wearing his fancy slacks and a dress shirt. Their eyes locked, Keyes somehow instinctively knowing they were family. Keyes had looked enough like his mother for Clyde to see the family resemblance, but for him, Clyde represented hope and he'd never had that before.

"He should have." Clyde nodded. "But he wanted your mother's social security benefits."

"I don't even think that was it. He hated me and wanted me to pay. I was a fuckin'— Sorry. I was a reminder of bad shit that went down." He skirted the part he had learned about his mother whoring around the club. Of course, he'd always suspected, and Clyde probably did too, but he didn't need to say it to her brother. Hell, he wished he didn't know. "Fox told me a couple of months ago that Smoke wasn't my father, and he knows it. I guess they all knew it. I've had time to think about that. It explains a lot. I think he wanted me to pay for what she did."

Okay, that was straight off the cuff, out of his mouth before it registered as a thought. Clearly, he was holding on to some emotional baggage. He still couldn't seem to use his mother's name out loud. Where his father was a vindictive brutal bastard, his mother was a meth head who had lived her life as if she had a death wish—which she finally accomplished.

"I suspect so too. Have I told you about the conversation we had about you coming to live with me?" Clyde asked, pushing off his desk, going around the front to pull his lunchbox from a side drawer. Keyes only shook his head, waiting for the response. "He had some derogatory things to say about my intentions with a young boy and my sexual orientation."

Clyde was gay, so of course his evil-tongued father would have something like that to say. "I'm sorry…"

"Son, you don't have to apologize for that man," Clyde said, nodding him toward the classroom door. "Walk me outside."

Keyes did, following behind his uncle until they were out in the deserted hall. Clyde locked the door behind him.

"Keep talking. Tell me what's on your mind."

His fingers were back in his pockets as they walked toward the same door he had entered through. "I haven't seen my old man in months. The last time I did, though, I put my hands on him. He was frail but that goddamn mouth of his— Sorry," he said, looking over at Clyde, who nodded. "He threatened me, and I lost my shit, not terrible, but enough that I lost some control."

And there it was again, more of the emotional baggage he'd been harboring, pretending all the hate in his life didn't bother him. It did, weighing so heavily on him at times he couldn't breathe.

"It's understandable. I've always been amazed by the strength of your character, a far lesser man would have caved before now," Clyde said, pushing open the outside door for Keyes. "But you need to be careful, Keyes. He's a trigger. You need to be aware and mentally prepared if you see him again. He's not worth going to prison for."

"Should I go see him?" he asked, getting to the very root of this visit. The reason he'd sought his uncle out in the first place. Clyde would always tell him the right thing to do.

"I don't know, son. That's up to you," Clyde answered seriously, reaching into his pocket and pulling out a set of keys. He came to a stop on the sidewalk in front of his car. "What does your heart say to do?"

"I can't get a good read on it. I'm afraid I'll feel guilty later, and it'll eat at me," he answered. He did that shit all the time. He hated that about himself.

"Well, if you feel guilty for any reason where that man's concerned, then I'll probably have to kick your butt," Clyde said teasingly, and that made him smile, momentarily lightening his downward spiraling mood. "It sounds like your decision's made, just ask yourself what you hope to gain. If it's any sort of apology, then you're wasting your time."

"Nah, nothin' like that," he said, pushing his fingers in his pocket. "I was just…you know. I don't know. It's the guilt."

"You'll make the best decision for you. I have faith in that. Then I want you to be done. Let it go. Get on with your life and leave the past in the past. I'll be here for you always, but nothing good will come from bringing all that baggage into your future." Clyde had always given him the best advice. He nodded to let his uncle know he understood. Knowing his uncle was there for him made his heart happier too. Clyde was always going to make sure Keyes chose the path of right. He appreciated that in the man. "Now, this is the second time I've seen you with a haircut and a trimmed beard. Have you met someone?"

A flush of heat rushed up his neck, but he rolled his eyes and ran his fingers through his hair, hoping his uncle didn't press the subject.

"You have met someone. I wondered why you weren't around as much as normal. I thought the club had you busy."

Yeah, he wasn't doing this with his uncle. Fox had had a pretty keen eye too. Did he have a big red pointy sign above his head announcing he had a boyfriend? Whatever. Alec wasn't up for discussion, so he pivoted on his heels, going toward his bike. "I'm not talkin' about this with you."

"Why not?" Clyde asked, following behind him.

"Because," he said, reaching for his helmet before Clyde could demand he use one for protection.

"Tell me about him, Key. It's a him, right?"

How they had ended up on his sexuality when he'd come there to talk about his father was beyond him, but Clyde was tricky like Alec. Keyes and his uncle could be talking about what kind of pizza to order, then all of a sudden, his brain-ninja uncle could twist the conversation in a direction Keyes wanted no part of—like right now. Clyde could fuck with a guy's head that way.

"Even if you won't tell me, you've eased my heart. I'm happy you've found someone that makes you smile like that," Clyde said.

That sneaky son-of-a-bitch got him right in the feels. He chuckled to himself and mounted the bike with his helmet tucked under his arm.

"I'll tell you this. He's got a '65 Shelby Cobra," Keyes said, waggling his brows, proud of his own redirect in the conversation.

"No kidding," Clyde said in awe. "I'd like to see that. Have you driven it?"

"Nah, just touched it. Changed the oil once. It's badass, like real badass." He nodded confirmation of his words and slid the helmet on.

"Maybe we can talk about everything later." Clyde pivoted, then did a full swing back, facing him. "Can you have dinner tonight?"

"Sorry, I'll have to take a raincheck. Gotta get on the road."

Clyde nodded. "Let me know how it goes with your father."

Keyes nodded and started the bike. Clyde knew, probably before Keyes even did, that he'd go see that sorry old man at least one last time. It made his stomach sick, but it was the right thing to do. He guessed. Lifting a hand to return Clyde's wave, he backed his bike out and hit the road, first to the clubhouse, then to Alec's. It was later than normal, but that didn't matter to him, he'd ride for however long it took to get back to Alec.

The clock on Alec's computer monitor switched from seven fifty-nine to eight o'clock. He reached for his phone to check to see if he'd somehow missed a message from

Key. He hadn't. Key was late, and for a man who lived by an insanely structured routine, that was weird. His mister had also been quiet today. Key hadn't returned a text or call since this morning.

The knots in his stomach tightened in nervous expectation. Besides the worry that something was off, he and Key had a lot to celebrate tonight.

Leaning forward, Alec reached for his keyboard, accessing a local traffic website to look for any possible accidents. He let out a sigh. Just normal congestion for this time of day. Nothing that would indicate an accident with injury.

Like he'd done over and over this evening, Alec pushed back in his office chair, this time staring at the flashing green and yellow dots outlining the highways in the DFW area and stuck his fingernail in his mouth, gnawing at the corners. Yeah, something was off. Had the club connected the dots? The sudden ring of his phone startled the shit out of him. Without checking caller ID, Alec answered blindly with his Bluetooth. "Alec Pierce."

"You busy?" Reed Kensington asked, causing Alec to sit up straighter in his seat, grabbing a pen for absolutely no reason at all.

"No, not at all. What's going on?" Alec asked, and immediately regretted that question. When trying to impress a man he had the utmost respect for, maybe he should have gone with a "*How are you,*" or "*This is a pleasant surprise.*"

"I'm behind. I opened your email and started to respond, but decided to call instead. I hope that's all right," Reed said in the cultured way he spoke. "I'm coming to Dallas in a couple of weeks. I'll get you the exact dates, but I'd like to meet with you face-to-face to discuss some possible employment opportunities."

"Great," Alec said, then cringed again. As a trained communicator, he should have a much larger vocabulary than the words rolling from his mouth. "What's bringing you to Texas?"

"If you remember, Layne's corporate offices are somewhere down there in your general area. Without going into too much detail, I haven't yet found the right person to head up my Arik Layne Properties account. I've been overseeing their business myself."

Alec had forgotten Arik Layne's offices were in the DFW area. He quickly typed into his search bar to pinpoint the exact address while trying to hold his excitement at bay. To see Westlake, Texas, appear on his screen and see it was in fact local to him had Alec spontaneously replying as if he'd just been offered the job. "Wow, that would be perfect."

Reed chuckled, probably at his assumption not his eagerness, and added, "Honestly, you and I are very much on the same page. I've got to fill this position or risk my husband divorcing me for all these long hours and long-distance trips I keep having to make."

"I wouldn't be available until maybe mid-December at the earliest, but most likely, the start of the year. Is that a problem?" Alec asked, completely lost to the possibility. This would truly allow him to stay in the area while also working toward his career goals. No more DA's office, no more politics. The salary they had discussed when Reed had first approached him about the job over a year ago could support them very well. Damn, maybe he could truly be seen out with Key. That made his heart sore as his overeager head raced through what had to happen to get this done.

"If we come to an agreement, I'd probably like to begin transitioning you right away. Only as much as you can handle until you get out of your current situation, but I'd like to see you ready to take over the account starting January second. Arik's got a lot planned—he's a force who doesn't understand the word no. You'll have a team, they're currently officed here with me in DC, but they're already planning their relocation to Westlake in January. I'm getting ahead of myself. Are you familiar with that part of DFW?"

Alec shook his head as if Reed could see him. "No, but it's not a problem. It's a distance, but I'm planning to sell my place anyway. Based on the Google map, it looks like the kind of area I was hoping to relocate to. I wanted some land."

"Listen, I'm changing the subject. My father called tonight. He heard you were pulling your nomination," Reed said, dropping that unexpected bit of news. Alec hadn't told anyone, not even Key. The leak had to have come from his father's side.

"I was given strict orders not to say a word until after the election," Alec said, wondering how in the world this was going to come back and bite him.

"Nothing stays a secret in DC, you know that. My father knew I was scouting you, so he called."

Oh man, whoever Alec's father had trusted had clearly sold him out, but he was certain he could already feel the weight of blame being placed on his shoulders. He was always the easiest target. The slight beep sounded through his Bluetooth causing Alec to look down at his notifications. His front gate was opening. Good, Key was home, one less thing to worry about.

"For the record, I think it's a smart move. Your talents are better served in the private sector. I'll forward my itinerary. See when you can get free, and we'll talk more then."

"Thanks, Reed. I've regretted turning you down," Alec replied honestly, hitting the power off button to his monitor and pushing his office chair backward.

"No, thank you. Talk later." The phone disconnected as Alec grabbed his Robin mask and gloves, quickly putting them on to greet his man. His newest concern rested in how best to tell Key about all these changes. Should he talk about his changes in baby steps or dump everything out at once? He'd have to decide, but first, Gabrielle had secured Batman and Robin costumes. He had been dressed in this silly costume for two solid hours, waiting for Key to arrive.

Maybe he could talk Key into a little role play tonight. Shit. Key in spandex. That thought had him double timing toward the back door.

The weight and feel of his cut sliding across his back had always been like slipping into a second skin. He had donned the leather vest for his brief stop by the clubhouse to show his face around. His brothers' spirits were low. His father was well-loved in the club. As much of a motherfucker as his father had been toward him, he was as great and loyal toward the other members of the club.

Normally, he'd have stored his cut during the ride to Alec's place. His colors a big red target for any law enforcement he passed along the way, but not this time. Today was different. He had needed the reminder of who he was and where he belonged. Thank God it worked. When he'd first shrugged the cut on after a month-long absence, the leather had felt wrong. It took a second of adjusting the fit to realize the vest wasn't different, he was, and that had been a total mind-fuck on top of a string of mind-fucks he'd encountered today.

After parking in his regular spot, Keyes shrugged off his cut, staring at the colors he'd been so proud to receive. That same pride had lessened, and he wasn't entirely sure why or how he truly felt about the change. So little seemed to matter anymore. His focus rested on two things: spending the best quality time he could with Alec and then getting back to Alec after they were forced apart by their responsibilities.

This wasn't going to end well for him. If he were smart, he'd get his head straight before it was too late. He heard the back door open and quickly folded the leather vest, looking over his shoulder. He stopped short at what greeted him. An uncontrolled and much needed laugh erupted. His mister stood in the doorframe in the perfect Robin pose, and boy, did his heart need that release of tension. The image just tickled him into a good mood. He absently draped the vest over his arm, going straight for his guy.

"What're you doin'?" he asked, taking long strides toward Alec, not willing to wait another second to have the man in his arms.

"Holy Halloween, Batman," Alec said, assuming the position, feet planted firmly on the ground, legs spread apart, hands fisted at his waist. Robin never looked so fucking sexy.

The pressure of his dick pushing at his zipper had him adjusting himself as he stepped eagerly into Alec's personal space.

"You're hot," he teased, grinning at Alec as he wrapped an arm around Alec's waist as his lawyer remained in character.

"Come on, Batman! To the Batcave, my engine needs revving." Alec laced each word with dramatic emphasis as if he were in fact the boy wonder.

Keyes wondered if Alec had any idea how he lightened his heart. He grinned, tipping Alec's head back for a kiss on his lips.

"I think Robin was a smaller guy than you," Keyes said, keeping Alec close against his body so he could grind against the thickness trapped in the brightly colored tights. The kiss and dry humping was enough for Alec to break character. Keyes celebrated his victory when Alec greedily devoured his mouth then slid his palms down to grip his ass, pulling him in tight before breaking the kiss.

"You like?" Alec asked huskily, lifting his face for another kiss then another.

"I like a lot," he growled, tossing his cut over the patio chair to better keep Alec flush against his chest. "I needed this with the shit day I had."

"Hmmm." Alec's eyes narrowed. Right when Keyes thought Alec was going to step over their imaginary line of what could and couldn't be discussed between them, the man nodded at him and simply said, "Then I'm glad you're finally home."

CHAPTER 15

Key's soft moan woke Alec from his light sleep. He held still, listening long enough to make sure Key was okay before he relaxed back into the soft bed. Probably a bad dream. He fluffed the pillow and tried to get comfortable enough to fall back to sleep. After a few minutes, he realized that was going to be harder than he thought, so he lay there, listening to Key's even breaths and let his mind wander.

Alec considered himself one hell of a lucky man to have Key in his bed and in his life. The man was perfect in every way. Loyal and strong even though he'd been through hell. Key was a good man despite his circumstances. A biker that most tried to avoid. His mind drifted to the image of Key in his riding leathers, the way the leather fit his body like a glove. And the hair—Key had the silkiest hair he'd ever touched.

He needed to stop thinking about how perfect Key was and get some sleep. Alec sighed, closing his eyes, determined to put a halt to the stirring in his groin.

It didn't work. When he shut his eyes, the only thing behind them were images of Key's trusting blue eyes, staring back at him, thick, silky hair falling over firm broad shoulders as they made love. He loved the way Key's body fit so perfectly with his.

Don't go there, don't even start. Go to sleep.

His lover's breathing picked up, and Key moaned again. Alec's eyes popped open, he recognized that moan. This time the sound was a hell of a lot more sexy than alarming, and it vibrated through Alec's body before caressing his balls. His dick had agreed with the assumption and turned hard as fucking stone in an instant. Even after all this time, he couldn't get enough of Keyes Dixon. Alec slid his legs along the cool sheets, trying to find a comfortable position without waking Key. He had to find some perspective where the man was concerned. The biker kept him in a state of constant arousal. Alec kicked at the cover and snuggled deeper into the bed, trying to will away his arousal.

So innately aware of Key, he swore he could feel the exact point where the heat from his lover's body merged with his own. Now, Alec was completely wide awake and frustrated. Fuck it! He slid his hand down to grip the base of his dick, adding just a hint of pressure. Maybe then he could get his dick to submit so he could get back to sleep.

Who was he kidding? He needed some relief, or he wasn't ever getting back to sleep.

Key made a noise between a groan and a moan and Alec's dick jerked happily at the sound. Fighting this was futile, and it only made sense to rub one out and hopefully he'd be sleeping like a baby in no time.

He scooted closer to his dreaming lover, snuggling his back against Key's warm chest. Alec bit his lip to hold in a groan of his own as Key's erection greeted him, searing his flesh as it slid along the crevice of his ass. He pushed back, rubbing against the hot thickness of Key's dick. Fuck yeah, this wouldn't take long—he was horny as hell. The pressure from his hand made his eyes roll back into his head as he stroked his own cock. Thank God they slept naked, because he needed the skin on skin contact with Key. His eyes drifted shut as he twisted his wrist, adding that extra move to the already satisfying strokes.

He shifted his hips, sliding his ass back and forth over Key's shaft while working his own cock with a tight fist. He envisioned Key thrusting into him while holding him down on the soft mattress, giving deep, gratifying thrusts that made him quiver with delight. Alec didn't slow his hand when Key tensed behind him, nor did he stop the movement of his hips. He was too lost in his fantasy to stop now. Strong palms slid over his ass cheeks. Then demanding fingers pressed into the flesh of his hip. Key's pelvis surged forward, and he might have heard a whimper as Key's hardness ground against his ass.

Oh. Yeah. He had zero guilt whatsoever about selfishly wanting his lover to wake. Now, the man was and doing exactly what he'd wanted, Key's body setting his ablaze.

"Fuck, babe." Key's hot breath ghosted across his neck as strong arms pulled him closer, the heat from Key's broad chest searing Alec's back. "Slow down. Don't finish before I can get in you."

The firm pressure at his back only intensified the rush of blood surging in his veins.

Alec angled his head to the side to kiss his lover. Key's lips found his, tongues tangling, as they devoured each other's mouths. Alec broke from the heated kiss. He needed their physical connection, wanted Key in him to help quench the need building in his core. But he was so worked up he feared he might not be able to obey Key's command.

"Need you in me." His ass clenched as he practically begged Key to slake the fire burning him alive.

Key shifted to grab lube without saying a word. The click of the lid filled his ears as he scooted back in search of Key's warmth. The shock of the cold lube on the pad of Key's fingers made him jump, but he quickly succumbed to the pleasuring caress of the digits circling his hole. Key breached him with the tip of his finger. In and out. So good. But it wasn't enough, he craved more, he wanted to be fucked.

"Just fuck me," he begged. Alec's fist clamped around his cock. He just about came when Key sank two fingers all the way in him, brushing against his prostate. Holy mother of God, he had to get Key inside him. "Want your cock."

"Is that what you need?" Key's low growl vibrated through his balls and had his dick weeping with desire, pushing him even closer. Alec groaned. The fucker just wanted to hear him beg.

Those fingers pushed back into him and his ass clenched around them. Key pulled back then pushed in three, sending an onslaught of intensity along his channel.

Wicked fingers moved in and out of him, only making his need build. He craved the burn of Key stretching him—every inch of Key filling him and making him whole as the line between pleasure and pain blurred. Key continued edging him, had him open and ready, leaking like a faucet.

"Babe," he whined. Excitement fluttered in his belly when Key withdrew his fingers and he heard the crinkle of the condom wrapper as Key retrieved it from somewhere on the bed.

He didn't want to miss any part of the action and watched over his shoulder as Key rolled the condom on. The bed dipped as Key scooted closer to him, grabbing his thigh and pushing it up. That move made his cock jerk. He loved when Key took him like this. The air was cool against his exposed flesh. He pushed back against the heat of Key's cock teasing his hole, hoping to hurry the process along. Finally he reached behind Key and sank his fingers into the meaty flesh of his ass to pull the man's hips to him. Alec needed their connection like he needed oxygen.

"Fuck…fuck, fuck," he panted. The sting of Key's thick cock stretching him was exquisite. His breath hung in his throat as Key pushed into him. The intensity had him digging his fingers deeper into the flesh of Key's ass as he filled him with all that delicious hardness.

"You good?" Key paused as if allowing him a second to adjust. The tingle along his spine had his hips already rocking, seeking pleasure. He shoved back against his lover, urging Key on.

"Yes, so good." He couldn't help the words falling from his lips as Key started to move. Pleasure built along his channel and deep in his core as Key's thrusts became the drug he craved. Like a junkie he was so fucking strung out over this man.

Slow, sweet, and tender, his big biker made love to him. Key's cock brushed over his prostate, sending sparks traveling through Alec's body like red-hot currents of electricity, lighting him up and making him squirm for more. Key's hips rolled into him over and over. His orgasm built with every thrust. Key's hand joined his and stroked him in time with the cadence of his hips.

"Kiss me."

Alec turned his head to capture Key's mouth. Key's lips pressed against his, and he slid his tongue across the plump flesh before pushing inside. Their tongues slid together in a fevered kiss as Key fucked him with an intensity that had them both panting and groaning in ecstasy. He loved letting go, letting Key give him what he needed. Somehow his beautiful biker always knew.

The warmth of his impending orgasm flowed through every cell in his body. The pleasure his lover gave him had his body trembling and on the brink of exploding. He wanted the feeling to last forever.

Only Key could make him feel this way. Key's breath became his breath as they swallowed the little sounds the other made. Sweat slicked their skin as they rocked against each other. Every movement held the promise of release.

"So good, Alec," Key groaned huskily against his ear. Key's beard scraped along his neck as his lover pushed into him one last time, sending another shudder of pleasure rushing through him that made his body convulse with gratification.

"Yes," he said as the oxygen was pulled from the room, burning his lungs, and spots danced before his eyes. Key's cock twitched deep in his ass and his own dick jerked in his palm as the last of his seed coated their hands.

"That was a nice good morning," Alec said as warm lips pressed against Keyes's chest.

"I was dreamin' I was doin' you," Keyes rumbled lazily, basking in the relaxation of his orgasm. His fingertips trailed up and down the sexy dip in the small of Alec's back. "Can you see the time?"

"You did do me, and it can't be time for you to go." Alec playfully nipped at his chest. Where Keyes hadn't had the motivation to move, Alec somehow did and lifted just enough to angle his head in such a way to see the alarm clock on the nightstand.

"You have some time. It's four forty-five," Alec said and laid his head back on Keyes's chest, keeping him pinned to the bed. "Talk to me."

"About what?" he asked, sleepily. He should get up, otherwise he'd risk falling back asleep. Fifteen minutes wasn't anything more than the amount of time he'd need to go back to sleep then be pissed off he had to wake back up.

"Anything. Why were you late getting home last night?" Alec asked on a yawn. Keyes smiled to himself. Alec was fighting sleep too. He bent to kiss the top of Alec's head.

"I had a drive-by yesterday afternoon," he answered, resting his chin against the top of Alec's head, remembering a time when Alec would have played twenty questions to try to understand what he meant. It seemed they might have evolved until Alec's head lifted, and the concerned look on his lover's face startled him.

"Everyone okay?" Alec asked.

Keyes chuckled at the horror reflected in Alec's face. Okay, maybe Alec still had a little trouble deciphering his comments.

"Not that kind. The prez and Mack stopped by the shop." Keyes stared up at the ceiling while keeping a steady, comforting glide of his fingertips up and down Alec's back. Funny, all the anxiety he'd carried all day yesterday had vanished. Even mentioning Fox stopping by the shop hadn't caused the worry to return. Alec was fucking magic.

Where Keyes didn't worry, Alec did. A warm hand slid across his chest, and Alec lowered his chin to stare up at Keyes's face. He could see the questions forming in Alec's intense gaze while his brow creased together with more concern than moments ago. "And?"

Keyes gave a long pause as he decided how much to say. He never spoke of his father—not at all—and he had said nothing to Alec about his cancer. Admittedly, their lines were blurring. They shared more and more with the other, but old habits die hard, and in the end, Keyes hesitated to say more.

"You can trust me, Key. I won't ever repeat anything you say. I give you my word," Alec assured, reading his silence with bullseye accuracy.

"The easiest part of the day was the tire shop picked up in a major way. I guess the local news reported on the federal raid bein' dropped and the customers came back. I barely had a break for most of the day," he said, lifting to move Alec off him. Keyes scooted across the mattress to sit on the side of the bed, stretching and letting out a long yawn before rising to his feet. Then he stretched again, wishing more than anything that he could climb back in bed with Alec.

"That's great. Can you handle the extra workload?" Alec asked. All his guy did was roll from one side of the bed to the other to better face him as he walked toward the bathroom.

"I guess that's the other good thing I did." Keyes stopped at the bathroom door, turning back to the bed. "Louis is takin' on more duties, and I hired one of his buddies. I can't partner with him because I partner with the club, but he's officially the manager and gonna close five nights a week. He'll take all day Sunday. I'll take all day Saturday so our day off together doesn't get too fucked up," he added, then pushed off the door, going for his toothbrush. By the time he finished scrubbing his teeth, Alec was there with a towel, leaning back against the counter.

"Keep talking. I feel like there's more you're not saying."

Keyes rubbed the towel over his face and beard as he spoke. "I don't know, but I suspect, even with the increase in business, that'll help me get out of there a little earlier. I can roll by the club more than I have been and still get here by six thirty or seven." Keyes pushed the edge of the terry cloth under the cold water, wincing as he then ran it over his dick. Not one of his better ideas. He sucked in a sudden breath as his balls and dick protested the cold cleaning.

"Sounds like a productive day. What does that have to do with Fox and Mack stopping by?" Alec asked, leaning his bare ass against the sink. Clearly, Alec's lines were blurring too. Either he wasn't picking up or didn't care about the *that's-all-I-want-to-say* vibe Keyes was laying down between them. He pinned Alec with a pointed stare, one that left his mister completely unfazed, before rolling his eyes.

"Bullshit with my old man." His father was a downer and a deadbeat lowlife asshole. Keyes flat didn't want anything that hateful man's name conjured anywhere near this home.

"I'm not fond of your father. He's not coming back to the tire shop, is he?" Alec asked, trailing behind Keyes as headed for the closet. "Alexa, turn on the bedroom lamps."

The lights came on while Keyes pulled his underwear and socks from the dresser drawer.

"Nah, he's not comin' back." That was truly no longer a worry. From that angle, his glass was half full.

When in the world Alec had ever voluntarily woken before five in the morning was beyond him. He had also never dressed a man before, but he did this morning. While Key put on his socks, Alec went to the closet and pulled out a pressed pair of jeans and an equally pressed T-shirt, bringing them both to Key. "These work?"

"Yeah, whatever's good." While Key continued to dress, Alec searched for his work boots and belt, hoping to keep his man openly confiding in him. He did feel as if Key continued to hide something from him, mostly likely about his horrible father, but he wouldn't press for more there. Key liked to do things on his own terms, and more than anything, Alec wanted Key to trust him, and he was, which was enough for right now.

"I have some news," Alec announced, bringing to Key the belt and boots he'd found. Alec then grabbed a robe, only because the mornings had turned a little chilly. He needed to remember to adjust his thermostat.

"Okay, but first, tell me about the costume," Key said, using his chin to hold his T-shirt up while he threaded the belt through the loops.

How had he forgotten the purpose of the costume? He would have thought sitting two hours in the hot spandex, waiting for Key to come home last night, might have been enough to keep him on task, but the hi-honey-I'm-home make-out session, ending with dinner in bed because Key had thought that was Alec's attempt at role play, had been enough to make him forget the party.

"A friend of mine from the office, remember the one who had the engagement party?" Alec waited for Key to nod before he added, "She's having a masquerade party on Saturday night. It's the perfect decoy for us. We can dress up and go out together—very covert. My housekeeper secured us Batman and Robin costumes," Alec said, waggling his brows, and took a seat on the edge of the mattress.

"Except I can't go…" Key said, the bed dipping as Key dropped down to pull his boots on. Alec got stuck on the "I can't" portion of his lover's refusal and heard nothing more. He had expected Key to scoff at their going out in public. He'd even prepared for all of Key's reasons, but the "I can't" meant something altogether different.

"What? Why not?" he asked, feeling his body deflate in disappointment.

"We're havin' a club party—a barbeque fundraiser. Part of the reason for the prez's drive-by yesterday was so that he could personally ask me to come," Key explained, glancing up as he pushed the jeans down over his boots. Whatever he saw froze Key in mid-motion. He stayed bent over but continued staring at him.

"No," Alec said lamely, his feelings suddenly hurt. He had already planned the whole night in his head, even talking himself into getting a hotel in the Uptown area. Two separate, but adjoining rooms. It made so much sense to him. "Saturday's my night."

"I can't blow this off. It's a club celebration because the fed's case dropped. I think they're expecting the DA to stop her bullshit too, which will make business start rampin' up again. Weekends'll be harder to make happen—especially during the holidays. That's why I got Louis closing," Key explained, as he sat straight up. Alec stared at Key as the man ripped the metaphorical rug out from underneath him.

Wait. Did Key just in a roundabout way say he wouldn't be coming around as much on the weekends?

No. That was their time together.

"Babe, I'm disappointed. We won't have another chance this great," Alec said, rising and walking the length of the bedroom. He needed distance to help him think straight.

"We'll have next Halloween."

Alec went utterly silent, turning to stare at Key. It was silly how much he'd started looking forward to the idea of them going out together. If the costume party worked, then the doors were opening for them in other areas too.

"Stop lookin' so hurt. You go. Have a good time."

"When will your party end?" Alec asked as Key stood and headed toward him. Alec held his ground, but stuck out a hand, keeping Key at arm's length.

"It'll be late," Key's said, respecting his boundary up to but not including his hand. Key curled his long fingers around Alec's, drawing his knuckles up for a sweet press of lips, which somehow made his feelings hurt worse. "I should probably stay at my place Saturday night, maybe get a few extra hours in at the shop, see how much business actually returns."

"You still have your place?" Alec asked, clearly feeling very emotional. Of course, he knew Key had possibly kept an apartment closer to his club, but his feelings were still stupidly hurt. Alec took a sidestep away to try and gain control of all these negative emotions. Key held on tight, moving with him.

"You know I have my place." Key's tone was gentle, and maybe held hints of understanding.

His mister broke the imaginary line and stepped forward while pulling Alec into the circle of his arms. Alec was speechless and couldn't muster the strength to protest. His great start to the day had crashed and burned in a matter of seconds.

"Stop lookin' so hurt. You know I haven't given up my place. I need a place to crash closer to the club. You know all that," Key explained and tugged Alec's rigid form closer. Key's calloused palm cradled his cheek, and his lover's thumb slowly caressed across his lower lip. Alec had been full steam ahead, quitting his job, moving them away from all the hustle and bustle that caused them chaos, creating a new life for both of them while Key was talking about spending more time with a group of men that never fully accepted or appreciated him. It cut Alec deeply. He wanted to take care of this man, be Key's reason. Come to think about it, Key hadn't texted or messaged him all afternoon yesterday. He was later getting home last night with no explanation. Now, he talked about reducing their time together over the weekends. Each action seemed so much more significant.

"Stop whatever you're thinkin' that's makin' you look so sad. I'm sorry I can't go. I really am. You know when the club calls, I gotta go. It's my responsibility. I took an oath." His biker tried to re-explain the stupidity of his life, and Alec didn't want to hear anymore. Not right then.

He nodded and pulled from the man's hold. It was dumb his feelings were so hurt, but they just were. Alec started for the kitchen, passing the Robin costume draped over the sofa as he went. Alec went straight for the Keurig, turning the power button on early.

"So, you'll be coming over every day after you've handled your club business?" Alec asked, when he heard Key's footsteps coming toward him. He pushed the fill button before going for the new thermos he'd picked up especially for Key.

"My plan. Sunday's here though."

Alec stared at the slow trickle of coffee filling the cup and nodded again.

"I made plans the weekend before your birthday. Do those need to change?" he asked, finally glancing over at Key who faced him, his hip resting against the edge of the counter. The man had brushed his hair. It looked as soft as silk, a stark comparison to the tangled mess sweeping through him.

"You don't have to do anything for my birthday," Key said, coming to stand beside him. His strong palm settled on the small of Alec's back. "Don't be hurt."

"Do I need to change them? It's a simple question," he replied, his tone a little more clipped than he'd intended. "Never mind. I'll change them. Your Red Bull's in the refrigerator." Alec placed the empty thermos in front of Key before leaving him standing there, walking back toward the solitude of his bedroom. "Have a good day."

Alec didn't stop until he reached the bathroom. He brushed his teeth, surprised at how seriously upset he was. It was crazy how irrational he'd become. Of course, he knew the seriousness of Key's loyalty to his brothers. The club was going to be a continual problem between them, and more telling, the club would always come before Alec.

Alec reached for Key's discarded towel when the man himself came cautiously through the bathroom doorway. Alec didn't acknowledge Key. Instead, he turned away, reaching for the shower faucet.

"Alec, what's wrong?" Key asked, his own frustration clear in his tone.

"I just keep trying to move us forward only to be reminded we're still exactly where we were." Alec sighed as he let the robe fall to the floor. He kicked it out of the way with his foot then reached out to adjust the temperature before stepping under the spray. Key gripped his arm, keeping him there.

"I don't know what that means." Key's voice and demeanor radiated confusion and possibly some hurt of his own.

Alec looked everywhere except at the man himself. He never wanted Key hurt by another person again, but he wasn't ready to let go of this pain. In the end, Alec shook his head, tried hard to form a smile that he was certain didn't reach his eyes, and lifted his gaze to his lover. "I'll be all right. I'm just disappointed. I'll be more forthcoming next year so you have time to plan. Get on the road before the traffic gets too bad."

"Okay."

Alec started to step away again, but Key held tight to his arm. When he looked up, Key was there, lips puckered, initiating a goodbye kiss. Key usually gruffed about the kiss, but not this time. It did lessen the pain in Alec's heart. He placed his hand on Key's cheek and tilted his chin, making Key come more than halfway to meet him. The kiss was brief, the gaze afterward lingered.

"Have a good day. Text me when you get to work."

Key didn't let him go. He could feel his hesitation.

"Go. I'll be fine."

Finally, Key nodded and left Alec standing there staring after him.

CHAPTER 16

Saturday night

Keyes rolled his bike to a stop in the middle of his old man's empty driveway. He stared at the dilapidated house he'd grown up in, and his gut twisted. Everything inside him screamed to turn around and leave this place. He was a fundamentally different man than everything this house represented. Instead, he lifted his foot, easily finding the kickstand to his Harley and let the bike rest as he hiked a leg over the seat.

"You're a pussy," he hissed to himself as he continued to hesitate before finally starting for the front door. He took each porch step, remembering how many times in his life he'd been banished to this front porch. He had spent countless nights cowering in a corner, locked out of his house, scared out of his wits at every sound or small rush of wind that rustled the leaves on the large oak trees. He got through those scary nights with a promise to himself: once he got out, he would never come back. Those bad memories had him pausing with his hand on the front doorknob. Maybe he should leave, but in the end, he didn't and pushed open the door to walk inside his father's house for what he prayed was the very last time.

A prospect was kicked back on their old blue tweed sofa with a television remote in hand. The guy lifted his gaze to Keyes when he entered. He stared at Keyes, looked him up and down before slowly getting to his feet. Contempt shone in the young man's eyes, most likely poisoned by his old man. But the kid kept his mouth shut, smart enough to know one negative vote by Keyes and he'd never become a full patched brother of the club.

Keyes wasn't going to miss all the subtle disrespect he got from this pack of lousy prospects scouted by his old man. For the first time, the idea of a future where he was judged on his own merit, not from the vitriol that rolled so easily from his father's evil tongue seemed achievable.

"He back there?" he asked the prospect, skirting the coffee table, going toward the bedrooms.

"He doesn't want you here," the prospect said, the contempt in his eyes coming through in his voice. Keyes glanced over his shoulder. The prospect stayed rooted in his spot, confirming Keyes's initial thought that the kid wasn't stupid. While that gaze tracked him, Keyes ignored his warning completely. He passed his old bedroom and the numb feeling from days ago washed back over him. Rage, hate, or joy were all emotions he thought he'd feel during the many times throughout his life he had envisioned his old man's death. Never once did he see himself devoid of all feeling. That shit wasn't good.

He pushed open the master bedroom door to see his father lying in bed, his bedroom cleaner than Keyes ever remembered seeing it before. There was an older woman in scrubs sitting in a chair close to the bed. Her gaze lifted to him, otherwise she stayed quiet as he walked straight to the edge of the mattress.

His old man was an emaciated shell of the person he'd once been. The apologetic looks each of his brothers had given this evening when updating him on his old man's condition seemed a bit of an understatement. Now he got why gulps of beer and liquor were slammed after talking about their brother's condition. Smoke's breathing was shallow and labored, his skin a grayish, sickly color, and he looked much older than his late fifties.

Keyes let out a sigh, committing this moment to memory. He didn't know what he had hoped to accomplish by coming there this evening. In hindsight, he should have just stayed at the barbecue. It was this numbness that freaked him out the most. Honestly, the lack of emotion was with everything in his life. Well, everything except Alec.

He should be with Alec right now. Alec hadn't shaken that funky attitude of sadness since the other morning. Instead of ditching the barbecue to come see his old man, he should have met up with Alec. What had he been thinking? Why had that never occurred to him before right now? Keyes reached for his phone as movement caught his eye. The woman in the chair rose, going for the bed.

"Mr. Dixon, it's all right. Your son's here. You're his son, right?"

He had no idea how she would know such a thing, and Keyes swung his gaze to his father who was staring straight at him. For as frail as he was and the sheer volume of morphine he was no doubt on, there was still no mistaking the magnitude of hate in the old man's eyes, and it was all directed at Keyes.

Keyes met his father's glare. "I came to say goodbye."

His father moved, not much more than a twitch, but the old man tried. Keyes could see the agitation building in the movements before he began coughing.

"Mr. Dixon, calm down." The nurse grabbed his father's shoulders as the prospect launched himself through the bedroom door.

"I told you he didn't fuckin' want you here. Why couldn't you honor his last fuckin' wish, man?"

Keyes stepped back as the prospect rushed to the bed. He watched the two try to calm his ailing father. It took less than a minute more for Keyes to decide to leave. He was through the house and out the front door, dragging in gulps of fresh air as the boulders on his shoulder, weight he didn't even know he carried, lifted off him. He gripped the railing, closing his eyes as flashes of his life played out like a full-length feature film behind his closed lids. Images of his mother—the good memories, her laughing happily with him while watching cartoons, *Samurai Jack* to be specific. His father taking the seat next to her on the sofa, his arm coming around her, his hand landing on top of Keyes's head. His mother made a badass spaghetti dinner that he would eat platefuls of in one sitting, a recipe she had learned from her mother.

Maybe Clyde knew that same recipe. How had he never thought to ask?

Keyes opened his eyes and lifted his gaze, staring out at the darkened front yard. He wanted to leave this all behind. He'd done what he came to do. His mind drifted to Alec and his anxiety evened out. This was what Alec did for him—made him see the world with hope. Alec showed him everyone had value. Alec gave Keyes value.

He pushed off the railing, looking back at the broken-down home he hoped to never see again. The sorrow radiating off this piece-of-shit house was all he now saw.

His gaze went to the corner of the porch, the exact place he'd cower for wetting the bed. Who did that to a scared little boy? The flash of sudden anger built so quickly Keyes fisted his hand and drove it into the siding before he even knew what he was doing.

He seethed, his breath coming in hard gasps. He was losing it over something that shouldn't hold power over him any longer. Keyes forced himself to take a huge mental step backward. What the fuck was he doing?

Clyde told him to be done, and damn it, he needed to be fucking done. As he ate up the distance between the house and his bike, he shed the anger as fast as it had appeared. His heart regained the steady beat of anticipation, hope, and a brighter future. That was what he had waiting on him at home. *At home.* The words echoed in his head. With a promise to himself, Keyes mounted his bike. From that day on, he was only going to allow himself to look forward. He was going home to Alec. Jesus, that felt good to say.

Alec sidled up to the bar, sliding between two of his work colleagues, one dressed as Wonder Woman and the other as Spiderman. He lifted a hand toward the busy bartender, snagging his attention before lifting his glass. He got the nod that let him know his drink was on its way, so he downed the remaining vodka tonic as he turned back to the crowd of costume-clad partygoers.

When he lifted the glass to his mouth and ended up getting nothing but ice, he realized how much he'd had to drink this evening. Alec had driven to the masquerade party, only planning to stay for a short time before returning home and pouting because he hadn't gotten his way. Key hadn't come with him. But this little get-together had turned out to be a far better time than he had anticipated. He truly missed socializing, and all those warm feelings led him to drink more than he should have if he planned to drive home after the gathering.

What he couldn't get past was Janice's superior party planning skills. This little bar in the Uptown area of downtown Dallas was a great place to just be. Alec was super comfortable and looked down at his watch to check the time, only to be reminded he wasn't wearing one this evening. "Robin…right? Where's your Batman?"

His gaze shifted to the Wonder Woman beside him, and he grinned, running a hand down the tight-fitting bodysuit. He wasn't a hundred percent certain anyone would know who he was supposed to be since he'd ditched the face mask and cape over an hour ago.

"He got called to the Batcave. I'm solo this evening." He'd made that comment over and over since he'd arrived. He probably should have gone with Key's Batman costume instead of sticking with the Robin one, but he'd been in full-on fit mode and purposefully chosen to go without his counterpart.

The guy she was with, who was dressed as a Dallas Maverick basketball player, was also grinning at him, and he happily stuck out a hand toward the man. "I'm Alec Pierce."

"Jack," the guy said, cocking a head toward Wonder Woman. "I'm Eva's husband."

Ah, Eva. Yup, maybe he knew that. She was one of Janice's friends. They worked together in Janice's division. Eva's hand came up when Alec released Jack's handshake. "We haven't officially met. I'm Eva Covington."

"I'm Alec."

"I know. Janice talks about you all the time. You're being nominated for a federal judge seat, right?" Eva asked, turning her head between Alec and her husband as though filling him in on the big news.

Alec's happy slipped a notch, and his grin faltered as the bartender placed his drink in front of him. "That, I unfortunately am." He grabbed the glass, taking a hearty swallow.

"He's part of the Pierce family. His father is a congressman, right?" Eva continued, letting her husband in on all his dirty little family secrets. Any remnants of the grin he'd held for the last hour fell away.

"Unfortunately, that's the case," he said, mimicking his last words with an exaggerated nod. Luckily, a hand came to rest on his shoulder before running down the length of his arm. He turned, again lifting the glass to find Janice had come to stand beside him.

"You're having a good time."

The smile instantly slid back in place. "I am. Officially met Eva and Jack here."

"Well, that's good." Janice laughed and shared a look with Eva that Alec interrupted to mean "Men, what do we do with them," before she turned to the side, revealing the sombrero wearing Spanish hottie behind her. "I want you to meet my neighbor, Sean Romero."

A tipsy Alec must be a friendly guy because he stuck his hand straight out again as the room wobbled just a bit at his full body turn. The dizziness was a little unexpected. It might be in everyone's best interest for him to switch to water. A drunk Alec hated clothing, and there wasn't much more to remove from the one-piece bodysuit. "It's nice to meet you."

"You too. You seem to have a knack for getting the bartender's attention. Can you get me a glass of pinot noir?"

The handsome guy lifted an almost empty wine glass in Alec's direction by way of a salute.

"Sure, I can. Hang on." Alec turned back to the bartender who still happened to be in front of Jack.

"I heard. I'm pouring now." The glass was instantly handed to Alec who carefully extended it to Sean. "You need anything?"

"Probably a glass of water." The turning might be too much, the dizzy feeling increased substantially.

"You need anything?" the bartender called out to Janice.

"No, I'm good." She raised a hand to the bartender, but spoke to Alec. "I've got to get back to the door. My guests are starting to leave. I just wanted you two to meet. Sean is a stockbroker and my next door neighbor—I said that already. You both had dates that were no-shows." She looked like she let the obvious, not-a-secret-at-all cat out of the bag. "Sorry. See? I've had too much to drink already. I've said too much, but I think you two have a lot in common, and I'm ducking away before I say how much I'd love for you two to date." This time her oversharing was purposeful going by the faux surprised look she gave, and Eva laughed as she practically jumped off her seat.

"We're going too," she said, grabbing her purse.

"It was nice to meet you," Jack said, again sticking out his hand to shake Alec's.

Janice ducked away with Eva and Jack following, and Alec shook his head at her silliness. When he got bumped, he realized he was taking prime real estate away from other guests trying to get to the bar. Alec grabbed his glass of water and started to step away, bumping straight into Sean who had moved in closer.

The movement may have been natural, but the stance was purposeful, something a solid player would do, one that Alec himself had probably done in another time of his life.

The wine sloshing out of Sean's glass did nothing to dampen the sexy let's-fuck grin aimed right at him. Sean was Alec's height and build, handsome in that forbidden, sinful way with all his well-groomed dark good looks. Alec had always had a weakness for dark-haired guys, and Sean was the cream of that crop. Texas sure had a way of growing some hot-ass men. No doubt the guy could probably burn up his bed, and if Alec were single, they wouldn't be standing there wasting time.

"Sorry," Alec said, slipping to the side to give them room when Sean didn't move. He'd gotten so close he could smell his Clive Christian cologne. Oh hell, this Sean was damn good at the instant seduction. Alec had always had a preference for that particular brand. That dark sultry gaze followed him, and Sean did little more than turn, not moving a step out of the walkway to the bar. He was suave and smooth; again thoughts of his own past came to mind. Suddenly, Alec regretted drinking so much. His playful happy had sent the wrong vibe, and he quickly blurted out, "I have a boyfriend."

"So do I," Sean said indulgently, taking a sip of his wine. "I think Janice's guest list included couples. Where's your guy?" His voice was as smooth as his looks, stirring Alec's traitorous dick.

"Working." Alec gave his prepared explanation then took a long drink of water. Luckily, the guy's dark piercing stare released him, and he was able to take a literal as well as a figurative step backward. Juggling both glasses in his hand, Alec downed the vodka then slipped the empty glass on the bar. He kept the water, looking around for a clock. He found a small one hanging on the wall behind the bar. It was a little after eleven and his fun evening out had come to a crashing halt. Alec's gaze again connected with Sean's, and it held. He had enjoyed the simple gathering, more than he probably should have, and that was mostly likely due to the way he limited his surroundings to his home and that awful job.

The guy smirked as he looked Alec up and down. "You're new at this—the relationship thing?"

"I guess so," Alec answered truthfully.

"We're open. We've found it's the best of both worlds. My place is close. Wanna get out of here?" Sean had absolutely no shame in his game. He said the words like they were the most normal suggestion in the world, something Alec should take pleasure in accepting.

The old Alec wouldn't have let this much time pass before heading out the door. The new Alec was glad he and Key had defined their relationship rules early on. Many men had no problem sharing. Alec apparently wasn't one of them.

"No," he said flatly and stepped aside again, setting the water glass on the bar top. "We're exclusive, and I was just about to hit the road."

"Too bad," Sean said in what sounded like true disappointment. "That changes, you know where to find me."

The guy was unfazed and in control, much like the old Alec. It would be so easy to take this guy up on his offer. Easier to have someone like Sean in his life. Instead, he left the guy standing there and motioned for the bartender to cash him out. Alec pulled his wallet, pocketed his credit card, and quickly scribbled out a tip and his name across the bottom. The bartender had stored the removed portions of his costume behind the bar and slid those to him.

When he turned away, Sean was still standing there. "This isn't part of the pickup? You're serious?"

"Absolutely serious and exclusive." Alec found power in those words. One thing he learned about Sean, the man knew exactly where to stand to be in Alec's way, forcing Alec to move around him again to leave.

"Lucky guy."

He wasn't sure Key felt that way, but he did.

"I am." When he was sober, he'd have to examine all this uncertainty. Until then, well, he guessed he was going home to an empty house. At the door, he looked back, and Sean was standing there, watching him. He must have sensed Alec's hesitation and lifted his glass, giving him a sexy grin. Man, Alec could have gone to town using that hard body. Instead, he pushed through the door without seeking out Janice for a proper goodbye, walking to the valet.

"Do you have your ticket?"

"I think I've had too much to drink. Is the car secure if I leave it overnight?" Alec asked, looking around for the parking lot.

"It's in the private parking lot behind the building. We don't normally have any problems. We have a security guard here overnight."

"Cool," he said and palmed his phone to pull up his Uber app. Luckily, there was one nearby. Once he was in the backseat of the car, he sent a quick message to Janice. It was lame, but he didn't want to have to explain his sudden departure.

"*I had a lovely time. Thank you for inviting us.*"

There. That seemed like enough. He pushed send.

Alec looked around the car then out into the night.

Alone again.

He'd been having a good time and bolted because he got freaked out over some guy hitting on him. No, he got freaked out because he saw his past in front of him. What he'd now be if he hadn't met Key. He was ridiculous. Maybe these prickly feelings were the need to run. Alec had his new course. He was a new man and needed to figure himself out as this man. Alec leaned his head back on the rest and ignored the slight spin as he let the motion of the car lull him into sleep.

CHAPTER 17

Keyes blew through the open gate, squeezing the brakes as he trailed behind a car taking the circle drive to the front door of Alec's place. He pulled alongside the car, got a good look inside as Alec opened the backdoor with a giant grin plastered on his face. Alec's mouth was moving, but Keyes couldn't hear a single word until he cut the bike's engine, and by then Alec's arms had snaked around his neck. Between the intense smell of alcohol on his breath and his eyelids drooping to half-mast, Keyes figured his tights-wearing superhero was drunk. He absorbed Alec's body weight as he let the bike rest on its stand and the car left them both standing there in the driveway.

"...then you were here like I needed you to be." Alec lifted on his tiptoes, pressing a sloppy kiss to his lips.

"Where's your car?" he asked after Alec gave him a second simple kiss, coming closer to actually hitting the center of his lips.

"You don't listen." Alec grinned at him, seemingly content to stay like that forever. Keyes rested back on his seat, drawing Alec closer. He was fine with that idea. It was a little chilly out, but Alec had wormed his hands and arms inside the leather riding jacket to circle his waist. He was honestly okay with just about anything that involved this man and caught Alec's wrist as he slid his hand up to his chest. He brought Alec's palm to his lips, pressing a kiss there as drunk Alec did his normal thing, using all those words to explain in great detail about his night as if Keyes was living it in real time with him.

"...and then you were here. I think we've hit that mental telepathy thing. You knew I needed you."

"Why did you need me?"

Alec gave him a pointed look and pushed back. "You didn't listen."

"Maybe not to all of it," he said cheekily, keeping hold of Alec's wrist as he turned toward the house. Keyes climbed off his bike and followed, Alec threading their fingers together. "Tell me again."

"My car's at the bar," Alec slurred, unlocking the front door. "I drank too much." He pushed open the front door, quickly disarmed the home alarm and stepped back into Keyes's arms, sliding his palms up his chest to thread through his windblown hair. "I've changed so much since meeting you. Janice tried to set me up with this guy, and I completely freaked out."

Keyes brow furrowed as he digested Alec's unguarded words.

"His name was Sean, and he was in an open relationship. It's certainly not the first time I've been propositioned by someone in a relationship, but now that I'm in a monogamous one, I just felt like I shouldn't be there any longer. I wanted you there to defend my honor."

While Alec spoke, he urged Keyes's head down by pulling at his hair, a move Keyes generally loved, but since he didn't like one single word coming out of Alec's mouth, he fought the gentle tug. Oblivious to Keyes's downward spiraling mood, Alec lifted on his tiptoes to press their lips together. Alec leaned flush against Keyes, his arms circling his back. Keyes gripped Alec's hips, ready to push him away to finish this conversation when Alec's tongue darted out, licking across his lower lip, demanding entrance. Damn it, he loved that move, even more than he disliked Alec's words.

Torn between the hot kiss that was sure to end in a blow job and the knowledge that Alec had gone to a party tonight to be set up with another guy... Yeah, blow job first. Suddenly, he went from mouthing Alec's cheek to nothing but air. His hand, the one he had lifted to Alec's chin to better tilt him just to the right angle was now in Alec's hand, his guy's thumb slid over his swollen, bruised, and raw knuckles. Keyes let out hiss at the painful exploration and tried to pull his hand away.

"What happened tonight?" Alec didn't wait for an answer, stepping back from his hold to get a good look at his knuckles. "You've been in a fight. Why did I get drunk tonight? You aren't answering. This is why I hate that club. At some point, you're seriously going to be injured. You can't risk yourself like this."

"What? It wasn't a fight," Keyes declared, watching Alec eye him then throw up his hands in indignation, his face contorting from anger to anguish in five seconds flat. Alec took another step away from him.

"Of course, it was. Your knuckles don't just get torn-up for no reason. I know what a fight injury looks like." Alec wheeled around, his hand going to his mouth as if he were at a loss for words. Without warning, he threw his hands in the air once again. "Why did I drink so much?"

Alec pivoted on his heels, stalking toward the kitchen. Keyes followed slowly, wondering what in the hell just happened.

"Alec…"

He noticed a first-aid kit his drunk lover had placed in the middle of the counter close to the coffee pot that started its drip as Alec downed gulp after gulp of water from a glass. When he was done, he pushed the glass under the coffee drip and took the cup. His foot bounced as he motioned for Keyes to take a seat. He didn't. Alec had caused doubt and anxiety to rush through Keyes, and he came forward, trying to understand why Alec had gotten so angry.

"What happened?" Alec demanded.

"What's goin' on with you?" he asked, stopping about a foot and a half in front of Alec. "Did you cheat on me?"

"What?" Alec exclaimed, sounding like that was the most absurd suggestion he'd ever heard. He took a step backward as Keyes came forward. "I would never cheat on you. Why would you even ask such a thing?"

"I thought Janice knew you had a boyfriend," he said and held his ground.

"No, you can't divert me." Alec shook his head, reaching for Keyes's hand before pulling it under the cabinet lighting. "We're not going there right now. You didn't even clean the blood. It's trailing down your hand and arm. What happened?"

"Alec, I'm sorry—"

Alec cut him off, throwing out an arm to block his retreat.

"Key, answer the question. What happened tonight? You can't just go all willy-nilly anymore. It's not just you

you have to think about. What would happen to me if something happened to you? I wouldn't even know if something happened to you until you didn't come home and I had to search for you. I'm sick of the damn boundaries between us. You can trust me, tell me what happened." Where Keyes had wanted to move away from Alec, Alec left him standing in the kitchen, pacing to the middle of the living room then spun around, squaring off with him. His guy was serious. The look etched on his face was a cross between anger and intense hurt. Alec folded his arms over his chest, his right leg bouncing. The only thing off was the Robin costume Alec still wore.

Keyes narrowed his eyes, trying to catch up. He took a couple of steps toward Alec who just tilted his head, his jaw tightened and one eyebrow cocked. He'd never been so effectively stopped in his tracks before.

"My father's dyin'," Keyes said after a deep exhale.

Silence held between them for several heartbeats.

"I can't pretend to be sorry," Alec blurted, his face going through a range of emotion. His unguarded words seemed to have startled him and his arms tightened over his chest. "I'm sorry I said it like that. What's happened?"

"Lung cancer. He's in hospice. He's been there a few weeks, I guess. The party tonight was also a fundraiser for his medical bills."

Alec didn't lose his seriousness as Keyes took tentative steps closer.

"I'd been warrin' over whether I should see him again. It's been eatin' at me, so I decided to go."

"You were brave to do that to yourself," Alec said, his gaze softening as he searched Keyes's face. "So, you went. How did it go?"

"As expected. He hates me as much as I hate him, but he's real sick—obviously. When he saw me, he somehow managed to get all agitated even doped up like he was," he explained, slowly taking a few more steps toward Alec, encouraged when Alec didn't move away. More than anything, he didn't want to fight with Alec. He never wanted to fight with his guy. Alec was his solace in life.

"Then how did your knuckles get torn up like that?" Alec's leg doubled time, the tap echoing in the silence between questions.

"The side of the house when I was leavin'. It wasn't that big a deal. I didn't even realize I'd drawn blood," Keyes said, flexing and balling his hand. He looked down at his scarred, calloused hands. He'd fought his way through life. This was nothing but another day to him, at least the pain he'd felt had chased the numbness away.

"How did you feel?" Alec's voice was softer now, causing him to look up and step forward again.

"I didn't feel anything. I thought I'd feel differently." Keyes placed his hand over his heart, the thump beneath his palm acknowledging the organ was there even with the complete lack of emotion he had about his old man. "Just emptiness. I was empty inside. Nothin'."

"I've experienced some of that with my family." Alec's brow wrinkled, and he nodded like he was digesting that bit of information. Keyes waited for whatever question was coming next. "Then what made you punch the side of the house?"

"I don't really know. I hated that man my whole fuckin' life, but when I was starin' down at him, that was all gone. I think because of you. It freaked me out how much that I didn't care. None of that mattered anymore, and I couldn't even hate him. And before you ask why, I don't know. I just know it does, and I know you're responsible for lessenin' some of my hate. You're a real good guy who makes me a better dude. That's all I got, Alec. When I was leavin', I thought about bein' a kid and all the confusion and pain and humiliation I'd suffered at that house. I drove my fist through the sidin', but the anger didn't help and the old feelin's that I was nothin' came back. I came straight here because I feel better here." Man, he hoped Alec understood because that was all he had by way of an explanation.

Alec's leg continued to bounce as he stared at him. Alec remained silent as if he were digesting everything he'd been told.

"So, who's this dude you were set up with tonight?"

Alec's shoulders slumped. He rolled his head between his shoulders, clearly trying to relieve some of the sudden extreme tension that formed between them. "Absolutely no one, Key. I had a freak-out of my own. When the guy hit me up for a hookup, I realized how completely I didn't want anyone but you. I'd been drinking and I've never been in a relationship before you, I felt like I was compromising us by even being asked that question. It was strange and unreasonable, so I left and came home."

"I'm here every night," he said, instead of saying what he really wanted to say—*You're just now figuring out you don't want anyone else?* He didn't want to fight anymore, but goddamn, he wanted to know what Alec would say to that.

"I know." They stared at one another several long seconds before Alec spoke again. "Let this be enough where that awful man's concerned."

"That's what my uncle said too." Keyes still held his distance, the imaginary line in the sand between them now seemed carved in stone.

Alec's jaw clenched, his voice back to strong and unyielding, hard and determined. "I want to be the one you come to. I want to be your sounding board. I appreciate you have your uncle, and I'm not trying to come between the two of you. I just want to be your person. Your everything."

"You are. And I want that too." Keyes waved his hand between them. "You know that. I want this. The same. You know."

Alec nodded. After a moment more, he smiled. It took a second more for the grin to turn genuine, and he stepped forward. Keyes did too, meeting him halfway. "I do know. This was a good step in the right direction."

"Yeah. So about that guy…" Keyes had let Alec sidetrack him, but he couldn't let it go. His primal instincts where Alec was concerned reared, knowing it wouldn't take much to corner this stranger and make him shit his pants for hitting on what Keyes had claimed as his. A small part of the old Keyes relished the idea of scaring the shit out of that loser. "This Janice knows you have a boyfriend, right?"

"Stop, the guy was just being a guy, and I certainly wasn't interested in breaking these vows we've made to one another. Get territorial in the bedroom. I found the flaw in this costume, probably the reason I was able to get it so late in the season. I have to completely disrobe to go to the restroom. It's a pain in the ass. I was getting the strangest looks standing in my underwear in the bar's bathroom," Alec said, wrapping an arm around his waist and starting toward his bedroom. "You'd have thought they'd've figured that out. It's not a new costume."

Motherfucker, now he was jealous over the costume. Keyes gave Alec a questioning side-eye, absolutely not fucking liking a lot of the things Alec was saying about his night out. "Yeah, I don't like you undressin' in a public bathroom either."

"Then next time, you better be there to protect my virtue." Alec winked, moving ahead of him, motioning for him to get the zipper at his back.

"Virtue?" he teased, his mood instantly lifting. From the stories Alec had told him from the past, he wasn't sure that word could apply to Alec.

"Just go with it."

CHAPTER 18

Halloween

How could he ever make Alec understand that birthdays weren't a thing for him? Alec had sent a text message wishing him a happy birthday—not one time, but once every hour, on the hour for the past *eight* hours. On top of that, Alec had had delivered a balloon bouquet and some sort of cut fruit in a vase deal to the tire shop. His confusion had only increased when he'd figured out the driver wasn't there for a tire change but to deliver something to him. That was a first, never in his entire life had he ever had a gift delivered to him before. Keyes accepted the item only because it was shoved into his chest, then he stood there with everyone around gawking at him. He didn't even know what to do with the thing, so he set it on his father's bench and let anyone who wanted a piece have one, because seriously, besides the somewhat healthy Alec, who could eat all that fruit?

At Alec's insistence, he'd left work earlier than usual. He didn't stop by the clubhouse even though it had become customary for him since the fundraiser. Instead, he drove to Alec's place, currently rolling through the neighborhood, watching the children all dressed up in their Halloween finest.

This was a holiday he never participated in except a few times in elementary school when he'd had a teacher with used costumes and he'd get to dress up for the day. Those memories brought a smile to his lips and a clench to his heart. He had enjoyed the costume parades where they stopped by each classroom and received candy. It was like a birthday party just for him. He would hoard those treats, not letting anyone know he had them, eating a piece a day until it was all gone.

Alec normalized his life in that same way. He settled down the destructive side of Keyes's personality. Alec made him understand that normalcy was truly achievable for men like him. As Keyes turned into Alec's driveway, he wondered what Clyde might have to say about these changes in him since his uncle had been trying to drill those lessons into his hard head since the day they'd first met.

This evening, he didn't have to slow his ride to wait for the gate to open. Alec had the house decorated to the hilt, draped in over-the-top decorations, turning the front yard into a graveyard and the outside of Alec's beautiful house into a haunted mansion, all for the neighborhood children to have a great time when stopping by to ask for their treats.

With the glares he had gotten while driving past the soon-to-be trick-or-treaters, he wasn't quite sold on Alec's theory any of those parents were going to let their children stop by Alec's front door this evening. For close to a year now, he'd watched the adults in this neighborhood grip their children's hands a little tighter or usher them in the opposite direction as he drove past. That attitude wasn't going to magically disappear, but it also hadn't dampened Alec's expectations either. Alec had meticulously prepared for the night by buying hundreds of king-size candy bars. Then yesterday, he came home with three hundred one-dollar bills just in case the candy ran out due to Keyes's inability to keep his hands off the children's treats. His mister was hilariously cute over this holiday.

A little surprised Alec wasn't already waiting out front for the kids to arrive, Keyes drove his bike around the back corner of the house and stopped short, abruptly halting his bike at the sight before him. In his regular parking spot sat a big black tricked-out pickup truck. His gaze shifted to the house. Alec didn't come through the back door, ready to greet him like usual. Keyes's gaze cut straight back to the truck. Who was here? His heart amped up and an uneasy feeling stirred in the pit of his stomach.

Keyes slowly pulled his bike forward, looking over the nice ride until he stopped closer to the garage and cut the engine. He knocked the kickstand in place, looking over the sleek new paint job. The truck had to be close to new, and his gaze went back to the house. Who the hell was there? Should he go inside or take off—probably take off before he was seen. He reached for his phone to see if Alec had sent him a message, warning him away, when he heard the kitchen door open.

"Dammit."

Keyes jerked around to witness Alec coming to a sudden stop with a giant red bow in his hands.

"I started the Halloween music early, so I didn't hear you arrive." Alec then darted around his bike, quickly running forward to drop the bow on the hood of the truck. Throwing his hands in the air, he yelled, "Surprise!"

Keyes still had no idea what was going on. He had come off his bike, helmet left on the seat, and stood there staring at Alec before looking back over his shoulder to see who was inside the house.

"Surprise, Key. Happy Birthday!" Alec sing-songed, causing him to look back at Alec then around the truck as Alec's hands flew out in a Vanna White sweeping motion.

"Who's here?" he asked and again looked back at the house before angling his head to see inside the windows.

"No one's here. This is your birthday present," Alec explained. He about hit the ground before whipping back toward Alec, his lover's hands still motioning to the truck.

He blinked as understanding seeped in, and he immediately recoiled from the obvious implication. Keyes shook his head at Alec. "You gave me a fruit deal at work."

Alec's arms dropped, and he honestly looked crestfallen.

"You don't like it. It took me some time to find, but when I saw this truck, it screamed your personality." Alec had kind of deflated in front of him, but Keyes had all he could handle with the floodgates of his anxiety bursting open. "You can go down to the dealership and pick what you want. I should have just arranged that from the beginning."

"You can't give me a truck," he said incredulously. His gaze left Alec's, going to the beautiful, shiny black decked-out Ford F-250 4x4. He knew the price tag on this truck was stupid as hell.

"Of course, I can," Alec said, hesitantly perking back up.

"Alec, it's too much," he said, walking the length of the pickup and around the tailgate. Dev would totally prank him with something like this before offering to buy him a beer at the clubhouse where the liquor ran freely. Keyes looked down at his shaking hands. He quickly balled them into fists.

"It most certainly is not too much. You're putting all these miles on your Harley driving back and forth…"

Keyes admired the paint as he walked around the hood of the most perfect truck he'd ever seen. God, it was a beauty, and his heart soared at such a thoughtful gift. The rush of such exorbitant highs and lows left him uncertain as he looked back at Alec and repeated, "You can't give me a truck."

Any lingering dejection in Alec turned to frustration. "I've been planning this for a month. I thought you'd be pleased."

Again, all Keyes could do was blink as his heart drummed in his chest and his breath became harder to catch. Whatever Alec saw had the man rushing toward Keyes, his tone was forceful yet super calm. "Babe, you need to stop. You're flushed. Just take a minute and breathe."

He didn't. Couldn't. Panic raced along his skin, making him dizzy. Alec's expression changed to worry as he gently ran a hand over his back. "Breathe, Key. You're safe. Nothing's changed."

Darkness crept around the edges of his vision as he stared at the truck.

Shit, he was going to pass out.

"Head between your legs," Alec instructed, pushing him down. He bent, only because the fall would be shorter when he did in fact pass out. He watched Alec's fancy loafers move away from him. Seconds later, a chair pushed at the back of his legs. Keyes sat, bending his body forward, lowering his head between his legs, and closed his eyes.

He was a full patched member in a one-percenter bike club. He fought badass motherfuckers all the time. Hell, he *was* a badass motherfucker. Yet, this sophisticated man buying him a shiny new pickup truck brought him straight to his knees.

What. The. Fucking. *Hell*...

"Just breathe. Do you need a paper bag?" Alec asked at his ear while the man's steadying palm caressed his shoulders.

Keyes concentrated on filling his lungs as the pressure from Alec's comforting hand disappeared. A minute later, a brown paper bag was shoved under his mop of hair. "Here, babe. Breathe into the bag for me."

He did, because he didn't know what else to do.

Maybe as much as five minutes later, he angled his head enough to venture a look at the truck. "You can't buy me a truck," he repeated and lowered his eyes again to stare at the concrete of the driveway.

"I can though. It's in your name or will be when you sign the paperwork." Alec squatted in front of him, sweeping Keyes's hair to the side of his head.

"What're the payments?" he asked, just turning his head to see Alec's beautiful face.

He should stand. His ego required he get back on his feet and face this like a man. Grown men didn't cower this way, and he had never chickened out of a fight before in his life. Even with the self-lecture, it still took a second for him to push his back against the seat.

"It's a gift. There're no payments," Alec said, his hand going to his knee. "You're shit at receiving gifts."

He didn't say a word, just turned again to stare at the gorgeous truck. Birthday presents came in little boxes that a person unwrapped. Clyde gave him a birthday present every year. Sometimes he put them in those pretty bags with paper poking out of the top. When he'd sent gifts to Clyde and to Dev's two daughters, he'd selected the gift wrap option. Birthday gifts came in boxes, not driven into driveways and parked there. This was too much.

"Come on. Come see the inside. It's loaded." Alec went for the driver's side door, opening it wide while Keyes stayed where he was, unable to see inside the cab. "Or not. We'll do baby steps. Come to the house. We'll come back to this later."

Away from the truck sounded great. Being hit with so many emotions had completely thrown him for a loop. Keyes rose, pleased he was steady on his feet. Alec was there by his side, wrapping an arm around his waist that he interpreted as support more than affection as they walked together toward the back door. Keyes wrapped his arm around Alec's shoulders, drawing him flush against his side.

"If you'd prefer something different, we can return the truck and keep looking. It's close to winter, and you drive through all the elements to get here every day. What if this winter is unusually cold? I can't bear you battling all this intense Texas weather any longer."

"It's a truck," he said and pushed open the back door, encouraging Alec inside first. He didn't go. Instead, Alec crowded him, wrapping both arms around his waist, coming chest to chest, and lifting his chin.

"Nothing gets past you. Now kiss me." When he didn't immediately kiss Alec, his puckered-lipped boyfriend lifted a brow in challenge. Keyes rolled his eyes before he obliged with a simple press of his lips. "The trick-or-treaters'll be here soon. I thought we could have dinner afterward unless you're hungry now. Your choice. I have ribeyes for the grill."

Alec finally moved, stepping inside the house. Keyes couldn't help but look back at the badass pickup. Who gave someone a truck like that as a gift?

"Come on in." Alec's hand tightened on his wrist, tugging him all the way through the doorway. "Don't freak out again. I also have a birthday cake. I made the oatmeal cake my grandmother used to make. I wanted to spruce it up, but ultimately kept it the way she made."

Keyes stood at the back door, staring out into the driveway, wanting to go back out and take a good long slow perusal of the truck. Based on what just happened, he should probably do all that alone. Alec came in behind him, wrapping his arms around his waist, his lips pressing against his shoulder. "You know, it's okay to like the truck and accept it. I love you, and whether you say it or not, you love me. This is what we do for one another."

His hands slid along Alec's arms until he threaded their fingers together. It was easier not to look at Alec when they spoke of something so generous and personal. "I can't afford to buy you a car that you'd drive."

Alec laughed at him, definitely not with him, which might have been the only thing to pull him from the trance the confession held him in.

"I'm not driving in the rain to spend the night with you. There's a difference. That gift benefits me as much as it benefits you. Now, you could say you like it," Alec encouraged, turning Keyes toward him and away from the truck.

"I do. It's a lot to take in." He did love the truck. His uncle was usually the only one who ever remembered his birthday. What seemed a bigger deal to Keyes, and sent his heart racing, was knowing Alec had taken time to think about him to help make this day special. That was huge.

"You're welcome, and it's very practical." Alec's excited grin helped settle his heart, even if he knew practical would have been covered with an older used vehicle.

The doorbell rang and everything about the teasing, casual Alec changed as he jumped around and started jogging through the house toward the front door. "Don't go look at the truck until we go together!"

Keyes stayed at the backdoor, again turning toward his birthday present. He propped a shoulder against the doorframe, transfixed by the most spectacular vehicle he'd ever seen. Alec had given him the perfect truck for his birthday. His heart filled with warmth at the unbelievable generosity of his lover.

CHAPTER 19

Count this as another first given to Alec by Mr. Keyes Dixon. Alec loved Halloween and he loved the little trick-or-treaters. It was late in the evening, full darkness had descended well over an hour ago, but the children dressed in their fancy little costumes lingered in the streets. So Alec stayed outside his gate, his empty candy bucket at his feet, and continued handing out his dollar bills. There wasn't a single moment of the whole night he hadn't loved. From his badass biker hyperventilating over his birthday present to every version of Marvel superhero and Disney princess imaginable to the hesitant little hands reaching for their treats, Alec sat, enthralled by the whole experience—even the poop emoji he'd seen. Why someone would dress their kid up as poop, he'd never understand, but to each his own, and the little guy had been adorably sweet.

Unfortunately, Key had been right all along. Even though his neighborhood was packed with children, and he'd done everything he could do to invite and entice them to celebrate Halloween by stopping at his house for a treat, the whole street seemed to avoid his home. After the first brave costume-clad youngsters came by, no one else had ventured his way. Alec had stood at the door with his lights all on and watched the sidewalks fill with children and their parents—all bypassing his home.

Alec had whined to Key for about ten minutes before the man had shoved Alec's oversized bucket of candy into his chest and grabbed a patio chair. He escorted Alec to the end of the driveway, right past the gate, where the children and their parents had no choice but to interact with him. Then Key left, telling him to have fun, and boy, did he.

Tonight marked the exact day Alec had become fully domesticated. Blaine would die if he saw him now. On that thought, he grabbed his phone and took a quick selfie with his empty treat bucket at his feet. He sent the snapshot to Blaine. Alec scrolled through their old text messages and chuckled. Their message history was hilarious. Blaine sent him regular pictures of his pretentious parties, and Alec sent victory pictures of his empty Halloween treat bucket. As far as he was concerned, he was the clear winner in the race of life, beating Blaine hands down.

"Ready to come in?" Key asked from the gate. Alec glanced up and down the sidewalks lining the neighborhood. There were only a few stragglers left because it was a school night or so he'd been told over and over again by the excited little trick-or-treaters.

"Yep," he said happily and reached for the empty bucket before getting to his feet.

"You have a good time?" Key asked, coming for his chair.

"I did. It was great fun. I wish you had joined me," Alec said, letting Key take the chair as they walked side by side up the long driveway toward the back of the house.

"They wouldn't have even stopped on the sidewalk if I was out there with you. I freak 'em out."

Alec no longer doubted the truth of those words, so he didn't argue. Instead, he let the magic of the night cement his future.

"I wanna move us to a place that better suits the both of us. A place that the neighbors don't freak when they see you. Somewhere we're both comfortable." Alec side-eyed Key, trying to gauge his reaction, surprised when Key busted out with a hearty laugh.

"There's no place you and I both fit. You're the only person who doesn't seem to understand that," Key said, hooking an arm over Alec's shoulder.

"You're right. I do disagree." And he did. Wholeheartedly. He saw their differences, but that was what made them stronger. Besides, he was just discovering himself. Who knew how different they truly were. Only time would show Key how right they were for each other. Alec wrapped his arm around his lover's waist and snuggled in closer. They walked together in silence for three maybe four steps before Alec decided he might as well lay it all out. His decisions also affected Key, and he wanted to be the one to tell him. "I'll be officially removing my nomination for the federal judge seat next week. I've already told my family."

"You did? How did they take it?" Key's forward momentum slowed, and he turned toward Alec. The look of uncertainty that haunted Key when they spoke of his family was right there on his biker's face. That was one thing about spending the last year with this man, holed up only in his house, Alec had gotten to know Key intimately. He knew Key's triggers, and clearly, he'd hit several of them this evening.

"With all honesty?" His love gave him a continued side glance that he interpreted to mean absolutely. "It went as expected. I've most likely severed ties with them."

"You okay with that?" Key asked, his steps slowing even more.

"More than. It's been freeing, if that makes sense. I've also crafted my resignation letter to the DA's office. I haven't submitted it yet, mainly due to the one case I mentioned before, remember?" Alec hadn't given many details to Key, but his guy was listening now and nodded once. "I'm meeting with Janice—she's the one that invited us to her party." Alec waited again until Key gave another nod.

"Yeah, the one who tried to fix you up with that loser."

Alec just rolled his eyes.

"Stop. You'll like her, I promise. I'd like her to volunteer to oversee things until the transition of the file is complete. I crossed lines with this case. I think it was the little girl. She's so sweet but seems so scared."

"You're a good dude," Key drawled with authority, making Alec smile. Man, he was loving his life right now. Just walking in the dark with this special man by his side made him feel so damn good.

"Thank you. I like your little compliments. They seem genuine." Alec hip-checked Key then gave him a playful grin. "So I'll submit my resignation in the next couple of weeks with a month's notice, then I'll be free."

"Big steps. Sure you wanna do all that?"

"Well, there's more. My dream job, the one I turned down to move here is open again." Alec studied Key as he said each measured word to gauge his reaction.

"So, you're leavin'?" Key stopped dead in his tracks, his tone and stance tense, full of accusation as he turned toward Alec. He sensed Key's protective walls rising, and Alec hadn't had to deal with those in months. He wanted to say something smart, remind Key of the beginning of this conversation, the part where he wanted to move to a place that suited them both. Alec must not have answered fast enough because Key pivoted around, leaving him in the driveway alone. He watched Key take long strides toward the back porch and garage.

"Babe, the job's here in North Texas. I'm not leaving. I wouldn't leave you." He said the last words with more emphasis as he trailed slowly behind Key. Life changing events and Key didn't always make for a smooth course. When he rounded the corner of the house, Key was standing in the drive, his hands on his waist.

"Why are you doin' all this?" Key asked with loads of that heated biker attitude.

"Lots of reasons," he said, coming to stand directly in front of Key.

"Any of those reasons because of me?"

Alec just blinked at such an absurd question. "All of them are because of you, because of us. And don't have another panic attack. I'm just filling you in on some changes I'm making. That's it." Alec sidestepped Key, going straight to the house. When he pushed through the back door, his mood lifted, touched to find Key had been busy in his absence. The steaks were wrapped in foil, resting on the stove, all the sides were out and ready to eat. Key had even fixed Alec his favorite cocktail and left it sitting on the center island, ice melting, as condensation gathered on the glass.

"No…" Alec said as he turned. Key was so close, and the heat of their bodies mingled. "I'm supposed to be doing all this for you tonight. It's your birthday."

"Is all that what you want?" At those words, Alec lifted his hand, tenderly cupping Key's bearded cheek. He slid his thumb over his lover's lips and stared deeply into his blue eyes.

"Absolutely, one hundred percent yes. I've felt alone my whole life. It's the only reason I can come up with for letting my family use me like they have. Then I met you and I'm not alone anymore. It was you, not them, that I came to Dallas for."

Key's face softened. "I get it. I'm there."

He took that to mean that he had found a home in Alec too. At least, he wanted to believe their truth was very aligned to one another.

"I've always thought we were more the same than different."

Key remained silent while the sexiest smirk crossed his lips. After several long seconds, the tension in his face vanished as the biker tilted his head to kiss his upturned lips.

"I had a real nice time tonight. I'm glad you pushed me out to the street to hand out candy. It was fun. But I think the perfect ending to a Halloween birthday would be celebrating with ice cream and birthday cake in bed."

"What about dinner?" Key asked, looking over at the containers and foil-covered plates scattered on the counter.

"That can come afterward." He shifted so that his hips and swelling cock pressed against his lover's groin. Key's enticing grin spread slowly across his face, his heated gaze made his dick even harder. "We can have dessert first."

"I'd be into that, but I'd be more into havin' your ass in that fancy truck you got me." The wicked gleam in Key's eyes made his ass clench in anticipation.

"Umm…and there's that. Let's go!" Alec left the bucket on the counter, grabbing his drink as he went for the lube and condoms. He was back in five seconds flat. "We're good to go." On the way outside, he stopped abruptly in sudden indignation, Key bumping him from behind as he threw an accusing glance over his shoulder. "You looked at the truck without me, didn't you?"

Key only grinned and gave him a little shove between his shoulder blades to get him moving. Alec moved in such a way that Key hooked an arm over his shoulder, again walking side by side—hip to hip—to the truck. The romance of the night fueled each of his steps. Key surprised him by turning, resting his ass against the side of the truck, drawing Alec to him.

"So, you like it?"

"Of course." Key nodded, his cool hard-edged biker seemed to struggle at keeping his excitement under wraps. Key's thighs relaxed, and Alec pushed his knees through the opening to angle his body down the length of Key's body.

Yeah, no doubt he loved the badass truck, but it was the man standing in front of him who took the cake. That beautiful, proud smile made his head spin and his heart pound against his ribs. Alec Pierce consumed him, even more now that Keyes has seen the pure joy twinkling in those expressive eyes in response to his answer. Alec was so fucking sexy, hanging on to his every breath, waiting and watching to see if Keyes would finally accept the present.

"I'm pretty sure I'm gonna love christenin' it even more." He tilted Alec's head up and dipped his own, growling against Alec's lips. "Thank you."

Alec's eyes darkened with desire as Keyes hovered right there. This was where he had to agree with Alec, when they made love, they were so in sync, more the same than different. Keyes's dick drove the thought home by pushing annoyingly against the front of his jeans, threatening his plans for a slow, steady seduction. He took notice of the telltale hitch in Alec's breathing and the sexy as fuck way Alec drew his lip between his teeth in anticipation. Yeah, his guy was right there with him.

Alec hiked up his shirt, slipping the supplies into the waistband of his pants with a dick-pleasing little wink. He tugged the black Henley T-shirt over his blond head and dropped it to the ground next to the tire. Keyes groaned at the sight of Alec's bare chest in the moonlight and made his move, reaching for the flat brown disk, managing to pinch the tempting nipple before Alec grabbed his hand and pushed it down to his rock-hard cock. Fuck yeah, his man was as excited as he was.

"Mmm…I love how hard you are." Keyes squeezed the thick shaft in his palm, and Alec moaned his approval. "So fuckin' perfect." He bent in, licking across the flat brown disk then sucked the pebbled bud between his lips before flicking it with his tongue, drawing a ragged groan from his lover.

Alec tugged him up and his lover's soft lips brushed across his before taking his mouth in a demanding kiss that made his heart rate soar and his head swim.

Keyes deepened the kiss, wrapping his arms tightly around Alec, keeping him pinned right there. Every part of him wanted every part of his lawyer, and his sexy as fuck man met him move for move. Alec pushed him against the side of the truck as he took control of the kissing, eating at his mouth as they rutted wildly against each other.

Holy hell, his balls were going to fucking burst if he didn't hurry up and get this show on the road. Keyes broke from the kiss, gripping Alec's forearms, trying to slow them down as he took a step back hoping the distance would be enough as he ordered, "In the truck." The look of incredulity flashing on Alec's face made him chuckle. He got it, but the sooner they were in the truck the better for them both.

Keyes knew his lover couldn't be trusted to keep his hands to himself, but he let go of one of Alec's arms to tug open the door handle of his new truck, and sure enough Alec's hand went straight to Keyes already leaking cock. "Motherfucker!" The damn door was locked.

If Alec heard his little outburst, it didn't stop his lover's advances as he took the opportunity to attach himself to Keyes, kissing and mouthing his neck while those damn hands caressed their way over his body. Alec knew him too well, Keyes had to get them inside the truck or he'd lose the battle right there in the driveway while he frantically patted his front pockets in search of the key fob.

"It's locked," he managed to say, his body strumming under Alec's skillful assault. "I don't have the fuckin' key."

Alec's lust-filled gaze lifted. Keyes couldn't resist the temptation and leaned down to kiss Alec's passion swollen lips.

"Other door." Alec pulled from his hold, removing his warmth as he took determined strides to the other side of the truck. Keyes adjusted himself, took in deep breath of fresh air, and tried hard to control himself before he followed.

Alec lifted the handle...nothing. Best laid plans and all that. They both started laughing when they realized the driver side door was locked too.

"I'm not waiting for you to get the key." Alec's fingers were already at Keyes's hips, unfastening his jeans, and had him halfway freed from the restrictive material before his brain got on board with the new plan.

"But the truck..." He hissed as Alec's long sure fingers wrapped around him and started stroking. Fire boiled though his veins, and he canted his hips, pushing forward into the tightness of his lover's grip. "Fuck the truck."

"Round two?" Alec murmured against his neck. Since he'd stupidly left the key on the counter, it sounded like a perfect plan. "Now I understand the guys at the club who couldn't quite make it inside the truck because they were so hot with each other."

"Right," he agreed, eyeing the small patch of grass next to the drive.

The plush grass cushioned his knees as he dropped to the ground at Alec's feet. He removed the small foil packets from the waistband of Alec's jeans, shoving them in his own pocket for later as he wrapped his arms around Alec's waist and mouthed his stomach. Keyes inhaled, drawing Alec's scent in deeply—all arousal and all man, his man. Damn, such a heady mix. Alec was fucking intoxicating.

The need to feel him on his tongue had him eager to free Alec's cock as he sucked marks on the exposed skin below Alec's belly button. He kissed and nibbled his way across Alec's stomach and over his hip bones, before nipping at the material keeping him from his prize.

"You're so fuckin' sexy." Just a little taste of this gorgeous man before he took his ass was exactly what he craved. "Wanna taste you," he said, mouthing Alec's hardness through his jeans, smiling at the fingers already twitching against his scalp.

"Yes." Alec's hips shifted forward as Keyes drew back to see the reveal. The hiss of the zipper and the sound of their heavy breathing were amplified in the cool October air. A dog barked in the distance several houses away, but other than that, the neighborhood was quiet.

They were hidden from view from any nosy neighbors, which he knew with certainty because he and Alec had fucked on this very spot, several times over. Tonight though, he couldn't promise they wouldn't be heard. The need to push into Alec under the night stars had his dick leaking and his balls aching to be emptied. His feelings for this man overwhelmed him on most days. Today, even more so. His man took such good care of him on his birthday.

"Suck me." Alec gasped as Keyes worked his lover's pants and underwear down to the top of his thighs, exposing a gorgeous, thick cock that he planned on thoroughly taking advantage of.

"God, you're hot like this. All hard and leakin' for me." He stopped to take in the man in front of him, running his hands down the sides of Alec's thighs. Keyes leaned in and pressed a kiss to the spot where Alec's thigh met his groin. Keyes drew back, resting on his heels to look up at the only man who would ever own him. The man was so fucking perfect it made him crazy with need.

Damn, saliva filled his mouth at the sight of Alec's erection jutting from the dark blond thatch of hair. He loved the fact that Alec didn't overly trim or wax anywhere. He loved the rasp of hairs against his face and palms. Keyes raised up on his knees and grabbed Alec's ass, kneading the globes as he pulled him close enough to have his way.

He curled his fingers around Alec's thick shaft, admiring the bead of precome that glistened invitingly on the tip of Alec's cock. Keyes couldn't contain himself any longer. He stroked Alec a few times then dipped his tongue into the slit, stealing the pearl of moisture before taking the man to the back of his throat.

Keyes loved the salty taste of Alec's flesh gliding over his tongue. And the feeling had only intensified over time. He bobbed his head, concentrating on taking Alec down his throat. Alec held his head and thrust roughly into his mouth, gagging him. He grabbed Alec's hips and to give himself time. Tears welled in his eyes and ran down his cheeks, but he regained his composure and relaxed his throat, allowing Alec to do what he wanted and fuck his mouth.

The rougher Alec got, the harder Keyes's dick grew. He'd admit he got off on Alec's rough side; it only made him want to please his lover even more.

He caressed Alec's balls, delighting in the soft wrinkled skin that drew up against his lover's body accompanied by the little grunts and moans every time he rolled them in his palm.

Lifting his hand, he pushed his fingers between Alec's parted lips, letting the man get them good and wet, loving the way Alec's tongue curled around his fingers. The suction alone had him moaning around Alec's shaft, remembering exactly how amazing those lips and that suction felt on his cock.

He pulled away from the warmth of Alec's mouth and slid his wet fingers up Alec's crack, toying with the soft flesh around his opening before breaching him with the tip of his finger. Alec thrust wildly the deeper Keyes pushed his digits into his tight ass.

He took his time and worked him open using his fingers, adding another digit, until he was fucking Alec with three. He pressed lightly against the spongey knot, intent on drawing another sweet moan from those sexy lips.

"Oh, God…baby. Stop. I'm gonna come. Give me a minute." Alec's fingers tightened in his hair, sending a sharp bite of pain along his scalp as his lover pulled away.

Alec lowered to the ground in front of him, his dick bobbing enticingly, but Keyes didn't reach out to stroke it. He neared the edge too and had to have the minute to get himself under control. Alec's lips found his.

"Fuck me, baby."

"Turn around," he ordered, but then kissed Alec one last time before he could comply. He retrieved the lube out of his front pocket, his hands shaking with his need as he pushed his jeans down, allowing the fabric to bunch at his knees as he scooted closer behind Alec's parted legs.

As Alec situated himself, the tease wiggled his ass impatiently. Keyes rolled the condom down his cock, and with his teeth, he ripped the packet of lube open then spit out the corner as he squeezed the slick gel on his fingers.

Alec tensed as Keyes used his finger to push the cool lube into his lover's heat. He bent forward, kissing the warm skin of Alec's back, before running his nose up the side of Alec's neck, drawing in his fresh, clean scent. "God, you smell fuckable."

Alec's husky chuckle rumbled against his chest. "Fuckable?"

"Mmm-hmm. Extremely…fuckable," he confirmed against Alec's ear as he slid his cock up and down Alec's crease. Keyes positioned himself, and Alec leaned forward, his hands dropping to the ground to maintain his balance. Oh yeah, the bent position made it even easier for Keyes to enter Alec.

A small desperate whimper escaped his lips as Alec's body yielded to his and he pushed past the outer ring of muscle. All that welcoming heat engulfed him. The restraint it took to keep from slamming his hips home bordered on complete torture. Sweat beaded on his forehead and his legs shook as he fought for control, but Keyes held himself still, letting Alec's body adjust to the invasion.

"Fuck." Alec breathed out and started to move, forcing Keyes to hold his hips still.

"Need a sec." He was too turned on, without a minute to settle himself, he'd come before he got Alec off. Once he regained his composure and the overwhelming urge to come subsided momentarily, he moved in and out of Alec's body. Slow and deep, the heat drawing him in and squeezing him until he couldn't hold back any longer and started to fuck his lover with renewed intensity.

"Right there, baby." Alec panted.

Alec moved with him. Sex was a spiritual thing with them. Their chemistry had always been so perfect that he was sometimes afraid it couldn't be real. Alec moaned as he pushed in, rocking his hips deeper and faster, needing to feel Alec quiver around him.

He braced himself, using the side step of the truck for balance as he slammed his hips into Alec's body faster and faster. Keyes let himself go, pumping mindlessly into all that tightness. Unintelligible words and mumbled sounds fell from Alec's lips that he couldn't quite make out but fueled his need for more.

Keyes gathered Alec into his arms and pulled his lover up, thrusting with purpose as Alec's back met his chest. Alec angled his head and insistent lips met his, parting instantly to welcome his tongue inside. Alec's tongue slid along his, teasing and probing. Damn, the man could kiss. Alec had him balancing on a thread. He wanted to crawl into Alec's soul and stay there forever. No one could make him feel like this, so powerful, yet completely out of control.

"You make me mad with need. Want you to feel half of what I feel when I'm with you." He slid his hand down Alec's stomach and took his man's leaking cock in his palm. Keyes stroked in time with his thrusts. "I've never felt as needy as I do with you. I could stay buried in you like this forever."

If only he could. It was just a matter of time before he succumbed to the intense pleasure vibrating though his body. His resolve slipped away with every thrust of his hips.

Alec shouted his name as his dick jerked against Keyes's palm and hot come warmed Keyes's fingers. Alec's ass clenched around him, making stars cascade through his field of vision. White-hot fire shot up his spine and curled him over Alec's rigid form as he sank into his lover one last time. His orgasm hit him like a bullet train, almost causing him to black out from the force of his release.

Key's dick slipped from his ass, and even then, Alec had to wiggle to wake his heavy biker from the trance he'd fallen into. He jerked and grunted, using Alec's body to help lift himself up, his brawny arms then circled Alec around his waist like a vise, pulling him along as he sat back on his heels. Then he buried his face in the crook of Alec's neck.

Yeah, he liked Key just like this. Alec's hand came up, his fingers tangling in Key's long hair as he kept his man right there with him. "You're incredible. Had I known, I would've given you this truck months ago."

He got the desired results—Key chuckled almost silently and those sinful lips pressed against his skin, heating a path to his ear where he whispered, "Thank you. I'm sorry about my freak-out."

Alec tucked his chin to his chest and smiled, letting Key's warm breath and strong hold caress across his soul. Dear lord, he'd found his perfect one.

"Let's go inside. You're starvin' me."

Neither made a move, though. They stayed just like they were.

"Maybe just five more minutes."

CHAPTER 20

Alec sighed as he stood backstage with his siblings and their significant others, waiting to take the stage at his father's political watch party where Representative Pierce was humbly accepting his party's nomination, again. Apparently, Key wasn't the only one of them to be pressured into doing things based on guilt.

How Alec had let himself get roped into this was truly beyond him. His parents hadn't even asked him to attend. His father's campaign manager had phoned a little over five hours ago, wondering why he hadn't made it to Austin yet. Out of nothing more than guilt—absolutely not because of his father yelling at him in the background—Alec had dropped everything and rushed out the door, driving through rush hour traffic from downtown Dallas to Austin, Texas.

He'd barely made it on time then had to rush through the bowels of the rented convention center to stand with his family, waiting for their cue to take center stage with their father. The stress of the drive was nothing compared to the tense, awkward silence greeting him now. Not one single member of his family or extended family spoke to him. The pack stood huddled together about ten steps away, and there might as well have been a concrete barrier separating them. Alec stood to the side, phone in hand, staring at the screen while his entire family pretended he didn't exist. He didn't even rank high enough to get an occasional disapproving glance. They paid him no attention at all.

Alec checked the time on his wristwatch. How was it already ten forty-five at night? He couldn't help the glance toward his joyfully exuberant siblings, or the anger building inside him—maybe more a self-loathing than anything else. Why did he always drop everything to do their bidding when they called?

To avoid an unwanted scene, one fueled by all these hurt feelings he was experiencing, Alec opted to have Key there with him for support. He could get through anything with his biker only a screen away.

With phone in hand and a freaked out Key on live feed, he used his Bluetooth in his ear to talk. On poor Key's behalf, his guy had no idea what was going on. Alec wouldn't give his family the satisfaction of explaining for fear they might overhear his feelings had been hurt. Key looked skittish as hell, clearly afraid he might be seen, but Alec protected him from view, stepping as far away from everyone as he could and spoke of nothing important—the traffic getting to the venue, the suit he'd chosen to wear which also happened to be the one he wore to work that morning, and his plans to stay the night in the Hilton right across the street from the convention center. What he should be doing right now was booking a room. With his family's attitude, he had no doubt they hadn't thought to include him in their reservations. Hell, they hadn't even offered a lame apology for failing to inform him sooner of his mandatory participation in tonight's event.

"Okay, let's go," his father's event coordinator ordered, drawing back a side curtain.

"Are you ready?" he asked happily, staring into the phone. His badass biker looked paler than he had on his birthday, like he was truly going to pass out this time, and Key immediately started shaking his head.

"No, I'm not fuckin' ready, Alec. I'm hangin' up."

"I promise to make it worth your while when I get home," he said in his sexiest voice, not caring that he'd stepped within hearing distance of his oldest brother. He refused to be dissuaded by the hateful stares that instantly came his way. He didn't need any of them in order to have a family of his own. He adored the man staring back at him from the lighted screen. Key gave him the strength and courage to stand tall and let the rest go. His lover had such a genuinely alluring way of being the perfect partner who offered him everything he'd ever wanted in a relationship. His beautiful man, who happened to be wearing a ball cap backward on his head—a look Alec loved—had, in fact, not hung up the phone as he'd threatened to do at least twenty times in the last several minutes. Instead, he moved his body out from in front of the camera. Alec stared at the messy bed in Key's apartment, wishing he were in it. The television playing in the background relayed the election results and the night's win by their beloved representative Pierce. That was another point in Key's favor—he'd tracked the results all night long, keeping Alec up to date as he'd driven to Austin.

"Don't do this, Alec," Key growled.

"I love you too, honey." Key's startled eyes and stress-etched forehead came back into view, looking at him as if he'd lost his mind.

"What the hell kind of response is that?"

"Mmm." Alec stood at the back of the line with his heart pounding but feeling stronger than ever when his family was introduced. Cheers erupted as they walked out on stage. "Here we go!"

Key disappeared again, and in his ear, he could hear the delay on the event from Key's television. This hadn't been the landslide win his father had expected. The challenger had done a good job of building a destructive campaign against his father's lack of action, but in the end, his father had prevailed, and the ten or so thousand people in attendance tonight seemed excited.

Alec smiled, waved, and took his place in line, congratulating his father who smiled brightly at him, shaking his hand in a happy, hearty pump. He bet that killed his old man.

"That's your fake smile." Key yelled the words in order to be heard over the continued cheering. Alec dropped his phone inside his suit coat pocket, taking so much comfort in Key being there with him.

"You bet," he said, pretty certain he couldn't be heard.

"The screen's gone black. Can you still hear me?" Key yelled again. "Nod if you can."

Alec nodded, and maybe ten seconds later, when the crowd quieted to let his father continue speaking again, he heard Key's encouragement in his ear. "You got this. Keep that smile on your face. You look hot as shit."

A genuine smile tugged at the corners of his mouth at Key's appraisal. The brother who had so intently ignored him backstage, knocked him in the arm, pretending some sort of comradery as Key said, "You're the best lookin' one of the bunch. I bet they fuckin' hate that."

"You're good for my ego." Alec kept his smile plastered on his face not because he had to but because Key made him smile.

"What?" his brother asked, stealing some of his happy.

"Ignore him. Focus on me. Want me to sex-talk you right now?"

Alec laughed and shook his head no. To get a hard-on on stage would be horrible when his father's team replayed this night, picking apart every detail for the future.

Key laughed about ten seconds later. "Okay, lift your hand and wave to me."

He did, using the moment to look out over the crowd and wonder how the people gathered there would voluntarily choose to vote for his father.

"Okay, jump up and down."

"I'm not doing that."

"Flip off your father and punch your shitty brother in his smug face—that's what I'd do if I were there." The sinister tone Key took felt protective even if the words were shouted at him. But the place was settling down to listen to his father's over inflated ego go on and on about his win. Alec looked at the camera and lifted his finger to his lips, then gave a wink. Ten seconds later, Key chuckled into his ear. "Sorry."

"No problem. You're helping. I wished I could do exactly what you suggested," he said a little louder than a whisper.

"I've never watched anything like this before. I think you're tryin' to make me civilized."

Alec couldn't help the sudden burst of laughter. Both his mother and brother gave him questioning glances, and his father stopped midsentence to look back at him, uncertain what prompted such a response. That just made his grin brighter and his giggle continue.

After the delay, Key started laughing in his ear. He must look more ridiculous than he realized. That was all right too. Music playing and he looked around, his family had started toward his dad, so he followed, again shaking his hand. To Alec's surprise, his father clasped an arm around him, giving him a side hug, and he waved out to the audience. The campaign's photographer was there, snapping their happy picture of family unity. Such a fucking lie.

Less than twenty seconds after they were backstage, hidden behind the curtain, his father started in on him. "I'm getting past tired of your antics. Do you know what they would have said about me tonight had you not shown up?"

"I didn't know. It never even occurred to me that you'd want me anywhere near here tonight," Alec stated, immediately on guard and defensive.

"I doubt that very seriously."

Alec narrowed his eyes, wondering what he meant by that.

"Ryan, not here. He's always been rebellious. We know what to expect with him," his mother said, laying a guiding hand on his father's arm.

"What a fuckin' dick." Key's voice filled his ear. "Fuck that fucked-up shit. Now I seriously wanna lay that motherfucker out."

Alec watched his father roll his shoulders and shake his head at Alec in disgust before turning away. He wrapped an arm around his mother's waist and one around his sister's shoulders. His family was so in sync they just knew to move together, taking many steps away from him. Alec stood there, staring after them, and released a pent-up breath. Only then did he notice the staffers standing around, staring at him as if his very presence dampened the enthusiasm of the win. He tucked his chin to his chest and took off in the other direction, the way he'd come in.

"Why're you quiet? You're never quiet."

Because he had nothing to say. He had dropped everything he had planned, canceling an evening meeting with Reed and ditching his time with Key, all to come when his family called. It had taken him hours to get from Dallas to Austin during that time of day, and he was left with the same deep down hurt feelings he always had after being around his family. When would he ever learn? It seemed he wouldn't. He'd always be just like this where they were concerned.

"Are we still on video? Pull the phone out. Let me see you."

He pushed open the door to the convention center's main hallway, seeing a sea of voters making their way out of the building. They were happy, excited their candidate had won, and he saw the recognition on many of their faces as he passed by. Alec pulled the phone from his pocket and pretty much ignored everything around him except for Key's handsome face staring back at him with concerned eyes. That was the same expression he gave when Alec was upset over something and Key was lost as to how to help. He guessed that fit right now to a tee.

"I like when you wear that ball cap backward with your hair loose. You're hot."

Key nodded, a slight smile curled at the corner of his mouth, but he didn't let the compliment sidetrack him. "You're upset."

"I'm tired," Alec said and looked around for a side exit. He pushed open the first door he found, stepping out into the night, immediately searching his surroundings to try to get his bearings. "And I can't believe I have to be on the road in less than six hours to drive back to Westlake to meet Reed. It was dumb to come. I should've just said no."

"Hell yeah you should've said no to those fuckin' jackasses, but you're too good a man to leave 'em hangin'. It's that damn sense of loyalty you're cursed with."

Alec grinned at Key's astute assessment. He'd always thought he was fair. Times like these made him doubt himself though.

"Want me to come there? Or better, I could grab Dev and we could go fuck up some of their shit, just tell me where they're stayin' or tell me where they live. If they're there, they can't be here. Dev's been restless as fuck. He needs the outlet and you can trust he earned his fuckin' nickname."

Alec smiled at the sincerity in Key's tone and started around the building toward his car. He looked down at the screen, grinning at the visual image Key painted then narrowed his eyes as he realized Key might truly be serious. That was the dark side coming out in Key. Although it was incredibly sweet that he'd risk himself like that to support Alec, he had no doubt with even the smallest hint of a go-ahead, Key would do exactly what he'd just offered.

"I love you."

"How does that answer anything?"

"You know how it does. Thank you for wanting to defend me," he said, cutting through the grass toward the parking lot.

Key just stared at him with that same fierce expression he'd had when hatching his plan.

"What helps the most is to have you with me, even if it's on the phone." Alec made a beeline straight to his sports car, getting himself completely shut inside before he let his shoulders slump and scrubbed a hand down his face.

"How far is the hotel?" Key asked. Alec lifted his eyes to Key and his heart settled.

"Just around the building. You helped me, Key. Thank you." His finger went to the screen to run the tip along Key's cheek. "You need to sleep. I'll call you when I get on the road in the morning."

"No, call me when you get to your room." Key nodded, leaving no room for any action other than what he suggested.

"I'll text you then call in the morning. Go to bed. I love you."

He got his standard "Mmm" before Key said, "I got a better idea. Why don't I stay on the phone until you get in your room?" Key pushed back on his bed, scooting to the headboard. Alec shook his head at his mister who tried to care for him and decided to let it happen. Alec pressed the button, starting the car, and pulled out of the private parking lot. He loved that man, and he was so glad they were opening up to one another.

CHAPTER 21

"So, you've rented office space here?" Alec asked, tucking his hands in his slacks pocket as he walked side by side with Reed Kensington through Arik Layne's wing of the Layne Construction corporate offices.

"Somewhat renting, yes," Reed answered vaguely, holding the door open for Alec. He walked into an elaborately decorated office suite with a large mahogany desk in the center stacked with papers, blueprints, folders packed full, just everything conceivable piled on top. A small dark-haired woman sat commandingly behind all those stacks, phone to her ear and a finger swirling in air as she looked directly at Reed and continued talking.

"That's Iris," Reed said, and Alec lifted a hand her direction, giving a small wave. She smiled but stayed focused on the call, then bent her head to jot down notes with a pencil he hadn't seen her holding. "This is where our team will office."

Alec followed Reed through a side door that, from the outside, looked just like one of the many single offices he'd seen during the campus tour, but it wasn't. He was greeted with another small reception area. Four open doors ran along the back and side walls. Alec sidestepped Reed and went for the one of the center offices with an open door to peer out a large window.

"Great setup," Alec said as he walked into the spacious office that overlooked a small pond complete with a family of ducks enjoying the water. "What an impressive complex."

"One of the benefits of working with a construction company." Reed followed, hovering just inside the doorway. "This would be yours."

Alec nodded, keeping his gaze focused on the pond, trying to keep his enthusiasm in check. What a beautiful setting, far better than the fifty-year-old office equipment and dingy white walls of his current workplace. He also liked the idea of being off the Escape property site. There was too much distraction at the resort, the constant playful and enticing activities Arik Layne provided his guests could prove too tempting. They had work to do, apparently loads and loads of work if that front desk was any indication. He and his team would need to keep a single-minded focus if they were going to accomplish it all.

After a moment, Alec nodded. He easily envisioned himself here, saw his team with perfect clarity in his mind. "I see myself here," he repeated aloud for Reed's benefit.

"That's hopeful."

Alec looked back over his shoulder to see a grin crinkle the corners of Reed's eyes. This time, Alec stuck his hands in his slack's pockets and followed Reed back out into the reception area.

"From the first minute we talked law, all those months ago, I envisioned you in this spot. I think that's why I held this open. No one seemed to be the right fit."

"Thank you. That's nice to hear." Alec reached up to turn the light switch off and stopped mid-motion as the lights automatically dimmed. Very efficient, which also seemed to describe everything Arik Layne touched.

"It wasn't necessarily meant as a compliment," Reed said drolly. "It took you long enough. I was getting tired of waiting. So, do you have any more questions?"

Alec thought over the last four almost five hours of his interview. For a man who could find questions in anything, he had nothing left to ask. He and Reed thought so similarly that his potential new boss had over explained, covering all of Alec's bases. Even the salary was better than he'd expected, no negotiations required.

"I require a lengthy noncompete," Reed said as Alec came to stand directly in front of him. "Arik's a dear friend of mine. I've known him since I was a child. He likes a chase, and he'll most certainly try to lure you away. Now, he wouldn't know what to do with you after he got you, but that rarely seems to matter to him."

Alec chuckled, understanding the eclectic personalities of men in power probably better than any other person on this planet. His whole life had consisted of countermove after countermove. Taking this job would be a tremendous amount of work, maybe more than his current caseload in CPS. He'd be required to travel, not more than sporadically, but he'd have to fly across the world without much notice. The spontaneity of the job had its disadvantages, but Alec loved international law. He loved the complexities and detailed nuances. He loved the challenge of battling against set precedents and coming out the victor.

Alec heard a puppy yapping in the distance. The sound drew both Reed's and Alec's gazes toward the open door of the suite as someone entered the front room. Reed started chuckling, shaking his head as he turned back to Alec. "That's probably Arik. I heard about their newest addition—a puppy. Alec, I'm not rushing you, but Arik'll be here in a minute. Can I introduce you as head of legal?"

His heart leaped at the opportunity. This was exactly what he wanted. In fact, he wanted it so badly it made him nervous to accept. What if he couldn't handle such a job? He had a badass education to back him up, but he hadn't done much with it since graduation. His family had washed their hands of him. If that hadn't been made clear enough from his reception last night, he'd gotten a lengthy email from his brother after Alec had checked in to his room. Apparently, his abrupt laughter on stage had been ill-timed and had interrupted his father's stated declaration to follow his southern roots in every decision he made. Alec's brother hadn't minced words, making sure Alec knew what a failure he was. What if that were true?

Stop. If nothing else, Alec would put in enough hard work to beat the lousy opinion his family had of him. Besides, Westlake, Texas, was exactly the kind of area he'd imagined for himself and Key. This place was perfect. Everything was falling in line just as he had hoped. His dreams were within his reach, if only he'd reach out and grab them.

When he heard someone walking their way, Reed lifted his brows, and Alec gave one single nod of acceptance. Reed beamed at him, clapping his hands together then patting him on the shoulder as he turned toward the door. "Great."

"Do we have our guy?" Arik Layne asked.

Arik was as handsome as he'd been told. Very well dressed, bold and loud, owning the room both figuratively and literally. But the little puppy in his arms commanded all the attention. The little thing was tiny, wide-eyed, and very alert. Arik's affection for the puppy showed in his constantly stroking fingers, caressing the little one's head.

"We do," Reed answered proudly. "And I'll need a contract review to cover his enormous salary."

"Well, that's not gonna happen," Arik said dryly, his fingers momentarily pausing over the puppy's head. "I already pay you an arm and a leg and what most certainly feels like my left nut as it is." Arik seemed to dismiss Reed as he came toward Alec with his hand extended in greeting. "Arik Layne. Apparently Kensington does have what it takes to land you. I was afraid I was going to have to go around him and close this deal."

He couldn't help the laugh, Arik was so damn charming. He bet there wasn't too much that didn't just land at the guy's feet.

"Alec Pierce, and the pleasure's all mine." The handshake was solid, and Alec nodded in the puppy's direction. "Who's this?"

"Right now, his name's Little Bit," Arik said, lifting the puppy for a full inspection. "He was the most lively of the bunch, put himself out in front of the other puppies, always garnering the attention. He reminded Kellus of me, or so he said. Which honestly, I don't see at all, but he's ours as of yesterday. Kellus is my husband."

The puppy's whole body lifted when he turned his head toward Arik and barked. The puppy seemed fearless and in control of the room. Of course, Alec didn't know Arik well, but he saw the connection between the puppy and the man.

"Kellus is coming by to get him. He had his first vet visit today, but my husband had a delivery."

"Where did you get him?" Alec asked, reaching over to rub his tiny head. Little Bit yapped at Alec, then ducked his head for a thorough petting.

"Kellus's parents have a batch of them. They have two Bostons, a male and female. Apparently, something didn't take when they had her spayed. It was a surprise pregnancy." The puppy was so damn cute. His most immediate thought was Key and how his big guy would look holding such a little puppy in his arms.

"There're more puppies?" Alec asked as the idea formed. Were he and Key ready for such a big step?

With a mental shake of the head, Alec scolded himself...again. He had lectured himself for the length of the drive between Austin and Westlake to not let his thoughts shift to his lover during this interview. Key was a thought-robber, and Alec had to start putting the man in his place if he truly wanted to accomplish his goals for their relationship.

Even with the mental reminder, Alec couldn't let go of the image of Key holding the little puppy as protectively as Arik. Key would scoff at the idea of adding a dog to their lives, but Alec's gut said Key would care for and guard the animal with his life.

"Oh yeah, I believe they have three more. They're just six weeks right now. Kellus's mom is having a hard time letting them go. She wants to ensure they're going to good homes," Arik explained.

"I'm interested in one," Alec said, throwing caution to the wind. The pup seemed to move into his touch, causing Alec to smile.

"Here hold him. Just be careful, he's particularly bad about wetting."

Alec took the puppy whose little body quivered until he tucked him against his chest. He was adorable, and as sweet as he could be. Alec wondered if Key had ever had a dog of his own before. Alec never had. His grandfather had some, said one of them was Alec's, but he only saw him a few times a year during school breaks.

"So how about an early dinner to celebrate?" Arik asked and clapped his hands together, startling the puppy who reacted with an adjustment in his arms and a solid round of yapping. Alec wasn't sure what made Reed laugh, the dog, Arik's eagerness, or Alec's sudden need for a puppy.

"You gotta be careful of Layne, here," Reed said to Alec and hooked a thumb in Arik's direction. "He eats all the time. You'll gain twenty pounds the first month working here if you eat every time he wants to eat."

"I'm a food connoisseur," Arik confirmed with all authority, but his focus remained on the dog until Alec relinquished Little Bit back to Arik who carefully placed him on the floor and followed behind him.

"He's a garbage disposal is more like it."

Arik looked down at his watch and lifted his gaze while lowering his voice as if he were afraid to be overheard.

"No, really, Kellus is due here any minute to get Little Bit, and he's back on one of his strict plant-based diets. Let's go to dinner. It's close to five. We can be done by seven. Say yes." As if on cue, the main door to Arik's suite opened, and the newly quieted pup started yapping again, bouncing forward toward the sounds of people talking in the front room. "That's him. My treat. The Iron Maya's new menu is excellent," Arik whispered, staring at both of them, nodding to encourage their agreement.

Reed laughed uproariously, looking over at Alec and stating loudly, "You good for dinner?"

"Sure. I just need to make a phone call."

"Do that," Arik said excitedly and maybe with a bit of relief in his tone. "Take whichever of these offices for privacy then come meet Kellus." Arik was already scooping the puppy up while pivoting on his heels to head toward the main room.

"You're his excuse, so make it quick," Reed whispered, inclining his head before following Arik out of the office. Alec gave a nod while pulling out his cell phone. He looked around the office suite as Reed left. His hopes were so high at the opportunities being presented to him—maybe too high. But, man, this was coming together so fucking well... He grinned at how easily that word filled the inside his head. He'd need to be careful of all the swearing he had started. With the thought of Key, he quickly pulled up his contacts to call his mister.

CHAPTER 22

Keyes yanked up the front zipper of his Carhartt and tucked his hands inside the coat's pockets, staring out at the ominous clouds gathering above. A cold front, the first of the season, was expected—scratch that, a cold front had arrived, and it looked like rain. So much in fact that his parking lot had cleared out, not even a straggler left behind.

"Get everything inside, boss?" Louis asked.

"Yeah," he answered and started for the row of lift jacks along the outside wall of the building. Louis immediately barked out orders to the guys, getting everyone moving as thunder rumbled in the distance. He barely heard the phone ring, and by the time he pulled his cell out of the back pocket of his jeans, it was on its fourth ring.

"Hello," he barked over the rumble of the weather and started to grab the handle of one of the lifts when another of his staff came from behind him and took it from his hand.

"Hey, you," Alec said happily which was an incredibly good sign for as low as his mister had been this morning.

"How'd it go?" he asked, stepping under the awning as the first fat rain drop hit his face. He surveyed the parking lot, making sure all his equipment was inside before giving the thumbs-up to lower the overhead door as he stepped fully inside the building through a side door.

"Really good. I informally accepted the job."

That slowed his long stride to a stop.

"You didn't expect an offer today, right?" he asked, surprised.

"No. It's been a great meeting. I love this area. I think we could live out here."

Keyes remained silent. If he hadn't already known, he had learned since meeting Alec that he didn't adapt super well to change. As all of Alec's ideas and hopes firmed into reality, Keyes found himself unsteady. The silence he usually used whenever Alec talked about his plans proved ineffective at conveying his anxiety over such sweeping changes when they needed to keep their relationship hidden.

Keyes didn't know much about Westlake other than Texas Motor Speedway was somewhere around there. He and Dev had gone to NASCAR events a couple of times, and it was fucking far, but he suspected distance wise that Westlake and McKinney were about the same amount of miles from his shop. Traffic sucked either way he went.

Alec's laughter brought him back to the conversation. "You make me laugh when you get so silent. I spooked you," Alec declared confidently.

"No…" He tried to deny it. He wasn't necessarily scared, just needed a minute to settle into the idea, which spoke volumes to the comfort and care Alec handled him with.

"It feels like a longer drive, but I think it's about the same for you. Listen, babe, I called you because I've been invited to dinner with Reed and Arik Layne, the property owner. I'll be late at best. I didn't want you to worry," Alec said.

"I was gonna text you." A crack of thunder clapped hard, sending a rolling vibration rumbling through the street.

"What was that?"

"Thunder. It's startin' to rain." He looked over at the guys standing inside the warehouse, just kind of gathered together, and he nodded toward the parking lot, encouraging them to head out for the day. "I got a text. We got church tonight. I gotta go."

"What's goin' on with that?" Alec's voice filled with concern.

"Don't know. We're all expected to be there. I was thinkin' I'll probably stay down here though," he said, except he hadn't thought that at all. Last night sucked. He hadn't slept well without Alec there with him. He worried, and he liked it so much better knowing Alec was safe at home, and he was the one being called away.

"The meeting'll run so late that you can't come home afterward? I miss you, Key," Alec whispered, his happy tone turning to disappointment.

"You go enjoy yourself. Celebrate. You deserve it," he said.

"I'm gonna miss you," Alec said again quietly.

"Hmm," he murmured and tucked his chin to his chest, stepping out of the way as the guys left through the door he'd entered.

"I think that *hmm* means you're gonna miss me," Alec said, and Keyes gave a chuckle.

"Hmm," he murmured again in response, and Alec laughed.

"Okay, well, if anything changes, come home. We have a lot to celebrate. Or I could even come to you, but I know you won't let me."

"No, not a good idea. So, does this mean you're puttin' in your notice?" he asked, lifting his head, looking around the warehouse, so self-conscious of even indirectly talking about the DA's office out loud.

"Yes. By accepting this job, I've agreed to hit the ground running by January second. Listen, I've got to run. Call me later," Alec said.

"You call me when you're finished," he shot back and reached inside his jeans pocket to make sure the key fob was there. "Congratulations."

"Thanks, babe. I love you. Bye." The phone went dead as he pivoted around, heading back out the door. Louis was waiting for him on the other side, everyone else must have scattered.

"I'm headin' out too. The storm's supposed to last. Go home," Keyes suggested as the driving rain picked up in intensity. He got a lifted hand response, and Louis darted out of the building in the opposite direction of Keyes's new truck. He followed suit, locking the door then running across the parking lot as the clouds opened up, dumping a shit load of rain on him.

Keyes hurriedly jumped in the truck and hit the start button, staring out over the building. They needed something, maybe off to the side, that protected cars from the elements and kept business operating during bad weather. Maybe start with something big enough to hold a couple of vehicles. Make it covered, see if it was even needed. He dropped the gearshift into reverse and backed out, wondering what something like that would cost. Business was better, maybe he could afford it now. It'd be nice if he could start collecting a real paycheck again.

As he drove toward the club, he thought about what it would take to accomplish. He could ask his brothers tonight. With the club's help, he'd just be out the cost of the material. Couldn't be that hard. Keyes contemplated the ins and outs until he pulled into the parking lot of the clubhouse. He quickly shrugged off his warm Carhartt and donned his cold leather patch.

The rain hadn't quite made it to the clubhouse, and while walking inside, he used his phone to google the different kinds of designs available for what he wanted. His eyes locked on a rectangle awning setup that helped with wind gusts…

"Hey, man."

Keyes stared down at one of the prospects that sometimes hung out between Fox's shop and the clubhouse. He'd probably been introduced before, but Keyes had no idea of his name, so he lifted his chin and watched the guy open the clubhouse door for him. "Lookin' good in the new ride."

Keyes looked back at the truck, then again down at the guy. His brow furrowed. What a kiss-ass thing to say. That made him take a closer look at the guy, making sure he committed him to memory, just in case he made it out of the prospect stage.

"Right," he said, stepping through the door, turning back to the open room of the club.

"You're here early," Ace called out from behind the bar where Keyes found a stool and took a seat then resumed searching on his phone.

"Not by much. The rain shut us down early," he mumbled, taking the Bud Light put in front of him. "Know anything about an outside bay I could add to Tires?" he asked before taking a long drink. Even with the cold weather outside, the cold beer hit the spot.

"Talk to Hound. He's got a buddy," Ace suggested, resting two arms on the edge. "Or we could just add it. They have those pre-made kits. I wouldn't suspect it would take more than an afternoon."

"That's what I was thinkin'," Keyes said, tipping the bottle back for another drink.

"Hey," Dev said, taking the stool next to his. He reached over and instinctively slapped his buddy's hand, their standard lifelong greeting.

"Do you have time to fit me in?" Keyes asked, typing with his fat thumbs until he pulled up a picture he saved of a tattooed angel he wanted inked.

"Sure." Dev took the phone, getting a closer look. Keyes had been thinking about that particular design for a while now. This would be a first for him. He hadn't actually picked any tattoo currently marking his skin. He had always left it to Dev's discretion. "Where?"

"My back. Like across my upper back. I want the wings to tip out on my shoulders," he explained as Dev reached for his beer.

"Let me see," Ace said, taking the phone.

After Dev took his first drink, he said, "Yeah, it'll cover what's already there. I'll have to alter the design in the wings, but it needs to be big to look badass."

"Yeah," he agreed, taking the phone from Ace who gave him a nod he interpreted to mean he'd made a good choice.

"Send that to me. I'll work something up. When's Thanksgivin'?" Dev asked, looking at him, and he just shrugged. He had no idea of the date, and they both looked at Ace.

"I think in a couple of weeks, right?" Ace said, and Keyes again used his fat thumbs to pull up the date on his phone.

"Yeah, in a couple weeks," he replied.

"Can you come over Sunday?"

Alec would shit if he missed their planned day together, but he'd have to get used to it. The week and weekend before a holiday were always busy for the tire shop so he'd need to get this tattoo done before then, otherwise it might be January before he could carve out the time. People liked to buy all those fancy tires for their kids for the holidays. He wasn't sure Louis had enough of a salesman side to his personality. He didn't see him able to convince the customers to buy from their shop over the bigger name companies.

"I'll be busy with family matchin' ink from about next Tuesday through the Thanksgivin' weekend, so come early Sunday. Plan the time, it'll take me a while. Saw that new truck. That little kiss-ass said it was yours."

It took a second to mentally shift with the sudden change in subject. Keyes hadn't even considered the truck when driving over. Instead of acknowledging the new truck, he stuck with the kiss-ass part. "Yeah, little fucker. He's not gainin' favor with anyone, is he?"

"Your old man loves him," Dev said, tilting the beer bottle up for another drink. Keyes gave a humorless laugh and drained his beer. "All his recruits are just like that. Gainin' favor? Who says that shit?" Dev asked, laughing straight at him. "Tryin' to class us up?"

That was the other thing about spending time with Alec. He could tell his vocabulary was changing too.

"Fuckin' cold as shit out there." Mack came barreling through the front doors followed by Ray-Ray, Chain, and Hound. Keyes pushed off the stool, greeting his brothers with a round of fist bumps and hand slaps. He repeated the motion several more times as everyone started filing in. The clubhouse seemed to shrink in size whenever all the brothers were there. Fox came through last, phone to his ear with one hand and a finger shoved in the other. As everybody greeted each other, Fox's intense gaze landed on him, and his gut twisted. Fox looked away, over his shoulder, back to Ace who stood behind the bar.

His shit officially freaked as Ace yelled, "Church."

Oh fuck, what did that mean?

"Come on, man." Dev's arm locked around his shoulders, drawing him toward the meeting room. His most immediate concern was Alec. What if the club knew? Keyes jerked free of Dev's hold as Fox came in behind him. Keyes had become fucking lazy and content with his hiding. His pistol was locked inside the truck. It should be on his body. His heart sped up in panic, drowning out everything, even as Fox's hand rested reassuringly on his shoulder, giving a squeeze.

"Give me a sec." The hand squeezed again, and Dev looked over, catching the gesture. Keyes's intense gaze locked with Dev's. Surely if he was about to get the beatdown of his life, Fox wouldn't be so kind.

"Whatever you tell him, you can damn well tell me," Dev said with all the attitude that was Devilman. Keyes watched his buddy's chest swell in indignation. *Yeah, let's see how long that lasts if Fox brings Alec into the mix.* About half his brothers were already inside the meeting room, the other half turned at Dev's outburst.

"Holy hell, Dev. What the fuck's wrong with you?" Fox hissed.

"You can't just single him out—" Dev started, and Fox cut him off.

"Goddammit, sit your ass down," Fox ordered, grabbing Dev's collar and shoving him down on the barstool. Hmmm, that move changed things. Dev was known for his explosive personality. In all these years, Keyes had never seen Fox manhandle his son, not ever. While the action was wrong, it eased him. If this were about Alec, he imagined the brothers would already be beating his ass by now.

"Fuckin' pain in my goddamn ass," Fox grumbled.

Keyes slung out his arm, stopping Dev from rising as Fox turned to all the brothers then back to him and Dev. If his arm didn't keep Dev down, he suspected it would be two against the club. That wouldn't turn out good for either of them.

"Keyes," Fox started.

He looked up to Fox again who stood solemnly staring at him.

"That was the chick from hospice. Your old man passed."

Keyes blinked as the strange calmness from before washed over him. Relief blanketed him like a second skin. They hadn't found out about Alec. He closed his eyes, cocking his head to the side as the fear slid away, leaving optimism in its place.

"He don't give a shit. That sorry old man needed to die," Dev mouthed, clearly not reading the room. The rest of their brothers were in instant grief. Fox's vibrant eyes flashed on Dev, his jaw locked and his fists balled. Fox cared about Keyes's father. They were brothers with a long history and a deep friendship.

"Close your fuckin' mouth," Fox snarled, pointing a finger in his son's face, and Keyes clamped a hand down on Dev's shoulder to hold him in place.

"Is that why we got called to church?" Keyes asked, trying to defuse the anger between father and son. As far as he was concerned, his father's passing meant things just got easier in some respects and a lot more complicated in others. On one hand, he could start rebuilding his life without the constant insults. On the other hand, his dad had inadvertently given him an excuse to spend time away from the club which strengthened his relationship with Alec. The fear he experienced when seeing Fox walk through the door and look directly at him needed to be a reminder not to get too relaxed where Alec was concerned.

Keyes watched Fox take a mental step back before he took a full physical step away.

"No." Fox shook his head, wiping the anger from his eyes before he continued, "We've got other shit to talk about or I'd let us go. Smoke was our brother. We might've disagreed with him, but he was still one of us, and I gotta go deal with him first. Mack, ride with me. This reconvenes in two hours." Fox motioned toward Mack before looking down at his watch. "Be back here by eight."

Dev grabbed his arm as Fox turned to Keyes. "You have a need to deal with his body? Plan the funeral?"

"Not particularly," Keyes answered honestly, hoping the club hadn't expected him to. He was sure Fox had been made aware of his father's request that he take no part in the funeral, so he had to be asking out of respect. Fox gave a nod and started for the clubhouse door.

"Good?" Dev quietly asked when Fox left them standing there. Keyes gave him a look of hell-yeah-he-was-okay, and Dev slapped him on the back. "Let's go eat. My treat. The fuckin' dick is dead. And for what it's worth, man, I hope you know you're nothin' like him. You're strong where he was so fuckin' weak. And I know you, so when the guilt comes, and it's suffocatin' you, you better fuckin' know you don't have a goddamn thing to be guilty for. It's time to leave all that shit in the past and give yourself permission to breathe."

Keyes nodded and ducked his head, avoiding all the stares directed his way as they left the clubhouse. Let them think he was overcome with whatever the fuck they thought.

Maybe this was what freedom felt like, and it felt fucking good with the potential of great.

CHAPTER 23

Alec drove slowly down business highway 287 in Waxahachie, Texas, listening to GPS as he tried to read the street signs in the dark, not wanting to miss his turn. Of course, there were no street lights this far out. The angry wind whipped through the trees, fall leaves flew in every direction, and the unsteady street signs danced under the force of Mother Nature. He couldn't see a thing.

"Turn right in…" Alec flipped on his blinker and took the turn, hoping Google Maps hadn't screwed up again. For his first attempt, he'd been looking for a particular chocolate shop, a place Kellus had told him about, and ended up at what he could only describe as the neighborhood crack house. He hated being lost. It was already close to eight o'clock in the evening and seemed incredibly rude to show up much later than this, no matter if the sale had been pre-arranged.

Funny though, the Westlake area considered itself country living. Alec just shook his head. *This* was true country. Smaller homes on large chunks of land and lots of fencing indicating animals needed to be kept in. Not just pets lived around here.

Maybe as far at two miles down this side road the GPS alerted him of the upcoming address. It still took several hundred feet before he saw the mailbox. The address had been scratched off, which was about right, nothing could be easy. Alec came to a stop in front of the property. The home sat some distance off the road. Luckily, the porch light flipped on. He took that as an invitation and turned into the driveway, hoping he'd gotten it right. If not, he hoped he wasn't met with a shotgun for trespassing at such a late hour. Both seemed equally possible out here.

There didn't seem to be any clear parking guidelines. Alec pulled his sports car off the gravel drive and parked to the side of the house behind one of those Texas-sized trucks he saw all over the place and grabbed his coat. He got out, quickly slid his arms in, and pulled the full-length coat around him, throwing the wool scarf over his shoulders to ward off the icy chill in the wind as he started for the front door. Whoever said DFW didn't get cold was an absolute idiot. It was freezing outside. The cold wind made him shiver as he took the steps up the porch. Just as he reached up to knock, the door opened and a woman in her night robe motioned him inside with a warm friendly smile.

"Get in here. It sure is cold out there," she said, closing the door behind Alec before she asked, "You're Kellus's friend?"

"Yes, ma'am," he muttered, which was not something he said often. It just felt right to say now to this woman who somehow commanded his respect even in her night clothes. "I'm Alec Pierce."

"I'm Kristi. This is Paul."

Alec looked over to a tall man who was passed out asleep on an oversized La-Z-Boy in the living room a few feet away.

"Did I keep you up?" Alec immediately asked in a hushed tone, feeling like such a heel for coming so late. He should have waited until the following day.

"No. He's always out then up early. I'm the opposite. This is perfect, and you don't need to whisper. He won't hear a thing. A bomb could go off and he wouldn't wake." Even with the encouragement, Alec still couldn't find it in him to speak in a normal tone, so he nodded and smiled, hoping that was enough.

"Come on back here. They're in my back room."

Alec followed her down a long hall. All the doors were shut, even the last one at the end of the hall.

"I saw Little Bit. He's adorable. He stole my heart," Alec said.

"He is a cutie. Their mama's done with 'em. She wasn't a very good mom to begin with."

Alec had no idea what to say to that and opted for quiet again, wondering if that was one of the reasons Key always stayed silent.

She opened a door, revealing a room with both a table lamp and a heat lamp on. Alec skirted around her to the side of a large cardboard box where he saw three black and white marked puppies.

"See? She won't even get inside there with them."

Mrs. Hardin pointed to the cute Boston terrier lying on top of the bed. The dog must have known she was being talked about, because she rose then shook herself before jumping off the bed and exiting the room. Alec caught it all in his peripheral vision as his focus landed on one puppy who was staring up at him intently. The longer they were locked in the stare, the more he fell in love with that curiosity. The sweet little puppy cocked his head to the side, watching him. He held the pose until it proved too much, and the puppy tipped that direction, falling over on his back. That funny little guy had Alec grinning.

"Take your time. There's no pressure. I'll keep 'em all. My family just doesn't need to know my plan."

"Yes, ma'am," he said again, unwrapping the scarf and tugging off his coat. He tossed both on the bed before he dropped to one knee and stared at all three of the puppies. Alec reasoned he and Key needed a male. It just seemed easier, but as he stared at the one still focused on him, he wasn't certain that truly mattered.

"Hey there," he said, rubbing his cold hands together. That garnered all the puppies' attention, and Alec's grin spread. They were adorable. Not near steady on their feet, they toppled over each other to get close to him. He reached in, taking the one who'd been so attentive from the beginning. He lifted the puppy to his face and received a soft little yap. This one didn't even seem nervous to be held. Alec tucked the pup to his body and reached a hand over, petting the tops of the heads of the other two.

He had doubted this idea almost from the moment he committed to drive to Ellis County tonight. Even as he'd walked up to the house then to the bedroom, he hadn't been certain he needed a puppy at this time in his life. Adding a dog to his and Key's relationship, giving Key this pup, seemed a symbolic gesture of tying them closer together as they moved forward with their lives. Bringing an animal in the mix might even be stronger than wedding bands and vows. This puppy represented a joint commitment to care for another living being. It spoke volumes to his feelings and seemed right in line with the changes Alec was making.

Doubt was always there. Key wasn't much different than when they first met. It was Alec pushing for them to share a life together. Key still hadn't added a voice to his feelings, but Alec, as he did almost every day, pushed all those minuscule details aside. Actions spoke louder than words, and his lover's actions showed commitment and dedication. They just did. The man drove as much as ninety minutes, twice a day, to spend alone time with Alec. That said what the man couldn't.

"So you want to go home with me?" Alec whispered to the content puppy in his arms. His answer came by way of the puppy laying his head down on Alec's forearm before his whole body followed. The little one seemed to know exactly where he wanted to be.

"All right then, you're ours." Alec rose to his feet and reached for his coat. He was already so taken with the puppy that he didn't want to set him down long enough to put on his coat, so he shrugged it on while keeping hold of the dog. Alec reached into his pocket, pulling out the key fob to start the car, wanting the heater to warm the interior for their new arrival. The dog was so small Alec was afraid he'd lose his body heat quickly in the cold weather.

Alec carried the dog out to the front room where Mrs. Hardin was sitting in a La-Z-Boy next to her husband, watching television. When she saw them, her face grew excited. "You found one?"

"I did," he said, reaching in his side pocket for his wallet.

"Here, I have a blanket and a carrying case ready just in case," she said, rising to her feet. She took the puppy still resting on his arm. "You picked the last male."

"I hadn't even looked. He spoke to me from the minute I walked in," Alec explained, truly not caring in the least the sex of the animal.

"I thought for sure he'd be mine. He's kept his distance from everyone."

Alec was counting out his cash and looked up in surprise. That hadn't been his experience at all. Maybe destiny brought them together.

"How much do I owe you for the carrying case?" he asked.

"Nothing at all. He's also started his shots. The paperwork and a small amount of puppy food is inside here," she said, pointing to an envelope on the coffee table. Mrs. Hardin carefully wrapped the dog inside the blanket. The puppy kept his eyes on Alec the whole time. He placed the cash on the coffee table and tucked his wallet back in his back pocket before he took the envelope.

"I can carry him," Alec said when she started to put him inside the case. "It's cold out there. I'll get the case in the car and put him inside. I have it warming," he explained, folding the envelope to place in his side pocket.

"Very good then. I hope you get as much love from him as we have ours. They're wonderful little companions, smart and loyal." She carefully handed him back to Alec. He beamed at the Boston, now wrapped up like an Eskimo. Mrs. Hardin couldn't have been kinder as she handed off the case and opened and closed the door for him.

Once Alec got the puppy tucked away in the passenger seat with the heater blowing directly on the shivering bundle, he hit the road. Maybe ten minutes into the drive home, Alec split his attention between the Boston and the road as the blanket start unraveling and the little guy leaped from its hold, shaking his head. He was fierce, not frightened in the least. He looked all around until he found Alec then lay on the blanket, his head turned toward him.

"It seems you've been waiting on me. Or me waiting on you," Alec said, sticking his finger through one of the holes in the case, absently petting the little guy's soft head. He had a good hour and a half drive home that may have taken almost two with as slow as he drove. He had precious cargo in the car, and that seemed to change everything for him. Again.

"Church!" Fox called out, walking through the clubhouse about an hour later than he'd originally set for the meeting. Slowly, his brothers filled the meeting room. "Take a seat. We got shit to talk about," Fox ordered, taking his place at the head of the table. He dropped a heavy file on the worn wood but offered nothing more.

There was grumbling between the brothers. It was late for some. Others had spent the last three hours drinking, but for Keyes, he was just glad that no one was treating him any differently, and for the first time in his life, his old man wasn't there, throwing homophobic insults and making sure every one of his brothers heard shit about him.

Once the guys got settled, Fox started the meeting, going through the required protocol until the floor was given to him. He stood at the head of the table, looking at each brother before he pushed the file folder into the center of the table, older photos scattered across the top. "This shit came in the mail today. No idea who or where it came from."

Fox leaned over, and with a swipe of his hand, the pictures spread all over the table. Keyes wasn't close enough to grab one, all he could see were the photos were all of a younger Ray-Ray with a woman, the same woman in each shot.

"What the fuck's this?" Ray-Ray asked, defensive as hell. His chair scraped across the floor as he stood, reaching over the table, picking up several photographs.

"You tell us," Fox suggested, crossing his arms over his chest.

Mack rose, ran his hands over some of the pictures, shoving one particular one to Ray-Ray. Keyes looked around at the other members, but they looked about as confused as he felt when Ray-Ray shouted, "What the fuck, man? You gotta fuckin' give me more than this."

Whatever was going on, Mack seemed to clue in based on the anguish crossing his face. He dropped back into his chair, cursing loudly as Fox tossed out a piece of paper that had been underneath the file folder. Ray-Ray took it, and within seconds, he shouted, "Motherfucker!" And kicked at his chair, sending it slamming against the back wall.

"What the fuck's going on?" Hound asked.

"I didn't know," Ray-Ray said immediately, his burst of attitude turned to justification as he stared at Fox. "I swear to God I didn't fuckin' know. Honest, the whore was a fuckin' stalker."

"Goddamn, Ray," Mack said, crossing his arms over his chest.

"I fucked that whore a few times in the early nineties, man. She was a college chick that kept showin' up everywhere I was," Ray explained, shock in his eyes and desperation in his voice as he looked at each of his brothers, trying to make them understand. "I fucked her. She wanted to be fucked. I swear to God I didn't fuckin' know."

Dev rose from his seat, reaching across the table to rip the sheet of paper out of Ray's hands before taking his seat again next to Keyes. It took a second before Dev muttered the apparent sentiment of the meeting and handed Keyes the typed note. "Motherfucker."

Keyes read the aloud. "Donice Twiford—senior, University of Texas Dallas—current Dallas County District Attorney."

Whoa. That was a huge blow, and it took a second for the words to sink in before the room erupted in utter fucking chaos.

"I didn't know who the fuck she was," Ray exclaimed, backing against the wall.

"The shit you didn't," Hound yelled, and Chain had to hold the brother back as he tried to climb over the table to get to Ray.

"Fuck you," Ray-Ray yelled, his worry escalating to straight up anger as he got in fight mode, ready to take them all on if need be. "You remember every bitch you fuck?"

"I remember that goddamn bitch. She was over here lookin' for you for months," Hound said, and Mack gave a well-placed string of curse words to show he seconded Hound's statement.

"Then you fuckin' remember more than I fuckin' do," Ray shouted, his face turning beet red, his chest expanding and deflating with every breath.

"Goddamn's fuckin' right," Fox said. The prez was usually the one trying for order, but he was rounding the table with hands fisted. He was going for Ray, and Mack had to jump between the two men to stop Fox's advances. "This is why she's fuckin' on us. She's got a goddamn vendetta against you, asshole."

"It's not my fault. It could be any of us," Ray yelled.

Dev sat closest to Ray and had had enough. His buddy exploded. Luckily, Keyes was on it. Dev got one unexpected sucker punch in, sending Ray flailing against the wall before Keyes grabbed hold of his arm and collar, pulling him backward.

"Let me fuckin' go. Fuck you, asshole," Dev yelled at Ray. "You got us all fucked to shit this year. We're losin' our hold on this goddamn city, every other fuckin' club is gettin' our business…"

Dev clawed at Keyes to get back to Ray, ready to beat the shit out of the guy. Luckily, Chain and Hound were there, helping Keyes keep Dev off Ray.

"Stop," Fox bellowed, clearly getting a hold of himself. "Calm the fuck down. Everybody, calm the fuck down!" With help, Keyes pulled Dev back to his seat, shoving him down. Hound stayed on one side of Dev, Keyes on the other. The blame could happen later. They had to figure out a way around this.

Fox gripped the table, lowering his head, digging his fingers into the hard wood as he took a deep cleansing breath. Ray was the last one to take his seat, pushing it against the wall to keep an eye on everyone from a distance. Ray's nose and lip were bleeding, and he winced when he lifted an arm to wipe at the blood. No one else did shit to help the guy.

"We now fuckin' know what that bitch's problem is, but so do other people. There's a lot here, and I don't fuckin' know what to do with it," Fox said.

When Ray started to reach for a picture, Fox barked out, "Keep your fuckin' bloody hands off them."

Ray pulled back and finally Ace took the bar towel from his back pocket and threw it at Ray.

"After I got this in the mail today, I went to our attorney's office. She says we have Twiford, but we gotta wait. The club needs to keep a unified front, keep our shit clean for a minute fuckin' more, because we don't know who else got this information or what the motivation was in sendin' it. Hell, this could have been some fuckin' message from that bitch. We don't fucking know nothin'. If we aren't the only ones that got this shit, that means the media's gonna be all up our asses. If we release this ourselves, that means the news media's gonna crawl up our asses. If nobody else has this, then we release it on our terms, when we're ready."

"I swear to fuckin' God I didn't know," Ray repeated again, his voice distorted by the wadded up towel at his nose.

"Dammit, Ray. It took me a fuckin' minute, but I decided I didn't think you did," Fox said, but his jaw clamped shut as he stared daggers at Ray, and Dev released another string of profanity. Keyes held tight to the back of Dev's shirt, and Fox looked over at his son. "Calm the fuck down, Dev."

Oh man, that tone sent them back to schoolboy days, getting their asses handed to them for doing something wrong.

"So, do we all agree to keep this under wraps and see what happens?" Fox asked.

"This means we're layin' low a-fucking-gain," Dev yelled the words, bending in toward Ray.

"Pretty much, and no one lays a hand on Ray," Fox declared, giving another disapproving glance Ray's direction.

"How the fuck was I supposed to know that crazy stalker whore would wind up in this position?" Ray snapped, looking at the guys.

"Because we fuck club whores. Ain't none of us chasin' after college bitches," Hound yelled, and that got a rousing chorus of agreement, even from Dev which seemed a hard conflict of interest since he lived with a registered nurse.

Keyes's gut twisted at the inner turmoil. In all these months, nothing had really changed at all, except now, he was so far past the concept of letting Alec go that he'd spill his brothers' blood to keep Alec safe. Someone, somewhere was going to figure him and Alec out, and when they did, he would be sitting in Ray's position, blindsided. His palms grew sweaty with worry.

Stop, Keyes. Stop.

"How did I have any control over that? She's a fuckin' skank, was back then and still is now," Ray yelled, raising the anger level from about a seven to a solid nine.

"Goddammit, I said stop. We got other shit to talk about, and I'm not goin' on until everybody fuckin' agrees to lay low a little fuckin' longer. Does everybody goddamn agree?" Fox shouted angrily. A round of grunts was the only acknowledgement he would get.

"Next. We got some differences of opinion on who we are."

Keyes raised his brows at that. He had no idea what Fox was talking about and crossed his arms tightly over his chest.

"Hound, take over."

"Dammit, Fox. I don't want to follow that fucker," Hound yelled the last word.

"Tell 'em," Fox growled after maybe as much as a minute of complete silence.

"Some old lady was bein' harassed. I took care of it," Hound declared in an end of story kind of way that in no way explained how that made the club any different than minutes before.

"How's that?" Mack asked, skeptically.

"Vigilante shit that could've gone wrong," Fox answered, standing to his full height, crossing his arms over his chest.

"But didn't," Hound said, giving a full-attitude nod, daring any of them to say differently. "The cops came out, took a report, and thanked my ass for helpin'. She's blind and someone was robbin' her regularly, and I caught the motherfuckers."

"Hound thinks this is somethin' we could lend a hand in to get a better relationship with the cops," Fox explained and tossed out a hand toward the still scattered photos on the table. "We could use the fuckin' law on our side."

That got a round of grunts both for and against the idea.

"I ain't interested in what no fuckin' cop thinks about me," Ace said.

"Somethin's gotta give. This year's sucked," Chain added, driving the point home by hitting the table with his fist.

"It's been the worst fuckin' year in club history. Money's down by half," Fox explained.

Keyes nodded his disgust, but he really would have thought they were down less than half, and that was factoring in Fox's secret deals. His business savings account was depleted. He'd been digging into his saved cash just to make ends meet since the raid. If they went through another round of negative press, he didn't know how the tire shop would survive.

"I don't understand how gettin' friendly with the cops would increase income," Dev said, disbelieving.

"It wouldn't, but maybe the cops would keep some of this shit off us," Hound explained, and his tone sounded like he thought the rest of the brothers were a bunch of dumbass school children staring blankly at their teacher. "That's half the fuckin' battle anymore."

"The only way we get out from under this crap is for that intel to go public," Dev challenged, motioning to the pictures in the middle of the table. He had cooled down enough to point at the photos without lunging for Ray. "We need to leak it. Give it to the cops that gave Hound a nod.

They'll be the heroes in this deal, and they'll owe us or so they'll fuckin' think."

Dev was met with silence.

"Noted," Fox said, but shook his head no. "We're gonna wait like our fuckin' attorney advised. And I agree with her. We gotta see how many of these packets are out there and what's their purpose. Devilman, you ain't wrong, son, and I agree with your approach, but let's give this a week, maybe two, to see what shit hits. If this is still silent at the end of fourteen days, we'll decide the next course of action. The way I see it in my head, we go confront that bitch straight up and threaten to leak it to the news if she doesn't back the fuck off ASAP," Fox explained, and got a round of nods and another chorus of grunts. Fox pointed to the photos on the table. "That shit's gonna destroy that loudmouth bitch."

Destroying DA Twiford seemed to draw the most favor from his brothers based on the new round of *fuck yeahs* going on. "Now about Smoke. We got a graveside service in seventy-two hours. I tried for faster—couldn't make it work. I've already sent out a notice and enacted a truce. We'll see who comes. If the local news stations hit Ray-Ray's girlfriend, we meet that day. If not, we're back here at noon on Saturday. Funeral's at two."

That received a unified round of *rest in peace*. Chain squeezed his shoulder, but otherwise he was left completely alone which was exactly what he wanted. Fox ended the meeting and Keyes got to his feet, the only thing on his mind was whether he should go to McKinney tonight.

"Let's go draw your design, man. Have a beer," Dev said, shoving his chair under the table.

"What about your chick?" he asked, following Dev out of the room.

"She thinks I'm out for a while," Dev said, slapping his father's hand as they passed by. He felt Fox's attention on him. He figured most of the older brothers worried about him being a ticking time bomb. He just flat wasn't. The relief had only grown, making even his concern over being in Ray's position lessen. He'd hated his old man with a vengeance, and now he was gone.

"Cool," he finally said and lifted a fist to bump Fox's extended knuckles.

CHAPTER 24

Juggling an armful of pet supplies, Alec came through the garage door as Olivia darted through the living room, her hands stretched out. "Let me help!"

"How is he?" Alec asked, handing the bags full of dog toys, collars, leashes, just everything the new addition to their family might need. When she took those, he was better able to get a hold of the twenty-five pound bag of dog food he'd felt compelled to buy.

"He's sleeping in your closet, like you asked," Oliva said, taking the bags to the kitchen island.

"Did he settle in or does he seem scared?" Alec asked, bypassing Olivia and going for the kitchen pantry. That was where people kept their dog food, right?

"Not at all. He loves that house shoe you gave him. He climbed right on top to sleep."

Alec left the dog food in the pantry, going for the sacks. He hid those before digging inside the bag for a couple of the items he purchased. "Can you wrap these for me?" he asked. "The wrapping paper is…somewhere."

"In the hall closet, and yes, I'll leave them there."

"Perfect," he tossed over his shoulder as he went for his bedroom closet where his baby Boston had naturally seemed to gravitate to last night then again this morning. Alec quietly opened the door, peering around the doorframe, staring down at the little guy who slept inside a paper lined box. His soft house shoe had been an immediate favorite, and he was, in fact, sleeping soundly on top of the shoe. He had a blanket in the corner and small bowls of food and water.

Alec had learned last night that puppy sleep was a different beast altogether. Twice over the course of the night, Alec had freaked himself out when he woke to check on the little guy and he'd just seemed to melt away, losing all the bones in his body, passing out fast asleep on his back, and nothing seemed to wake him. The first time, he'd actually grabbed the dog up, startling them both in his panic. It had taken a full hour for Alec to fall back asleep, only to be awakened again with the same fear.

As much as he regretted having to leave, Alec quietly shut the door and headed back out to find Olivia. "I'm going. I'll be gone about three hours. Keep an eye on him, and can you please take him out to potty like we discussed?"

"My sister's dog was potty trained in two weeks," she stated proudly, something Alec found incredibly hard to believe, but also had no knowledge-base on potty training anything.

"Thanks, Olivia. The caterer should be here about three. They know what to do, just let them in if I'm not back, and call me if you need me. If Key gets here early, do everything you can to keep him out of the bedroom," Alec instructed, reaching for the key fob in his slacks pocket.

"Mr. Key never comes inside," she said in that same proud tone. "He won't see him."

Alec didn't doubt that for one minute. On the rare occasion that Key beat him home, his mister was always out somewhere on the property. The only time Key willingly came indoors was to follow Alec in or to grab the keys to the locked garage holding his prized automobiles. Key had recently taken over their care, and he wasn't sure they had ever been treated so well. He changed the oil every six weeks like clockwork. It didn't matter that the Shelby was driven less than two miles between changes and his Maybach was driven by Alec as far as the grocery store and back, Key never missed an opportunity to tinker under their hoods. Maybe he should put the puppy in the garage. Key would definitely find him faster.

"Thank you for all your help," he said as his phone rang. He answered through Bluetooth while walking toward the back door. "Alec Pierce."

"Hey you," Janice said. "I'm returning your call."

"Keep your ears open," he said, cheekily. Alec grabbed his suit coat off the kitchen chair, doing a quick glance to make sure the envelope with his resignation letter was still inside.

"Oh, it's today. Goody. Did you remove the b-word from your letter?" she asked, chuckling.

"I regretfully did," Alec acknowledged, and it *had* been with deep regret. The word fit the DA better than any other he could think of.

"How did yesterday go. Did you get an offer?"

He liked Janice so much. She was such a good friend, maybe better than even Blaine, and she was very down to earth. Her soon to be husband owned a lawn care company, so he suspected Janice would have no problem with Key's blue collar background.

"I did and accepted on the spot with no regrets."

"Great! Alec, this is going to be life-changing for you."

"Absolutely, it will. I'm on my way in," he said, getting behind the wheel of his car. "I've got a couple of things to tie up first, then I'll submit my resignation, so maybe in about an hour and a half. Keep your ears open and let me know what you hear," he said, pulling down his long driveway.

"On it, and listen, Alec, I know you've stuck around because of the Cummings case, but Betty Young agreed to take the case for criminal. She'll do her absolute best for you. I'll work with her and stay on it, I promise. Let this be enough," she said. Her voice had lowered, and he smiled at how well she knew him when she really had no idea the truth behind what he had done.

"You're a good friend," he said, starting the car.

"Remember that. I'll call you if I hear anything. Bye."

Alec slipped the car into gear, pressing on the gas as he drove down his driveway. Janice had never known the half of it, but he appreciated her efforts nonetheless. He drove through his neighborhood toward the highway, marveling at how well his dreams were falling into place. Now, he just needed Key to relax and let things happen. Honestly, he didn't see that happening, but maybe... Alec just shook his head, needing to be forward thinking and completely prepare for all Key's arguments. That had his grin growing. Life was never going to be dull with that man.

Alec stood in the window overlooking his patio with the puppy in his arms, waiting on his lover. Adrenaline strummed through his body, making his leg bounce with the anticipation of the night. The most current obstacle in his way was that it was already six thirty and Key was nowhere to be seen. He supposed that was most likely traffic's fault. Key had opted for the truck due to yesterday's rain, which at the time, even being in Austin with his awful family made Alec unreasonably happy. Then came the text about the time it took Key to get to the shop. On his bike, he could zip in and out of traffic. He used high occupancy lanes and rode the line between vehicles to help cut his driving time. The truck didn't allow for those conveniences, and that wasn't anything Alec had anticipated.

When the truck turned the corner of the drive and pulled toward the garage, Alec found the other fault he had with the truck. The pipes of the Harley were so distinctive they could be heard from miles away. Not so with the truck, and Alec dashed from the window toward his bedroom, carefully placing the puppy in his box.

"Be good. Stay quiet," Alec instructed then paused, looking down at the puppy as if he might somehow respond. Turns out, he didn't need to ask. The little guy had been up with Alec for hours, so he eagerly curled up on his house shoe and closed his eyes. Alec carefully shut the closet door, hoping to save the surprise. He left the bedroom, shutting that door behind him as Key opened the back door.

"Alec!"

"I'm home. Come in," Alec said quietly, moving around the furniture toward the kitchen. "You're later than normal. I was getting worried."

"It's the truck. I had to fight the traffic. It sucked," Key said, hooking a thumb over his shoulder, coming to a stop as Alec approached.

"Hmm, I bet. I'm sorry," Alec said, placing both hands on Key's pecs, lifting his chin for a kiss. Key didn't hesitate as he shrugged off his coat, dropping the Carhartt on the back of a kitchen chair—which seemed to be its regular hanger.

"I should clean up," Key said, and Alec looked down at Key's work clothes. That was something else he hadn't prepared for that threw an immediate wrench in his surprise plan.

"Well, you can't do that," Alec said and stopped speaking before he finished the sentence, racking his brain for something more to say.

"Why?" Key stood directly in front of him, his hands going to his waist with attitude.

"I've done some planning and preparing...a surprise. You can't go in the bedroom." That had Key furrowing his brows. "I can get your clothes and you can go upstairs."

Key continued to eye him, then looked around the kitchen. His gaze landed on the several covered dishes warming on the stove before he turned back to Alec. "What're you up to?"

"Let me get you a change of clothes. Shower if you must, but make it quick and in the guest bathroom. I'm ready to get started." Alec moved quickly, careful to open and shut doors as quietly as possible. He went for the closet. In stealth mode, he tiptoed inside, keeping his eyes locked on the sleeping puppy, ready to leap and grab him if he woke. He slowly reached for a pair of jeans then for one of Key's tight-fitting tees, a favorite of Alec's because it brought out the unusual color of Key's eyes. He made an executive decision to forgo underwear or socks and shoes. Those would just be wasted time in removing.

His heart was pounding, and once he closed the bedroom door behind him, he gave himself a good internal laugh at his ridiculousness. Such a dork. He should just show Key their new puppy and stop playing games, but seriously, where was the fun in that?

Alec put the clothes on the kitchen bar, watching Key drop two bacon wrapped shrimp in his mouth. He covered his mouth, and said, "I love those things."

"They seemed like something you'd like. Go," he said, pointing to the stairway at the front of the house. "Use the upstairs bathroom and hurry. I'm starving. I missed lunch."

"I'll just change down here," Key said, going for the hall bathroom.

"Good. I'll get you a drink and set the table." His anxiousness was showing. Key even gave him an odd look and placed a palm on Alec's chest—Key's way of checking his heart rate. It had to be elevated, no news there.

"Get," Alec said and cocked his head to the bathroom. After Key shut himself inside, Alec rolled his eyes again at his own stupidity, then headed for the liquor cabinet. He poured himself a shot just to relieve his nervousness.

Alec remained antsy even though he'd gone through two full glasses of wine in less than thirty minutes. Clearly, he had something big to share, but he was doing his normal stretching out the anticipation thing he got a big kick out of. So, Keyes sat in a state of tension, because this could go two ways. Either the surprise was really great or he'd be dropping his head between his knees, praying he didn't pass out. Man, Alec could stress him the fuck out as much as his brothers did.

"When are you gonna tell me what's up?" he finally asked, shoving his plate back a couple of inches to rest his forearms on the table.

"I'm nervous, and I'm messing this up," Alec answered, adding a second helping to Keyes's plate.

"Nothin's messed up," he assured him, trying for encouraging, reaching for the shrimp Alec added to his plate. "You went to a lot of trouble for a weeknight dinner. It's nice. Just tell me what's goin' on."

Alec put the spoon back inside the bowl and raised the napkin from his lap to his lips. He then reached for his wine glass before sitting fully back in his seat. Keyes watched Alec gather himself and followed Alec's lead, mimicking his actions by picking up the glass of water nearby before taking a hearty gulp.

"Well, first, I tendered my resignation today," Alec said.

"How do you feel?" Keyes watched Alec closely. He doubted the resignation had anything to do with his current state of anxiety.

"Good. Really good." Alec nodded then nodded again. "I also formally accepted the new job. I signed my offer and emailed it back to Reed."

Keyes's smile erupted at that news. He pushed his chair back several inches and reached for his pilsner, lifting the glass in toast to Alec's huge accomplishment. "That's great. Everything was like you wanted?"

"Better than. It's ready to pick up and run with. The money was right. I toured the Layne Construction campus—it's beautiful. I'll office there and couldn't ask for better. Are you familiar with the Westlake area?" Alec asked. It wasn't the first time Alec had brought up Westlake, but it was the first time he'd questioned him about the area.

"NASCAR and country. That's all I really know."

Alec grinned at him and nodded, staying silent.

"So, when do you start?"

"Soon. I'll begin immediately learning the ropes and transitioning files over. I'll be super busy until the end of the year. Some of my staff will be relocating from the DC area. I'll have to go up there for a couple of days...soonish. My official start date is January second but Reed's secretary has already started making contact. My last day in the DA's office is December fifteenth."

"That's great. Will they pay you for the work you're doin' now?" he asked.

"Oh yeah, the salary started today," Alec added with an exaggerated nod.

"That helps."

"It does. You know, I've been vocal about my shifting priorities since we met. I'd like us to live off what I make."

Oh, the topic just took an unexpected turn. No... The talk of money stressed him out. His shop barely covered the cost of Dev's crappy one-bedroom apartment. He'd hired all those workers to help cover all the time he was gone. He'd be forced to dig into his super-secret funds before too much longer. Keyes couldn't see ever making much more than he made right now.

"I should be helpin' pay the bills around here," he found himself saying, thinking about the money he made from Fox's side deals. He lifted his beer, taking a drink, wondering if those secret runs would continue once the club was able to shake the DA and could once again be a little more open with his brothers.

Yeah, the idea of losing that extra money had him tipping the beer, draining the glass.

"Why in the world would you ever pay a bill here?" Alec's cool demeanor morphed to a look of disbelief, as though the suggestion were absurd. "You kept your apartment. You haven't officially moved in."

"Most of my shit's here," he stated matter-of-factly, rising, taking his plate and glass to the sink, going for the refrigerator for another beer. "I just keep that place for show. I come here every day."

Why was he arguing against the out Alec had just given him?

"Where did you sleep last night?' Alec countered.

That stopped him and his bravado in his tracks. Damn. Keyes looked up to see that familiar cock of Alec's brow, proving he knew he'd won that argument.

"If you lived here, it wouldn't have mattered what time you got out of the meeting last night, you'd've come to your home. Same with me going to Austin. You didn't stay here while I was gone. If it were your home, you'd be here."

Keyes eyed Alec closely, some of the happy from minutes ago was gone. Okay, this conversation had taken a wrong turn somewhere. He sucked at the twenty-question game Alec pulled off so easily. On that theory, Keyes remained silent until he took his seat, and then teased Alec, hoping to turn this night around.

"You think you're so smart. Keep goin', what's goin' on tonight that you're still hidin'."

With a cocky little move, Alec popped a shrimp bite in his mouth. His nervousness was gone as he reached for the wine bottle and poured himself a refill. "I think we can stay right on the *you think I'm so smart* for a minute more. Let me bask in my victory."

That was one of Alec's finest qualities. He didn't allow himself to wallow in anger or stay upset for long, and Keyes barked out a laugh, choosing to contradict him. "I think I said... you think you're smart."

"You've been hanging out with me too long if you're picking apart every detail." Alec stood with the wine glass in hand, giving him a wink as he bent over, coming within inches of his lips. "Come on. I have more to say. Let's do it in the bedroom." Alec took his hand, pulling on him until he reluctantly rose. If sex were involved, he'd have gotten a kiss. So, he was back to wondering what the hell was up as he grabbed his beer for liquid courage.

Funny, he was a badass biker who had people scattering when they saw him, yet this refined man who had never seen the end of a fist somehow regularly brought him to his knees, and he didn't even seem to care. He voluntarily let Alec continually surprise him even though he fucking hated being surprised, and that was because it made Alec happy. When Alec encouraged the twist of their hands, entwining their fingers, Keyes let that happen, too, even as his anxiety built at a rapid pace.

"You've been busy."

"I didn't like sleeping alone so I stayed awake," Alec said, his voice growing quiet as he got closer to the bedroom.

"Quit tryin' to sex talk me," he teased, and Alec shot him a brilliant smile over his shoulder as he opened the door. Alec stopped right inside the door, and Keyes craned his neck to see inside. His anxiety immediately lessened. Wow, okay, he could be into this. Alec had gone all out in the romance department. Rose petals carpeted a path to the bed, the only light in the room came from the soft glow of candles, very soft classical music played and champagne sat chilling in the bucket along with several longneck bottles of his favorite beer.

He guessed Alec was breaking their recently established no sex after eating rule. "Why did you do all this?"

"The night requires romance." Alec didn't let him go, moving forward, guiding him toward the edge of the bed. There had to be a hundred candles flickering, all over the bedroom. "I got you a gift. Sit down."

Oh hell, another gift. His anxiety swirled as he lowered to the edge of the mattress, his body tight with tension. Why was Alec buying him more gifts? He hadn't bought Alec shit since they'd started dating. Now he'd be two down. Keyes stared at the small brightly wrapped boxes Alec extended. He hesitated. Small things could be as expensive as the big things. He didn't take the gifts immediately. Instead, he looked up at Alec and asked, "What's goin' on?"

"Seriously, play along." Alec ignored his question and placed the gifts in his hand. When he started to say he'd gotten that ridiculous gift sitting out in the driveway, Alec shook his head, and nodded to the present in his hand. "Unwrap."

Keyes leaned over, placing his bottle of beer on the nightstand, then reluctantly unwrapped the box as Alec left him sitting there. Alec got a new job and he got a gift? That made no sense at all.

"Keep going," Alec encouraged quietly from the closet door. Keyes lifted the lid to find a small leather collar and leash inside. It took a second for him to digest, then suddenly he better understood what tonight was about. Sex toys. They were celebrating Alec's good fortune and taking their relationship to the next level sexually. He nodded— totally into the idea as long as he wasn't the one tied up— and immediately reached behind his back to tug his T-shirt over his head. Whew, all the anxiety fled. He'd dodged a bullet in this deal.

CHAPTER 25

Alec pushed open the closet door. The little pup was curled on his new doggie bed and had somehow managed to wrestle and move the house shoe over to the bed with him.

"Sorry to wake you, but it's time," Alec whispered, marveling like he'd done every time he picked up the tiny puppy at how small and light he was. "I have a feeling you and he are going to be the best of friends."

Alec came out with the puppy tucked against his chest to discover a shirtless Key unbuttoning his jeans, the collar and leash lying on the mattress behind him. What in the world about his gift had made Key disrobe?

"Baby, I have someone I'd like for you to meet," he announced as he walked across the room. He came to a stop in front of Key.

The range of expressions crossing Key's face might have been comical in another situation. Key took a step back, legs hitting the mattress as Alec stepped closer.

Wanting to avoid any potential panic attack, Alec carefully handed his precious cargo to Key.

The dog wasn't much bigger than Key's work-roughened palm, and for the first time since Alec had met their little guy, the puppy began to shake. Maybe it had to do with the fierce expression marring his lover's handsome face.

"Take him, babe. He's ours."

Key finally accepted the puppy, his strong arms cradling the little guy, bringing him to his chest. Key's still tense gaze lifted to his. He didn't need words to understand the question, but Key's focus immediately shifted his attention back to the dog, his thumb rubbing across the pup's tiny head.

The sudden doubt over what he'd done in bringing the dog home vanished. The puppy looked up, craning his neck until Key bent in enough to look the dog in his face. The little guy gave Key that same soul-touching gaze he'd given Alec last night. Key slowly sat on the edge of the mattress, his whole attention fixed on the bundle in his hands.

Alec circled the bed and kicked off his shoes before climbing on the mattress from the other side. He purposefully stayed silent to give Key a moment as he stretched out across the end of the mattress, resting his head on his hand, and waited for whatever was to come next. It took some time for his big, rough and tumble biker to form any words.

"What's his name?" Key asked, looking down over his shoulder. Alec patted the bed beside him, encouraging Key to move closer.

"I don't know. What should we name him?"

In true Key fashion, it took time for him to turn, then to carefully and gently place the puppy on the bed between them before stretching out on his side to face Alec. The puppy turned a full circle then yapped at a rose petal that had followed Key onto the bed.

"I thought that was for my dick," Key grumbled, pointing at the collar and leash on the edge of the mattress. It took a second, but when it hit him, Alec couldn't help the laugh. That possibility had never occurred to him. He excitedly filed away for later Key's apparent willingness to play. "What's goin' on?"

Alec's heart was so full in that moment. He stared at his man as warmth washed over him. Their love, at least for him, was a forever and always kind of love. Alec reached across the bed to take Key's hand. They both grinned when the puppy went on the defense, turning to yap at their joined hands. "Key-baby, I want a life with you. I want a family. I want to be your reason, and in return, you be my reason. These changes I've made, they're to remove some of our obstacles and to keep us together—you know all that." Alec nodded toward the now wide awake puppy that growled and jumped on their hands. "He's to help remind you of where we are, and that we're here, waiting on you to get home."

"Alec..." Key's expressive face softened as he tightened his hold on Alec's hand. At the same time, the rose petal moved, and the puppy turned his attention from their joined hands. His bark was so powerful it lifted his front paws off the bed—the perfect mood lightener. The sudden outburst had Key grinning from ear to ear. They watched as the little guy dove for the petal, missing his mark and landing straight on his face. "He's perfect."

"That's what I thought too."

"What's his name gonna be?" Key asked, releasing Alec's hand to pet the puppy. "I always wanted a dog growin' up."

"Me too. I've never had one. You name him." Alec encouraged, wanting more than anything for Key to name this little guy.

"What do you think?" When the puppy steadily got to his feet, Key ran his fingers along the mattress toward the little guy, watching the puppy back away until he finally gathered enough courage and held his ground. What sounded like a mix between a yelp and a growl was all the warning he gave as he leaped forward, attacking. Key chuckled as he moved his fingers across the bed again and the puppy backed away.

"He's got a ways to go before he's a fierce guard dog."

Alec laughed, watching the puppy brave up and attack before scurrying away when Key did it again. Alec had done the right thing; his heart filled with the perfectness of the moment.

"When I was a kid, there was a stray in my neighborhood. I named him Nash. It was short for Nasty because that's what everyone called him. I loved that dog."

Alec didn't question anything about the stray, especially while watching Key's expression turn nostalgic. He'd learned those stories ended with his heart breaking for the little boy.

"Perfect name. Nash, it is."

Key grinned at the same time something caught the pup's attention. It took a second for Alec to realize it was a candle's glow flickering on the bedspread, drawing Nash's attention this way and that, causing Key to laugh straight out loud.

"He's perfect." Even Key's loud outburst didn't sway Nash from his pursuit of the shadows crossing the bed.

"He is." Alec reached out again, taking Key's hand. "He needs you here, babe. He needs this to be your home."

"Alec…"

"No. Listen to me. When I was in Westlake yesterday, I saw our future so clearly there. We don't need all this house or this pretentious neighborhood. I see a large backyard, a huge shop, a place to store all our vehicles, for you to work on your bikes, and lots of land separating us from our neighbors," Alec explained, painting a mental image of his dream with Key as he spoke.

"Alec..." Key said softly. "What would your family think?"

"Who took care of me when I was with them? You saved me from falling into a deep depression after spending twenty minutes with them. I don't care in the least what they think."

"Alec..."

"No. I anticipated the skeptical look, but I won't be swayed. I see us as long-lasting, maybe even becoming a family. You, me, this little guy, and possibly children someday." Maybe he'd gotten ahead of himself and said too much as Key moved back several inches, instantly raising those concrete barriers between them, completely separating him from Alec. "No, babe, listen to me. You know you feel it too. I've changed. You've changed. My world's gotten much smaller, but given me so much more in return—it's given me you."

Key started to rise, scrambling to push himself off the bed. Alec reached out, palming Key's cheek, his thumb smoothing over his lover's beard. Alec's gentle touch stopped Key with as much power as a forceful hold, which showed just how much his big strong biker truly respected him.

"I can't ever make you understand. I'm a biker. That's what I am. That's all I'll ever be," Key said, desperation in his voice.

"Have I asked you to change?" Alec asked, looking down at Nash who sat watching them, his big brown eyes shifting between him and Key.

"Yesterday, the club found out Ray had dated that DA bitch like twenty years ago, and I had to hold Dev back from whoopin' his ass," Key explained, his gaze imploring Alec to understand.

"So that's true?" he asked, lying back down on the bed, throwing out his arm to stop the curious pup when Nash bounced up, leaping forward to chase another flame.

"You knew?"

"Yeah, for months. I thought it might just be gossip floating around the office." He drew Nash back toward him, and Key closed the circle, getting the little guy back between them.

"Why didn't you tell me?"

"We don't talk like that to one another and never about club business. I'm surprised you said this much to me," Alec explained, lifting on his elbow.

For the first time since Key had spoken in detail about his club's business, he looked shocked he'd let so much out and went immediately on the defensive. "I'm not talkin' about the club. I was trying to explain what they'd do if they find out I'm with you. I regularly plan for the moment I learn they know…"

"Babe, stop putting all that between us. Stop. Let me love you. Let me take care of you. Whether you believe it or not, it's true, love will take care of everything else. It already has. We'll keep to ourselves, tucked away. No one will know." He cupped Key's neck, drawing him in for a kiss. "Just let this happen. Be in this with me. We'll figure out the rest, just like we've been doing."

Nash attacked Alec's shirt sleeve as he leaned in for another quick kiss, drawing their attention his way. They both looked down when their tiny puppy growled. "He's precious."

"He's a fighter."

"Like his new daddy," Alec teased, lifting his chin again to seal the tentative agreement with a kiss. This kiss lingered, and he felt Key give in even as Nash set his sights on a new target, the tattoo on his lover's chest. Key's genuine laugh, the one that melted his heart, broke the kiss as he looked down at the dog, scooping him up. At the same time, his biker rolled to his back, lifting the puppy high in the air. Nash barked several times, seeming to say he wanted back down on Key's level.

Alec watched the scene, loving the raw emotion pouring from Key. It was these little moments that neither of them had ever truly experienced before that were now tying them so closely together. Key lowered Nash who instantly attacked the tattoos on his chest again.

"Hey!" Key yelped, covering his nipple where Nash had set his sights. "He fits us."

"There was no question to me. I saw him, he saw me, and that was it. I didn't know if he was male or female. I didn't care. I knew instantly he was ours," he explained, stretching back out on the bed, loving the idea of lounging and watching his lover play with Nash.

"He's got papers?" Key asked, glancing over.

"Yes, and he's had his first shots. Olivia's been taking him outside to potty train him every thirty minutes. We kept that up until right before you arrived," he explained, reaching over to pet the little guy.

"He seems awful young to potty train," Key stated while letting Nash bounce around on his chest.

"That's what I thought, but apparently that's not the case."

Key executed a fluid body roll, lifting off the bed with the squirming pup in his grasp. "Let's take him out then."

Alec followed, then accepted the puppy as Key grabbed his T-shirt. He pulled the shirt over his head before taking the dog back. Alec was seemingly forgotten and forced to trail behind Key who murmured sweetly to Nash as he headed to the back door.

"Does it matter where?" he asked, looking back over his shoulder and stopped before opening the back door.

"We took him to the patch of grass by the back door," he said. Key pulled open the door, his hands protectively cupping Nash to keep the chill off him.

"Did he go?"

"No, not for me, but he did for Olivia." Alec called out to Alexa to turn on the porch lights before going to stand beside Key who put the dog down and stood directly over him, staring down, waiting right there with Nash.

"Go potty," Key urged.

But that didn't happen. Nash was so full of personality. He attacked the grass with such a force that his body rolled over his head, landing him on his back, causing Key to burst out in a hearty laugh as he tucked his fingers into his jeans pocket.

"Do you think it's too chilly for him?" Alec had no real idea, but reasoned the temperature had warmed back up today, and the ground shouldn't be cold at all.

"I think he's okay until he goes."

Alec slipped a hand between Key's arm and body until he could wrap himself around his waist. Key caught on nicely, opening to hold Alec there against his side. Nash on the other hand quickly shook off his fall, getting back on his feet, and attacked the grass again.

"Thank you," Key said quietly.

"Thank you," he replied and squeezed Key a little tighter. Seconds later, Nash squatted. "He's doing it."

"Just luck," Key announced, but Alec heard the pride in his voice.

"It's a start. That's how I got you." He rested his head on his man's shoulder, content to stay like this forever.

CHAPTER 26

"I got a dog," Keyes mumbled, chin to his chest, his eyes screwed shut, trying to think of anything other than motherfucking Devilman hitting the bones of his fucking shoulder as he etched the wings across his back.

"Yeah?" Dev said, distracted as he focused on his work.

"Yeah."

Maybe as much as fifteen minutes passed with the buzzing of the gun drowning out the hard metal music playing overhead—at least for Keyes. The volume had been turned up, Dev liked it loud when he worked, but for some reason this tattoo hurt worse than any of the others he'd had.

When Dev lifted the gun for a moment, Keyes added, "I named him Nash."

Minutes passed until the gun lifted again, and Dev said, "Nashtayyy." That made him smile, remembering how he and Dev used to talk to the stray dog before Keyes's mother had the city come pick him up. "I was gonna name my son Nash."

"Yeah." Keyes had forgotten that part of the plan. Both of Dev's girls were supposed to be boys, per Dev, not by any testing. Each time, Nash was going to be part of their names.

The gun started to buzz. He ground his teeth and closed his eyes, waiting for Dev to lift the gun again. He had no idea how much time passed until the machine turned off. Keyes lifted enough to look over his shoulder. "Done for today?"

"Yep. I got it down. Lots to fill in, but that'll come. The outline's down. Looks kickass," Dev said, pushing back on his stool.

"What's it look like?" he asked, standing but still straddling the seat.

"Cool as fuckin' shit. It's a badass design. Here." Dev handed him a mirror. Keyes took it and twisted toward the back wall, angling the small mirror to see the freshly inked tattoo. His back burned like fire licked his flesh, but Dev was right, the angel and his expansive wings were the shit.

"I like the way he's got his elbow on his knee and his head down like that. It's like he's thinkin'," he said, studying Dev's work. The whole design was amazing. The angel's body fit in the center of his back. The angel was on one knee, his elbow resting on the other with his forehead leaning on his fist. He was cool as shit on his own, but it was the angel's wingspan that truly made this design remarkable. Dev seriously knew how to work an ink gun. The wings encompassed older tattoos, which he couldn't tell were ever there, and spanned from one shoulder to the other. The whole tattoo took up the upper half of his back.

"We gotta wash it," Dev said, getting to his feet. For some reason, that was always the suckiest part for him. He stayed still, letting Dev do his thing. "So, gettin' a dog means y'all are what? Like together, together?"

Keyes kept his head bent, studying the lines on the linoleum at his feet. "I don't know. He's pushin' for that."

"When am I gonna meet him?" Dev asked, and he had to concentrate on the words not the sting coming from his back.

"I don't know. I can't see how it's gonna work."

"It's worked for a while," Dev said, bending around to look him in the face.

"Yeah, but he wants more. That's the part I don't see happenin'."

"More's not always bad, buddy."

Keyes looked over his shoulder as Dev gently applied an ointment over the design.

"Don't look at me like I'm crazy. We're young, but we've been club our whole life. I get that at some point life's gotta open up—especially for you. You're never gonna be able to mix business with pleasure even with your fuckin' old man dead."

"I wish they were more like you," he said quietly, talking about his brothers as he turned back to the front. Honestly, it was beginning to feel like his heart was being ripped apart every time he had to leave Alec and keep their relationship hidden from everyone else in his life.

Hell, he spent more time with Alec than he'd spent with anyone, including Dev, in his whole life. Keyes was proud that a guy like Alec wanted to spend time with him. He had even started catching glimpses of the future Alec kept rambling on about. He resented the idea of club business picking back up and taking more of his time, the time he spent with Alec.

On the other hand, if he wanted to be what Alec needed, he had to start putting some serious time in at the tire shop. He had to recover financially, which meant he had to be there to make it all happen. Between the club and his business, he didn't see how he'd have any free time ever again.

"Man, this is gonna be the shit. Keep it covered through the night," Dev instructed. Keyes sucked in a breath when the cool clear wrapping hit his skin.

"I thought it was like an hour," he said when Dev pushed back again to reach for Keyes's T-shirt.

"Changed it. Had a client get a badass infection."

Keyes rose, picking up the mirror again, getting a good look at the tattoo one last time. It really was already perfect. He placed the mirror on the chair and took the T-shirt. Slowly and carefully, he pulled it on then reached for his wallet. He dropped five hundred dollars on the seat.

Dev looked down at the cash then back at him as if he were flat ass crazy. "What's that for? I ain't takin' that."

"Sure you are. You were here all day," he replied, tucking the wallet back in his back pocket. "It ain't anywhere close to how much it's worth and you know it."

"Not takin' your money," Dev argued, picking up the cash as he circled around the chair coming toward him. "Mom wants to know if you're comin' over for Thanksgiving."

"I'm gonna say probably not. We cook a lot," he said, grinning as he backed out of the office. Dev thrusted the folded bills and a box titled Ink Oil into his chest.

"You ain't a cook," Dev countered incredulously, letting the items tumble from his hands, leaving Keyes to scramble to grab the box as he let the cash hit the floor.

"Yeah, he cooks and I clean," he replied, twisting around, grabbing his coat off the rack in the front lobby. At the front door of Fox's shop, he was suddenly hauled backward by his shirt. Dev shoved the money into the waistband of his underwear. The tenderness of his back held him captive, allowing Dev to win the battle of the money.

"Not takin' your money. Let that heal, then we'll keep goin'. I want to shade it in," Dev said and shoved him out the door with a boot to his ass.

"Thanks, man," he said, turning back to see Dev shutting the door in his face. He lifted a hand. Dev did, too, through the glass in the door. Man, Dev was such a good friend.

And that was fuckin' Alec in his head, defining all his relationships like that. He swiveled, tossing the jacket around himself, carefully angling his arms to catch the sleeves. It was cold and he had a long ride ahead.

"Come on, Mr. Nash, do your business," Alec encouraged, wrapping his arms around his chest, trying to warm up. The weather was seriously bipolar in Texas. This morning, it was almost eighty degrees—hence his current state of attire, a T-shirt and shorts. Now, it had to have dropped twenty degrees, which may only mean it was somewhere in the low sixties in temp, but the chill nipped at his skin.

The pup started to do his business, but stopped and barked, hopping out of the small section of grass and heading toward the driveway. Of course, Nash had heard Key before Alec did. Alec swooped up the pup, putting him back on the grass as the bike's pipes grew louder and the front gate started to open. At this point, Nash was barking like crazy, well past the point of finishing his business, and Alec had to again scoop the puppy up, who tried to leap out of his hands when he finally saw Key round the corner.

As busy as Alec was transitioning files and learning the complicated ropes from Reed, his heart connected with this moment, making everything occupying his head fade away. Nash was taken with Key as much as Alec was and, although his big biker had never admitted it—which was clearly his way of things—his guy was equally as taken with Nash. From the minute Key arrived home, he commandeered the dog, keeping him nearby until he was forced to leave the next morning.

In Key's quiet way, he left the bike, his stride full of sexy swagger as he walked straight to Alec, taking Nash from his hands before leaning over and placing a kiss on Alec's waiting lips.

"How was work?" Alec asked, slipping his arms inside Key's open jacket.

"Mmm," Key muttered, bringing Nash to his face, giving their puppy a toothy grin before rubbing his head. "Did he do his business?"

"Just maybe started to when he heard you."

"Did he use your shoes again?" That had Alec's smile falling to a frown. Nash seemed to have a thing for his shoes—different ones for different things. His expensive Italian loafers were better than any puppy pads at drawing Nash to them.

"I spent the morning moving everything up off the floor after you left. I've got to remember not to kick my shoes off anywhere and forget them. They're like magnets to him," he said as Key placed the puppy back on the patch of grass.

"You should've figured that out with the house shoes." Key chuckled, shrugging off his jacket to give to him.

"I thought he liked the softness." He hesitated but did take the jacket when his lover wrapped it around his shoulders. That was one of the little things that made Key special. His burly biker was always a gentleman.

"They ain't that soft. Go inside. I got this." The temperature seemed to be dropping even further, and if nothing else, he could grab his long coat. He returned Key's jacket and started to go when he spotted the tape on his man's neck. He reached up, pulling at the collar, and saw the plastic wrapping.

"Did you get a new tattoo?"

Key looked at him and smirked, which was Alec's clue he was missing something that Key thought he should know.

"What?"

"You're fishin'," Key said and rolled his eyes.

"Does that mean you got the tattoo for me?" Alec asked, narrowing his eyes as he tried to get a good read on his mister.

"I thought I'd at least make it inside before you noticed."

Alec started across the walk with every intention of turning on the outside lighting to help get a better look at the tattoo then changed course. Dusk had already settled over them, and he really wanted to see what Key had designed for him.

"Get in the house. I have to see this," he ordered, darting back to where Key had been standing, scooping up Nash, and still managed to make it inside and turn on the kitchen lights before Key ambled through the doorway.

"Maybe I don't wanna show you," Key teased, humor in his voice as he shut the back door behind him.

"Is it really for me…or about me?" he asked, placing Nash on the pee-pad he'd placed close to the back door.

"I don't know. You tell me." Key was hard to read on a normal day, but when he tried to be mysterious, he was infuriatingly cryptic. Alec hurriedly pulled out the kitchen chair Key had used to drape his jacket over and ushered him to sit.

"Alexa, turn on all the lights in the house." Every light in the house lit up like a football stadium at game time.

"Whoa," Key muttered, just like every time Alec used that function. He tended to agree, but he just pointed to the seat.

"Take off your shirt and straddle it."

Key gave him attitude, lifting a brow and purposefully taking his sweet time to shrug off the T-shirt while facing Alec, continuing to effectively block his view. Key winced a couple of times, and Alec did have sympathy, but his eagerness got the best of him. He grabbed the T-shirt from Key's hands and tossed it on the table.

"You're killing me. Turn around," Alec ordered. Key's blue eyes met his, and he swore that, after this, he was going to kiss that sexy smirk right off Key's handsome face. Key shook his head and used his finger to motion for Alec to turn around.

"I'll tell you when to turn back," Key teased.

"What? No. I wanna see." Alec stood his ground until Key lifted both brows and waited him out. So, begrudgingly, Alec finally turned, crossing his arms over his chest, tapping his foot with anticipation. "I can't believe you didn't tell me about the tattoo. I tell you everything."

He heard the chair scrape across the tile floor, and he twisted around only to find Key still standing. "No peekin'."

"You're driving me crazy!" Alec complied with Key's request, but the curiosity was killing him. "You have five seconds."

When he turned back, Key was straddling the chair, his back to Alec, watching him through the reflection in darkened glass of the window. Alec froze at what he saw. The massive tattoo was stunning, the detail incredible. How in the world did that magnificent tattoo represent him in any way? "A fallen angel?"

"No."

Alec moved closer, completely drawn to the image, taking in the finer details of the intricate design. He lightly ran his fingertip over the tip of the right wing.

"Explain this. Why?"

Key shifted in the chair, moving to where his legs were on one side, and Alec moved with him, staying at his back.

"It's the defender of mankind. I looked up the meaning of your name and it fit," Key explained. He looked back at Alec, but winced and gave up, turning forward again. Nash came running, nipping at Key's steel-toed boot.

Alec crossed his arms over his chest, remembering a time when he was a young boy. He and his grandmother had spontaneously looked up the meaning of his name. That night, she and he had decided when he grew up, he should go into law. She'd convinced him it was the best profession to help him live up to his name. He'd forgotten that precious memory and had to swallow the sudden lump forming in his throat.

"This is how you see me?" he asked, his voice small even to him.

"Kind of," Key answered and turned around, reaching out to clasp Alec's hand before he was able to cross his arms over his chest to help hold himself together. "You okay? You look weird."

"I'm stunned," he said, knowing that simple word didn't begin to describe all this emotion rolling through. Key's hand tightened on his. His gaze lifted to Alec's and he saw worry reflected there. A concern for Alec, just the way Key always cared for him with such a sweet gentle need to ease any anxiety Alec may have.

"Don't be freaked." Key searched his face, and that seemed enough to knock Alec out of his awestruck trance. He gripped Key's hand and brought it to his lips, softly kissing Key's palm before lowering to kiss his upturned lips.

"I'm the exact opposite of freaked out," he said against Key's lips and lifted a few inches to stare Key intently in the eyes when he asked his next question. "Is that how you see me?"

"I might not have chosen all this exactly." Key nodded toward the interior of the house then slid a hand across his chest. "But I mark my body with significance. No matter how this turns out between us, I always want you with me. You've had the largest impact on my life. I wanna remember everything about this time, so I made it the biggest ink I could."

Alec couldn't help the well of tears as he tugged Key from the chair, sealing this moment with a sweet lingering kiss. He stayed there, carefully wrapping his arms below Key's waist. His eyes closed with his mouth against the man he loved.

"I never want to lose you," he whispered.

This time, Key moved and cradled his face with his palms.

"It's not supposed to make you cry." Key tilted Alec to better look him in the eyes.

"I feel so loved. I've never felt so loved."

Key's mouth lowered, his tongue pressing along the seam of Alec's lips. Alec opened and put everything he had in that kiss. Key moaned and held his face tighter as if he couldn't get enough, and he kissed him with a fervor that made Alec melt.

Just as suddenly as Key had kissed him, Alec found himself sucking air. Key was gone from his hold. When the lusty haze started to clear, he realized Key was reaching for his phone in the back pocket of his jeans. There was a purposefulness on his face that had the fine lines at his mouth more pronounced.

"I've got someone for you to meet. Can you go?" Key asked in a rush, the phone going to his ear.

The words were unexpected, and it took Alec a second to understand. His brow furrowed and slowly his heartbeat started to pick up. *Someone* meant another person knowing about the two of them. Key had resisted that from day one.

Maybe he'd misunderstood.

"Hang on for a sec," Key said into the phone, staring at him as his brows lifted in question.

"Sure. Yeah. Now?" he asked. He glanced down at his casual clothes and touched his face. He hadn't shaved this morning, because he had spent the entire day working from home, preparing for the tedious week ahead.

"Uncle Clyde, you busy?" Key asked, staring at Alec. The uncle… Key wanted him to meet his uncle. "I've been busy, but I think I got plans for Thanksgivin' this year so go do whatever or maybe you can be a part of our plans if you want, but listen, I got someone I want you to meet." Key grinned, and Alec wished he could hear what was being said on the other end. More importantly, this was Key's family, and he hadn't showered today. Alec darted toward the bedroom, leaping over Nash who yapped at his sudden movement. "Yep. Like an hour and a half. Is it too late?"

Alec was in and out of the shower in record time, already toweling off and going for the sink when Key came to the bathroom door, carrying Nash. "I thought we could take Nash. Show him off."

"His carrying case is in the garage. Are we taking my car? We're riding together, right?" Alec asked, toweling off his wet hair. His eyes connected with Key's in the mirror.

They were at another unexpected turning point, and this one meant so much more, because for the first time, Key had initiated this major step on his own. More importantly, Key seemed so calm about it all.

"Yeah. You wanna drive? Or we can take the truck, whichever," he said casually, Nash gaining all his attention as he rubbed the puppy's head.

"I'll drive. You drove all day. Give me a few minutes. I won't be long." Alec yanked the brush through his hair, adding product with shaky hands. His normally calm, cool, and collected demeanor had vanished. He was so excited that it made him nervous. When he reached for his toothbrush, Key was back with his house shoe in hand, the one Nash loved. Their eyes locked in the mirror again, this time Key gave him a genuine smile. It eased Alec. He wasn't sure why, who knew what that grin truly meant, but he didn't care. Tonight, everything was changing—again.

CHAPTER 27

    Alec had no idea where he was. Based on the distance they'd traveled, Cedar Hill, Texas, wasn't too far south of downtown Dallas. Twenty minutes max down Hwy 67 and a few turns here and there and they had traveled into a beautiful, rustic setting. Clusters of oaks and stately pecan trees peppered the gentle rolling hills, but he was more surprised by the sheer volume of cedar trees in this area. It was shocking how things could change in such a short drive. The tranquility he felt here made no sense, because less than two miles away was a thriving small town with tons of retail stores. Yet none of the bustling city seemed to touch this small, private patch of the land.

    "It's remarkable out here," he said, breaking the silence in the living room.

    "It's why I stayed." Key's Uncle Clyde represented everything good for Key.

    Clyde was a mild-mannered man with a genuine kindness to him. Maybe not right at this moment, but it was easy to see the man loved and cared for his nephew as if he were his own son.

"I wasn't expecting this," Clyde said honestly from his chair in the living room with Nash resting happily in his lap. Their puppy preferred the constant petting, nudging Clyde's fingers with his nose when they stopped moving.

He had to give it to Clyde, he never missed a beat. Key had come straight inside the house, not really even giving his uncle as much as a greeting before proudly handing Nash straight to the man. The pride on Key's face when he'd presented their puppy then introduced Alec to his uncle was something Alec hadn't seen before in his guy.

His palm was sweating because he hadn't let go of Key's hand since the initial introduction when he had shaken Clyde's hand. Alec now sat somewhat comfortably beside Key on the sofa. His nervousness hadn't diminished, but he hoped he was doing a reasonably good job of hiding it, sweaty palm and all.

"I figured you'd like him. He's like you," Key said confidently, looking over at Alec with a wink and a nod. Key didn't seem to see or read his uncle's hesitation.

"How did you two meet?" Clyde asked.

"He had a flat," Key replied. His lover said the words with a bit of pride, maybe because he'd saved the day that night and sealed their fate.

"You've known each other awhile?"

"About a year, right?" Key asked, turning those vibrant eyes his way before bumping him in the shoulder. "You're never this quiet."

Alec just smiled, so much emotion passed between them in that brief exchange that he wanted to pull Key in for a kiss. Instead, he turned back to Clyde and said, "A year in January. For at least the last six months we've been together just about every day."

"So why all the secrecy?" Clyde asked as he rocked his chair slowly back and forth. Nash seemed to love the movement. Alec filed that bit of information away. They might need to get a rocking chair. The puppy laid his head on his paws and settled down.

"It's complicated," Key answered, not expanding past those two words. Clyde stayed silent, staring between the both of them, clearly waiting and wanting more of an explanation. When Key didn't say anything, Alec sighed. Clyde would never have a good impression of him if they walked away without confiding in the man. More so, Alec could see the unconditional love between Clyde and Key. He didn't want to leave tonight and have Clyde worrying about Key's wellbeing any more than he already did.

"The secrecy is because I'm with the Dallas district attorney's office or I was with the DA's office—my last day is December fifteenth," he explained, watching Clyde's eyes go wide and the motion of the rocking chair coming to a sudden stop.

"You're kidding me, right?" Clyde said, his tone clear that he found no humor in what was being said. Key's uncle grew immediately defensive, and although Alec loved the protectiveness, he didn't like all the skepticism now directed his way.

"We've been very careful to keep our relationship hidden," he started before Key cut him off.

"He's worried about what happens if the club finds out." Key tried to explain Clyde's reaction and concern to him. Alec wasn't entirely sure that was Clyde's primary concern, but the gentle sweep of Key's thumb sliding over the back of his hand helped calm him.

"As I should be," Clyde said, his eyes hard with concern.

Key suddenly got up off the sofa and walked over to his uncle, lifting Nash. "He's on a schedule. I'll take him out. Y'all talk so you can quit givin' each other all those weird looks." Key carefully cradled Nash in his arms as he walked to the front door. He turned and looked back over his shoulder at Alec. "Might as well tell him who your old man is. I guess get it all out now. Clyde's trustworthy."

The front door shut behind Key, and Alec stared at Clyde who got to his feet. He walked across the living room to the liquor cabinet. After pouring and drinking down a hearty sized drink, he turned to Alec and lifted the bottle. Good idea. Alec nodded and got to his feet too.

"I have to admit, I was nervous coming here."

"I'm nervous now that you're here," Clyde said, handing a cocktail glass over with a shot or two of straight whiskey. "So, who's your father? The Dallas chief of police?"

"It doesn't matter who my family is. We have no real relationship to speak of. They're a non-factor in any of this. They'll never know Key. As it turns out, I'm a huge disappointment to them," Alec explained, swallowing a gulp of the whiskey, reveling in the burn.

They stared at one another for several long seconds before Clyde nodded, accepting his answer. Thank God. He might have given the older man a heart attack if he knew the truth.

"My nephew's a great guy. Turned out that way despite all the crap thrown at him. God knows I worried. But he's smart. He's a motorcycle mechanic, first in his class. He rebuilds bikes, and they're beautiful pieces of artistry. I don't think anyone in that club understands how talented he is or they would never have him changing tires for a living. He's dedicated to those bikers. I think more than they are to him. You'd be just the excuse they needed to hurt him," Clyde said honestly, fear in his tone.

"He's told me it would be rough, but he's been more worried about me than himself," Alec said, taking another drink of his whiskey.

"They harbor immense hate for people like you. They believe the law's out to get them. That there should be no consequences for their actions, even though they're the ones breaking the law. If they think you're getting in their way, you might not survive," Clyde added solemnly and turned to pour himself another drink.

"I'm trying to remove the obstacles in our way. I've quit the DA's office—I only stayed this long because of Key. I've accepted another position as head legal counsel for Reed Kensington's Arik Layne Properties account. He owns the Escape Resort properties, and the headquarters are local," Alec explained, wanting to help ease Clyde's fears or at least let the man know how seriously Alec took Key's welfare. "I want us to move out to Westlake together."

"What does Key have to say about that?" Clyde asked as he downed the amber liquid he'd just poured.

"Nothing. Absolutely nothing," he answered, after realizing the truth to Clyde's answer.

"Alec, you understand what you're dealing with, right?" Clyde asked, placing his glass on the small bar top.

"I understand Key. I know he's a good and caring man. Perhaps a little rough around the edges, but a good man— better than most."

"That didn't come easy for him. When I found him, he was barely in school, close to living on the streets even though he technically lived with his father," Clyde explained, his expression growing hard as he stared unseeingly at Alec.

"He's told me you were responsible for getting him through school and you pushed him to get his mechanics license. He gives you credit for all his successes." Alec watched Clyde grow more agitated. The man paced the small room. The silence thickened, and he could sense Key's uncle held back everything he wanted to say. He stood in his spot and watched as the other man worked through his demons with another long pause. Alec had no idea what to do or say to ease the heaviness hanging between them. Then Clyde suddenly turned back to Alec and gave him a hard stare.

"The first time he spent the night here in this house—No, let me go further back. I'd given Key a phone in case of an emergency. He kept it hidden from his father. One night that sorry man had beaten Key up pretty badly and kicked him out of the house. Keyes called me. I picked him up. He was about ten years old at the time. That night, I heard the front door open about three o'clock in the morning. Thought it might be a burglar so I got out of bed to check it out. I found Keyes outside. His clothes were wet. He'd had an accident in the bed during the middle of the night. I felt so sorry for him. He looked so young and scared, so lost. See, ever since he was a small boy, he had wet the bed, and when that happened, no matter the time of year, he was put outside for the remainder of the night. And bless his little soul, that child believed that being shoved outside was a normal punishment for having an accident in bed. That broke my heart," Clyde explained, disgust and pain clear on his face.

Alec's heart hurt hearing that story.

"Even after I explained how things should be, the boy still hid a backpack behind one of my porch chairs with a change of clothes and a blanket for when it was cold outside," Clyde continued. "At ten years old, he'd spent so many nights on the front porch that he had already gotten into survival mode. Key's life has been all about surviving. He's never owned more than he can fit inside a duffel bag, and I'd venture to say, he's saved as many dollars as he possibly could. He knows what it's like to be hungry and abused and sick with no medical care, yet he still turned out to be a man who could display a deep pride in something as simple as having a small puppy."

A lump swelled in Alec's throat as those words broke his heart. The wonderful man caring for their small dog outside that door had been through hell. Alec hurt for the man he loved. His gaze moved to the big window in the living room. Key was there, walking slowly along with Nash. He was such an unassuming man. His hands were in his pockets, his ball cap turned backward. That was a new look that Alec loved, especially when his hair was loose and flowed down his shoulders. It occurred to him he hadn't seen Key pile his hair on top of his head in a good while. He actually couldn't remember the last time he'd seen Key do that.

"I only want to make his life better. If he would leave with me, I'd take us far away from here. I'd make a life for him that he deserves. I love him with all my heart."

Clyde was silent, and after several moments, Alec lifted his gaze back to Clyde who pleaded for Key. "Please don't jerk him around. He's come a long way and deserves an easier life."

"He's brought me a long way. Given me something to work for." Alec gave a small smile, knowing no truer words had ever been spoken. They both looked over at the front door when Key came through, talking to Nash in his version of a baby voice, giving the dog encouragement for doing his duty. Alec's gaze snapped back Clyde's way, who had lifted his brows at what he was seeing, a small smile touching the uncle's face.

Key looked at both of them in confusion. His brow furrowed as he fixed his gaze on Alec, but spoke to Clyde. "I was hopin' I could go show Alec the shop. Maybe take him for a ride back there."

"Do you want me to watch him?" Clyde offered as he went for Nash.

"Yeah, if you don't mind." Key carefully handed over Nash then went to an entryway closet and pulled out two leather jackets.

"Of course not. Take your time," Clyde said, putting Nash on the floor. The puppy promptly leapt toward Key, face planting in all his eagerness to get back in Key's hold.

"He likes his daddy," Alec teased, the moment going a long way in relieving some of the anxiety Clyde had managed to instill in him. Key handed him the coat and scooped Nash up again to give him back to Clyde. "And he doesn't walk much when Key's around. He's a bit spoiled."

"He's little," Key justified as if there were no other reasonable explanation, never once admitting to the notion he might be spoiling Nash. "Wear this. We'll walk." Key left him standing there as he started for the kitchen but stopped abruptly in his tracks and turned back to look past Alec's shoulder to Clyde. "I forgot to tell you, my old man died."

That was news to Alec. His stomach sank as his gaze darted to Key, studying the way he looked at his uncle. Alec turned back to Clyde who remained stone-faced and didn't offer a pretend apology or condolences. Neither spoke. Finally, the older man only nodded. Alec could feel the finality in the way Key returned the nod.

Whatever passed between the two men was over and done in an instant. Key showed no emotion. Alec, on the other hand, wasn't sure how to feel. When had this happened? Why hadn't Key said anything to him? Had he been a bad boyfriend because he hadn't asked?

"Take your time," Clyde said and settled back in his rocking chair with Nash. He lifted the remote, but Alec noticed he didn't turn on the television. Instead, he watched as Key came back to help button Alec's jacket. Those were the little things Key did for Alec all the time. He took care of Alec even in the smallest details. Those thoughtful assists were becoming more and more prevalent with each passing day. Alec finally dropped his hands to let Key finish fussing over him.

Key didn't say anything as he took Alec's hand and led him through the kitchen and laundry room and out the back door. They trotted down a set of steps, Key walking with purpose, pulling Alec along behind.

"Where are we going?"

"Watch where you're steppin'. There's ruts and shit out here." Key didn't answer his question. The man didn't waste his words. Alec had been with his biker long enough to know he would eventually get the answer he sought.

"You didn't tell me about your father." Direct was the best way to approach the subject. Alec picked up his steps, matching Key's long stride in order to keep up with the brisk pace.

"I thought I mentioned it."

Alec shook his head and looked over to say he hadn't when he stumbled over the raised edge of a rut. *Shit*! His heart sped up as he almost lost his balance. He tightened his hold on Key to help keep him on his feet. When balanced again, he added, "You didn't."

"Probably because I don't care. He hated me. Didn't want me there…at the funeral, you know." The callousness of Key's words weren't convincing. Alec didn't press it, especially after hearing what Clyde had to say about Key's childhood. The man was gone, and hopefully, the pain of Key's childhood could die with him. When Key was ready to talk, he'd be there for him.

Alec took a good look around. It was nice out here, quiet and homey. He wanted a place like this for Key and himself, minus the ruts. The property had tons of trees, and fallen leaves rustled loudly as a gust of cool air sent them swirling around. The heat from Key's body deflected the chill in the air and made it perfect. The full moon's light filtered through the trees, giving a soft glow to the area around them.

"So, Cedar Hill's an accurate name for the town. Lots of cedar trees."

"Hmm. Used to be a lot fuckin' more of them until they carved out all that land for the mall," Key said disgustedly. Alec wouldn't have suspected a different answer from his always outside boyfriend.

"I didn't see the mall. I saw a Target," Alec said.

"Yeah, it's a big shoppin' center behind the Target. All the trees keep it from bein' seen."

"I like it out here." Just beyond the trees Alec noticed a small clearing, giving way to a small warehouse style shop. As they approached, a light flashed on, brightening the area near the building.

"My mother's parents owned this property. My uncle bought it from them. It was built in the seventies," Key replied.

"Are they still alive?" Alec asked, coming to a stop at a side door that sat just to the left of the double overhead sliding door.

"Yeah, they live in Florida, I think." Key took a set of keys from his pocket, working the series of locks on the side of the door. "I never met 'em."

Many of the pieces of Key's past had come together with Clyde's short explanation of Key's childhood. This fine man truly had so little to build off of. How Key had managed to become a good and fair man defied reason. A protectiveness grew inside Alec, something that made him want to reach out and wrap his arms tightly around Key and promise to never let anyone hurt him again. The only thing that stopped him was the fear Key would consider that pity. It wasn't, not at all. Like everything else between them, these strong protectionary feelings were grounded in love.

Key pushed open the door and walked inside ahead of Alec. With the flick of a switch, overhead lights popped on, showing three bikes inside. Two were older and in pristine condition. One was the sexy black bike Key had been on the first night they'd met. There were also well-organized rows of tool boxes and tools and a table with engine parts scattered across the top.

"It's my place I told you about," Key said, going for the black street bike that had appeared in Alec's fantasies a couple of times since their first meeting. "This is where I used to come to spend my free time before I met you."

"Did you rebuild this?" Alec asked, walking to an older Harley, remembering what Clyde had said.

"Yeah." Key's voice softened, giving Alec a glimpse of the pride Key held in the craftsmanship of his rebuild. Alec ran a hand over the seat.

"It's incredible." It truly was.

"Wanna take a ride?" Key asked, moving toward him, helmet in hand. Alec took the helmet, reveling in so many of his dreams coming true so unexpectedly tonight. He watched Key roll the sleek black bike out the door before following him, trying to etch every single moment into his heart. He wanted to remember it all.

Key lifted his long hair, gathering it together to tie in a low ponytail. He tucked the ends in his jacket before zipping his jacket as far as it could go. The man was amazing. Just being here with him right now meant the world to Alec.

"Do I get on back?" he asked after Key straddled the bike. Those thick thighs evoked all kinds of ideas as Key patted the seat.

"Yeah." If his tone wasn't enough, Key smirked as if that were a given.

"I haven't ridden on the back of a motorcycle before." Alec rambled as he got situated, his nerves on edge, the adrenaline pumping through his veins had him all kinds of chatty. One thing for certain, he really liked Key's warm body pressed between his thighs. Alec wanted to wrap his arms around his man too, barely restraining himself as he remembered Key's freshly tattooed back. So, he sat back, keeping distance between them. "You aren't wearing a helmet?"

"Most of the time on this bike and about half the time on the others. I know these roads like the back of my hand. I'm not gonna race anyone. Not tonight. I want you to wear one though."

Alec wanted to disagree but didn't. Instead, he just did as Key requested and shoved the helmet on his head. Key started the engine, let the bike rumble, and grabbed both of Alec's thighs, pulling him tighter against his body.

"I don't want to hurt your back." Alec resisted the urge to grind himself on Key. It seemed all his fantasies were coming true and his body stirred, but he could behave. He'd get his when they got home tonight.

Key looked back over his shoulder and smiled, his teeth extra white in the bright moonlight. "You ain't gonna hurt me. Ready?" he asked, squirming between Alec's spread thighs as if to prove his point.

"Ready." If Key kept rubbing up against him, he'd be ready to ride something other than the bike.

Key didn't acknowledge his arousal, just revved his engine and called back over his shoulder, "Then hold on."

And he did. Key drove them off the property along a small dirt road, speeding up when they turned onto a country road. Key was right, he did know these roads. They dipped and curved, Alec following the lead of Key's body until the single lane blacktop became a two-lane concrete road. The air rushed to meet them, fresh and crisp. The scenery slid past them in moonlit shadows. It was them, the night, speeding down a shadowed tree-lined road, the glow of the moon guiding their path. He felt free, his nerves long since vanished. This was unbelievable. This whole night had been such a treasured surprise. Alec wrapped himself around Key, trusting every dip and sway the bike made. Key was made to ride, and Alec was certain he was born to be on the back of this bike with this man.

Their momentum ebbed, the bike came to a crawl until Key veered off the road, taking a turn into an empty service area. Key followed the small drive up the side of the hill and executed a quick turn then came to a complete stop at the end of the empty lot.

"That was amazing," Alec yelled, taking off his helmet while Key cut the engine. "Man, I can't believe we've never done this before."

After knocking the kickstand in place, Key held out an arm to help Alec off the back. Key stayed sitting in the seat, staring past Alec, out into the night. He turned, following Key's line of sight to take in the view. They were high on the hill, and the way the trees split, he could see for miles and miles. Alec's heart was pounding; he loved this moment. He faced Key, thankful his lover had shared this with him.

"You love it out here, don't you?"

"Yup."

Alec looked out over the night again, trying to see the tranquility from his lover's perspective. "You were made to ride."

"Mmm," Key muttered, drawing Alec's attention back to him. Alec stared at the handsome man who met his gaze. Seconds passed before Alec took the steps separating them. He couldn't stand not being able to touch Key.

"What happened tonight? Why did you get the tattoo today?" He lifted his hand to Key's shoulder, toying with the hair that had escaped during the ride.

"You're—"

Oh no, Alec cut him right off. "Don't say fishing. I'm not. I'm trying to understand. You've been resistant to us, like you've waited for something, then tonight you've suddenly broken all your hard rules. Why?" Alec asked, tucking those long pieces of hair behind Key's ear. "Be honest."

"I don't really know except it seemed like you were changin' your shit, so I needed to change some of mine." Key's hand went to Alec's waist, tugging him in closer.

Alec waited for more, but when Key remained silent, he pressed his lips to Key's and said, "I can question you, but I'd rather you keep explaining on your own."

Key stared at him for so long he thought he wouldn't say more. As Alec opened his mouth, warm fingers touched his lips, silencing him. "I know I don't belong in your world. Hell, you damn sure don't belong in mine. We don't go together, not really, but you're always there, ready to defend me. You're the most important thing that's happened in my life. I wanted to remember."

"It's a compliment that you see me as a defender," Alec said, not really the explanation he was hoping for, but he went with it as he ran his fingers through Key's beard.

"It's what you are. I wish you saw yourself like that," Key said, his gaze holding Alec hostage, willing him to agree. Oh man, Keyes Dixon was being sweet tonight, and Alec forced himself to stay focused, to hear everything Key was trying to say between the lines.

"And why the ride tonight?" he asked, leaning into Key, desperately needing to be closer.

"I'm claimin' you." The image of Key as a caveman pounding the swell of his chest immediately came to mind. A thrill shot down his spine and he could feel himself flush. More than anything, Alec wanted to be claimed by this man.

"And that means what to you?" Alec asked, prodding.

His lover's brows lifted, and the cocky biker had the audacity to smirk at him. "I thought you spoke fluent biker." He'd needed that. Alec busted out with a huge grin as he let Key keep talking. "It means way back when we first hooked up, I claimed you. You're mine, and you belong on the back of my bike."

"I'm yours?" he asked, unable to stop his grin from growing. Key just shook his head, giving him the *you're crazy* eye roll. "And my place is on the back of your bike. All bikers do that with their significant other?"

"Yeah, somethin' like that." Key's smile widened. "And I like you there."

"Me too." Alec pressed his lips to Key's who opened enough for him to slide his tongue along the seam before he moved a fraction of an inch back and pressed their foreheads together. "It felt right to be with you back there."

"What'd you and my uncle talk about?" Key asked. Not necessarily the direction he would have gone in that moment, but he'd let Key guide the conversation this time. So again, Alec went with it.

"He's worried about our safety," he answered honestly, their breath mingling with how close Alec stayed to Key.

"I'll protect you. I won't let 'em near you. I already decided that." If Key's hands weren't already on Alec, his biker would probably pound his fist in his palm, driving the point home with a show of force that matched the resolve in his tone.

"I know you will. I've been thinking about some private security when you're not around. Your uncle helped me realize the true dangers," Alec said and affirmed right then to move forward with that plan. He wanted to protect Key as much as Key wanted to protect him.

Key's hand slid suggestively down Alec's ass, his chin lifted in defiance as he spoke. "You're first to me. I'll protect you."

Alec melted into his lover. He believed every word Key spoke and wanted nothing more than to let him. "I know you will."

"I do want what you want, Alec," Key said, taking his lips. The distraction had an instant hypnotic feel, and he opened, meeting Key's velvety soft tongue with his own. Key lifted a hand to his neck, those strong fingers angling Alec while he reached an arm around Key's neck and fought the questions bouncing around in his head.

Damn it. Alec pulled away to look at his lover. "You do want the same things?"

"Yeah."

As Alec started to move back to the kiss, Key's penetrating stare focused on his lips until it suddenly lifted to meet his. That intense gaze pinned him in place inches from Key's face, stopping his movement. "I love you. I pretty much always have. I'm sorry it's tak—"

Alec took the rest of those words from his lover's tongue. Those three coveted words echoed in his head as he devoured Key's mouth in a fevered kiss.

CHAPTER 28

At first, the all-consuming love in Alec's kiss startled him, only to firmly nestle into his overfilled heart. He'd told the truth—finally—and was truly sorry for waiting so long. Alec deserved those words, but he had been selfish and foolish, holding on to them out of nothing more than fear. Afraid if he said them out loud he'd somehow lose their magic…and lose Alec. He'd wake up from this unbelievably fantastic dream. That it would all disappear in front of his eyes, because Alec was so much more than he deserved.

The pressure of Alec's palm gliding over his aching erection had the air hanging in his throat. He moaned into his lover's mouth. "You make me so fucking hard."

He'd meant every word he'd said. Alec was his, and in return, he belonged to Alec. There was no longer a choice in the matter. He tilted his head, holding Alec by the neck, driving his tongue deep inside the far reaches of Alec's mouth. Keyes devoured his man, wrapping one strong arm around Alec's waist, tugging him flush against his chest. He needed the physical connection in that moment more than he had ever believed possible.

It was Alec who tore free of the kiss, gasping for air as his mister's body trembled with every breath. Keyes nipped at the soft skin on Alec's neck while Alec's skilled hand continued the dick-teasing massage between his legs.

He eagerly mouthed a trail to his lover's ear, and in a whisper said, "Want you in me, Alec. I need to feel you." He practically begged, the desperation overriding any common sense. They were hidden well enough that if a car happened by, they would have plenty notice.

"What if someone…" Yeah, they were exactly on the same wave.

"We'd see them first." Keyes rushed to assure Alec as he swatted Alec's insistent hand away from his overly eager dick and unbuttoned his jeans then lowered the zipper. All while Alec's sweet puffs of breath coated his face, his mister refused to move even an inch away from Keyes.

Fuck it. He didn't care if anyone saw them. All he knew was he needed Alec like he needed breath, so he grabbed Alec's face between his palms and pulled him back for a quick press of the lips before he instructed, "Now, claim what's yours."

"Babe, you're killing me." Alec groaned, before eating at his lover's mouth like a greedy man. Keyes slid his hands under the warmth of Alec's jacket and found the waistband of his jeans, slipping his fingers inside. With a flick of his finger and thumb, he popped the button and eased the zipper down to free Alec.

There was no hesitation on Alec's part. His lover finished what Keyes had started and shoved the pants down enough to expose his thick cock that stood erect and inviting in the bright moonlight, begging to be touched and stroked.

Keyes grinned at the bold move and did the same, pushing his pants to his thighs, freeing himself from the binding material. The cold breeze blew over his heated skin, sending his balls looking for warmth and a shiver racing up his spine.

"You cold?" Alec stepped closer.

"I won't be if you'll quit talking," he murmured against Alec's lips.

Alec took charge and kissed him back. A lazy, drugging kind of a kiss that he easily lost himself in. Kissing Alec sent a wave of pleasure coursing through him that flowed all the way to his balls.

Alec's warm fingers found his cock as he, in turn, slid his hand over the head of Alec's wet tip. "So fucking hard for me."

He nipped at Alec's lips. The playful bites turning into rough licks and hard kisses as he thrust his cock up into his lover's snug palm. Keyes broke from the kiss, eager to rush things along. "Bring anything?"

"Sex wasn't the first thing I thought of when you said you wanted me to meet someone." Alec pecked him on his lips before pulling away with a throaty chuckle. Alec wrestled his pants back up and did a quick search of his pockets, finally pulling something from the pocket of his billfold.

"This is all I've got," his sexy lawyer announced as he held up a single foil packet of lube. The implication caused his breath to heave from his lungs. Bareback; his fucking heart soared.

"I haven't been with anyone since we met." The words rushed out. He wanted Alec to take him bare. Truth be told, he hadn't been with anyone months before he met Alec, and he'd been tested since then.

"Neither have I, and I wanna fuck you on this bike so bad," Alec said, moving in closer. "But not here. I have to take my time with you, especially if we go bare." Alec pushed his pants down his muscular thighs again before hauling Keyes snugly against him and grinding their stiff cocks together. "Just the thought of pushing into you with nothing between us…makes me so fucking hard my balls hurt." Alec ripped the corner of the packet and drizzled the gel in his palm as Keyes's heart shifted into overdrive. "Don't worry. I'm going to make you come before we head back to your uncle's house."

Hell yes, he wanted that too. Keyes slammed his eyes shut, and his breath escaped in a pleased hiss as Alec took both of their dicks firmly in hand and slid his fist down his shaft, forcing their cocks together in the most delicious way.

"Fuck yeah," he panted, totally on board with the idea. He was fucking game for anything Alec had in mind. "Completely naked, skin on skin on my bike." The words conjured all kinds of depraved images. Fire rushed through his veins at the thought of the cold metal biting into his flesh as Alec fucked him, and his ass clenched and his dick jerked in excitement at the image. Alec's heated flesh felt amazing against his, singeing his skin in a white-hot rush of pleasure that had his balls drawing up against his body.

"You'll never look at that bike the same after I have my way with you," Alec promised against his lips, the man's grip growing tighter and rougher on every stroke. The intense rhythm drove him to the edge.

"Anything you want." He would have agreed to run through the police station covered in nothing but rainbow glitter and steal doughnuts out of the breakroom, if Alec had asked at that moment. The feelings Alec brought out in him were unlike anything he'd ever experienced and made him all too eager to explore every last one.

The sudden rush of blood from his brain left him fuzzy. He couldn't think. Especially not with the way Alec was kissing him. Fuck, he was trying not to embarrass himself by coming too fast, but as usual, Alec could take him from a five to a ten in a matter of a few seconds. He was so lost to the man.

"Feels so good, Alec."

They found a rhythm that had his toes curling in his boots and his hips moving of their own accord as Alec's fist drove him closer to his orgasm. He strained against his body's urge to give in to the pleasure vibrating through him. Alec swallowed his moan, kissing him as if his life depended on their connection. With every twist of Alec's palm, his orgasm built with overwhelming intensity.

He dropped his forehead to Alec's and added his hand to the mix. Their warm breaths combined in white puffs that disappeared into the cool night air.

"Wanna watch you come, Key."

Pleasure churned in his balls and radiated through him in mind-numbing waves of intense pleasure that locked his muscles in place and made his knees weak. He absolutely wanted to give Alec everything he'd ask for.

A deep rumble erupted from Alec's chest and the firm grip quickened when the man took his mouth in a soul-claiming kiss. His orgasm swamped him, the weight of it almost bowling him over.

Their combined release spilled over their hands, a few warm jets escaping, painting the dark leather with perfect ribbons of white.

When his breathing finally slowed, and he was certain his legs would hold him, Keyes lightly brushed his lips over Alec's. "I love you."

"Say it again, please."

"I love you, Alec Pierce."

"God, I love hearing you say that." Alec's silly grin filled him with a sense of pride, and it felt amazing. "Let's get Nash and go home. I want you all to myself. I'm not finished with you." Alec licked across his lips, sending an excited thrill down up his spine. "Not by a long shot."

"You always have the best ideas." He held his hand up and looked down at his jacket and grinned, pushing to his feet. "Have a couple of those handy towelettes in that wallet?"

CHAPTER 29

Apparently being in love and loved in return made Alec a crazy, silly man. He had more work than he could possibly do with less than two weeks before his last day with the district attorney's office and exactly two weeks and a day before he started his new job where he had already learned his biggest obstacle wasn't the ever-changing landscape of international law. Instead, it was Arik Layne himself. Since the first day they had met, Arik was a force to be reckoned with and had pushed and pushed until he had Alec starting right away and meeting with his board of directors that very same day.

Instead of dealing with any of the mounds of paperwork on his desk, Alec was out in the garage, sitting on an uncomfortable stool, looking down at Key who was, at the moment, on all fours. Maybe the problem was he liked that position too well to leave—his grin grew at the idea—or maybe it was because the idea of spending even a minute of their precious time together out of Key's company was more than he could bear.

"Do you need your gloves?" Alec asked, torn between watching Key change the oil and transmission fluid oil on his Harley and the cuteness of Nash attacking Key's shoestrings, continually pulling them free of the tight lace Key had to keep retying. Apparently, Nash had a real thing for shoes.

"Fuck no, I don't need gloves." Key's hands stopped moving, and he looked up over his shoulder. His sweet biker explained his hard-edge tone, "That *fuck* was because the fluid's not that hot, not because of the suggestion."

Alec smiled back at Key. It had been over a week since he'd seen the tattoo, met Clyde, and finally gotten his *I love you*, and Alec wasn't certain Key had left his thoughts for one single minute since. Without question, Alec had never been happier in his life. His world began and ended with those blue eyes staring up at him, waiting for his acknowledgement, so he nodded and winked. "I didn't take offense."

Key went back to turning the wrench. Alec had gotten a lesson in changing bike oil and transmission fluids today. Key had meticulously schooled him on every step, and Alec had listened, insanely interested in anything that came from his biker's mouth.

"Watch him."

Alec got off the stool, reaching for Nash as Key moved the oil pan to a new position under the bike and did a twist of his hand. He had cat-like reflexes, barely getting a drop of transmission fluid on his hands before it dumped down into the pan. That was a pretty remarkable skill since the second the plug was freed, nothing stopped the flow.

Key pushed away, knocking his ponytail back over his shoulder as he reached for a shop towel, wiping it first over his hand then over the plug he held. "Need a new O ring."

"I'll get it, where?"

"I got it." Key stood, going to the tool box in the corner. "Clyde texted me today. He said that dressin' you made was the best he ever had."

"He sent me that text too. I think he's just being kind. The dressing seemed dry to me," Alec said of his attempt to cook a turkey and dressing, southern style. Clyde had joined them for Thanksgiving, giving Alec the perfect chance to finally use his dining room table. He had cooked for two days straight, made enough food to feed an army, so pleased to be cooking for his new family.

"Nah, it was good. I liked it. I want that for my birthday next year," he said, rummaging through one of the drawers in the toolbox.

"What're we doing for my birthday?" Alec asked.

He watched Key's shoulders tense, and his hands paused. Alec felt some of Key's walls materialize between them. Not a lot of them, nothing like before, but enough that Alec could sense Key's hesitation. Hmm, he wondered why exactly.

"I'm takin' that day off," Key said, not looking up, and his fingers stayed still.

Key had opened up on a very small scale about his cash flow problems at the tire shop by saying he really hoped the Christmas shopping season would turn things around for his small business. The reciprocation of birthday gifts wasn't something Alec had considered when buying the truck. The *give equally* factor had never occurred once in selecting the truck. He studied Key as he walked back to the bike and dropped to his knees on the other side, partially blocking Alec's view.

"I was hoping to sneak in another ride for my birthday. I bet when you look down over the hill you could see all the Christmas lights below."

Key said nothing, but he suspected some of the shielding might have lifted as Key nodded. "Can you hand me the three-eighths Allen?"

"Sure." Alec scooted off the stool as his phone vibrated in his pocket and the Echo beeped.

"What's that?" Key asked, looking up over the bike.

"I connected my phone to the Echo so I can talk hands-free. I think that means I received a text," he said to Key's raised brow. "Alexa, read my text message."

Her automated voice started reciting the details of the message. Alec handed Key the tool bit for the wrench and started back around to his seat when he heard his mother's name as the sending contact. He hiked his leg over the stool, before flipping a playful Nash to his back, letting him attack his hand as he held the small pup and listened to the message.

"Alec, this can't come as a surprise to you. Your father and I have done quite a bit of soul-searching and we've decided it's in our best interest and our health to discontinue our relationship with you. You've always been a struggle for us to understand, and frankly, a constant source of disappointment. Your rebellion has grown old and tiresome. We can't abide the man you have allowed yourself to become. December will be your last allowance installment, I encourage you to spend it wisely. There will be no more. Good luck to you. Please respect our wishes by making no further contact."

Alec stared at the device, disbelieving his ears, not realizing that Key had risen and walked toward him until he came in his line of vision, drawing Alec out of his trance. His mister looked so concerned that Alec tilted his head, looking past Key, back to the bike to see what might have happened.

"You okay?"

Alec glanced back at Key who stood inches from him.

"They have never given me an allowance. Not ever. In school, my extra money always came from my grandparents. How don't they know that they've never given me an allowance?" It was mind-boggling to him that they'd never bothered to make sure he had what he needed. It incensed him into deep anger and hurt for the little boy he'd once been, looking in on a family unit he didn't understand and could never get on the same equal footing as his selfish, spoiled siblings.

Key just stared at him and nodded. Nash chose then to practice his attack skills and bit down on his hand. Alec yelped, grinning down at the squirming puppy trying to right himself in Alec's arms to better reach his hand to bite again.

Oh man, that was the sweet reminder he needed. Whatever had happened in the past brought him to this moment, to his new family who loved him for him. This time, when he reexamined his feelings, he sensed a genuine transformation building inside him.

"You're naughty." Alec lifted the ferocious pup to his face. Nash barked. "And pretty adorable."

Key's caring hands covered his as he held Nash. Alec lifted his grin to Key who still had the worry lines etched in his face.

"Don't worry. I'm good. Oddly, my only care seems to be the normal sibling rivalry. I'm tired of being hurt by people who don't want me when I have everything right in the world standing in front of me."

Key's hand went to Alec's cheek, his thumb moved slowly back and forth across his skin, his loving gaze never left Alec's.

"Kiss me, then go back and finish the bike. It's Sunday and we have a lot of leftovers to eat. I googled all the ways to use that turkey meat. I guess a fifteen-pound turkey was probably too big for the three of us."

"My old man hated me, and there was never any denyin' it. Told me so every day of my life. Your family's so much worse, because they treat you differently in public, like they're truly proud of you and that has to give you false hope that their act could possibly be real."

"You're a wise man. I know *this* is real," Alec explained, cupping Key's hand still at his cheek. "We've got enough going on right now that my emotional plate is full—full of you and this guy. Now, tell me you love me."

Key rolled his eyes and removed his hand, giving him a quick kiss before stepping away. "I figured I'd say it once, you'd know, and it would be over. So why am I sayin' it like every hour of every day," he teased, going back for the bike.

"Because I waited so long to hear it."

"Then record me, so I can stop sayin' it and you can keep remindin' yourself," Key replied, his voice laced with humor as he started working again.

"I know you're teasing, but that's a good idea just in case you need reminding." He flipped Nash over in his arms, and the puppy wasted no time in attacking his hand again as he scooted off the stool. "I'm taking him out then warming up leftovers if you're not too sick of them." Four days of eating the same thing every day was getting a bit boring.

"Bring your work into the livin' room. We can watch a movie. Your pick," Key offered.

"Wow, I get to pick? You must really feel bad for me. What if I make you watch the history of the sewing machine?" Alec teased at the garage door.

"Then the plan might alter," Key said distractedly, his whole concentration back on the bike.

"Let's go do your thing, Nash," Alec said, stepping out into the cool evening. He refused to get emotionally down about his family. This was for the best. If they hadn't liked him before, wait until they saw him now. That made him smile as he rubbed Nash's head and set him on the ground.

CHAPTER 30

Keyes reached for the remote, pointing the control at the television while pressing the power button. Wincing as he took a seat on the sofa, the thin material of his well-worn T-shirt offered little comfort for his still tender back against the leather. It had been a few days since he'd gotten the new tattoo and the son-of-a-bitch was starting to itch and bugged the shit out of him.

Alec had sent one cryptic text message a couple of hours ago about being late due to a work emergency. His mister had worried over Nash being home alone for so long. Keyes didn't bother teasing Alec about being overprotective. They both seemed to take Nash's potty training and loneliness seriously. Keyes found no other solution except to bail on work. So he'd rushed straight home to watch over their little guy.

Keyes flipped channels, searching the local news stations on Alec's five million channel television. Nash, who played rambunctiously on the sofa nearby, barked. He cut his gaze to see the puppy facing off with him, trying to gain his attention. He was a stinker, one Keyes found hard to ignore.

"You talkin' to me? You wanna be a badass, huh?" Keyes dropped his hand to the sofa cushion, wiggling his fingers to play the hand-monster game. Nash willingly played this particular game for hours on end. When the puppy almost backed himself straight off the edge of the cushion, Keyes kicked up a leg to keep Nash from falling. The little ball of energy didn't seem to notice he'd just been saved from a tumble and continued the attack on his hand.

"Ouch!" Keyes yelped, spinning Nash a different direction while keeping his fingers away from the pup's mouth. "Your little teeth are sharp."

The fearless Nash was back in attack mode, yapping at him to keep up the action and stay in the game. He was so damn lost to this life. If he had worked a solid eight-hour day in months, that'd be a damn shock. Just the drive time to and from home fucked up his work schedule before he ever did things like sit for a tattoo all fucking day long or rush home because a puppy needed to be let out.

"Maybe you need to come to work with me some of the time," he suggested to the growling puppy. He flipped Nash to his back, keeping him caged in and squirming. The little pup calmed as Keyes rubbed his belly.

"After the surprising turn, you see Dallas ADA, Alec Pierce, exiting the courthouse. He doesn't look happy, Tom." At the mention of Alec's name, Keyes lifted his gaze back to the screen and pointed a finger toward the television.

"See your daddy?" he asked Nash.

Keyes's heart clenched and sort of dropped just staring at Alec. He was such a fine-looking guy, all polished and sophisticated in his snug-fitting suit—that visual never got old. Keyes read the bottom of the screen, trying to catch up on what was going on and why his gorgeous guy was on TV.

"*Donald Cummings released today*" was the caption running along the bottom of the screen. The cameraman zoomed in on Alec and the woman walking by his side. Alec looked angry and tense, his head slightly bent as he blatantly ignored the news team covering him so closely. He spoke to the woman beside him, who wore the same expression. They both moved past the waiting press, refusing to speak with any of them.

Keyes pushed the rewind button, taking the segment back to the beginning to try and better understand what was going on. The best he could tell, this sounded like it might involve the guy Alec had worked hard to keep behind bars. Somehow, Cummings had unexpectedly been released. He watched Alec trot down a set of steps and disappear around the corner of the building. The screen then filled with a mugshot of Donald Cummings.

What the fuck?

Keyes paused the television to get a closer look. The guy looked familiar, like real familiar. He kept the guy's picture on screen as he reached for his cell phone and dialed Devilman.

"Hey, man," Dev answered on the first ring, the hard rock music from the ink parlor blaring in the background.

"You near a TV?" he asked, still staring at the guy. No question, he'd run across this Donald Cummings somewhere before. Hell, it could have been anywhere, maybe even a convenience store for all he remembered.

"Nah, I'm workin'. What's up?"

"Hang on. I'm gonna send you a picture." Keyes pointed his phone toward the television and snapped the photo of the mugshot. He sent the picture to Dev in a text message. "Tell me when you get it."

Seconds passed with only rustling sounds coming through the phone from Dev's end before he was back. "Yeah, dude, that's that guy that used to hang around all the time at the clubhouse. A fuckin' douchebag your old man found. No way he's gettin' his patch. You remember him, right? Hang on." The music faded only to be replaced with Harley pipes. Dev must have stepped outside, but Keyes wasn't certain which one was easier to hear over. "He was always up your old man's ass. He'd share his old lady around. You and I thought he was real fucked up."

Yeah, okay, he kind of remembered.

"Your old man had a hard-on for him—no offense. He'd claim shit like that dude was the son he never had—no offense, again."

Oh fuck yeah, now he remembered. He'd swept those memories and the hurt he'd felt under the rug, or so he'd thought. His father had paraded that loser around for days to get under his skin. He hated that motherfucker.

"I don't know where his wife is, but he's been terrorizin' his kid." Keyes racked his brain, trying hard to remember exactly what Alec had said about the guy.

"Sounds like he's right up your old man's alley then."

That caused a humorless huff while he stared at the frozen mugshot on the screen. "Can you get me his address?"

"Yeah. I got someone in the chair, but I'll text my mom and get back to you. I gotta go. This bitch doesn't look happy with me stoppin'. She's fuckin' staring holes through the damn window," Dev said.

"Later." He disconnected the call and didn't allow himself to overthink. He had the power to help Alec in this deal, and he was going to, fuck the questions that might arise. He didn't see it taking much. He could toss out a few threats and do some shoving around with promises of more to come if the guy didn't stop his shit with his kid. Keyes took Nash to his doggie pen. He didn't like being the one to cage their little guy. Nash's big brown eyes always looked so sad when the gate locked him in. "You're gonna have to be good until we get home."

As he dressed in his leathers for the long ride, he decided not to text Alec. The less he knew, the better. He'd take care of things on his own. By the time he had made it back to downtown Dallas, Dev had sent him the address and asked if he needed a backup. He didn't respond. Instead, he drove straight to the address Dev had indicated.

He pulled through the front entrance of the apartment complex and rolled to a stop, the vibration from the bike rumbled between his thighs as he scouted out the area. The place was a fucking dump. Until he met Alec, these were the kinds of places where he always hung out. The whole complex was run the fuck down and that looked to have happened about thirty years ago. Peeling paint, broken shutters hanging lopsided on the building, zero landscape, and what had to be the entire population of the community loitered around outside—not in a good, let's have a neighborhood party, kind of way. No, everyone looked straight-up thug.

Keyes eyed the different groups as he rolled past, following the numbers high on top of the buildings. He drove all the way around to the back of the complex before he found the building he was looking for. He popped the curb, driving his bike along the sidewalk dividing the individual apartments. He dropped his kickstand in place directly in front of Cummings's door.

He centered himself. He hadn't needed his inner badass biker in a long time, and he wasn't sure he needed him now.

If the guy wanted in his club, he'd have respect for a patched brother. Maybe he could skate on intimidation, effectively threaten this douchebag with just his status. He could then follow up with the prez in the morning. The club wasn't opposed to slapping around their old ladies, or their kids for that matter, but they also didn't need any more trouble right now. He could ask Fox to reinforce his message with this guy.

He took the three or so steps to the front door and balled his fist, beating on the dingy metal barrier. He heard someone right on the other side and paused, fist still in the air. The door opened, and a half naked dark-haired chick stood on the other side. Keyes ground his jaw, hating the sudden trip down memory lane—his mother had looked just like her. Keyes furrowed his brow.

"Where's Cummings?"

"Whoa," she said, her brows lifting as she looked Keyes up and down then stepped back, opening the door wider. Keyes stayed on the threshold, scanning the small living space. Cummings lay sprawled out on the sofa maybe fifteen feet away. Keyes took the step inside, the strong smell of weed hanging heavily on the air. This Cummings looked different than his mugshot, his head was shaved and he'd put on some muscle. He had that menacing prison vibe and a stare aimed directly at Keyes.

Keyes ignored the hard stare, scanning the rest of the room until he spotted the Disciples of Havoc prospect patch hanging on the back of a chair, letting him know he'd come to the right place. He'd apparently been elevated to a prospect at some point. His irritation spiked as Cummings broke the number one cardinal rule of all prospects when he didn't show respect as Keyes entered the room. The disrespect crawled all up his spine. Prospects always acknowledged when a patched brother entered any goddamn room.

"You need to get to your fuckin' feet," Keyes commanded. All Cummings did was lift the leg hanging off the edge of the sofa to cross his ankles.

"Dory, get me a beer," Cummings drawled in a lazy redneck kind of way, ignoring Keyes altogether.

"He need one?" she asked, stepping a little too closely to him as she twirled her wannabe mermaid hair. The smell of cheap perfume stung his nose when she stepped past him toward the small kitchen.

"Nah, he ain't stayin'. This is Smoke's queer boy." The room grew still as the words scraped through the air like nails on a chalkboard. The girl stopped in her tracks, staring between both men. "Remember the dick suckin' fag Smoke used to talk about all the time?" The prospect's gaze remained locked on his. "This is him...in all his cock-sucking glory."

"Donny, I don't need no trouble," she cautioned, edging her way to the opening of the kitchen.

"Ain't no dick here for you to suck, queer." Cummings's voice dripped with disdain, but it was the sneer curling his lips that grated up his spine.

He took a deep breath and stepped closer to the smart-mouthed prospect. "I'm here to tell you to stay the fuck away from that kid of yours before you fuck her up."

"Pussy."

"What'd you say?" Keyes growled, his intentions imploding in that five second pause.

"I said you're a fuckin' pussy."

Keyes shook his head, biting back his anger as the thought of a sweet little girl being terrified by this pig ripped at his heart.

The prospect jumped off the couch, catching him by surprise when Cummings grabbed a Lucille-style baseball bat from a spot behind the couch. The guy was smarter then he'd anticipated, with all his fake lounging around and shit. A mistake Keyes wouldn't make again.

"I'm gonna make a special visit to see my little girl just as soon as I beat your homo ass."

Over his dead body. Rage fueled Keyes's steps as he stalked across the small room toward Cummings. The stupid fuck had a lot to learn, and Keyes figured today was just as good as any to take him to school.

"That's right. Come get some of this, fag." The dumbass hauled the barbwire wrapped Louisville slugger over his shoulder, readying to swing.

Was this loser serious?

Keyes's level of pissed off shot through the roof.

"You sorry son of a bitch, I came here to fuckin' warn you to stay the fuck away from your kid, but you're pissin' me the fuck off," he roared.

The stupid motherfucker hadn't been listening, because he swung the bat. Cummings's whole upper body twisted around, the force of the swing throwing the guy off balance. Clearly, the douchebag had never been in an actual bar fight. Taking his chances, Keyes lunged at the asshole, easily manhandling the barbwire wrapped bat out of Cummings's hands.

What Keyes had in height and strength, Cummings had in quick and wiry. The guy darted under Keyes's arm while Keyes attempted a swing of his own, clipping Donald in the side as he fled across the living room. Keyes jerked around, taking long strides, pointing the bat at Donald as he spoke. "You can bet your ass your fuckin' days with Havoc are numbered, but that's not gonna fuckin' stop me from fuckin' your shit up if you go anywhere near your kid again."

"I don't take orders from fags," Donald said and spit at him, challenging him.

Man, what the fuck was wrong with this guy? Logic screamed at him to toss the bat on the sofa and take off, let the threat resonate and do its job, but he just couldn't get past the slurs. He'd put up with that shit his whole adult life. The same hate he'd found in his father's eyes so many times stared back at him with malice. All of that contempt should have died with his old man.

As if in slow motion, Keyes watched the guy reach behind his back. Instinctively, he knew the scumbag was pulling a weapon. There was no hesitation on his part, Keyes charged forward and swung the bat with every bit of brute strength he had, knocking the pistol from Cummings's hand before he was able to truly take aim. The gun exploded somewhere behind Keyes and he lost his shit.

Momentum from the swing pulled him forward as he brought the bat back around to catch Cummings in the ribs. Lucky for him the hit did the trick, stopping Cummings in his tracks, sending him staggering back. Shock flashed across his face right before Donald crumpled and dropped forward, clutching his side. Keyes released the bat, grabbing Cummings by his dirty wife beater, driving his fist straight in the guy's startled face. "Call me a fag now, motherfucker!"

He saw nothing but red as his father's abusive slurs echoed in his head. The pain of his past threatened to suffocate him, pull him down. He unleashed his pent-up aggression on Cummings, purging the demons of his past with every fall of his fist. No child deserved to grow up terrified or hated by their father. He had no idea how long he pounded the scumbag when the screaming seeped past his anger. Slowly, he came back to the here and now, to the crappy apartment with the disrespectful prospect battered and bleeding, trying his best to cower away from Keyes's death grip-style hold.

Keyes released the little shit, and Cummings dropped to his knees doing a piss poor job at shielding his face and head. Whatever had snapped in Keyes's head righted itself. He drew air into his burning lungs, his focus now drawn to the screaming woman who stood with several other people in the front doorway, one with a phone in his hand pointed straight at him.

Shit.

Keyes started to turn away then stopped. He lowered his face to Cummings who tried to scramble away. He took a moment to wipe his bloody knuckles across the tank top as he issued his last warning. "Don't make me come back here."

To make sure the scumbag understood, Keyes grabbed the nasty ass vest slung over a chair. Hell would freeze before he left that prospect patch behind.

"You'll have to go through me to lay claim on this." No way was this guy ever coming back to his club. All the bystanders but the female gave him a wide berth, quickly rushing out of his way as he left the apartment.

He was back on his bike, hitting the street within a minute of leaving the apartment.

Keyes raged at himself to calm his ass down as he broke seventy on a side road. This wasn't the type of neighborhood where residents called the police when shit went wrong. The cops didn't get in a hurry to answer a disturbance call in this part of town. That small bit of knowledge calmed him, and only then did he let himself take a good, long breath. That breath had him pulling off the road into a vacant parking lot. He left the bike running as he stared at the prospect vest he had hastily shoved inside his leather riding jacket. Every bit of pent-up anger hit him hard as he ripped the prospect patch off, tossing the blue-jean vest to the ground.

He had lost his shit in there, something he never allowed himself to do, but goddamn, he had made a promise to himself the day of his old man's funeral. He would never let anyone disrespect him again. Not anyone, for any reason. Apparently, that was a vow he planned to take to his grave.

Keyes took another deep breath and pushed the patch inside his leather jacket for safe keeping. If he were smart, he'd go straight to the club right now and hand it over to Fox or Mack, but by God, he didn't think he could walk into that clubhouse and look at his so-called brothers who had willingly let his old man treat him like shit all those years, at least not right now.

He shook his head, trying to rid himself of those destructive thoughts. He just couldn't seem to shake the pissed off resentment he had toward his brothers right now. He was so fucking tired of the name calling and insults, and tonight showed him that his old man's ghost still lingered all around him.

Instead of risking an outright brawl at the clubhouse, Keyes pulled his phone free and messaged Dev. "*I fucked up. He's beat down. I have his patch.*"

"*Cummings?*" Dev replied within seconds.

"*Yeah. With witnesses.*"

"*Fuck, Bro, what were you thinking?*" The blood gathering at Keyes's knuckles ran down his hand, leaving a warm trail over his tender skin.

"*I got his patch. Whatever happens, he ain't gettin' this one back.*" As he waited for Dev's reply, his phone rang. Dev's name popped up on his screen. He swiped to answer, lifting the phone to his ear. "Yeah."

"Lay low. If you need somewhere to go, come to Holly's." Dev's voice was low and serious, showing his concern.

Having a secret place to stay wasn't a problem at all. Funny though, Alec was the whole reason for this trip, and he hadn't considered him once since arriving at Cummings's stupid apartment. "Tell your old man for me?"

"Fuck, man, I should've gone," Dev said, regret lacing his words.

A bitter laugh welled in his chest. "He'd be dead right now if you went. My old man was spewin' out of his goddamn mouth. Pissed me the fuck off."

"I knew I hated that motherfucker," Dev growled. Whether motherfucker meant his father or Cummings didn't seem to matter, and Keyes swore he heard the sound of Dev's knuckles cracking in the background.

"Yeah, I'm out," he said and ended the call.

He settled back in his seat, rolled his tight shoulder muscles before he pushed the kickstand back in place and drove straight to Alec's. The front outside lights of the house were all off, not the normal inviting home he usually drove up to. Keyes rolled down the long driveway, spotting Alec through the windows taking long strides through the house. Keyes parked his bike in its regular spot and was barely off the seat before Alec threw open the back door, calling out to him.

"A biker assaulted Cummings," Alec said frantically, and Keyes nodded, never breaking stride as he by passed Alec, heading straight through the still open back door. There was no hesitation on Alec's part as he easily shifted around to stay right on his heels. "Alexa, turn on all the lights."

The room was immediately bathed in bright light as Keyes shrugged out of his jacket, the prospect patch falling to the floor at his feet. The leather sleeve of his riding jacket scraped across his raw knuckles causing the bleeding to begin again.

"Dammit, Key, what the hell did you do?"

Alec reached for his throbbing hand, but Keyes sidestepped him again, going for the sink. He flipped on the hot water and waited for it to warm as he let the fresh blood drip into the empty basin. The knuckles on his right hand were a torn-up mess. They would definitely be tender for a while. Alec stayed close, hovering at his side, reaching for his hand again but Keyes didn't readily hand it over.

"It's club business, Alec."

"Fuck club business. Are you hurt?" For the first time since he'd arrived home, he cocked his head Alec's direction where he held a clean hand towel in his hand. The heavy concern caused deep worry lines to wrinkle Alec's forehead. Nash had finally made it to them. In his peripheral vision, he'd watched Nash trying to keep up since he'd walked inside the back door. Nash yapped at Keyes's feet, his tiny face craning to better see them until the puppy lost his balance and toppled over.

Even with Alec's aggressive outburst, the two of them instantly calmed his ravaged soul. The settling peace was immediate and thorough, the mounting weight of the evening's emotional toll lifted off Keyes. Instinctively, Keyes lowered his face, rubbing his bearded cheek against Alec who brought his hand up to cup Keyes's cheek, turning him to better look him in the eyes.

"Tell me you're all right."

"Of course." He let a deep sigh out as he moved to kiss Alec's lips. He stayed in Alec's face, staring at this perfect man, basking in the soothing comfort that was Alec Pierce. "He just pissed me the fuck off and I lost it." He let out another lengthy sigh then dunked his hand under the running water.

Keyes jerked his hand back at the sudden burst of pain and took a closer look at his knuckles.

"Goddammit." Removing the dried and oozing blood hadn't improved the look of his hand. And if his hand was this torn up, he must have done some pretty serious damage to Cummings.

"Let me get the first-aid kit."

For Alec, Keyes suffered through the pain of washing his hands with antiseptic then wrapped the towel around his knuckles as Alec dumped the contents of a first-aid kit on the counter. Keyes gathered Nash up with his left hand, taking a barstool as Alec sifted through the small packages.

"Put your hand up here," Alec instructed, his head reeling over the possibility of what this might mean for Key. He quickly scanned the directions on a can of antibacterial spray, not really seeing the instructions, his whole concentration demanding his internal panic stay at bay. It was damn hard to do. The word of Donald Cummings's brutal beat down had gotten to Alec too fast. If the authorities didn't already know about Key's part in the incident, then they would as soon as Donald regained consciousness.

His heart started racing again, thinking over what would happen to Key. A premeditated fight with a state's newest informant, granted full immunity for his willing cooperation. No right-minded judge would ever see the coincidence in a patched Havoc club member going after

Cummings for any other reason than Cummings planned to rat the club out.

"Stop fussin'. I'll be all right." Key's voice jarred Alec from his downward spiraling thoughts. He looked up to watch Key set Nash on the counter, boxed in with his arms, before he unwound the towel from his hand. The knuckles were still bleeding, and he quickly placed the towel over the cuts, adding pressure, trying to stop the flow as he rewrapped his hand.

"What were you thinking? He's dangerous, Key," Alec scolded, dropping his trembling hands to the counter, his shoulders slumped in uncertainty as he stared at his man.

"So the fuck am I, Alec." Key countered with just enough force in his voice to drive the point home. They stared at one another until Key rolled his eyes and reached for Nash, putting him back on the floor. "I came home early after I got your text. Me and Nash were watchin' TV and I saw you, and I saw him, and he used to hang out at the clubhouse. I recognized him. He's a prospect, and I'm not entirely fuckin' sure how that happened without my vote."

Alec waited for several long seconds for more of an explanation, trying to understand what Key knew exactly. He had been careful to never give too many details away. Had Key snooped through his files, found the clues that Cummings could be granted immunity? Alec rejected the notion as soon as the idea crossed his mind. Key wasn't the kind of man to rifle through Alec's private belongings.

When Key didn't say anything more, he took a deep centering breath, trying for calm as he questioned him. "Why did you go after him?"

"Dammit, Alec." Key's fist came down on the counter so hard the packages of the first-aid kit bounced. "All I was gonna do was tell him to stay the fuck away from his kid. I was gonna put some fear in him, then the fucker used my old man's words. All I heard was my father's constant badgerin', and I lost my shit. He pulled a goddamn bat then a motherfuckin' pistol, and I ain't playin' with that. My fuckin' father used a bat to enforce his vile words. I lost it."

Alec's heart pounded so loudly, he was certain he hadn't heard Key's words correctly. "Cummings pulled a gun on you?" All the worry Alec had reined in settled on the glaring fact that Key could have been killed tonight, forever taken away from him. His heart crashed to his feet. His knees threatened to fail him.

Key just gave a huff and rolled his eyes at something he clearly saw as absurd. "Yeah, stupid fuck tried to pull it, but I used his bat on him."

"Did the gun discharge?" Alec asked, carefully holding himself in check. He moved around the counter to stand beside Key, fighting his overwhelming need to reach out and touch his man.

"Stop lookin' so worried. Yeah, the gun went off, but I was never in danger. I could wipe the goddamn floor with that motherfucker." Key stated that with all certainty as he got to his feet, rounding past Alec. He watched Key carefully pick up Nash and nuzzle him as he went toward the living room. Alec stood there dumbfounded as Key looked back over his shoulder. "I was thinkin' about how much bigger he's gotten. He's growing up so fast."

"Key, are you telling me a gun fired at you this evening?" Alec asked, feeling the bile of panic clogging his throat. This was something Alec wasn't prepared for, reality staring him in the face.

"Alec, don't start." Key took a seat on the sofa. Alec followed, sitting on the coffee table directly in front of Key, reaching to place both his palms on Key's thighs. Every worry about what Key knew was now gone. If a stare could communicate anything, his was imploring Key to never allow himself to get in a position like that ever again.

"What would I do without you? I'd never get over the loss," he explained simply, his voice turning soft in its sincerity. "I couldn't live without you."

"That's dramatic," Key replied, clearly unimpressed with Alec's concern.

"Because it is dramatic." Alec pushed back, crossing his arms over his chest, holding himself together. They stared at one another for several long seconds while Alec willed his worried glare to penetrate Key's nonchalance. "Key." Alec sighed as all their differences settled heavily between them. "Baby...Keyes... I appreciate you wanting to help me, but you can't put yourself in harm's way like this, not anymore. Your life's bigger than just you."

Key only stared at Alec who couldn't find it in him to accept anything less than Key's oath to never do anything like this again. The quiet stare between them continued for some time. It wasn't until Key moved Nash and patted the cushion beside him that he knew he'd been heard. Not the vow he was hoping for, not by a long shot, but he'd take the invite. After a second of staring at the man who could have been so easily taken from him tonight, Alec did finally move, needing Key's comfort and reassurance more than ever. He took the seat next to Key, sitting as close as he could, letting the tension go as Key slid an arm around him, drawing him closer.

"There were people there watchin' in the doorway. How much trouble am I in?" he asked, kissing Alec's forehead.

"I'm not sure. I thought matters of the club stayed inside the club. Will he talk or keep to himself?" Alec asked, back to his original concern. Key's hold loosened, and Alec turned, angling his body to better see Key.

"Yeah, I thought about that on the ride back here. Normally they are club business, but he had no respect for me," Key said, his head lowered to the back of the sofa, staring at the ceiling.

"What will the club do if he talks?" Alec asked, watching the fine lines around Key's eyes become more pronounced. That question seemed to hurt Key more than anything else.

"Don't know. I wasn't in the vote to add him as a prospect." Key turned toward Alec. Such rawness reflected in that unguarded stare. Deep sadness lingered there, but something was off in the tone of his voice. Was it regret because things went sideways with the prospect? He seriously doubted it. Surely, the club would back a brother over a prospect. Alec knew Key well enough to know he was loyal to a fault when it came to matters of the club. They were family to him.

Key's words came rushing back along with the answer. Key hadn't been included in the vote. Betrayal...the word was a slap of disbelief. His foundation must have been shaken to the core with that knowledge. Damn, Alec had such ricocheting emotions tonight. His aggression spiked, and he wanted to watch them all burn for excluding this dedicated member who had been nothing but loyal to them.

"What's that mean to your overall future with the club?" Alec asked, lifting a finger to move a strand of Key's long hair that had fallen into his face. His fingertips lingered on his lover, caressing Key's bearded cheek until Alec lifted to press his lips to Key's in a soft kiss. "You aren't going to answer?"

Key shook his head no, his direct gaze unwavering.

"How badly was Cummings hurt?" Alec asked.

"I fucked him up." Key gave a satisfied nod as if he approved of his fighting skills, making Alec smile. He'd have to remember to coach Key if he did in fact have to go to court. Key needed to show remorse, not pride, in his actions.

"Any priors?"

"You never ran me?" Key asked, giving him a sideways glance as he picked Nash up.

"No, I didn't care. I had a hunch about you," Alec said, knocking him in the shoulder, letting their natural easiness soothe him at least for this minute. Alec leaned back into the crook of Key's arm, resting his head against Key's firm shoulder, bringing a tired Nash to his chest for warmth.

"That's not too smart, Pierce. I could've taken you for everything." Key circled a strong arm around Alec, drawing him closer as Key's hand came to rest protectively on Nash. They were a family. A loving, well-suited if slightly unusual family.

"I'd gladly give it to you."

The rumble of an almost silent laugh in Key's chest let him know what Key thought about that. "No priors."

"We've got to talk about this gun thing."

"It's club business. Dev knows. I'm sure he called his old man. Cummings won't rat me out," Key said, the confidence back in his tone which contradicted what he'd said just moments ago. Since Alec was solidly on the other side of that argument, he decided to prepare for the worst just in case.

"I'll call in some favors if necessary. I'm working the last week of my notice, so I'm not sure how much I can do, but I'll ask Janice to keep an eye out." Alec rose to his feet, deciding to take Nash to his doggie bed and then call Janice. She'd know best who he should beg to pick this case up the minute charges were filed. "I'll be back to bandage your hand."

"It's fine," Key said on a yawn, staying seated. His gaze tracked Alec until he was out of view.

"It's not, and we're not finished talking about this gun situation. I'll ride you about this, so much so that you'll stay out of situations like this just so you don't have to listen to me bitch." Alec was almost to the bedroom when he heard Key's response, which sent a grin spreading across his face.

"Oh hell, I know how much you like your fuckin' words, but my mind kinda stayed in the gutter after you offered to ride me."

CHAPTER 31

Keyes heard the sirens before he saw the lights. He dropped the tool in his hand as he instinctively knew they were coming for him. He wasn't giving anyone who might be trigger-happy a reason to shoot him. He straightened to his full height, moving back several paces while calling out to Louis to take care of the business as they'd discussed this morning. He had a few seconds, so he quickly opened his phone, sending a prepared text to his uncle, the one that said he'd been arrested and asked him to come bail him out with money from his stash. He made sure it went through before he dropped the phone in his pocket and lifted his hands high in the air and stepped out into the open as one squad car after another pulled into the parking lot of Tires.

Before an officer could step foot out of his squad car, Keyes dropped to his knees, hands still above his head with his chin to his chest. He'd had a hunch this would happen when the morning news aired the Cummings story. His name was never mentioned and the angle of the shaky camera recording failed to get a clear shot of him, but he'd fucked Donald up pretty bad in his fit of anger. It was just a matter of time before the weasel ratted him out. Apparently, his time was up.

Keyes was shoved to the pavement, a knee digging hard into to his back and a foot adding unneeded pressure to his neck, all in an effort to hold his yielding body in place. He blocked everything out, centering into himself. Alec took center stage behind his closed eyes as he complied with the officers' commands. The only regret he had about his actions was that Alec would be drawn into his shit show. Alec didn't deserve it. He was such a good man. The care he'd used to clean and bandage his knuckles while going on and on about him having more to consider than just himself brought a small hint of a smile to his lips.

The memory of Alec brushing the hair from Keyes's face as he cared for his hand shattered as cold bit into the bones of his wrists as his hands were handcuffed behind his back and he was hoisted up. That shit hurt like hell and he had to fight every instinct inside him to keep from tugging out of their aggressive hold which would also add resisting arrest to the litany of charges he suspected they had on him. He marched at an awkward angle toward the police car with his hair acting as a curtain, shielding his face from curious eyes while being shoved inside the back of the squad car.

This was his own damn fault. He shouldn't have lost his temper like he had yesterday. He was smarter than that. He damn sure shouldn't be sitting in the back of this fucking squad car with the lights flashing as they went toward the county lock-up. Had his life finally caught up with him? Would he finally go to prison for this? Keyes sighed. Probably. He didn't have the money or connections to get out and that bitch DA would make sure the book was thrown at him, make an example out of him. She finally had a hook in one of the Havoc club members.

Maybe the club attorney could put up a strong fight on his behalf. In his heart, he knew that wouldn't matter. He was going to prison. What would happen to Alec and Nash while he was incarcerated? Would that be the final straw? Would Alec wake up and see how poorly suited they were as a couple? Alec would be so fucking hurt by this. He grunted, staring unseeing out the side window. Alec ran fast and loose with his heart, no sense of self-preservation. Keyes had warned him over and over that he wasn't a good guy. He should have given Alec up instead of being so selfish.

Fuck, even being man-handled out of the cruiser and dragged inside the jailhouse, the only thing that caused pain was the thought of Alec moving on without him. They fingerprinted him, took his mug shot, and booked him in quick order. He wasn't given the opportunity to make his one phone call before being tossed inside a crowded cell— nothing new there. That would be an 'accidental' oversight later on down the line if he complained. He wouldn't though, the less he said the better.

Apparently, his reputation preceded him or the unfriendly glower on his face intimidated his cell mates. Two scooted off the bench where he chose to sit to keep his back to the wall. Good, he wasn't there to make friends anyway. Keyes rested against the wall and waited.

Hours had passed from the bullshit bail hearing that set bail at a crazy expensive amount for somebody who had just gotten into a fucking fist fight—that shit pissed him off more than the time it was taking to be released. He'd been waiting so long for his uncle to post bond that Keyes was certain he was staying the night.

Metal on metal signaled the cell door opening, then a cop yelled, "Keyes Dixon."

Every-fucking-thing the cops ever did concerning him included a minimum of three officers, this time included. All took measured steps backward as he walked through the cell door. Two had their hands on their weapons, eyeing him as if he were stupid enough to start shit in the fucking jailhouse.

The wait had been long and uncomfortable, his attitude was complete shit, and he growled a response when he was handed his jacket, wallet, and phone. He walked out to his Uncle Clyde standing there, looking haggard, worried, and uncertain as hell. He hated he'd put that concern on his uncle's face. Keyes scanned the waiting room to see Alec standing with an older man, the same one who'd introduced himself as his attorney at the bail hearing earlier. From where he stood, he took a better look at the guy who wore an expensive suit and fancy tie. The man held a briefcase in his hand and, from the familiarity he showed toward Alec, probably wasn't the free court-appointed attorney Keyes had initially thought he was.

On top of everything going on with Keyes, he didn't need the burst of jealousy slicing at his heart at seeing Alec and the other attorney standing so close. They looked good together too. Alec belonged with someone he could be proud of, not someone he had to bail out of jail. Keyes was a biker; he fit perfectly in this backdrop. The two men across the room dressed in expensive suits certainly didn't fit in the cold, dingy waiting area where they currently stood.

He wanted to drive his fist through something, anything. Jealousy was a funky little bitch, sliding in to take the top spot for fueling his anger.

"What're you doing here?" Keyes asked, walking toward to his uncle, but talking directly to Alec.

"He was here before I got here," his uncle answered, drawing all his attention back to him. "Dev, Mack, and Fox were here too. I don't know how they found out. Dev was causing a big scene, so Fox took him to get your bike."

Keyes cut his gaze straight to Alec. The jealousy dropped a notch as Alec's safety moved to the most important concern he had. Keyes felt his face tense. All that bullshit talk of him staying out of harm's way then fucking Alec shows up here at the same time as his brothers? Keyes somehow managed to hold tight rein on his anger and swung his gaze back to Clyde. "Did you get my money?"

"Alec got you out. He had already posted the bond before I could."

Fucking hell, the shit show just kept getting better. His jaw clenched tight but the fire breathing dragon was hard to tamp down. His gaze sliced back to Alec who stared boldly back at him. Every motherfucker in that jail cell was afraid of him, but not Alec, not even a little bit. It was Keyes who was scared to death of losing Alec.

In the hours Keyes had spent sitting on that fucking hard bench, he had devised his plan. He'd tell his brothers this wasn't about club business, that it was personal and shit had just gone sideways. That would make sense to his brothers why he'd called Clyde to bail him out instead of them.

Alec had put himself right in his club's path.

Keyes also hadn't wanted Alec spending any of his cash on him. This had been his decision alone. He'd fucked up. Now, all the ground they'd covered since they'd met led them right back to the beginning, when he'd felt like Alec was slumming it with the trash that wound up in county lock-up.

Fuck.

Keyes ground his teeth together and mumbled out, "I'll pay you back."

"That's unnecessary. Keyes, this is Marc Manners. He's agreed to take your case." The lawyer's hand came out, and Keyes stared at it, refusing the handshake until Clyde cleared his throat and whispered his name. Dammit. He finally reached out to clasp it, not looking the guy in the eyes.

He had to get the fuck out of here. There was too much bullshit emotion and spending the day caged like a motherfucking animal hadn't helped his perspective. He hated that shit, being stuck inside like that. No wonder convicts beat the hell out of each other.

Keyes took a step for the door, giving a side eye to the older attorney who had his head bent toward Alec, talking quietly. They looked so fucking pretty together. Keyes looked back over his shoulder to Clyde. "Can you give me a ride back to the shop? I'll call Dev to leave my bike there."

If Dev would even take his call. But if he didn't, Keyes would know for sure how far his brothers had gotten in trying to figure out who the fuck Alec was.

Why had Alec come?

"I will, Clyde," Alec answered, his voice hard, drawing every eye his direction. Alec held the attention of room and ignored Keyes like he had tried to do with Alec. Alec extended a hand to the attorney beside him. "Thank you for all you've done today. I'm not sure we could have gotten him out so quickly."

The older attorney looked like he had an infinite amount of patience. He was completely unfazed by Keyes's attitude. "Keyes, we'll need to meet in the morning. I've carved out time and scheduled with Alec."

Keyes didn't say a word, just kept walking toward the door.

"We'll be there," Alec said, again his tone was swift and firm, leaving no question as to whether what he said would be done.

"Call me when you get a minute. I want to know what's going on," Clyde said, inserting himself in the swirl of tension surrounding them that seemed to be multiplying by the second. Then Clyde said what Keyes should have. "Thank you for everything, Alec."

"I'm sorry you had to leave work. I didn't realize he called you or I could've stopped you," Alec said with attitude and accusation in his tone. They seemed to be following him, and he pushed through the door, seemingly ignoring everything as he scanned the parking lot and beyond, looking for any sign of his brothers.

The door swung shut behind him, momentarily drowning out their voices until Clyde was there, pulling him into a hug, a comfort Keyes didn't want and didn't deserve. He kept his body rigid but bent enough to allow Clyde his moment.

He didn't participate in any of the rest of the conversation as he walked the length of the sidewalk down the side of the building. He knew the club members' practices for surveillance better than anyone. They were sneaky bastards. There was no hiding in plain sight, which caused his anxiety to double.

Alec walked about three feet behind him, following as he turned the corner. Keyes scanned every direction, looking for threats.

"My car's this way." Alec took a step off the sidewalk, walking out in front of him. Keyes resisted the urge to grab his arm in a protectionary move and put Alec behind him. Instead, he double-timed it to pass Alec, walking several feet ahead of him. He heard the doors of the car unlock, and again, he scanned the entire parking lot from this new angle, his inner thoughts chanting a kind of prayer, willing himself to not miss one single detail.

As Alec opened the driver's door, Keyes lowered inside the vehicle on the passenger side. Instead of starting the sports car, Alec placed both hands on the steering wheel and stared out the front windshield as he said, "Why didn't you call me?"

"Why would I call you? Why are you here?" he asked in a sudden burst of anger, turning to face Alec.

"Because you went to jail today, Key." Alec swung his head Keyes's direction, but he might as well have said, "*You're the dumbest person on the planet, Key*" with all the condescension lacing every syllable.

"And you put yourself right in front of the club. They had to have seen you, Alec." He tried to mimic that same "you're dumb" tone, but failed.

"They can't possibly know who I am. I never spoke to any of them. Clyde handled the whole group. I stayed at a distance even as your friend got irate. They left pretty quickly after arriving. There's no way they could have known who I was or that I was there for you." Alec explained all this as if the notion was absolutely ridiculous, and he reached out to push the button to start the car, pressing the gas pedal to add to the loud rumble.

"Goddamn, Alec. This is serious." Keyes slammed a hand on the dashboard, drawing Alec's gaze. The lawyer lifted a brow and stared at him, a fire lighting in those green depths.

"I don't know that you understand how serious this truly is," Alec countered in that fucking way the man had of yelling without ever raising his voice, but Keyes wouldn't be sidetracked.

"Why did you come? They've seen you and that's all it takes. If I get locked up, I can't protect you, and I guarantee, they'll figure out who you are. Somebody in that fuckin' jailhouse is being paid by the club, and they'll rat you out in a hot second. We got eyes every-fuckin'-where," Keyes shouted, trying to make Alec understand he was playing with a loaded gun.

"I've worked the entire day trying to get you out of that place," Alec said calmly, but this time his tone carried a warning. "You should have seen the trumped-up charges they wanted to pile on top of you. You've got yourself in a situation where you can't even begin to understand the gift you've given that vicious DA."

What the fuck did that have to do with what he'd just said?

"You shouldn't have come," Keyes repeated, holding firm to his argument. They glared at one another, neither giving a single inch. Finally, Keyes rolled his eyes and gave in, facing forward to stare out the front window, refusing to put his seatbelt on as he crossed his arms tightly over his chest and fumed.

After a minute more, Alec put the car in gear and started driving them out of the parking lot.

"You're being mean. Why are you being so mean?"

Keyes stayed silent, staring out the window. He didn't know how to make Alec realize the threat was real.

"You're never mean to me. I did what I had to do. You have to see that."

Keyes narrowed his eyes and mashed his lips together to help keep his silence.

"I'll have security on me tomorrow then, is that better?"

This was what Alec did regularly, he underestimated the badass nature of his bike club. A little rinky-dink personal security company was child's play. They'd get past them before Alec could hit the panic button.

Maybe as much as five minutes later, Keyes forced the shift in his thoughts and grumbled out, "How much did it cost today?"

For a first time in their relationship, Alec remained quiet which told him all he needed to know. Alec was always chatty; he talked and talked and talked.

"I'm payin' you back. How much does that fancy attorney cost?"

"Why does it matter?" Alec finally asked, turning onto West Davis Street, close to the tire shop. "We've never let money get between us."

That did it. Keyes barked out a harsh laugh and turned Alec's way. "Money's always between us, Alec."

"Why are you being so mean to me?" Alec asked again, turning into the parking lot of Tires. The place was closed up tight—no one around. Keyes looked down at the time on the dash. When had it gotten so late?

"Stay inside this car, and if anything happens, do whatever it takes to drive the fuck away." Keyes got out of the car, his long strides carrying him to the side of the building. His bike was gone, but there was a note tucked underneath a rock where it usually sat. He went over to the spot and pulled the page free, seeing Dev's scribbled handwriting.

I got the bike at your apartment, locked up. We need to talk.

Dread built solidly in his gut. It was one thing to assume his brothers knew, another to have it confirmed.

He flipped around, jogging back to the parking lot. He stopped dead in his tracks at seeing only Alec's car in the lot.

Think, Keyes. Be smarter than they are.

He scanned every pebble in the parking lot, willing his brain to think.

Okay, there was no possible way Dev would have left a note or taken the bike to his apartment if he truly knew everything. If the club knew, his Harley would be at the clubhouse to draw Keyes there.

He stared down at the note again. Dev never used words like *we need to talk*.

"Dammit," he roared to the heavens. "Can't you give me a fucking break for once in my fucked up life?"

Think, Keyes.

He balled his fists, knowing he'd kill any of those motherfuckers for touching one hair on Alec's head.

That wouldn't be enough to stop them.

Stop the caveman bullshit and think.

He stared at the note again, reading between the lines. All right, if his brothers did in fact know, they could have ambushed him here—especially if Clyde called Dev and told him they were headed to the shop.

Alec was there, still waiting inside the car like he'd asked, staring straight at him. An anxiety-filled sigh escaped as he started that direction, opening the passenger door and dropping down inside. He had to get a hold of himself, a hold of this anger that wasn't helping anything, and think tactically. Of course, Alec would have shown up. He loved Keyes, and he did have the power to help or at least he'd think he had the power to help. Yeah, Alec was the kind of man who would have his back no matter the consequences.

Alec stared at him, and he stared at Alec. He needed to have more faith in Alec. And the fucking secrets between them needed to end. Too much was at stake now for Alec not to know everything, knowledge would help better protect him for the future. They needed to work together to figure this out, and as a tried and true loner, that was a damn hard decision to make.

"Dammit, Key, just talk to me." Alec fumed. How Key could be anything except proud of everything Alec had accomplished today was beyond him, and he refused to move his vehicle from the Tires parking lot until they settled this between them. He stared a hole though Key's profile as the man again ignored him completely, holding his phone in his hand, his thumbs moving across the screen.

When had Key become so proficient with a cell phone that he'd changed from using a single index finger for typing each letter to skillfully typing away using his thumbs?

"Did you hear me?"

Key's eyes narrowed and he continued to type. There was no question, Key was absolutely ignoring him.

Alec hated being ignored.

"I'm not—" Alec started through clenched teeth, but Key stopped him by way of his thumbs pausing and his head turning slightly toward Alec, not enough that he could see Key's eyes or his full face, but enough to make Alec pause.

"I'm worried about your safety." Key lifted his hand, stopping Alec when he dragged in breath, preparing to launch into why his safety was secondary to Key's wellbeing. "And I wanna pay you back for all of this. We have a club attorney. She's good. She can handle this, and she's not gonna cost me a dime, because of all the money I pay in…"

There was too much Key didn't know, and he clearly didn't understand the value of connections. Between Alec being in the politically connected Pierce family and Marc

Manners being as connected as it got in the Dallas-Fort Worth area, Key might truly have a chance at staying out of prison. Marc Manners was a badass. He made his deals with the justices while on the golf course or at Friday night poker parties. Marc was a winner—in everything he touched. Key needed him, and as long as Alec got this settled before his father found out how much he was tossing his name around, Alec might be able to keep Key from taking the fall for his entire club, something DA Twiford would aim for in a heartbeat.

"Baby, I promise you, your club attorney isn't Marc Manners. You have to trust me on this. I've watched miracles happen under that man. He doesn't lose. Period."

"Can you get us on the road? I don't want to risk anyone else seein' you." Key's head tilted fully away from Alec, and his thumbs again moved on the phone screen in his hand.

They hadn't resolved the fight between them, but they also were no longer sniping at each other. So, he depressed the gas pedal and pulled to the entrance of the parking lot.

"How much?"

He didn't pretend to misunderstand as he took his place in the line of crowded traffic on West Davis Street. Instead, he took a page from Key's playbook and remained silent.

Key lifted his thumbs, keeping his whole concentration on the screen. He didn't say another word as Alec tried hard to remember his way back to the highway while keeping an eye on the road and slyly trying to see who Key texted.

At the red light, Alec reached over, taking the crumpled sheet of paper sitting in Key's lap. Key's gaze followed as Alec read the quickly written note. "Who's this from? Dev?"

"Yeah," Key answered and lifted his phone, waving it at Alec. He refused to play the guessing game with Key right now, and reached over, grabbing the cell phone, quickly scanning the text conversation.

Key: "*You got my bike?*"

Dev: "*Locked up at your place. We need to talk.*"

Key: "*Yeah?*"

Dev: "*No more bullshit. Come to my shop in the morning.*"

Key said nothing more as Alec held the phone and another text came in.

Dev: "*I always got your back. You're my brother.*"

Alec's gaze collided with Key's who looked up at him with what he could only describe as deep relief in his eyes. His heart clenched and he gave a small involuntary smile. The last fifteen minutes was forgotten as he got lost in the beauty of his guy. The honking from the car behind them had Alec looking over to see the street light had turned green, and he quickly grabbed the wheel, accelerating through the intersection.

"Can we go by my uncle's place? It's like fifteen minutes from here. I gotta get something," Key asked, taking the phone, rising enough to push it back into his jeans pocket.

"Sure, Olivia's babysitting Nash," he added and got the desired result from his admission.

"No fuckin' way. You did not hire a babysitter for a puppy."

Alec's grin grew. Say what he would, Alec could hear the relief in Key's voice for that decision.

"I did. I didn't know how late we would be, and it just felt like the right thing to do. He's on his schedule, and he's not pottying in my shoes anymore. I've read that when they're left alone for long periods of time, they'll fall back into the patterns of being destructive. I decided a babysitter is less expensive than buying new shoes." Since he had no idea of the direction to Clyde's, Alec should be focused on the navigation, but instead, he took Key's hand in his. Key was slower to thread his fingers with Alec's, but when he did, it felt very much like Alec might be Key's life preserver. "Please stop being angry with me. I love you. I'd risk anything to help and protect you."

Key didn't say a word, but his lips lifted in a soft smile as he waved a hand to point Alec into the right-hand lane. Alec took the turn, heading toward Cedar Hill.

CHAPTER 32

"That's Clyde," Keyes said, using his key to unlock the dead bolt to the shop door as a clicking noise of the outside camera disrupted the quiet of the night.

"He's vigilant," Alec said.

"He's smart." Keyes tossed out the dig and looked back over his shoulder to see Alec lifting the collar to his suit jacket, wrapping it tighter around him to ward off the chill in the air. Keyes pushed open the door and walked inside ahead of Alec. Normally, he would have either had Alec wait in the car or ushered him into the room first, but even with Dev's assurances, paranoia ate at him. He went straight for the lights, flipping the overhead switch before doing a full-turn scan of the room, checking every corner to make sure they were completely alone.

"Come stand by this," he said, walking over to the small heater and flipping the lever to high.

He left Alec standing there, going for the safe he had in the corner. He removed the old tarp he used as covering and

357

bent at the knee. He turned the combination until the door popped open. He had four items inside. Keyes pulled out his pistol and tucked it inside his jacket pocket. Next came two boxes of ammunition, which he stuffed in the both pockets. While he trusted Dev with his life, he couldn't say that faith in Dev extended to Alec's safety. He was too precious to him to risk on assumption.

Keyes stuck a hand in the very back of the safe and pulled out a heavy metal box full of his cash. He rose, kicking the door of the now empty safe shut, listening for the automated lock that secured it back in place. He again started for the overhead light when he looked up to see Alec's concerned gaze on him.

"I'm not necessarily opposed to guns…" Alec started and Keyes cut him off. Of course, they'd never talked about weapons. He didn't see Alec as someone who would ever own a gun, but these were drastic times, and Alec was just going to have to learn to live it.

"Precautionary. If they were comin' after us, they already would have made a move." He adjusted his path, erouting back toward the heater. He reached down, shutting it off as he eyed his guy who hadn't taken his eyes off him since they'd walked inside. Alec looked uncertain and maybe hurt. Keyes had put both those looks on his face. Taking the moment wasn't the right decision, but hell, he'd been making bad decision after bad decision since he'd met Alec. Keyes caught Alec by surprise, cupping the back of his neck and drawing him forward for a hard, insistent press of lips. Alec eagerly reached for his waist, holding him there, kissing him again in just the same way.

"I love you. I can't stand us—"

Keyes's hand went to Alec's moving lips, covering his mouth to silence him.

"We'll talk at home." He left no room for discussion. He stared Alec straight in the eyes until he got Alec's nod. Alec tilted his chin, quickly kissing the hand still at his lips as he tucked in around Keyes, wrapping a strong arm around his back, removing all space between them.

"No more secrets," Alec said in a whisper. "We're past secrets."

"Yeah, we are," he easily agreed.

"Then I have a lot to say."

Seconds before he cut the overhead lights, he looked over to see Alec's eyes narrow and his jaw clench as he started for the door as though he'd made some resolution. For some reason, those words didn't have the same effect on Keyes. When didn't his lover have a lot to say?

The fatigue of the day wore on Alec. Although his decision was made, it still weighed heavily on his heart. Putting aside the ethical consideration of what he was about to do, the concern for how Key might react to his digging through his past was enough to almost keep him silent. But this was just too important. Key had to understand why he hadn't thought twice about putting himself in harm's way today, because this was all his fault.

Alec walked through the house, watching as Key pretended to ignore Nash nipping at his feet while he went from window to window, lowering the window blinds and pulling the drapes. Key was diligent in his task, but seemed to walk a little slower to let Nash catch up before he moved to the next window. It was sweet gesture, one that would eventually warm Alec's heart. His strong, mean biker was in fact fluffier than a teddy bear on the inside.

Key was so protective he left nothing to chance. On the long quiet drive home, Alec finally rationalized that Key knew they weren't in imminent danger. All the worry of their future from this point forward was being channeled into keeping Alec safe. So he didn't say another word.

He let Key busy himself while he gathered all his files on the Cummings case and dumped them on the kitchen bar counter then went to the refrigerator, pulling out two IPAs—Alec needed the liquid courage—and went for the drawer housing the bottle opener. He downed half the bottle in one long chug. His leg bounced, and he watched Key grab his metal box from the table and come to the kitchen counter, taking a barstool.

"I'll take Nash out, you stay inside. If somethin' does go down, you stay inside this house no matter what, lock yourself in an upstairs closet, and call the police." Key's words were ridiculous, and he had to know full well Alec would never leave him to defend himself all alone. "We need to get you security—like big security. I was thinkin' about your old man, he's gotta have like secret service security. Can you get them?"

The tension weighing heavily in the air lifted, making Alec smile. The relief slowed the nervous energy bouncing his leg as he shook his head. The secret service idea must have given Key hope, because when he said no, his guy's face crumpled. "I have someone to call for security and tomorrow's my official last day in the DA's office. I'm taking the personal days I've accumulated, so it should be easy enough to keep the house secure if I'm not leaving much."

"Tomorrow's your birthday too. I don't have a present for you. I was gonna do that today," Key confessed, and the same anger from when Key stepped out and spotted Alec in the detention facility's waiting room was back on Key's face.

"You staying safe and us working through this together is more than enough."

"No, it's not." Key's brows slid together as he shook his head. He lifted the large metal ammunition style box and put it right on top of Alec's files. "I'm recoverin' financially at the tire shop, but not enough to compensate for all the hours I'm gone to come here and all the staff I've had to hire to make up for me bein' gone. I've done some side work and saved. I was gonna get you a gift with this money. Now, I'm just givin' it to you."

So, money was in that box. Key reached across the counter to grab the beer bottle. "I'm pretty sure I'd've been shit at buyin' you a present anyway. Maybe this is just better."

"I would love anything you picked out for me," Alec said, working the intricate locking system on top of the box. He opened the lid to see stacks of hundred-dollar bills. Alec tested the weight with his hands. The box that Key so easily lifted was actually heavy and stuffed full of cash.

"How much is here?" he asked, fingering down several stacks, seeing nothing but hundred-dollar bills.

"Stopped countin' at one fifty," Key answered nonchalantly and tipped the bottle back to take a drink as his gaze stayed fixed on Alec.

"A hundred and fifty thousand dollars?" Alec asked, questioning the number. Key's hard-earned cash was sitting unprotected in a small safe on the back of his uncle's property? Anyone could have stolen this from him. "Is this from Tires?"

Key's jaw clenched, and he sat back on the stool, tightly crossing his arms over his chest. He wasn't going to answer, which was all the answer Alec needed.

"Key, it's all right. You don't have to say anything. What do you want me to do with this?" Alec said, shutting the lid and moving the box off his files.

"I want you to pay the attorney then I want you to use the rest to build that house you're workin' on because this place isn't right for you. It's too big and you need something homey that's comfortable like you are. When I go to jail, I want you to take my bikes and sell 'em. I'll make sure Clyde knows to give 'em to you. They're worth somethin'. It'll help pay you back for all this cash you're gonna be out, and I don't want you to feel bad about not waitin' for me." Key turned the beer bottle up and gulped the contents down. Alec watched his Adam's apple bob, completely confused by the sudden shift of topics. He'd been instructed to build their home then let Key rot away in prison and date someone else? Did Key truly see him as that kind of a man? He would never do that.

"I'm going to do what it takes to keep you out of prison…"

"No!" Key pounded the now empty bottle down on the counter, the dark expression back on his face. Key vigorously shook his head. "While I was sittin' in that cell, I thought about it. There's shit I don't know goin' on. There was no reason for him to spring free from jail like he did or act like he did to me. He was a cocky motherfucker and nobody acts like that unless they think they're above the law. That means I'm goin' to jail, for fuckin' sure." There was pain on his brilliantly reasonable man's face. How had he nailed it so completely?

"Key—" Alec said and stopped short. Again, much like he'd done several times throughout the day, Alec laid the blame squarely on his own shoulders. Had he not kept this information quiet, had he warned Key of the possibility, they wouldn't be in this situation today. Alec had stayed in the district attorney's office to protect Key, and when it came down to it, he had failed the only man he'd ever loved. It physically hurt him to think of letting Key down so monumentally.

"No, Alec, listen to me. I thought about breakin' it off with you, actin' like this time didn't truly matter, but it just does, and I can't fuckin' hurt you. It's like I physically can't cause you pain, so I'm not gonna pretend differently. You work your angles and do whatever you think's best. You pay that attorney whatever you pay, but in the end, when I'm sittin' in the pen, you gotta get over it and move on. Don't wait for me—one day's too long. You take care of Nash and you go find someone like that attorney today. You two look right together." Again, pain crossed Key's handsome face, his fingers curled into fists, and Alec swore he saw a well of tears forming in this generous man's eyes. He could see Key willing himself to be okay with everything he'd just insisted on. The battle was real and didn't seem to be working as raw anguish radiated off Key and he started to rise off the stool.

"Stop. Stay here. You're right on everything..." Alec felt just as out of control as Key, and his anxiety spiked as he pushed the files closer to Key. "You're right about it all, except how this is going to end between us."

Key needed to know this information, and no matter what, Alec would fight for them. Determination straightened his spine. He'd make the justice system work in his and Key's favor. He'd throw every single dime he had at keeping Key from being locked away. His gaze lifted to catch Key's as he reached over, opening Donald Cummings's file.

"So there is more, isn't there?" Key asked, his arms tightening against his chest, his big biceps bulging as he settled back in his seat.

"Yes," Alec answered with a single confirming nod. "You now know I've worked the case against Donald Cummings. I've told you bits and pieces, but not everything, not by a long shot. Those files hold the rest of the information."

"Tell me what it says. Hit the highlights," Key said, nodding toward the paperwork.

Alec took a deep breath to organize his thoughts then stared Key straight in the eyes as he spoke. "I've never lied to you about my knowledge of the DA's intent against your club. I didn't know why or what she's doing, but I found Donald Cummings when I entered CPS. At the time, all I knew were the problems between him and his daughter. For some reason, Donald's daughter reminded me of you."

"I didn't fuckin' know the guy."

Alec lifted a hand, silencing Key. "I would have resigned from the DA's office in July had I not been given this police report." He rifled through the pages until he found that initial report and handed it to Key. While he read, Alec spread the rest of its contents out, including pictures of Donald, his wife, and Key's father.

"Yeah, I know. I remembered seein' him with my old man. That's why I went," Key said, pushing the page to the side of the others.

"At the time, this police report hadn't been found by Twiford. Janice, my friend, stumbled upon it by accident on the day I drove past your shop, the day I won my argument to keep him behind bars after his probation violation. I had planned to quit that day, but this report stopped me, and it stopped me because of you." Alec crossed his arms over his chest, mimicking Key's stance, watching the confusion cross Key's brow.

"Why me?"

"Because when that information was found, Cummings would become the DA's missing link. She's been working to end your club. If she found a way to grant immunity to a member or a prospect of the Disciples of Havoc, she could finally have her break inside the impenetrable walls you guys surround yourselves with." Alec's nervous energy came back to the surface as understanding replaced the confusion in Key's gaze. Key dropped his arms to the edge of the counter and leaned forward, staring straight at Alec.

"That's what I figured when I was sittin' in that jail cell. I should've fuckin' thought about that before I went."

"No." Alec couldn't hold the direct stare any longer. He dropped his gaze as he shook his head, his leg double timing it now. "I should've fucking told you so you could be prepared if he ever got out. I realized that today. We've always been clouded where each other's professional lives are concerned; we've been so damn protective of matters that hold no real importance." Alec, frustration eating at him, lifted his gaze back to Key. He was just so damn sorry for what he'd done. "I ultimately caused this to happen. Staying with the DA was the wrong move. I should have told you, given you the heads-up that this could happen so you'd be on the lookout yourself. I don't know why I never considered that option."

"Because you're a good damn dude. You try to fix all the wrong. This ain't your fault or your fight, Alec." Key got to his feet, moving around the bar toward Alec.

"I wish that were true. I wish I could have seen past my own wants and desires and judged this appropriately," he said, the helplessness he'd fought against won as he stopped the movement of his leg and rested back on his heels, turning as Key came toward him. Key gripped his biceps in strong hands, running them from elbow to shoulder, trying to give him comfort. Alec couldn't lose Key, he just couldn't. That wasn't an option. It couldn't be an option.

"So he got some sort of immunity to rat us out?"

Alec stepped into the circle of Key's arms, seeing the wheels turning in Key's head as he stared down at the photos from the file. After a second, one of Key's hands went to the photos he'd scattered around, getting a good look at each one while his other hand drew Alec against his side, keeping him right there where his hand caressed across Alec's lower back.

"I ultimately don't know, but I'm certain he did. It's the only way he could have gotten out like he did," Alec said, picking up his beer bottle and taking a drink.

"This skank was at his house last night. I think she's also the one who was fuckin' my old man one night I went home. I didn't recognize her last night," Key said, flipping Keely's mother's mugshot around to face Alec.

"She's Donald's wife. She has a warrant for her arrest—skipped bail," he explained, looking over the young woman who looked harder and older than her years.

"Where's their kid now?" Key asked, back to examining the rest of the file.

"Even though it might appear I was waiting on you all day, I did leave for a while to take care of them when Marc had another appointment offsite. A friend of Janice's, Betty—the woman you might have seen on the news walking with me while leaving the courthouse last night. She's an attorney in the criminal division of the DA's office and she's agreed to take the case against you...and theirs. I like her. She's sharp and didn't waste any time taking care of the family. I feel confident she's their best hope. I'll make sure they know that Donald's wife is local and with him."

Alec watched as Key dug deeper in the file, and any hope he'd had that these answers would be enough for Key faded. Alec stepped backward the couple of steps to the refrigerator and pulled out two more beers. He opened each one as Key continued his search. Alec put the beer close to Key's hand as Key found the information on his father. How could he not? It was the largest stack of stapled papers in the folder.

He also found the unopened envelope with his name scribbled on the front. Alec remained silent as his heart drummed in his chest. Key went back to the barstool, thumbing through the stack, looking over each page in his father's file. The wait was a killer. Alec's anxiety was eating him alive.

"Please don't be angry. I didn't open your file, not because of the invasion of privacy, but because I couldn't take the pain of your life while reading your father's criminal history."

"They still have all my records on file?"

Alec couldn't help going around the bar any more than he could help reaching out and touching Key. Thankfully, Key put the file down and turned enough that Alec angled himself to stand between his parted thighs.

"They do." Alec ran his hands across Key's broad shoulders, cupping his neck, his thumbs massaging the soft hair covering Key's jaw. He saw vulnerability in Key as his lover reached for Alec's thighs, drawing him in closer. Key leaned forward, his forehead landing on Alec's.

"I never wanted you to know all that," Key's said quietly.

"We kept so much from each other—you more than me. I'm naturally inquisitive. I just didn't think I could handle it. I love you so much it hurts me to think of you being abused." Alec pulled back, then bent to kiss Key's still bent head as his fingers caressed across Key's long hair.

"He wasn't my father," Key said in little more than a harsh whisper, not looking him in the eyes.

"I suspected as much. When I saw him, I decided he couldn't be your biological father," Alec said, lifting Key's head to move closer. He held Key who wrapped those strong arms around him, pulling him as close as he could. Key's arms tightened as he rested his cheek on Alec's shoulder.

"I always feel like trash when I'm around you. I just can't make myself leave." Key's voice was filled with so much pain Alec didn't think he could handle another minute. He closed his eyes and drew Key as close to him as possible.

"Don't ever leave me." Alec pressed his lips to Key's hair. "Don't ever leave me, Key. I won't recover from losing you."

They stood there holding one another for several long minutes until Key gave a deep sigh and the arms around him relaxed. Alec wasn't in the same mindset. Key could do little more than tilt his head upward, because Alec was unwilling to release his hold.

"I beat the fuck out of the state's informant. No way they're not gonna see this as anything other than club retaliation. I'm going to prison, Alec." Key's strong arms tightened again.

"Let me handle this, babe." Alec threaded his fingers through Key's thick beard when he started to turn away again. He kept Key's head tilted even when his lover averted his eyes. "Promise me you'll trust me and let me take care of this. I made this mess; I'll get us out of it."

Key's gaze met his. "I trust you." Key shifted in his arms and concern rushed across his face again. "Are you sure you can't use the secret service?"

For some reason, it was just the unintended comic relief he needed. He let go of Key as he reached for his files.

"I'll call my security company right now."

Key gave a nod of approval, scooping up Nash who had apparently hovered around their feet. This might have been the first night since Nash arrived that he wasn't center of attention. Alec rubbed the little pup's head then tucked the files underneath his arm before heading to his office.

CHAPTER 33

As Keyes walked inside Fox's custom bike shop, he had to ask himself...if he wasn't afraid of anything, why was he nervous as hell? When the front door slammed shut behind him, the clanking of the bells hanging on the knob had him jerking his head over his shoulder in panic. Man, he'd been skittish since he left Alec's house this morning, much later than normal, due to his refusal to leave until Alec had his new security detail in place. He needed to calm his ass down or his nervous energy would make his brothers suspicious—if they weren't already, which brought the anxiety back full force.

"Hey, Key," Fox's old lady said, coming into the small showroom of the family owned business seconds before his hand landed on the door handle leading to Dev's ink parlor. His heart had leaped into his throat as if he were surprised to be greeted by the woman who had greeted him in this same manner every single time he entered this building.

Fuck, he was a wreck.

"Hey. Goin' to see Dev," he said and cleared his throat while doing a weird thumb motion over his shoulder toward Dev's area of their shared building.

"He's in the back with his dad. They saw you pull up. They're comin'." She came to stand right in front of him, running a warm, caressing palm down his forearm. "You doin' okay? I heard about yesterday. I wanted to come see you last night, but Dev said you were taken care of—your uncle was there. I hoped you went home with him last night."

"I'm fine. I just lost my temper." He spouted the lines he'd rehearsed over and over again in his head if any of his brothers asked about yesterday.

"It happens. Trust me. I know all about that." She gave a commiserating nod as Fox came through the only other door in the showroom, Dev following behind him. Keyes locked his guarded gaze on the two men. He took in their casual gait and the gentle smile Fox gave his wife as she again patted Keyes's arm. "Key, I'm gonna let you guys talk. Call me if you need anything, and come over for Christmas dinner. We'll have plenty."

He lifted a chin in acknowledgement with his eyes fixed on Fox. "Clyde told me you guys came up there yesterday."

Fox completely lost his casual swagger. Things took a different spin as he swung his head toward his son. "Goddamn Dev, actin' like a fuckin' ass or we would've stayed to take you home."

Not the first time Dev had heard those words, and his buddy was completely unfazed by his father's customary outburst. Devilman never looked away from Keyes. In all the years he'd known Dev, he generally had two types of looks: that of the joking, fun-lovin' guy who was always up for a good time, and the other that was red-hot, pissed off and everyone knew it. Today though, Dev had speculation on his face, and those eagle eyes focused straight on him. Keyes couldn't get a good read on his brother.

"We got Margo ready to go, but she said you're already represented."

Well hell, in all his planning, he hadn't come up with a reasonable explanation as to why he'd chosen not to use the club attorney. Fox's words didn't sound like a question, more an accusation, and Fox crossed his arms over his chest, his full attention back on Keyes. Dev mimicked his father's stance, crossing his arms over his chest, remaining weirdly quiet, waiting on his answer.

"Clyde called somebody. I don't know. He's freaked. I'm meetin' with 'em later. I'll let you know," he answered vaguely. He didn't dare say more, feeling like he was already rambling.

"Not sure that's gonna be good enough. This is club business. You know the rules," Fox said with a single nod, his biceps bulging as he shifted from one foot to another. That was the other fucked-up thing churning in his gut. How much did he tell his club about Cummings? They'd want to know where he got the information, and by God, he'd never tell them the truth.

If Fox wanted to talk club rules, Keyes had one to throw out—Donald Cummings had been voted in as a prospect without his approval. That broke every goddamn rule they had. The club bylaws were clear: patched members voted unanimously on new members, both prospects and full members, or the individual didn't make the cut—no exceptions. His brothers' betrayal festered in his gut.

Instead of saying any of that, Keyes held the argument and responded with an impromptu something he pulled straight out of his ass. "Nah, not really club business. I didn't know who he was, but he was terrorizing his kid."

"So, this was more of that vigilante shit," Fox said. Again, not a question, and Keyes would let him think whatever he wanted. It was as good a deception as any, and he reached inside his cut, pulling the prospect patch out of the pocket, handing it to Fox.

"Maybe, but he had no respect, sounded like my old man. I lost it, not club-related, just me pissed off."

Fox took the patch. His brow wrinkling at the material in his hand.

"Figured I'd take it back since I never voted him in."

He let that sit between the three of them. His club leaving him out had been a hard pill to swallow. All his lifelong lines of loyalty and friendship were blurring. This time a year ago, if Keyes learned there was a rat among them, it wouldn't have even been a question. Fox would know within minutes of him finding out. Today, he didn't know who to trust in a club that owned him body and soul. All he'd ever done was put this group of men above everyone and everything. Had they always kept him at arm's length not because of his old man, but instead because of who he was as a man? Had they used him for his strength and brute force like Alec had suggested before?

"You know better than most we ain't ever got between a brother and his kid, but the no respect bothers me," the prez said, tucking the patch in his back pocket. Yeah, Keyes wasn't buying that either. He'd never been respected. If this had been any other brother, they would have ridden out together last night to finish Cummings off.

Keyes's jaw ticced in aggravation.

Fuck. He wasn't feeling his brothers at all. What the fuck did that mean?

It meant Alec had gotten inside his head.

"I sent Ray-Ray over to the tire shop to help out. He says Louis's got your shit down, so don't worry about that. I didn't know how much time you were gonna need today," Fox said and lifted a hand to clamp on his shoulder. Keyes looked over at it and had to stamp down his need to move out from under the hold. "Don't worry about Cummings. I'll take a ride this afternoon, see where his head is. You'll decide how the club handles this one."

The back and forth inside his head made him feel like he was playing mental volleyball. Habits were damn hard to break, and the protect-the-club-at-all-costs habit went to the forefront of his thoughts. Fox going to Cummings would be the worst thing in the world to happen. Right as Keyes said an internal "*fuck it*," and started to spill Alec's secrets, the door rattled again, drawing all their attention that way. A small woman stood in the threshold, staring at them with a hubcap in her had.

"Mr. Fox."

The woman diverted the prez's attention and he turned to help his customer. Dev slammed both his palms on Keyes's chest, pushing Keyes backward a couple of steps until he spun him around, shoving him out the front doors. When they were about halfway to his bike, Dev grabbed his arm and twisted him back around, getting right in his face, not three inches separating them from being nose to nose. "All right, man, which one? The blond or the old man?"

Keyes narrowed his eyes, staring at Dev's excitement as a knowing grin tugged at the corners of his friend's mouth.

"What are you talkin' about?" he asked and took a step backward. Dev followed. Of course, he totally knew what Dev was asking, but fuck no, he wasn't answering, so he schooled his features and started to turn away, giving nothing up.

"Oh bullshit," Dev said, coming in and crowding him. The playful side of Dev was intrigued and there would be no stopping him until he had his answers. "Ain't no way you got the kind of money to hire that dude without the club backing you. After I got your bike, I came back and sat outside, watching that shit go down. Those two guys left for a while, not long, but long enough for me to see the older attorney get in a Benz S-class, and the blond in a fuckin' Ferrari. You ain't got the cash to hire either one of them, so you're fuckin' one, maybe both." Dev's newest burst of amusement was immediate as he laughed in Keyes's face. "Shit, man, I didn't think about that. You went kink on me, got you a daddy and a third."

Keyes stepped back again. Dev didn't follow, but his hand went out for a celebratory hand slap—one that Keyes left hanging.

"You don't know how much money I got," he grumbled, ducking his head, fighting his own grin. Dev's craziness was exactly what he'd needed. It also gave him confirmation that Dev had in fact gotten Fox and Mack out of there on purpose, which meant his brother still truly had his back. The relief was a bit staggering, and he lifted a hand, scrubbing it over his face. Fuck, he had needed the reassurance more than he ever thought possible. Keyes was truly beginning to believe he had misread every person in his whole damn life.

"I kinda fuckin' do know how much cash you have. You just bought that fuckin' truck when business has been shit, then yesterday, I figured out that older sugar-bear bought it for you. Then I saw the blond, and my money's on him. He's fuckin' classy-hot with all that rich, motherfuckin' swagger. I'd fuck his sweet ass."

Okay, wait a minute. Keyes slowly lifted his eyes, staring at Dev through his parted fingers still covering his face. The fuck? Keyes dropped his hand and stood to his full height. His glare pinning his buddy in place. "What the fuck did you just say?"

"You know I like some ass," Dev said, giving a knowing nod and throwing out his fist for a bump. Keyes left that one hanging too.

"No, that's somethin' I sure don't fuckin' know," Keyes said. He looked at Dev as if he'd never seen the man before.

"Sure, you do. All the time I fought the club about that shit. I'm not gonna be judged," Dev declared smugly, his chest swelling in his indignation. Keyes's eyebrows slid up. What the hell? This was news to him.

"I thought you were defending me," he said in an utter state of shock.

"Fuck no. I like ass. I just like the self-lubricating shit too." As if the last forty-eight hours weren't enough for Keyes, Dev blew his fucking mind. His mouth gaped open with no words coming out, because seriously, what the fuck? "I'd've fucked you, but you had head issues about it all, and man, I'm freaky, but you're my brother—like, real brother. Sibling shit only turns me on when it's not my sibling."

Keyes was struck dumb, and Dev let that hang between them, grinning like the fucking Cheshire cat.

"It's the blond, right? You've lost your shit over him. He seemed pretty fuckin' upset too. He's loaded, right?" Dev said so matter-of-factly, with no fear for the club or their patched brothers, just genuinely happy for him.

"Dev—" He looked down at the parking lot, kicking at some loose rocks. Fucking hell, the relief of someone knowing and just being happy that he'd found someone to love threatened to bring on the damn tears. His eyes welled up, and he lifted a hand, digging his fingers into closed eyelids, trying get hold of himself. What the fuck was wrong him?

"It's cool. I get it. If it were me hooked up with him, I would've told you—you know, best buds and all, but I get it…" Dev said teasingly, and Keyes raised his head back up.

"Fuck you, you would not have." He pointed his finger in Dev's face. "You never even told me you liked ass, so fuck you."

Dev's good-natured grin stayed plastered on his face, and he reached out again for their familiar hand slap. This time he obliged, feeling like he was finally on level ground again.

"I just didn't want you to fall in love with all this." Dev raked his hand down his body, causing Keyes to bust out with a much-needed laugh.

"Never say one word about him," Keyes said, somehow knowing in his heart his secret was safe with Dev.

"Man, I got my old man out of there so fast yesterday, and they know you're more tight-fisted than Warren Buffett. You got the cash to pay for that fancy attorney. I'll listen to the talk and give you the heads-up if anybody starts suspecting anything, but right now, you're golden. They didn't understand not usin' the club attorney, but I told 'em it was for the better, keep it away from the club until we decide what to do with that bitch. They seemed to buy it." Dev tossed out his hand for a fist bump, and Keyes obliged that one too.

"By the way, he wasn't a fuckin' prospect. Your old man gave him a patch so he could fuck his wife. I heard all that shit last night. I figured that was what my old man was gonna say to you before that chick walked in," Dev explained, staring him straight in the eyes. His gaze never wavered, and Dev was a fucking terrible liar.

Keyes nodded, instantly feeling better about that too.

"All right, man. Bring it in." Dev enveloped him in a tight hug. One he participated in, hugging Dev back. "Hope that fancy attorney can keep you outta jail."

Keyes took a deep breath, fought the indecision, and closed his eyes, gripping Dev tighter. "I got some intel last night. Shit I didn't know before I went over to Cummings's apartment." He turned until his lips were almost touching Dev's ear and whispered, "I need you to handle this without involvin' the club. Give me your vow."

Dev's body tensed. He released the tight grip he had on Keyes but stayed close as Keyes relinquished his hold on Dev. "'Course."

Keyes hated a goddamn rat more than anything, but he still paused. Alec's protection was everything to him. They had gone overboard this morning while hiring as much security to watch Alec as Keyes saw fit. Alec wasn't going to be able to take a leak without someone there, guarding him. Hell, Keyes had even suggested he stand lookout for Alec. There wasn't one motherfucker that would get past him if he were on guard duty.

But if his father had overshared with Cummings, then that could bring the entire club down, and the bitch DA would win.

Keyes reached out, cupping the back of Dev's neck, drawing him forward as he whispered, "Cummings got immunity to rat out the club. He's a protected informant. I didn't know when I went over there."

Dev's head jerked back as if he'd been burned, fire lit his eyes. Every single one of Keyes's movements became measured, including his hand sliding inside his jacket pocket to grip the pistol he had hidden there. Dev's crazy-eyed gaze stayed transfixed on his for several long seconds until his brows furrowed into a hard V.

Keyes gave a single nod.

The concern on Dev's face relaxed, the challenge was clear in the spark of excitement that split into a shit-eating grin. "Stay in plain sight." Dev reached out, whacked his arm while pivoting on his boot-covered heels. "Love ya, brother."

Keyes staggered under the weight of his relief. Out of everyone, it would have hurt the worst to know Dev hadn't truly been on his side. He was his brother. Keyes took several steps backward before he spun around, heading for his bike, letting Dev's unconditional commitment ease his heavy heart. Just maybe...

CHAPTER 34

Key lay stretched out on his side. His long body created a shell around Alec's work space on the living room floor, a spot he'd commandeered. They were close to the roaring fire, comfortable and cozy. Key had sweetly built the fire to keep him from getting a chill as he worked. The lights on the Christmas tree twinkled brightly, and the glow of the fire bathed the room in a warming light. Alec had been truly surprised at how much he had enjoyed the holiday decorations he had gone ahead with, even under the uncertainty of Key's arrest and the waiting game that had held them in a constant state of worry.

The blueprints for their new home had been pushed to the side. What weighed heavily on his mind now were the stacks of cash lying between him and Key. He'd counted fifty-three stacks, each with five thousand dollars. Alec did the math quickly in his head before lifting his eyes, staring at his biker who was resting his head on his hand, playing the finger monster game with Nash.

There were so many sides to this man. "You have two hundred and sixty-five thousand dollars here, Key," Alec said, sounding almost accusatory, even to himself.

Key's gaze lifted to his, showing exactly how uninterested he'd been in all this cash lying between them. "Is that enough to pay the attorney?"

"Are you serious? You won't even buy new hair ties and you have two hundred and sixty-five thousand dollars in a safe in the back of your uncle's property? Not even a wall safe. I could have carried the thing off." Yeah, that definitely came out as an accusation.

"Are you mad?" Key's hand stopped moving, letting Nash attack him as he stared straight at Alec.

No, he wasn't mad and did manage to shake his head no. In a relationship of constant twists and turns, this was another major shift in learning who Key was as a man. "You're a baller. My boyfriend's got money. Where did this come from?"

Key's face went through a range of emotions. As he said what he said, Key's playful grin spread across his face only to fall instantly when he again asked how Key had gotten this much cash. He masked his thoughts as he rolled to his back and started to rise.

"If it's not enough to pay for the attorney, I can sell a bike," Key added, reaching for his beer bottle on the coffee table. It was twenty-five degrees outside, the wind sounded like a blizzard had moved in, and Key had chosen a cold beer when all Alec wanted to do was snuggle on the sofa and stay there until this minute of winter blew through.

"This changes things. I'm intimidated. If you can get your hands on this kind of cash, you don't need me," Alec said, lifting to his feet as Nash attacked a stack of cash.

Key obviously thought Alec's words were the funniest thing in the world. He laughed one of his hearty laughs, drawing Nash's attention. Their pup leaped forward, double timing it Key's direction. Key's phone vibrated, and Alec followed him toward the kitchen where he pulled a new beer from the refrigerator. Alec wasn't nearly ready to let this go.

"I'm serious. That's a lot of cash. You can absolutely pay your attorney and build our house."

"I doubt that," Key said, twisting the cap off the bottle. With a well-practiced expert flick of his fingers, he sent the cap flying toward the trashcan, then he reached for his cell phone, charging on the kitchen counter, right as it started vibrating again. Alec stood in front of Key as he worked his phone with his thumb, and Alec's hands went to his waist as he stared at Key. More than anything else, Alec wanted to provide for Key. He was serious—that was what he saw as his role in their relationship. Key made them a family. Alec paid their way. He'd been working himself into the ground catching up on everything associated with Arik Layne Properties for the sole purpose of being their bread winner, wanting to give Key more.

Key's forehead crinkled, and he shook his head, drawing Alec's gaze down to the phone. He didn't necessarily intend to read Key's text message—it was more that it was right there in his face. The message came from Dev. He bent in more to see animated cats dancing in front of a lit fireplace. The perfect diversion. Alec turned his head to get a better look. The GIF seemed so out of place, considering it had been sent from the tatted-up man he'd watched throw one of the biggest fits he'd ever seen anyone throw while in the waiting area at the jail.

"What's that mean?"

"Don't know," Key replied and placed the beer on the counter to type. "He asked if we were home durin' the bad weather, and then that came."

"*We've been in the house all day—there's a chance of ice tonight. You need to stay in too.*" Alec watched as Key typed the words, pushed send, and the pending message dots started drumming, showing Dev was already typing back.

"*Yeah, we've been in all day—me, Holly, and the kids. No plans to change. Take care, brother.*"

Alec looked up to see Key's brows draw up in question while he stared at the phone screen.

"He likes cats?" Alec asked, taking the cell phone from Key's hand and going back to the GIF. He'd seen it correctly: three cats dancing to "Jingle Bells" in front of a fireplace.

"Not that I've ever known." Key grabbed his beer and the phone from Alec before bending, scooping up Nash, and going back to the living room. Alec trailed slowly behind Key, his gaze moving between the cash still on the rug, and Key's impressive back covered in a tight-fitting thermal long-sleeve shirt. Something wasn't right, maybe several somethings weren't right, but Alex couldn't quite wrap his head around what he was missing.

Key went to the television and grabbed the remote. Right as Alec decided to start questioning the parts he didn't understand, his cell phone buzzed. Key took a seat on the sofa, turning on the television as Alec went for his phone, surprised to see Marc's name crossing the screen.

He didn't hesitate to check his messages.

"You talkin' in here?"

The volume button that Key had been actively turning up started its descent. "No, I'll go to my office."

Alec read the message as he went. "*I sent you an email outlining the stipulations Judge Jenkins has added. He's ready to finalize, please advise. Alec, this is as good as its going to get. I strongly recommend Keyes agree.*"

Alec's mind raced as he jogged toward the front of the house and into his office. By the time he rounded his desk, his heart pounded, blood thundering so loudly through his veins his hands shook as he tossed the phone to the side of his monitor and quickly typed on his keyboard to open his email. In those few long seconds it took for the program to open, Alec dropped his chin to chest and willed himself to calm.

For the majority of last several days, he had diligently worked with Betty in the district attorney's office and with Marc Manners, trying to rush Key's plea deal along, not letting too much time pass for Twiford to blow this case up, but he'd never expected anything to happen this quickly. Betty could see the truth of the situation…that Key wasn't interfering with an informant. She'd agreed to reduce the charges to a misdemeanor and three years unsupervised probation. Now they just had to get it through the final judge sign-off.

With a click of the mouse, Alec opened Marc's email then the attachment. With each word he read, the pounding of his heart turned into a sinking feeling, his shoulders slumped a little further until he sat back in the seat defeated.

Alec lifted his gaze, re-reading the small paragraph written by the judge. Nothing changed over the second read through and he scanned the rewritten plea agreement attachment that included the stated changes. Keyes Dixon could have no contact with the Disciples of Havoc for the length of his probation period, which the judge had also expanded from three to five years.

The club was Key's life.

Alec was silent, bringing his chin to his palm, staring at the screen, his mind racing over the possibilities.

For Alec, this could be a chance to fight for their future—his and Key's. For Key...well, he would he see this as losing everything. The club was his foundation.

But if Keyes were incarcerated, he wouldn't have access to his brothers then or during any probation he received after release. That wouldn't change. And the risks of taking this case to trial were too great. Public opinion on the Disciples was too negative and that would flow through to the jury pool and influence not only the disposition of the case but also the sentencing.

Marc was right. There was no choice.

"All right," he muttered to the silent room before typing back a message of acceptance to Marc. He pushed send before he allowed his downward spiraling emotions to get the best of him. How in the world was he going to walk into the living room and tell Key he couldn't have anything to do with his family for five years?

The pit in his stomach grew. He felt sick. The guilt was back in full force. What could he say to help Key see this as anything other than his world ending? Even with Key's adamant instruction for Alec to handle the details of his case, would he actually agree to stay away from his brothers?

Alec looked at the door when he heard a quiet rapping from the outside.

Would Key ever believe this wasn't in the deal from the start? Anxiety rolled though him as the door pushed open.

"Sorry—you gotta see this," Key whispered, sticking his head inside the door.

"Come in. I'm done. See what?" he asked, confused why Key looked so eager with all the horrible news Alec had just received.

"I paused the channel. Come see." The excited Key left the room. Alec rose, and grabbed his cell phone, defeat heavy on his heart. He trailed after Key who stood behind the sofa with the remote in one hand and Nash in the other. When he came to stand beside Key, his guy pressed play. Alec was still distracted and hadn't really been paying attention when he heard District Attorney Twiford's name along with seeing several images of a younger Twiford hanging on to a Disciples of Havoc biker. She beamed brightly in every single picture. Key had told him these pictures existed, and Alec instantly perked up.

"Who released this information?"

"Doesn't say. It's exclusive breakin' news on Channel 8. It's got it all, Ray-Ray's name, her connection to the club. Said they contacted her office, but she's been on leave and hasn't released a statement."

Alec guessed this was the reason Twiford had been oddly absent from the office, giving Betty the chance to do what she had done with Key's case—Twiford must have known this was coming. Key sounded so happy. How long would that last?

Alec's phone went crazy in his hand, vibrating with alerts, most likely texts, and he opened his phone to see several messages. The first several were from Janice, but he bypassed those and opened the one from Marc.

"Got your email. I'm sorry we couldn't get this through the way you wanted. The silver lining, no jail time and no other stipulations other than avoiding club members."

Alec left that message and went to Janice's where she didn't mince words. *"Donald Cummings died in a head-on collision tonight—initial reports say weather was at fault. I just got an alert."*

The next text message from Janice read, *"Did you see Twiford dated the biker? WTH, Alec? So that was true?"*

The next text read, *"Betty just told me about the change to the plea. I'm sorry. *frowny face*"*

Key leaned over his shoulder, and Alec didn't try to shield his view from reading Janice's message. "What's goin' on? Why's she sorry?"

Alec had to tell him. It was now or never. He lifted his eyes, turning to better face Key while tucking his arms over his chest. How was he going to say these awful words to Key? For the first time since they'd met, Alex couldn't bear the weight of Key's stare and dropped his eyes to about Key's chin, taking a small step backward.

"First, Donald Cummings apparently died this evening. He was in a motor vehicle—"

Key nodded, turning away, his fingers steadily petting Nash.

"What does that nod mean?"

Key opened his mouth, and Alec lifted a hand, stopping him from speaking, knowing Key planned to say something like "club business" as a response.

"Don't tell me. If the police come to talk to you, don't nod or agree or offer any good riddance. You only say you want your attorney present, do you understand?"

"I was with my attorney all afternoon because of the weather," Key said cheekily, giving Alec his sexy smirk.

There was a clear tease in the words, but he didn't truly understand the joke, nor did he try. Key went around the sofa, dropping down on one of the cushions, completely missing the anxiety Alec was operating under—damn, he should be playing poker right now with as balanced and even as his face must seem.

"So the DA bitch is out, right? They aren't gonna keep her around like that, right? We're gonna be free of that bitch. She deserves what she's gettin'." Key kicked his legs up on the coffee table, looking smug as hell when he turned back to Alec who was moving closer to his lover—the least

Alec could do was to deliver the news while looking Key in the eyes.

"I can build business back up—it's already gettin' better—and then I'll make some money again. If you can keep me out of prison, that'll give me a chance to save even more." Key nodded to the large amount of money still stacked on his living room rug. Key's gaze swung up to Alec as he settled Nash on his lap. Whatever he saw made Alec doubt his poker face. Key sat up, dropping his feet to the floor, setting Nash on the floor beside his boots. "What's wrong?"

"I…" Alec couldn't say the words.

"Just say it. I'm goin' to prison, aren't I?" Key was up on his feet, moving around the coffee table toward Alec. Damn, it was hard to stay in his spot and not take a step backward.

"No." Alec shook his head as Key stopped less than a foot away. "No prison. Judge Jenkins has made a slight change. They do this all the time, Key. I had hoped my working relationship with the parties involved would be enough…" Alec stopped speaking again and shook his head. He finally took that step backward, averting his gaze down to his trembling hands. God, he didn't want to say the words.

"What is it?" Key asked and followed his retreat. Alec crossed his arms over his chest and forced himself to look Key in the eyes as he ruined his life.

"You can't have any contact with the club for the length of your probation."

"For three fuckin' years?" Key asked incredulously.

"Judge Jenkins is upping probation to five years. I'm sorry." Alec could see the anger building quickly in Key. He was helpless to know how to help.

"For five fuckin' years, I can't have contact with my brothers? That shit only happens after prison," Key roared, stepping into Alec. Anguish washed over Alec at the suffering he saw on Key's pained face.

"I didn't expect this, Key. I hoped me vouching for you and the agreement of the prosecutor would be enough for the judge to sign off."

Key threw his hands in the air, wheeling around and away from Alec.

"Are you fuckin' kidding me?" Key spun back, his face turning fierce as Key's finger pointed in his face. "Did you do this to get me out of my club?"

"Of course not. I just got the message. It was completely unexpected," he said, defensive at the heated accusation.

"What if I don't do accept the deal?" Key asked, leaving him standing there as he stalked past the kitchen toward his Carhartt slung over a kitchen chair. In one fluid motion, Key swung it over his shoulders, driving his arms inside each sleeve.

"Where are you going? It's cold and we're expecting an ice storm," Alec said, following Key, losing some of the pain he'd felt for his lover as he realized Key's intentions.

"Answer the question, Alec. What happens if I don't do it?" Key asked, stalking toward him. It took the reminder that Key would never lay a hand on him to keep him from moving away and cowering from the threat bearing down on him. "Fuckin' answer the damn question."

"We'll go to trial. Public opinion is still very much against your club…" he said, Key's face within inches of his own.

"Fuck, Alec, my goddamn business partner's the club. What about that?" Key didn't wait for an answer, he pivoted around, heading for the back door. The door burst open with a rush of icy cold wind as Key left the house.

"Key, don't leave. We'll figure this out together," Alec called out, rushing forward. The door slammed in his face.

Alec swung around, and a weight lifted from his shoulders when he spotted Key's keys on the counter beside his. He crossed his arms over his chest and worry raced down his spine. What should he do? Go after Key or give him space? He decided on the latter, at least for a few minutes, and looked down at his phone. He pulled up Janice's contact information. He needed the specifics on what the hell had happened to Donald Cummings tonight.

Keyes stayed tucked away under the cover of the cabana, pacing the length of the small structure. The wind was relentless, threatening to snap branches in its gusty wake. With the phone stuck to his ear, he listened to the fourth and final ring. Frustrated, he lowered the phone, but Dev finally answered.

"Hey," Dev said. "You get the dancin' cats?"

"Yeah." Keyes stopped in his tracks. He dropped his stare down to the polished concrete, wanting more than anything to ask the details of what Dev had done to help initiate the end of Donald Cummings's life, but a cell phone connection wasn't safe. Those answers would have to come later. He was already risking so much by calling his brother. A resentful sneer formed even as his brow wrinkled, adding venom to his words. "Saw the bitch got put on blast."

"Yeah, tired of her shit, for fuckin' sure," Dev said with an equal amount of disgust in his tone.

"Yeah." Keyes closed his eyes and lifted his head toward the covered roof. The anger fled, and he was left with a deep uncertainty. The silence between them hung like a weight around his neck. He had so many emotions rolling through him. He had to find the right words.

"Somethin's not right. You should be celebratin'," Dev said before he could gather his thoughts.

"Can't. Got a major change to my plea tonight. The fuckin' judge extended my probation and added that I can't have contact with the club for five fuckin' years. Could've told 'em to go fuck themselves, but I'd go to trial, and we both know I won't get a fair one. I'll go to prison." Somehow, saying it out loud made it seem so much worse. Keyes dropped his head forward from the weight of the words and balled his fist tight as pain lanced across his heart.

"Are you kiddin' me, man?" Dev shouted, and from the sound of his friend's voice, his anger shot to a solid ten on the Richter scale.

"I wish. It's all signed off, and I can't do anything about it." The range of emotions he was experiencing had him wanting to fucking cry in his indignation.

"Goddamn, that shit's not right. My old man suspected somethin' like this would happen, but I call bullshit. You didn't fuckin' kill a man," Dev said.

Keyes stayed silent, his heart hurt. What the hell did he have, who the fuck was he without his bike club at his back? A big black pit of unknowns threatened to swallow him whole. What did he do from here?

He didn't even realize he had said those words out loud until Dev answered, "I'll help you, Key. You ain't gotta go at this alone. I'm sly as a motherfuckin' fox. I got you, man."

"I been wantin' things I shouldn't want." Keyes opened up, letting his heartbreak guide his words. He shouldn't have ever started this with Alec. Once he moved over from the wrong side of town, there wasn't ever going to be a turning back. He was such a fool.

"Why shouldn't you want 'em? You're a good dude, man. Five years ain't that long. You know you'll have your place back when you're ready. We'll get you through this. I'll make sure of that." Dev's voice was strong, determined, and the exact opposite of the way Keyes saw things.

Keyes closed his eyes, letting the worry hang heavy on his shoulders. "I shouldn't've gone over there."

"Nah, I should've gone with you. You fuckin' saved the goddamn club—no tellin' what your old man told that piece of shit. He'd screwed us all sideways. You're a hero, man," Dev assured.

"Key." He looked up to see Alex standing two feet in front of him.

"Is that your guy?"

Keyes didn't respond. He stared at Alec who looked so hurt and lost, and every bit as confused as he was.

"Let him comfort you, man. I'll talk to my old man, give him the heads-up. I told him about Cummings—don't be pissed. He's the one who said you saved our fuckin' asses. Go talk to him; get a fuckin' blow job—that'll make everything a little easier to take. I'll handle the rest."

The phone went dead, but he was slower to lower his arm. Alec looked so pretty standing there, bundled in his long coat. Keyes was tired of seeing the constant worry in Alec's eyes. He was such a good dude. He didn't deserve all this bullshit either. Keyes had fucked up his own life, but he'd also screwed up Alec's life. For better or worse, they were in this shit together. Who would have fucking known this was how everything would all play out?

"I'm sorry…"

"No," Keyes interrupted, shaking his head. "No. I can't listen to you take responsibility for another goddamn thing I've done."

"Then come inside. It's freezing out here. Whatever you're thinking, we'll work it out together," Alec pleaded, the hurt in his eyes bordered on despair.

Keyes was tired of that too. He was always hurting Alec, causing him anger and confusion. He had to figure that shit out too. "There's no workin' this out together. There's never an *us* workin' it out together. It's always *you* workin' everything out, then takin' the blame when shit doesn't go right. This is on me, and I'm unemployed. I got nothin'. That club's all I got. It's everything, all the backup I have, and it's gone."

"That's not true, Key. You've got me." When every other person in the world backed away from Keyes's anger, Alec didn't. He took the steps separating them, coming straight toward Keyes.

"My choice is to either to risk prison or be a fuckin' jobless loser. Who's gonna hire me? How long are you gonna wanna be with a loser, Alec?" He knew the answer even if Alec pretended not to. He'd have a better damn chance to have Alec waiting on him for after prison than to watch Alec slowly fall out of love because he was nothing. He was always nothing. Every situation in his life brought him right back to zero.

Alec's palms trapped his face. Keyes tried to step away, not wanting the comfort this fine man wanted to give, but like normal, Alec held firm. "You so regularly undervalue yourself it's frustrating. You have value, Key. This isn't a door slamming shut on your life. This is an opening. You can literally do anything you've ever wanted to do."

Keyes stared at Alec as if he'd lost his mind, because clearly, he had. What the hell did that even mean? He couldn't do anything more than stay transfixed by Alec's simple hold of his face and stare at this crazy man. When Alec dropped his hands, it freed him to move. He shook his head and stepped away, pacing the length of the cabana again.

"You're a certified mechanic, Key. You work on Harley Davidsons. You refurbished an old bike—do you have any idea what I've spent on rebuilding old cars? Start a business. Hell, I'll be your partner. I've run in the circles of men with money who have a thing for anything with a motor. You do the repairs, and I'll bring you the bikes," Alec explained matter-of-factly, and Keyes wheeled around, standing at least ten paces away from that frustrating man.

"You don't fuckin' get it, Alec. You're gonna get sick of me. It's gonna happen."

Alec's face dropped, and he stepped forward while Keyes backed away, keeping him at a distance. Alec had to stop the bullshit and listen for once in their relationship.

"That's what all this is about?" Alec said, following him as he continued talking and Keyes kept moving away. Finally, Keyes held his hand up to keep Alec at a distance. "Key, that's my fear with you. At some point, you're going to open your eyes and see I keep wrecking your life. I'm the reason you're in this mess to begin with. It's me being me, trying to control everything, analyzing all my steps, and ultimately, failing at protecting what matters the most in the world."

His hand remained up, keeping Alec at bay. He had to skirt around the man who was determined to move step for step with him. "Goddammit, Alec, you always try to put yourself on my level and you can't."

"I know, that's what I'm saying. You're too good a man. All I have is that I love you and I'm trying and I'm sorry. I keep hurting you when all I want is to give you the world."

Alec looked so anguished that Keyes relaxed his arm, dropping his hand to his side. Weirdly, Alec didn't move forward, the invisible barrier holding between them. "I don't deserve a man as wonderful as you. I'm lucky."

"What?" Keyes said as if that were the most ludicrous thing he'd ever heard. Seconds passed as they stared at one another, both hurt, anxious, and their chests heaving from the stress of the moment. Their breaths mingled in the icy air as they stared at one another. Just like Alec always did, he eased the pain of losing the club, making it secondary to this generous man looking so hurt.

"For me, nothing's changed except I have one more thing I have to make up to you. I want us together. I want to marry you. I want a home and a family and a forever life with you. This last year has meant everything to me, and I never want to be without you—not ever. Be a mechanic, rebuild bikes, go back to school, tinker around the house. Hell, build our house. Do whatever you want, just do it with me by your side," Alec pleaded.

Keyes bowed his head, scrubbing a hand down the length of his face. There was no denying the anger and the panic of minutes ago had vanished in a flash. Alec hit many of Keyes's truths. He wanted the life Alec just laid out in front of him. He wanted it all with Alec.

No prison—that was a relief.

No club. Keyes narrowed his eyes, for the first time seeing the benefit of no longer having to hide Alec for fear his brothers wouldn't understand. There was relief there too.

He did like rebuilding bikes better than changing tires.

He was unemployed, but he could get work, especially with no felony conviction on his record. He'd never been one to shy away from hard work.

"Key, please say something. You're killing me. I'm sorry I didn't plan…"

Keyes lifted his head, and he broke the invisible barrier that kept them apart to cover Alec's always moving lips with his fingers.

"You gotta stop takin' responsibility for my shit."

Alec started shaking his head no, and Keyes added pressure to the fingers on Alec's mouth.

"And I think you're gonna get sick of me…"

Alec couldn't hold his tongue and started talking around the press of his hand. "I never want to lose…"

Keyes used his forefinger and thumb to mash Alec's lips tightly together. This loving man made everything better—he always did—and as far as Keyes hoped, he always would. Keyes stepped in, coming chest to chest with Alec, anchoring a strong arm around Alec's back to draw him closer. He stared deeply into Alec's sad eyes. Nothing had really changed. Someday Alec would get sick of him. Someday he would wise up and see them for what they were, but Keyes was helpless to do more than try to be a man deserving of Alec Pierce.

"I want those things too—all those same things you want."

Alec's eyes softened as he wrapped both arms around Keyes's waist.

"We'll figure it all out after I kiss you. I'm gonna remove my fingers. No talkin'."

Alec didn't listen, he rarely did. Seconds before his mouth touched Keyes's lips, he whispered, "I love you."

EPILOGUE

Nine months later

Devilman raised his head and stared Alec straight in the eyes, concern lowering his brow. "You know, more than half the people I do this to get divorced, and no matter what you put here, everybody's gonna know you were married. Ain't none of that fancy soap gonna' wash this shit off." Dev's brow lifted smugly as he delivered the final word.

Alec instantly grinned at the warning from the man sitting across the table from him, for three reasons. One, the permanent band being inked on his ring finger was already halfway finished. Two, there was never going to be a time that he allowed Key to leave him—that decision had been made months ago. Key owned him, end of story. And the third reason…he'd caught the devilish gleam in Dev's eyes, and it was obvious the guy was trying to get under his best friend's skin. Dev had caught on quick that Key could be a bit defensive where Alec was concerned, so the guy pushed the boundaries whenever he got the chance.

"Shut the fuck up and finish," Key growled, and Dev jerked from the kick Key had given his chair. Alec's eyes met Dev's and they both chuckled at Key's reaction.

"I'm just sayin'," Dev teased, grinning broadly. Alec watched the two men for a second then dropped his gaze to the freshly inked ring finger on Key's left hand. Just seeing the perfectly etched symbol had love and pride swelling in Alec's chest and joy filling his heart. The pressure of Key's strong hand on his thigh comforted him and reassured him with a gentle squeeze of solidarity.

Dev rolled his shoulders then his neck before the burning started on his finger again. He was ready to be done with this part. Devilman had been working diligently for hours. The guy was truly an artist and had unbelievable skill, not to mention the patience he'd shown during this entire process. First, he had worked on Key's massive back tattoo for a couple of hours before starting on Alec and giving him his first ever tattoo—Key's name in bold, fancy lettering, scripted directly over his heart. Now they were at the end, almost finished with the identical ring tattoos representing the vows they'd promised to each other in a civil ceremony held yesterday afternoon.

The fact that he had become comfortable with Devilman coming to their new home was a testament to how cunning and extremely sneaky the guy was. At least once a month since they had moved to Westlake, Dev somehow managed to make it inside Key's large workshop completely unnoticed by the elaborate security system Alec had installed on their fifteen acre property and, even more impressive, he'd made it past their always vigilant guard dog, Nash. His bark was definitely worse than his bite, all show and no action—but where the pup did excel was in clearing a room, even in his sleep. Alec cringed at the times he had suddenly woken to the horrible smells coming out of the precious dog who slept in bed with them every night.

Alec turned his attention back to Dev, watching as the guy skillfully worked the tattoo gun over his skin. He'd not fully explored Dev's covert techniques that allowed him to slip by undetected, but he now understood why Key had gotten so freaked out over his safety where the Disciples of Havoc were concerned. He could only imagine what those bikers could do with that kind of stealthy surveillance ability. Maybe he didn't really want the answers. Perhaps, there was something to be said about ignorance being bliss after all.

Alec had gotten past the initial worry and the unexpected twinge of jealousy that had sparked when he'd met his lover's best friend for the first time. It had only taken a couple of minutes of being in the same room with both of them for Alec to realize Dev wasn't who Key wanted. Dev was good-looking with that model surfer look, but edged enough on the hot, rough biker side you couldn't help but steal a second glance. Dev was definitely easy on the eyes, and even more surprising, the guy had a quick wit that kept everyone laughing. It was refreshing to see how close Dev and Key really were. The two men were truly like brothers. Key and Devilman were fluid and comfortable with one another, a familiarity that only came with time. They shared a bond closer than if they had actually been born family, a family which now included Alec.

Dev seemed to need Key's friendship as much as Alec needed Key's love. Alec was grateful Key had Dev. It had been Dev who hooked Key up with his first official custom bike restoration, and he'd just finished another one Dev had sent his way. Since that first bike, Key's new business had taken off like crazy with projects scheduled out for the next eighteen months.

As Alec had predicted, he and Key spent most of their time in this enormous workshop, Key building bikes and Alec enjoying his favorite pastime, drooling over Key building bikes. He wasn't complaining; he loved to watch Key do everything. They had also retained some of their old habits, like staying home a lot, and the always fun *naked movie nights*. Neither seemed to miss going out or having the public intrude on their sacred alone time, especially not after the long hours Alec spent working with Arik Layne Properties. The way he saw it, their time was their time. His time to be with Key.

"I thought you'd be a pussy," Dev said, breaking the moment of silence, never stopping the movement of his hand.

Alec looked over at Key, waiting to see if his lover would defend his honor. He usually did, but this time Key only shrugged at him. "It's fair. I wondered, too."

"Thanks, guys. I'm not some pansy," he said defensively.

"No, but you either love it or hate it." Dev raised his head to give a nod to what Key had said.

"I don't see myself getting a lot more, but it's okay," he replied, feeling somewhat pacified when Key squeezed his thigh again. Alec covered Key's hand with his, clasping his long fingers as they shared a meaningful glance—they did that a lot these days. He and Key had really fallen into a happy place, something real and binding. Their smaller three-bedroom home was perfect for them. He wasn't sure life could be better.

The security feed's alarm chimed and all three men shifted their gazes to the monitor mounted in the corner of Key's workshop. Nash came tearing in through the doggie door at about that same time, barking loudly to gain their attention.

He was such an odd dog. Nash was in warning mode. Their happy puppy seemed to innately understand Key was by far the bigger threat out of the bunch, so the warning came from Nash to Key, not Nash to the person who just pulled down their long driveway leading to their new farm-style home.

"It's Blaine." He recognized the top of his head as he stepped from the rental car.

"Did you know he was comin'?" Key asked, his guy tensing with uncertainty, instantly on guard.

"No, but I sent him a picture of the marriage license. I figured he'd show up sooner or later," he explained.

"Do I need to split?" Dev asked, concern flashing in his eyes as he reached over to shut off the machine.

"Keep going. He's cool, and it'll take him time to find us," he said, twisting his finger to give Dev better access. No way was he stopping until his entire finger matched Key's.

"He won't leave if you don't answer the front door?" Key asked as the buzz of the tattoo machine came to life and echoed off the walls as Dev settled back in to his work.

"Oh no, things like manners never stop him," he explained, getting a curious grunt from Dev.

Several minutes later, Blaine came closer to the shop door, no doubt lured all the way in by Nash. He would run out the doggie door, find Blaine, then scurry back to warn Key about the incoming intruder. They watched it all play out on the security monitors, the humor of the situation helping to relieve some of the tension that had suddenly formed between them. When Blaine came within feet of the shop door, Key patted his thighs, and the crazed dog jumped toward Key, landing on his lap, instantly curling up and settling down as if his job were complete.

"I've been searching for you," Blaine said snippily, busting through the shop door like he owned the place. He had all sorts of accusation and attitude aimed at Alec. This was Key's first time around Blaine since that first night they'd all met, because Blaine had decided to jet off for months at a time on some kind of fuck fest he called an enlightening-quest to help better find his inner self. Alec watched Key's brows furrow as he shifted the hand on his thigh to the back of his chair, putting a protective arm around Alec.

Dev's attention swung from Key toward Blaine, and he lifted his brow in amusement with just a hint of a smirk playing at the corner of his lips. This was going to be interesting, both Dev and Blaine were evenly matched in the sarcasm department.

"I know, we've been watching you." Alec pointed to the security monitor, a curl tugging his lips as his friend looked up, shook his head, then turned back to him.

"Why didn't you come get me?" Blaine asked incredulously as he stalked to the table, getting a good eyeful of what they were doing. Dev went right back to work, ignoring the newcomer's intrusion. Blaine pointed an accusing finger toward Dev. "Is he even supposed to be here?"

"Do you fuckin' see me here?" Dev quipped, never looking up from his work.

Alec laughed at the confusion coloring Blaine's face. He seemed to be trying to understand Dev's question and its obvious answer. When Key chuckled, Alec figured it was time to deal with the whole damn situation before it turned into a cock-measuring contest.

"What are you doing here?" he asked, nodding at the empty chair across from them so Blaine would sit and give the attitude a break.

"I'm here to be the best man," Blaine said nonchalantly.

"They already got a goddamn best man," Dev grumbled and rose from his task to give Blaine a very clear *I got this, back-the-fuck-off* glare.

Oh lord, all the testosterone in the place was practically tangible, and it wasn't coming from Key this time. Alec lifted his throbbing finger, studying the permanent band. Key cupped his neck and pulled him closer, then Key extended his hand to admire his inked finger alongside Alec's. The bands were gorgeous, and he couldn't be any prouder than he was in this minute.

"We're already married, guys." Alec tipped his head, meeting Key for a sweet and tender kiss. His mouth lingered on Key's a little longer than intended, but this was his husband. Man, he loved the sound of that, those words filled his heart with love and contentment. He still couldn't believe his good luck. His husband.

"Are they always like this?" Blaine asked.

Dev grunted. Alec took the sound to mean *absolutely*, but he was a little biased where Key was concerned.

He snuggled in closer to Key as his lover bent and whispered in his ear, "I think they're jealous."

Alec grinned at the twinkle in Key's eyes. God, he was so in love with this man.

The end

Discover the beginning, meet Alec and Key in *Havoc*

(Tattoos and Ties, book 1)
Now Available On Amazon

Follow Kindle Alexander to receive release day emails.
kindlealexander.com/contact-us

NOTE FROM
THE AUTHOR

Send a quick email to kindle@kindlealexander.com and let
us know what you think of Order.
For more information on future works click sign-up for our
new release newsletter or come friend us on all the major
social networking sites.

BOOKS BY KINDLE ALEXANDER

If you enjoyed *Order*
then you won't want to miss
Kindle Alexander's bestselling novels:

Reservations
Painted On My Heart
The Current Between Us (with Bonus Material)
Closet Confession
Secret
Texas Pride
Up in Arms
Always

Nice Guys Series
Double Full
Full Disclosure
Full Domain

Tattoos and Ties Duet
Havoc
Order

Join our new release email list to stay update on the exact
date.
kindlealexander.com/contact-us or follow us on Amazon.

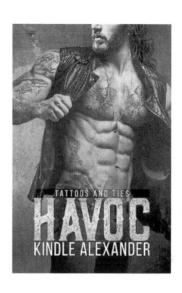

Havoc
(Tattoos And Ties, Book 1)

Keyes Dixon's life is challenging enough as a full patch member of the Disciples of Havoc Motorcycle Club but being a gay biker leaves him traveling down one tough road. With an abusive past and his vow to the club cementing his future, he doesn't believe in love and steers clear of commitment. But a midnight ride leads to a chance meeting with a sexy distraction that has him going down quicker than a Harley on ice.

Cocky Assistant District Attorney Alec Pierce lives in the shadow of his politically connected family. A life of privilege doesn't equal a life of love, a fact made obvious at every family gathering. Driven yet lonely, Alec yields to his family's demands for his career path, hoping for the acceptance he craves. Until he meets a gorgeous biker who tips the scales in the favor of truth and he can no longer live a lie.

Can two men from completely different worlds...and sides of the law...find common ground, or will all their desires only wreak Havoc?

KINDLE ALEXANDER

Reservations
Winner of the 2018 Book Excellence Awards
Elit Awards LGBT Book of the Year

Wildly successful entrepreneur, Thane Walker is stubbornly set in his ways and adamantly resists the shackles of commitment. He's seen enough unhappy endings to learn the best way to play is by keeping his men on the payroll.

Levi Silva's dream of graduating from one of the country's top medical schools is in his grasp, until news from home changes everything. Now, he's raising his two teenage brothers and trying to keep everyone's head above water, emotionally and financially.

When Levi's new job puts him in Thane's path, their chemistry explodes, but their fear of being involved in relationships keeps them apart. Unfortunately, despite the intense desire drawing them together, neither man can move forward until they get past their own...Reservations.

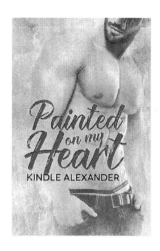

Painted On My Heart
Winner of the 2017 eLit Award Romance category
Winner of the 2017 eLit Award LGBT Fiction category

Artist Kellus Hardin let love and loyalty cloud his past decisions, a mistake he definitely won't make again. Now, lost and alone, he's left to pick up the shattered pieces of his broken heart while facing the truth of his reality.

Arik Layne exudes power, confidence, and determination. But when an encounter with the guarded artist shakes him to the core and alters all his future goals, he finds more than just his heart on the line.

For Kellus, opening himself to love isn't an option.

All Arik wants is to make the artist his.

Can love create a masterpiece when it's painted on your heart?

Always
Book of the Year 2014
Member Choice Awards
~Goodreads MM
Romance

Book of the Year 2014
~Sinfully Sexy Book

LGBT Book of the Year
2015 eLit Awards

KINDLE ALEXANDER

Born to a prestigious political family, Avery Adams plays as hard as he works. The gorgeous, charismatic attorney is used to getting what he wants, even the frequent one-night stands that earn him his well-deserved playboy reputation. When some of the most prominent men in politics suggest he run for senate, Avery decides the time has come to follow in his grandfather's footsteps. With a strategy in place and the campaign wheels rolling, Avery is ready to jump on the legislative fast track, full steam ahead. But no amount of planning prepares him for the handsome, uptight restaurateur who might derail his political future.

Easy isn't even in the top thousand words to describe Kane Dalton's life after his father, a devout Southern Baptist minister, kicks him out of the family home for questioning his sexual orientation. Despite all the rotten tomatoes life throws his way, Kane makes something of himself. Between owning a thriving upscale Italian restaurant in the heart of downtown Minneapolis and managing his long-term boyfriend, his plate is full. He struggles to get past the teachings of his childhood to fully accept his sexuality and rid himself of the doubts brought on by his religious upbringing. The last thing he needs is the yummy, sophisticated, blond-haired distraction sitting at table thirty-four.

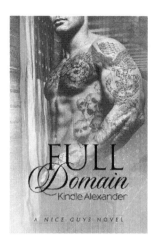

Full Domain
(Nice Guys 3)

Book of the Year, 2016
elit Awards

Honor, integrity, and loyalty are how Deputy US Marshal Kreed Sinacola lives his life. A former SEAL now employed by the Special Operations Group of the US Marshal Service, Kreed spent most of his life working covert operations and avoiding relationships. Never one to mix business with pleasure, his boundaries blur and his convictions are put to the test when he finally comes face-to-face with the hot computer geek he's been partnered with. Hell-bent on closing the ongoing case for his longtime friend, he pushes past his own limits and uncovers more than he expects.

Aaron Stuart strives for one thing: justice. Young and full of idealism, his highly sought after computer skills land him a position with the National Security Agency. Aaron's biggest hazard at his job is cramped fingers, but all that changes when he is drawn into the middle of a dangerous federal investigation. Aaron gets more than he bargained for when the FBI partners him with a handsome and tempting deputy US marshal. His attraction to the inked up, dark-haired man provides another kind of threat altogether. Aaron tries desperately to place a firewall around his heart and fight his developing feelings, knowing one misstep on his part could ultimately destroy him.

The solution isn't as easy as solving the case, which is treacherous enough as it is. But the growing sexual attraction between them threatens to derail more than just Kreed's personal convictions as he quickly learns temptation and matters of the heart rarely fit easily into the rules he's lived by. Will Kreed be able to convince Aaron to open his heart and face the fact that sometimes the answers aren't always hidden in code?

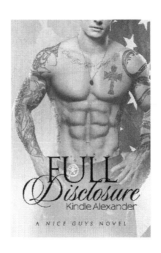

Full Disclosure (Nice Guys 2)
Book of the Year 2014 ~Sinfully Sexy Book

Deputy United States Marshal Mitch Knox apprehends fugitives for a living. His calm, cool, collected attitude and devastatingly handsome good looks earn him a well-deserved bad boy reputation, both in the field and out. While away on an assignment, he blows off some steam at a notorious Dallas nightclub. Solving the case that has plagued him for months takes a sudden backseat to finding out all there is to know about the gorgeous, shy blond sitting alone at the bar.

Texas State Trooper Cody Turner is moving up the ranks, well on his way to his dream of being a Texas Ranger. While on a two-week mandatory vacation, he plans to relax and help out on his family's farm. Mitch is the last distraction Cody needs, but the tatted up temptation that walks into the bar and steals his baseball cap is too hard to ignore.

As Mitch's case gains nationwide attention, how will he convince the sexy state trooper that giving him a chance won't jeopardize his life's plan...especially when the evil he's tracking brings the hate directly to his doorstep, threatening more than just their careers.

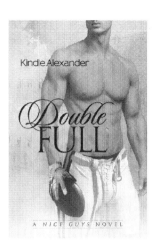

Double Full (Nice Guys 1)

Up and coming football hero, Colt Michaels, makes a Hail Mary pass one night in the college locker room that results in the hottest, sexiest five days of his young life. However, interference after the play has him hiding his past and burying his future in the bottom of a bottle. While Colt seems to have it all, looks can be deceiving especially when you're trapped so far in a closet that you can't see your way out. When ten years of living his expected fast-lane lifestyle lands him engaged to his manipulative Russian supermodel girlfriend, he decides it's time to call a new play.

Jace Montgomery single-handily built the largest all-star cheerleading gym in the world, driven by a need to forget a life-altering encounter with a handsome quarterback a decade ago. His reputation as an excellent coach, hard-nosed business man, and savvy entrepreneur earned him respect in the sometimes catty world of competitive cheerleading. When Jace learns of his ex-lover's plans to marry, his heart executes a barrel roll and his carefully placed resolve tumbles down without a mat to absorb the shock. Can his island escape help him to finally let go of the past and move his life forward?

Secret
Silver Award Book of the Year, 2015 elit Awards

Tristan Wilder, self-made millionaire and devastatingly handsome CEO of Wilder-Nation is on the verge of a very lucrative buyout. With tough negotiations ahead, he's armed with his acquisition pitch, ready to launch the deal of a lifetime. There's just one glitch. The last thing he expects is to fall for the hot business owner he's trying to sway.

Dylan Reeves, computer science engineer and founder of the very successful social media site, Secret, is faced with a life-altering decision. A devoted family man with three kids and a wife, Dylan has been living a secret for years. Fiercely loyal to his convictions, his boundaries blur after meeting the striking owner of the corporation interested in acquiring his company. For the first time in his life, reckless desire consumes him when the gorgeous computer mogul makes an offer he can't refuse.

"Mitch and Cody are perfect and so bloody hot, it made my iPAD melt."
~Jules Swoon Worthy

Double Full

"These two hunky men had me in tears, their love for one another is magical."
~Jennifer Robbins, Twinsie Talk Book Review

"Kindle Alexander sure can write a red hot sex scene like nobody else."
~Vickie Leaf, Book Freak

"Without a doubt one of the BEST m/m romances I have ever read."
~Mandie, Foxylutely Blog

Texas Pride

"I have a severe case of book hangover. Seriously readers – you need to read this book. Ten stars for me!"
~ Mandie, Foxylutely Blog

"Definitely a great read…I didn't want this sweet story to end."
~Christi Snow, Author